THE CAMBRIDGE COMPANION TO THE CITY IN WORLD LITERATURE

This book forges new ground in the relationship between cities and world literature. Through a series of essays spanning a variety of metropolises, it shows how cities have given rise to key aesthetic dispositions, acts of linguistic and cultural translation, topographic conceptualizations, global imaginaries, and narratives of self-fashioning that are central to understanding World Literature and its debates. Alongside an introduction and three theoretical chapters, each chapter focuses on a particular city in the Global North or Global South, and brings World Literary debates – on translation, literary networks, imperial and migrant imaginaries, centers and peripheries – into conversation with the urban literary histories of Beijing, Bombay/Mumbai, Dublin, Cairo, Istanbul, Johannesburg, Lagos, London, Mexico City, Moscow and St. Petersburg, New York, Paris, Singapore, and Sydney.

ATO QUAYSON is the Jean G. and Morris M. Doyle Professor of Interdisciplinary Studies, and Chair of the Department of English, at Stanford. He has published six monographs and eight edited collections. His latest book is *Tragedy and Postcolonial Literature* (Cambridge University Press, 2021). He is an elected member of the Ghana Academy of Arts and Sciences, the Royal Society of Canada, and the British Academy.

JINI KIM WATSON is Professor of English and Comparative Literature at New York University. She is the author of *Cold War Reckonings: Authoritarianism and the Genres of Decolonization* (Fordham University Press, 2021) and *The New Asian City: Three-Dimensional Fictions of Space and Urban Form* (University of Minnesota Press, 2011). She has also co-edited, with Gary Wilder, *The Postcolonial Contemporary: Political Imaginaries for the Global Present* (Fordham University Press, 2018).

THE CAMBRIDGE COMPANION TO THE CITY IN WORLD LITERATURE

EDITED BY

ATO QUAYSON

Stanford University, California

JINI KIM WATSON

New York University

CAMBRIDGE
UNIVERSITY PRESS

CAMBRIDGE
UNIVERSITY PRESS

Shaftesbury Road, Cambridge CB2 8EA, United Kingdom

One Liberty Plaza, 20th Floor, New York, NY 10006, USA

477 Williamstown Road, Port Melbourne, VIC 3207, Australia

314–321, 3rd Floor, Plot 3, Splendor Forum, Jasola District Centre, New Delhi – 110025, India

103 Penang Road, #05–06/07, Visioncrest Commercial, Singapore 238467

Cambridge University Press is part of Cambridge University Press & Assessment, a department of the University of Cambridge.

We share the University's mission to contribute to society through the pursuit of education, learning and research at the highest international levels of excellence.

www.cambridge.org
Information on this title: www.cambridge.org/9781316517888

DOI: 10.1017/9781009047883

First published 2023

A catalogue record for this publication is available from the British Library.

Library of Congress Cataloging-in-Publication Data
NAMES: Quayson, Ato, editor. | Watson, Jini Kim, editor.
TITLE: The Cambridge companion to the city in world literature / edited by Ato Quayson, Jini Kim Watson.
OTHER TITLES: City in world literature
DESCRIPTION: Cambridge, United Kingdom ; New York, NY : Cambridge University Press, 2023. | Includes bibliographical references and index.
IDENTIFIERS: LCCN 2022058992 | ISBN 9781316517888 (hardback) | ISBN 9781009047883 (ebook)
SUBJECTS: LCSH: Cities and towns in literature. | City and town life in literature. | LCGFT: Literary criticism. | Essays.
CLASSIFICATION: LCC PN56.C55 C365 2023 | DDC 809/.93358209732–dc23/eng/20230503
LC record available at https://lccn.loc.gov/2022058992

ISBN 978-1-316-51788-8 Hardback
ISBN 978-1-009-04861-3 Paperback

Contents

Contributors

HATICE AYNUR, PhD (1993) in Ottoman Literature, Istanbul University, was formerly Professor of Ottoman Literature at İstanbul Şehir University. She is currently a visiting scholar in the Research Institute for Languages and Cultures of Asia and Africa (ILCAA), Tokyo University of Foreign Studies. She has published works on Ottoman literature; Istanbul in Ottoman literary texts; architectural inscriptions of Ottoman lands; history of printed books and manuscripts culture in the Ottoman world. Recently she edited *Gölgelenen Sultan, Unutulan Yıllar: I. Mahmûd ve Dönemi (1730–1754)* [*Neglected Sultan, Forgotten Years: Mahmûd I and his Reign 1730–1754*] (2 vols., 2020), and coedited with Tülay Artan *Osmanlı Kitap Koleksiyonerleri ve Koleksiyonları: İtibar ve İhtiras* [*Prestige and Passion: Ottoman Manuscript Collections and Collectors*] (2022).

RUTH BUSH is Associate Professor in African and French Cultural Studies at the University of Bristol, UK. Her research concerns literary and cultural production, with particular interests in material print cultures, translation, gender, and institutions. Her first book was *Publishing Africa in French: Literary Institutions and Decolonization 1945–67* (2016). She has recently published *Translation Imperatives: African Literature and the Labour of Translators* (2022). She currently convenes a collaborative project on representations and lived experiences of universities in four multilingual, historically francophone, African cities (Dakar, Abidjan, Abomey-Calavi, and Yaounde).

PHILIP HOLDEN worked for twenty-five years at Nanyang Technological University and the National University of Singapore. His scholarship in auto/biography studies includes the book *Autobiography and Decolonization: Modernity, Masculinity and the Nation-State* (2008), and articles in major journals such as *biography*, *Life Writing*, *a/b: Auto/*

biography Studies, and *Postcolonial Studies*. He has published widely on Singapore and Southeast Asian literatures, is the coauthor of *The Routledge Concise History of Southeast Asian Writing in English* (2009), and one of the editors of *Writing Singapore* (2009), the most comprehensive historical anthology of Singapore literature in English. He is now an independent scholar.

MADHU KRISHNAN is Professor of African, World, and Comparative Literatures at the University of Bristol, where she currently serves as Director for the Centre for Black Humanities. She is author of *Contemporary African Literature in English: Global Locations, Postcolonial Identifications* (2014), *Writing Spatiality in West Africa: Colonial Legacies in the Anglophone/Francophone Novel* (2018) and *Contingent Canons: African Literature and the Politics of Location* (2018). She is currently working on a five-year project funded by the ERC titled "Literary Activism in Sub-Saharan Africa: Commons, Publics and Networks of Practice."

MEGAN JONES teaches in the English Studies Department at Stellenbosch University, South Africa. She has published widely on South African literature and culture. She is the author of *Everybody is Here: Reading South Africa through the 21st Century Township*, forthcoming in 2023.

ANNE LOUNSBERY is Professor of Russian Literature at New York University. She has published widely on nineteenth-century Russian prose in comparative context, most recently with a focus on symbolic geographies. Her most recent book is *Life Is Elsewhere: Symbolic Geography in the Russian Provinces, 1800–1917* (2019).

REINHOLD MARTIN is Professor of Architecture in the Graduate School of Architecture, Planning, and Preservation at Columbia University. He has published widely on the history and theory of modern architecture and urbanism, with a focus on the history of architecture, technology, and media. His books include *The Organizational Complex: Architecture, Media, and Corporate Space* (2003); *Utopia's Ghost: Architecture and Postmodernism, Again* (2010); *The Urban Apparatus: Mediapolitics and the City* (2016); and *Knowledge Worlds: Media, Materiality, and Making of the Modern University* (2021).

CHRISTOPHER MORASH is the Seamus Heaney Professor of Irish Writing in Trinity College, Dublin. His books include *A History of Irish Theatre, 1601–2000* (2002), *A History of the Media in Ireland* (2009), *Mapping*

Irish Theatre: Theories of Space and Place [with Shaun Richards] (2013), *Yeats on Theatre* (2021), and *Dublin: A Writer's City* (2023). He curated a series of audio plays, *Unseen Plays*, for the Abbey Theatre in 2021, and chairs the judging panel for the Dublin Literary Award, the world's richest prize for a novel in English. He was elected to membership of the Royal Irish Academy in 2007.

MARÍA MORENO CARRANCO (PhD Architecture, UC Berkeley) is a Professor at the Department of Social Sciences at UAM-Cuajimalpa, where she teaches courses in urban studies. Her recent publications include a coedited volume with Greig Crysler, *Spaces of Fear: Bodies, Walls, Cities* (2021) exploring the intersection of emotions and the built environment. She also coauthored the book *Mundos Habitados: espacios de arquitectura, diseño y música* (2020) with Rocio Guadarrama, departing from established frameworks for studying the creative city, and considering urban history, the particularities of the place, and the role of everyday practices. Moreno Carranco has extensively studied urban megaprojects and the effects of neoliberal globalization in the contemporary city.

NOOR NAGA is an Alexandrian writer. Her verse-novel *Washes, Prays* (2020) won the Pat Lowther Memorial Award and Arab American Book Award. Her novel *If an Egyptian Cannot Speak English* (2022) received rave reviews from *Kirkus*, *Chicago Review of Books*, the *Los Angeles Review of Books*, *Guernica*, the *CBC*, and *The New York Times*, which called it an "exhilarating debut." It won the Graywolf Press Africa Prize and the Center for Fiction First Novel Prize, and was shortlisted for the Scotiabank Giller Prize. She teaches at the American University in Cairo.

ANJALI NERLEKAR is Associate Professor in the Department of African, Middle Eastern, and South Asian Languages and Literatures (AMESALL) at Rutgers University, and coeditor of *Modernism/Modernity*. She is the author of *Bombay Modern: Arun Kolatkar and Bilingual Literary Culture* (2016) and has also coedited a special double issue of *Journal of Postcolonial Writing* on "The Worlds of Bombay Poetry" and a special issue of *South Asia: A Journal of South Asian Studies* on "Postcolonial Archives." In collaboration with Dr. Bronwen Bledsoe at Cornell University, she has created an ongoing collection of documents titled "The Bombay Poets' Archive." She is currently coediting *The Oxford Handbook of Modern Indian Literatures*.

ATO QUAYSON is the Jean G. and Morris M. Doyle Professor of Interdisciplinary Studies University in the Department of English at Stanford University, where he is also chair of the department. He has previously taught at the University of Cambridge, the University of Toronto, and New York University, and has held fellowships at Oxford, Harvard, Berkeley, the Australian National University, and Wellesley College, among others. He is the author of six monographs and eight edited collections, including *The Cambridge History of Postcolonial Literature* (2 vols., 2012), and most recently, *Tragedy and Postcolonial Literature* (2021). His book, *Oxford Street, Accra: City Life and the Itineraries of Transnationalism* (2014) was co-winner of the Urban History Association Best Book Prize (non-North America) in 2015.

JOSÉ RAMÓN RUISÁNCHEZ SERRA is a professor in the Department of Hispanic Studies at the University of Houston, where he teaches Latin American Literature and Theory. His recent publications include *Torres* (2021), where he delves into the dialogue between poetic and visual image, and the monograph *La reconciliación: Roberto Bolaño y la literatura de amistad en América Latina* (2019). He has coedited with Anna M. Nogar and Ignacio Sánchez Prado *A History of Mexican Literature*, *A History of Mexican Poetry* (in press), and *A History of Mexican Novel* (forthcoming).

BRIGID ROONEY is an Associate Professor (Affiliate) with the Department of English at the University of Sydney where she taught both Australian literature and Australian studies. In her research and publications on twentieth-century and contemporary Australian literature, she focuses on the role of literature, and especially the novel, in both figuring and shaping space, place, and social life. She is the author of *Literary Activists: Writer-Intellectuals and Australian Public Life* (2009) and *Suburban Space, the Novel and Australian Modernity* (2018), and with Fiona Morrison is currently coediting a volume of scholarly essays on the fiction of Eleanor Dark.

WEIJIE SONG is associate professor of modern Chinese literature and culture at Rutgers University, New Brunswick. He is the author of *Mapping Modern Beijing: Space, Emotion, Literary Topography* (2017), *From Entertainment Activity to Utopian Impulse: Rereading Jin Yong's Martial Arts Fiction* (1999), and *China, Literature, and the United States: Images of China in American and Chinese-American Novel and Drama* (2003), in addition to other publications and translations. His current research projects include "Ide(c)ology: Environmental Objects and Chinese Ecocriticism," "Chivalrous Psychogeography: Martial Arts, Avant-garde, Sinophone Cinema," and "Reviving Northeast China: Contemporary Literature and Film Beyond the Great Wall."

ROBERT T. TALLY JR. is Professor of English at Texas State University. His recent books include *The Critical Situation: Vexed Perspectives in Postmodern Literary Studies* (2023); *For a Ruthless Critique of All That Exists* (2022); *J.R.R. Tolkien's* The Hobbit*: Realizing History Through Fantasy* (2022); *Topophrenia: Place, Narrative, and the Spatial Imagination* (2019); *The Routledge Handbook of Literature and Space* (2017); *Fredric Jameson: The Project of Dialectic Criticism* (2014); and *Spatiality* (2013). Tally is also the editor of the *Geocriticism and Spatial Literary Studies* book series.

RASHMI VARMA teaches English and Comparative Literary Studies at the University of Warwick. She is the author of *The Postcolonial City and its Subjects* (2011) and coeditor of *Marxism and Postcolonial Theory: Critical Engagements with Benita Parry* (2018) and *End(s) of the Global City: Displacement, Disaffection and the New Ecologies of the Urban* (forthcoming, 2023). She has also coedited a special issue of the journal *Critical Sociology* on "Marxism and Postcolonial Theory: What is Left of the Debate?" She is a founding editorial collective member of the journal *Feminist Dissent* and has published numerous essays on post-colonial and feminist theory, activism and literature in edited volumes and journals.

JINI KIM WATSON is Professor of English and Comparative Literature at New York University. Her publications include *Cold War Reckonings: Authoritarianism and the Genres of Decolonization* (2021), which received honorable mentions for both the ACLA's René Wellek Prize and the MLA's James Russell Lowell Prize; *The New Asian City: Three-Dimensional Fictions of Space and Urban Form* (2011), and the coedited volume, with Gary Wilder, *The Postcolonial Contemporary: Political Imaginaries for the Global Present* (2018). She is a long-time co-convener of NYU's Postcolonial, Race and Diaspora Studies Colloquium, a research cluster for graduate students and faculty.

Chronology of Political, Literary, and Cultural Events

This chronology starts from the 1400s to mark the start of the Age of Exploration. We end the chronology in 2020 to indicate the palpable end of the world order that was marked by the declaration of the COVID-19 pandemic. We have tried to capture the diversity of political and cultural events that provide the inspiration and background to the city in world literature. While we have privileged the social histories of the cities that feature prominently in the Companion, we have sought to indicate developments in a few other cities that help to demarcate the interconnectedness of global developments, especially from the Global South.

When Nobel Prize winners are listed more than once, their dates of birth and death (where applicable) have been entered against their names in the year in which they won the prize. The dates of the founding of significant city newspapers and literary journals from various cities and regions has been provided, along with those for the most important literary prizes. The chronology is best read comparatively, with an eye to making connections between different parts of world literature.

Date	Urban Developments	Cultural and Literary Events
1400–1500		
1403	Beijing – city named Beijing for the first time	
1409	Dublin – first mayor appointed	
1420	Beijing – Temple of Heaven, Forbidden City, and Tiananmen Gate completed	
1421	Beijing – Ming Dynasty moves capital to Beijing	
1430	Joan of Arc burned at the stake	
1440		First printing press developed by Gutenberg in Europe (ca. 1440)
1453	Istanbul – Final Siege of Constantinople Istanbul – Capital of the Ottoman Empire relocated to Constantinople from Edirne	
1446		Proclamation of *Hunminjeongeum*, establishing Hangul script in Korea
1456		François Villon, *Le petit testament*; *Le grand testament* follows in 1461
1470		Gasparin de Bergame, *Letters*
1471	London – War of the Roses	
1477	Alexandria – Citadel of Qaitbay built	
1494	Treaty of Tordesillas: Spain and Portugal divide New World between them	
1495	Moscow – Kremlin completed	*Malay Annals/ Sulalatus Salatin* (*Genealogy of Kings*) (composed between fifteenth and sixteenth century)
1500–1699		
1503	Casa Contrataccion (Colonial office) founded in Madrid to deal with American affairs	
1509	Istanbul – Earthquake destroys Constantinople	
1514		*Septem horae canonicae*, first book published in Arabic type, published in Italy
1515		The Lateran Council's decree, "De impressione librorum," forbids printing of books without permission of Roman Catholic authorities

Date	Urban Developments	Cultural and Literary Events
1516		Thomas More, *Utopia*
1517	London – "Evil May Day" riots	
1521	Hernando Cortés assumes control of Mexico after destruction of Aztec state	Nguyễn Dữ, *Truyền kỳ mạn lục* (sixteenth century)
1522		Jacopo Sannazzaro, "De partu Virginis," religious poem fusing pagan and Christian myth
1526	Babar establishes Mogul dynasty in Delhi	
	First Battle of Panipat – Delhi under Mughal Empire	
1540	Afghan rebel Sher Shah becomes Emperor of Delhi	
1541	Dublin becomes capital of the Kingdom of Ireland	
1547	Moscow becomes capital of the grand duchy of Russia	Miguel de Cervantes Saavedra, Spanish writer b. (d. 1616)
1554	London – Wyatt's rebellion begins	
1555	French colony founded on the Bay of Rio de Janeiro	An Aztec dictionary published
1560	Municipal Chamber of São Paulo founded	Hsu Wei, *Ching P'ing Mei*, first classic Chinese novel
1561	Moscow – Saint Basil's Cathedral consecrated	
1562	Plague in Paris	
1564	Spaniards occupy Philippines and build Manila	William Shakespeare b. (d. 1616)
		Moscow – Moscow Print Yard established
1570–1600	New York City – Iroquois Confederacy formed	
1571	Manila – Intramuros founded	
1572		Luís de Camões, *Os Lusíadas*
1573		Isabella Whitney, *A Sweet Nosgay*
1574	Chinese pirate Limahong tries to take Manila	
1575–1600		Zahīr al-Dīn Muhammad Bābur, *Memories of Babur*
1578	Paris – construction of Pont Neuf begins	
1590	The Emperor of Morocco annexes Timbuctoo	
1592	Seoul taken by Japanese forces	Wu Cheng'en, *Journey to the West*
	Plague in London	
1593	Manila – Fort Santiago completed	

Date	Urban Developments	Cultural and Literary Events
1595	Dutch begin to colonize East Indies	
1596		*The Merchant of Venice* first performance (first print 1600)
1598	Moscow – time of Troubles begins Tang Xianzu, *The Peony Pavilion* Paris – Edict of Nantes	
1599		Thomas Dekker, *The Shoemaker's Holiday* London – Globe Theatre opens in Southwark
1600		Tang Xianzu, A *Dream under the Southern Bough*
1601		Bento Teixeira Pinto: "Prosopopya," first Brazilian Epic
1602		Tommaso Campanella, *City of the Sun*
ca. seventeenth century		Ajamı script spreads through Africa
1603	Lord Mountjoy conquers northern counties of Ireland	
1604		*Relation aller Fürnemmen und gedenckwürdigen Historien*, the first printed and circulated newspaper, debuts in Strasbourg
1604–05		*Othello* first performance (first print 1622)
1605	Barbados, West Indies, claimed as English colony London – Gunpowder Plot	Miguel de Cervantes, *Don Quixote, Part 1* Cervantes, *Don Quixote*
1606–07		*Antony and Cleopatra* first performance (first print 1623)
1607	Manila – San Agustin Church consecrated	
1610	Skirmishes between English and Dutch settlers in India	
1611	Manila – University of Santo Tomas established	*The Tempest* first performance (first print 1623)
1612	Moscow Uprising	
1614	Dutch settle on Manhattan Island	
1615		Cervantes, *Don Quixote, Part 2*
1620	Pilgrim Fathers leave Plymouth, England, in *Mayflower* for North America; land at New Plymouth, Massachusetts to found Plymouth Colony	
1625	London – Colonial Office established	

Date	Urban Developments	Cultural and Literary Events
1627–58	Shah Jahan (1592–1666), succeeding his father Jahangir, becomes Great Mogul of India	
1626		English author and traveler George Sandys makes first translation of a classic in America of Ovid's "Metamorphoses"
1630	John Winthrop, English Puritan leader (1587–1649), sails with Plymouth Company's expedition (Apr); arrives in Massachusetts with 1,000 settlers; founds Boston; 16,000 more settlers follow (–1642)	
1631		Paris – *La Gazette de France* begins publication
1632	Portuguese driven out of Bengal	
1634	Paris – first meeting of the Académie française	
1644	Beijing – Qing Dynasty moves capital to Beijing	
1649	Siege of Dublin	
1650	Dutch and English agree respective frontiers of their North American colonies	
1651	Beijing – Tiananmen built	
1652	Dutch arrive to establish settlement in Cape Town	
	Dublin – High Court of Justice established	
	Moscow – German Quarter developed near city	
1653	Mumbai – Taj Mahal completed	
1654	Treaty of Westminster ends Anglo-Dutch war; Dutch recognize Navigation Act	
	Portuguese finally drive Dutch out of Brazil	
1655	English capture Jamaica from Spain	
1656	Istanbul – Çınar incident	
1659	New York City – labor strike by bakers	
1661	Famine in India, no rain since 1659	
	Dublin city government established	
1662	Moscow – Copper Riot	
1665	Great Plague of London begins	London – *Philosophical Transactions of the Royal Society* begins publication

Date	Urban Developments	Cultural and Literary Events
1666	Great Fire of London	
1667	New York City – city becomes part of England per Treaty of Breda	
1668	British East India Company takes control of Bombay Mumbai – Royal Charter of March 27; Bombay Province created Mumbai – Establishment of the Western Presidency at Surat	
1669	Venetians lose Crete, their last colonial possession to the Turks	
1670	Spain formally cedes Jamaica to England Lagos – Iga Iduguran built	
1672	Mumbai – Consecration of the first Tower of Silence	
1680	French colonial empire is organized, reaching from Quebec to mouth of Mississippi River	
1682	Moscow Uprising	
1685	Some Chinese ports open to foreign trade	
1686	Federation of New England formed by James II in order to remodel British colonies in North America	
1688	London – Glorious Revolution	
1689	Natal becomes Dutch colony	
1691	New East India Company formed in London	
1693		London – *The Ladies' Mercury* begins publication
1695	Dublin – Four Courts built London – Government press censorship ends	
1698	Moscow – Streltsy Uprising	
1700–1799		
ca. 1701		Father Ximénez transcribes the Mayan epic *Popul Vuh*
1702		London – *The Daily Courant* begins publication
1703		Moscow – *Vedomosti* newspaper begins publication
1708	British East India Company and New East India Company merged	
1709		London – *Tatler* and *The Female Tatler* magazines begin publication

Date	Urban Developments	Cultural and Literary Events
1711	Rio de Janeiro captured by French	
1712	New York City – New York Slave Revolt Russian capital relocated from Moscow to St. Petersburg	
1719		Daniel Defoe, *Robinson Crusoe*
1722	New York City – Tuscarora join Iroquois Confederacy	
1725		Dublin – *Dublin Weekly Journal* begins publication New York City – *The New-York Gazette* begins publication
1726		Jonathan Swift, *Gulliver's Travels*
1728	Russian capital moved back to Moscow	Mwengo bin Athuman, *Utendi wa Tambuka* (ca. 1728)
1732	Russian capital relocated to St. Petersburg	
1733	London – Serpentine Lake created in Hyde Park	New York City – *New York Weekly Journal* begins publication
1735	Moscow – Tsar Bell cast	
1750	Beijing – Yi He Yuan (Summer Palace) commissioned	
1756	120 British soldiers imprisoned and die in India ("Black hole of Calcutta")	
1756–1763	Start of Seven-Year War between English and French in North America that leads to the English acquisition of Quebec	
1757	Battle of Delhi; Delhi under Maratha Empire	
1760	Dutch explorer Jakobus Coetzee advances beyond Orange River, South Africa	
1762–64	British occupation of Manila	
1763	British Proclamation provides government for Quebec, Florida, and Grenada	
1765		Paris – *Almanach des Muses* begins publication Hong DaeYong, *Damheon yeongi*
1768	Secretary of State for Colonies appointed in Britain	
1770	Dublin – City directory published	
1771	Dublin – City Assembly House built Moscow – Plague Riot	

Date	Urban Developments	Cultural and Literary Events
1773	Boston Tea Party (protest)	August Ludwig von Schlözer uses the term "*Weltlitteratur*" in *Isländische Litteratur und Geschichte*
1774	Quebec Act, to secure Canada's loyalty to Great Britain, establishes Roman Catholicism in Canada	
1775	Dublin – Four Courts Marshalsea founded	
		New York City – Bowne & Co. printers established
1775–83	American Revolution	
1776	New York City – Battle of Long Island	
1777		Paris – *Journal de Paris* newspaper begins publication
1780		American Academy of Arts and Sciences established
1783	London – *Zong* massacre trials held	
1784	Pitt's India Act; East India Company under government control	Phillis Wheatley, Black American poet, d. (b. 1753)
1785	New York City – New York Manumission Society founded	
	London – *The Times* begins publication	
1787	Constitution of US signed	New York City – *The Federalist Papers* begin publication
1788	Penal colony founded in Botany Bay, Australia	*Kālidāsa Shakuntala* translated into English by William Jones
	Paris – Bread riots	
1789–1799	French Revolution	
1789	French Revolution: French Royalists begin to emigrate	Paris – *Journal des débats* begins publication
	New York City – Yellow Fever epidemic	
1790	Canada Constitutional Act divides the country into two provinces, Upper and Lower Canada	
	Slaves revolt in French Santo Domingo	
1791	Society of United Irishmen Dublin branch founded	Cao Xueqin, *Dream of the Red Chamber*
1791–1804	Haitian Revolution	
1792	Denmark is the first nation to abolish the slave trade	Dublin – *The Flapper* begins publication

Date	Urban Developments	Cultural and Literary Events
1796	Dublin – Kilmainham Gaol opens Beijing – Edict of Peking forbids import of opium into China	
1797	Prospect, a western Sydney suburb, becomes boundary between colonists and indigenous Australians	Johan Gottfried von Herder, *Briefe zu Beförderung der Humanität*
1799	Paris – *coup d'état* of 18 Brumaire; Napoleon Bonaparte takes power	
1800–1849		
1801	Act of Union of Great Britain and Ireland comes into force Dublin becomes part of the United Kingdom of Great Britain and Ireland	New York City – *New York Evening Post* newspaper begins publication
1802	British colonial rule of India begins	
1803	Dublin – Emmet's insurrection	Sydney – *Sydney Gazette* newspaper begins publication
1791–1804	Haitian Revolution	
1807	France invades Portugal; dethroned royal family flees to Brazil	
1808	Sydney – Rum Rebellion	
1809		Washington Irving, *History of New York: From the Beginning of the World to the End of the Dutch Dynasty*
1810	Venezuela breaks away from Spain Simon Bolivar emerges as major figure in South American politics British seize Guadeloupe, last French colony in West Indies Revolts in New Granada, Rio de la Plata, and Mexico	
1811	Paraguay declares independence from Spain British occupy Java	
1812	US declares war on Britain Moscow – French invasion	
1813	Americans capture York (Toronto) and Fort St. George Mexico declares itself independent	
1814	Battle of Paris; Abdication of Napoleon	
ca. 1815–21		Ntsikana, "Ulo Thixo omkhulu"
1815	Paris – Battle of Waterloo	

Date	Urban Developments	Cultural and Literary Events
	Brazil declares itself independent from 1816 under Dom John	
1816	Argentina declared independent Java retaken by the Netherlands	
1817	Simon Bolivar establishes independent government of Venezuela	
1818	Chile proclaims its independence Border between Canada and the US agreed upon	
1819	British settlement established in Singapore by East India Company Florida purchased by US from Spain Simon Bolivar becomes President of Gran Colombia	Johann Wolfgang von Goethe, *Westöstlicher Divan*
1821	Istanbul – Constantinople massacre Peru proclaimed independent from Spain followed by Guatemala, Mexico, Panama, and Santo Domingo	
1822	Brazil becomes independent of Portugal	Mumbai – *Mumbai Samachar* (originally *Bombay Samachar*) begins publication London – *Sunday Times* begins publication Arabic printing press in operation in Cairo
1823	Guatemala, San Salvador, Nicaragua, Honduras, and Costa Rica form Confederation of United Provinces of Central America The Monroe Doctrine closes American continent to colonial settlements by European powers	
1824	Singapore becomes a British colony	Paris – *Le Globe* begins publication Glasgow Missionary Society publishes Xhosa orthography
1825	Bolivia becomes independent of Peru, Uruguay of Brazil Portugal recognizes Brazilian independence New York City – labor strike by United Tailoresses Society	
1826	Pan American Congress in Panama	Paris –*Le Figaro* newspaper founded

Date	Urban Developments	Cultural and Literary Events
	Istanbul – Auspicious Incident	Mexico City – *El Iris* literary magazine in publication
1827	Peru secedes from Colombia	Johan Wolfgang von Goethe first uses the term *weltliteratur* in a piece that appeared in the journal *Kunst und Altertum* (*Art and Antiquity*). He makes various subsequent remarks on the topic in various letters, diaries, and conversations between 1827 and 1831.
1828	Uruguay, since 1821 part of Brazil, becomes independent republic following Treaty of Rio de Janeiro	
1829	Venezuela withdraws from Gran Colombia to begin its independent existence	
1830	France captures Algeria Ecuador secedes from Gran Colombia and becomes independent republic Mysore added to Britain's possessions in India	
1831	London Bridge opens	Sydney – *Sydney Herald* newspaper begins publication Istanbul – *Takvim-i Vekayi* newspaper begins publication
1832	Singapore becomes center of the government of Straits Settlements	Dublin – *Dublin Penny Journal* and *Paddy Kelly's Budget* begin publication
1833	Mehemet Ali is given Egypt and Syria; founds the dynasty that rules Egypt until 1952 Mumbai – Asiatic Society of Bombay (Town Hall) completed	Rodolphe Töpffer, *Histoire de Monsieur Jabot*
1834	Sixth Kaffir War until 1835; severe clashes between Bantu people and white settlers on eastern Frontier of Cape Colony New York City – anti-abolitionist riots New York City – Convention for the Improvement of the Free People of Color held London – fire in Houses of Parliament	

Date	Urban Developments	Cultural and Literary Events
1835		New York City – *New York Herald* begins publication Philarète Chasles delivers lectures on "La Littérature étrangère comparée" in Paris
1836	Boer farmers launch "The Great Trek," systematic emigration across the Orange River away from British rule; founding of Natal, Transvaal, and Orange Free states	
1837	Chicago incorporated as a city; first city charter	
1839–42	Beijing – First Opium War	
1841	Dublin City Council established	New York City – *The New York Tribune* begins publication
	Britain's sovereignty proclaimed over Hong Kong USS *Creole* carrying slaves from Virginia to Louisiana is seized by the slaves and sails into Nassau where they become free New Zealand becomes British colony	
1842	Treaty of Nanking ends Opium War between Britain and China, and confirms cession of Hong Kong to Great Britain Sydney – city incorporated	
1843		London – *The Economist* begins publication William H. Prescott, *History of the Conquest of Mexico*
1845	Maori uprising against British rule in New Zealand	Singapore – *Straits Times* begins publication
1846	New York City – Constitutional convention	
1847	Liberia proclaimed independent republic	Prescott, *History of the Conquest of Peru* Chicago – *Chicago Tribune* begins publication
1848	New York City – Seneca Falls Convention Paris – 1848 French Revolution	New York City – Associated Press established Manila – *Diario de Manila* newspaper begins publication
1849	Britain annexes Punjab by treaty with the Maharajah of Lahore New York City – Astor Place Riot	

Date	Urban Developments	Cultural and Literary Events
1850–1899		
1850		Sydney – *Freeman's Journal* newspaper begins publication Shanghai – *North-China Herald* newspaper begins publication New York City – *Harper's New Monthly Magazine* begins publication
1851	Cuba declares independence	New York City – *New York Times* newspaper begins publication London – Great Exhibition
1852		Harriet Beecher Stowe, *Uncle Tom's Cabin*
1854		Sigismund Wilhelm Koelle, *Polyglotta Africana* Paris – *Le Figaro* begins publication
1855	Britain annexes Oudh, India and establishes Natal as crown colony	London – *The Daily Telegraph* begins publication Paris World Fair
1856	Istanbul – Dolmabahçe Palace completed London – "Big Ben" bell cast	Moscow – *The Russian Messenger* magazine begins publication
1856–60	Beijing – Second Opium War	
1857	Indian mutiny over British rule; siege of Delhi begins; Delhi captured; British enter Cawnpore	
1859		New York City – *Weekly Anglo-African* begins publication
1863	Shanghai International Settlement established Construction of London Underground (railroad) begins	
1867	Moscow – Einem brothers chocolate factory founded Singapore becomes crown colony of British Empire Singapore – Legislative Council of the Staits Settlements	
1870	Siege of Paris by Prussian army begins	Istanbul – *Diyojen* magazine begins publication
1871	The Great Chicago Fire Accra – Jamestown Lighthouse built	
1872	Moscow University for Women founded Dublin tramways begin operating	Tokyo – *Tokyo Nichi Nichi Shimbun* (newspaper) begins publication Shanghai – *Shen Bao* newspaper begins publication

Date	Urban Developments	Cultural and Literary Events
1875		São Paulo – *Provincia de S. Paulo* newspaper begins publication
1876		Istanbul – *Akhtar* magazine begins publication
1877	Istanbul – Central Committee for Defending Albanian Rights formed	Hugo von Meltzl and Sámuel Brassai found the journal *Acta Comparationis Litterarum Universarum*
	Chicago – Great Railroad Strike	
1878		Paris World Exhibition
		London – Electric streetlights introduced
1879	Sydney Riot	Istanbul – Society for the Publication of Albanian Writings formed
1880		New York City – Electric streetlights introduced
1881		David Gestetner patents his Cyclostyle stylus
1882	Dublin – Phoenix Park Murders	James Joyce, Irish novelist, b. (d. 1941)
	Istanbul Chamber of Commerce established	
1883	Paris – Orient Express (Paris–Istanbul) makes its first run	New York City – *Life* magazine begins publication
	New York City – Brooklyn Bridge opens	Oliver Schreiner, *The Story of an African Farm*
1884		Paris – *Le Matin* begins publication
1884–85	Berlin Conference (Scramble for Africa)	
1885	Mumbai – Indian National Congress founded	
	The Congo becomes a personal possession of King Leopold II of Belgium	
1886	Johannesburg township established by Boer government	Chicago – *Chicago Evening Post* begins publication
1887	First Colonial Conference opens in London	Johannesburg – *The Star* newspaper in publication
1888	Mumbai – Brihanmumbai Municipal Corporation established	José Guadalupe Posada Aguilar printer in business
1889	Paris – Eiffel Tower completed	
	Paris – First May Day celebration	
1890	Johannesburg Public Library opens	São Paulo – *O Estado de S. Paulo* newspaper in publication
		James Frazer, *The Golden Bough*
		Knut Hamsun, *Sult*

Date	Urban Developments	Cultural and Literary Events
1892	Dubai becomes a British protectorate	New York City – *Vogue* magazine begins publication
1893		Cairo – *Le Progrès Egyptien* newspaper begins publication
1894		Chicago – *Ženské Listy* women's magazine begins publication
		Lagos – *Lagos Echo* and *Lagos Standard* newspapers begin publication
1894–95	First Sino-Japanese War	
1896	Moscow – Khodynka Tragedy	
	Manila mutiny	
	Istanbul – Occupation of the Ottoman Bank	
	Johannesburg – Uprising against Boer government	
1897		Seoul – *Kurisudo sinmun* newspaper begins publication
1898	New York City Charter	
	Battle of Manila	
1899	London borough councils established	Alexander Veselovsky, "Tri glavy iz istoricheskoi poetiki"
	Mumbai – plague epidemic	Joseph Conrad, *Heart of Darkness*
1899–1902	Johannesburg – Second Boer War	
1900–1919		
1900	Beijing – Boxer Rebellion	London – *Daily Express* begins publication
		Solomon T. Plaatje, *Boer War Diary*
		José Enrique Rodó, *Ariel*
		Paris World Exhibition
1901		Nobel Prize in Literature is established
1902	Colonial Conference meets in London	British Academy established
	First meeting of Committee of Imperial Defense	J.A. Hobson, *Imperialism*
1903	Johannesburg – Sophiatown suburb developed	Prix Goncourt is established
	First Tour de France (bike race) held	
1904	Paris conference on white slave trade	Prix Femina is established
1904–08	Herreros and Hottentots revolt in German South West Africa	
1905	Moscow Uprising	Dublin – *Irish Independent* newspaper begins publication

Date	Urban Developments	Cultural and Literary Events
	Istanbul – Yıldız assassination attempt	Johannesburg – *Johannesburg Statistics* begins publication Chicago – *Chicago Defender* newspaper begins publication
1906		Tokyo – *Keijō Nippō* newspaper established Upton Sinclair, *The Jungle*
1906–09	US troops occupy Cuba after reconciliation following Liberal revolt fails	
1907		Rabindranath Tagore, "VisvaSahitya"(b. May 7, 1861, d. August 7, 1941) Rudyard Kipling, Nobel Prize for Literature (b. Dec. 20, 1865, d. Jan. 18, 1936) Dublin – Irish International Exhibition held
1908	Istanbul declared a province with nine constituent districts	Choe Nam-seon, "From the Ocean to the Youth"
	Leopold II transfers the Congo (his private possession since 1885) to Belgium	Tagore, *Home and the World*
	Union of South Africa established	Istanbul – *Karagöz* and *Jamanak* magazines begin publication
	Dutch establish rule in Bali Istanbul – The Young Turk Revolution	
1909	Johannesburg – Crown Mines Limited founded	Mohandas K. Gandhi, *Hind Swaraj*
		New York City – *New York Amsterdam News* begins publication
1910	Seoul – Japanese in power; rename city "Keijō"	Sydney – *The Sun* newspaper begins publication
	New York City – Manhattan Bridge opens	Istanbul – *Hikmet* magazine begins publication
	W.E.B. Du Bois founds National Association for the Advancement of Colored People (NAACP) Start of the Mexican Revolution	
1911	Wuchang Uprising	J.E. Casely Hayford, *Ethiopia Unbound*
	Beijing – Xinhai Revolution	Iliya Abu Madi, *The Memorial of the Past* Muhammad Iqbal, *Complaint*

Date	Urban Developments	Cultural and Literary Events
1912	Johannesburg – Alexandra township established	Léon Damas b. (d. 1978)
1913	Dublin Lock-out begins	Dadasaheb Phalke (dir), *Raja Harishchandra*
	Gandhi, leader of Indian Passive Resistance Movement, arrested	Tagore, Nobel Prize for Literature
	Beijing – Commission on the Unification of Pronunciation makes Beijing dialect national standard for spoken Chinese	New York City – *Vanity Fair* magazine begins publication
	Istanbul –Ottoman *coup d'état*	
1914		Gabriela Mistral, *Sonnets of Death*
		E.R. Burroughs, *Tarzan of the Apes*
		Lagos – *Lagos Central Times* newspaper begins publication
		Vladimir Mayakovsky, "Poslushayte!"
1914–18	First World War	
1915	Istanbul – deportation of Armenian intellectuals	Mariano Azuela, *The Underdogs*
	Istanbul – the 20 Hunchakian gallows hanging occurs	Cairo – *Arev* and *Housaper* newspapers begin publication
		Nikolai Bukharin, *Imperialism and World Economy*
		New York City – Knopf Publishing House founded
		Mariano Azuela, *The Underdogs*
1916	Sydney – Liverpool riot	Yi Kwang-su, *Heartlessness*
	Dublin – Easter Uprising	Vladimir Lenin, *Imperialism: The Highest Stage of Capitalism*
		Tagore, *Nationalism*
1917	Moscow – Bolshevik Uprising	Hô Chí Minh, *The Case Against French Colonization*
1918	Moscow becomes capital of the Russian Soviet Federative Socialist Republic	US Post Office burns installments of James Joyce's *Ulysses* published in *Little Review*
	Moscow – Left SR uprising	Petrograd – Vsemirnaia Literatura translation publishing house founded by Maxim Gorky
	British government abandons Home Rule for Ireland	Moscow – *Izvestia* newspaper in publication
	Istanbul – Occupation of Constantinople by Allied forces begins	
1919	Chicago race riot	Chu Yo-han, "Fireworks"
	Egyptian Revolution	Li Ta-chao, "A New Era"
	Peace Conference opens in Versailles	

Date	Urban Developments	Cultural and Literary Events
	Cairo – Ismailia Square becomes known as Tahrir (Freedom) Square	
	Istanbul – Turkish War of Independence begins	
	Beijing – May Fourth Movement	
1920–1939		
1920	Paris – League of Nations established	Seoul – *Chosun Ilbo* and *Dong-a Ilbo* newspapers begin publication
	Government of Ireland Act passed by British Parliament: Northern and Southern Ireland each to have own parliament	
	New York City – Wall Street bombing	
	Treaty of Moscow	
1920–33	Prohibition throughout the US	
1921	PEN International is founded	
	First Indian Parliament meets	
	Winston Churchill becomes Colonial Secretary	
	Britain and Ireland sign peace treaty	
	Lord Reading appointed Viceroy of India, succeeding Lord Chelmsford	
1922	Battle of Dublin	James Joyce, *Ulysses*
	Dublin becomes capital of the newly formed Irish Free State	Lu Xun, "The True Story of Ah Q"
	Johannesburg – miners' strike	
	Gandhi sentenced to six years' imprisonment for civil disobedience	
	League of Nations approves mandates for Egypt and Palestine	
	Arab Congress at Nablus rejects British mandate for Palestine	
	Mustafa Kemal proclaims Turkey a republic	
1923	New York City – city's first birth-control clinic opened	Paris – *Paris-Soir* newspaper begins publication
	Istanbul – Treaty of Lausanne	New York City – *Time* magazine begins publication
	Republic of Turkey established	William Butler Yeats, Nobel Prize for Literature (b. June 13, 1865, d. Jan. 28, 1939)

Date	Urban Developments	Cultural and Literary Events
	Turkish capital relocated from Istanbul to Ankara	*London Radio Times* begins publication
		Albert Sarraut, *The Economic Development of the French Colonies*
1924	Beijing Coup	Pablo Neruda, *Twenty Love Poems and a Song of Despair*
	Mumbai – Gateway of India inaugurated	London – British Empire Exhibition held
1925	New York City – Madison Square Garden opens	New York City – *The New Yorker* magazine begins publication
	Shanghai – May Thirtieth Movement	Thomas Mofolo, *Chaka*
1926	Beijing – March 18 Massacre	Ricardo Güiraldes, *Don Segundo Sombra*
	Guangzhou – Northern Expedition launched	Martin Luis Guzmán, *The Eagle and the Serpent*
		Thomas Mofolo, *Chaka*
1927	Shanghai municipality established	Taha Husain, *The Days* (vol. II, 1939)
	New Delhi founded	New York City – Random House publisher founded
		José Vasconcelos, *The Cosmic Race*
		Paris – Josephine Baker active
1928	Adoption of standard dialect and orthography for Swahili	Vladimir Propp, *Morfologija skazki*
	Johannesburg gains city status	Édouard Glissant b.
	Beijing – city renamed Beiping; capital moved to Nanjing	Mario de Andrade, *Macunaima*
		José Carlos Mariátegui, *Seven Essays towards an Interpretation of Peruvian Reality*
1929	South African Institute of Race Relations headquartered in Johannesburg	Mikhail Bakhtin, *Problemy tvorchestva Dostoevskogo*
	Paris – Nardal sisters open Le Salon de Clamart	
	New York City – "Black Friday"; the Great Depression begins	
	Chicago – St. Valentine's Day Massacre	
1930	Constantinople renamed "Istanbul"	Chinua Achebe b.
	Dublin – city boundaries expanded	Zaria Translation Bureau in Nigeria founded
		Négritude movement begins
		Mao Zedong, "A Single Spark Can Start a Prarie Fire"
		Nicolás Guillén, *Son Montifs*
		Aimé Césaire, *Cahier d'un retour au pays natal*

Date	Urban Developments	Cultural and Literary Events
1932	Indian Congress declared illegal; Gandhi arrested	Gregorio López y Fuentes, *The Land*
	Syndey Harbour Bridge inaugurated	Index Translationum is established by The League of Nations; subsequently passed on to UNESCO by the UN in 1946.
		Ahmad Shawqi, *Diwan*
1933	Philippines gains independence	Mulk Raj Anand, *Untouchable*
		Tewfiq al-Hakim, *The People of the Cave*
		Claude McKay, *Banana Bottom*
		Mao Tun, *Midnight*
		Gilberto Freyre, *The Master and the Slaves*
1934		Jorge Icaza, *Huasipungo*
		Alfred Mendes, *Pitch Lake*
1935		Jorge Luis Borges, *A Universal History of Infamy*
1936	Moscow Trials begin	Mao Zedong, *Problems of Strategy in China's Revolutionary War*
		Jayaprakash Narayan, *Why Socialism*
		Jawarharlal Nehru, *An Autobiography*
		Mani Bandopadhyay, *The History of Puppets*
		C.L.R. James, *Minty Alley*
		Lao She, *Rickshaw Boy*
		Munshi Premchand, *The Gift of a Cow*
1937	Beijing – Marco Polo Bridge Incident	World Congress of Universal Documentation held in Paris
	Dublin becomes capital of the newly formed Republic of Ireland	Hafiz Ibrahim, *Diwan*
	Mumbai – Indian provincial elections	Paris International Exposition
		R.R. Narayan, *The Bachelor of Arts*
		Siburapha, *Behind the Painting*
1937–45	Beijing – Second Sino-Japanese War	
1938		C.L.R. James, *The Black Jacobins*
1939	New York City – first World Science Fiction Convention held	Lin Yutang, *Moment in Peking*
		Stalin Prize is established
		Shanghai – *Shanghai Jewish Chronicle* begins publication
		Jorge Luis Borges, "La biblioteca total"
		James Joyce, *Finnigan's Wake*
		New York City –New York World's Fair opens

Date	Urban Developments	Cultural and Literary Events
		Margaret Atwood b.
1939–45	Second World War	
1940–1959		
1940		Dublin – *The Bell* magazine begins publication
1941	Battle of Moscow begins	H.I.E. Dhlomo, *Valley of a Thousand Hills*
	Manila City Hall completed	Edgar Mittelholzer, *Cortentyne Thunder*
		Ibrahim Tuqan, *Diwani*
1942	Singapore – Sook Ching Massacre	Jorge Amado, *The Violent Land*
	Manila – Japanese occupation begins	Albert Camus, *L'etranger / The Outsider*
	Mumbai – Quit India Movement declaration passed	Stefan Heym, *Hostages*
1942–45	Singapore under Japanese rule	
1943		Ishaw Musa al Husaini, *A Chicken's Memoirs*
		Eileen Chang (Zhang Ailing), "Love in a Fallen City" and "The Golden Cangue"
		New York City – New York Fashion Week begins
1944		José Maria Arguedas, *Everyone's Blood*
		Ismat Chughtai, *The Quilt and Other Stories*
		Jacques Roumain, *Masters of the Dew*
		Eric Williams, *Capitalism and Slavery*
1945	Moscow Victory Parade	Gabriela Mistral (b. 7 Apr. 1889, d. 10 Jan. 1957) wins Nobel Prize for Literature
		Gopinath Mohanty, *Paraja*
		Chicago – *Ebony* magazine begins publication
		Accra – *African Morning Post* newspaper begins publication
1946	Seoul National University established	Jawaharlal Nehru, *The Discovery of India*
	Singapore – Staits Settlements is dissolved; Singapore becomes separate crown colony	Peter Abrahams, *Mine Boy*
	Singapore – Legislative Council of the Colony of Singapore	Erich Auerbach, *Mimesis: Dargestellte Wirklichkeit in der abendländischen Literatur* (translated as *Mimesis: The Representation of Reality in Western Literature* in 1953)

Date	Urban Developments	Cultural and Literary Events
	Manila becomes part of newly proclaimed Republic of the Philippines	Miguel Ángel Asturias, *Mr. President*
1947	Independence of India; partitioned into India and Pakistan	Istanbul – *Şalom* begins publication
	New Delhi becomes the capital of India	Paris – *Présence Africaine* magazine founded
		Tennessee Williams, *A Streetcar Named Desire*
		Salman Rushdie b.
		Jawaharlal Nehru delivers, "Tryst with Destiny" speech
		Babani Bhattacharya, *So Many Hungers!*
		Birago Diop, *Tales of Amadou Koumba*
		Suryakant Tripathi "Nirala," *The Earthly Knowledge*
		Badr Shakir al Sayyab, *Withered Fingers*
1948	Capital of Philippines relocated from Manila to Quezon City	East African Literature Bureau founded
	Gandhi assassinated	
	State of Israel comes into existence	Aimé Césaire, *Soleil cou coupé*
	British Citizenship Act grants British passports to all Commonwealth citizens	Cairo – *Tchahagir* newspaper begins publication
	Seoul becomes capital of the Republic of Korea	Graham Greene, *The Heart of the Matter*
		Alan Paton, *Cry, the Beloved Country*
		G.V. Desani, *All About H. Hatterr*
		Saadat Hasan Manto, "Toba Tek Singh"
		Ernesto Sabato, *The Tunnel*
		Léopold Sédar Senghor, ed., *Anthologie de la nouvelle poesie negre et malgache de langue française*
		Jean Paul Sartre, *Black Orpheus*
1949	Beiping renamed Beijing; becomes capital of People's Republic of China	Istanbul – *İstanbul* newspaper begins publication
	People's Government of Beijing established	Paris – *Paris Match* magazine begins publication
	Seoul Metropolitan Government founded	Miguel Ángel Asturias, *Men of Maize*
	Apartheid program established in South Africa	Alejo Carpentier, *The Kindgom of This World*

Date	Urban Developments	Cultural and Literary Events
	Holland transfers sovereignty to Indonesia; France to Vietnam	Khalil Mutran, *Diwan*
	India adopts constitution as federal republic	V.S. Reid, *New Day*
		Ma'ruf al Rusafi, *Diwan*
1950	Second Battle of Seoul	Pablo Neruda, *Canto général*
	Singapore – Hertogh riots	Octavio Paz, *Labyrinth of Solitude*
	Mumbai – Bombay Province becomes Bombay State	Doris Lessing, *The Grass is Singing*
		Aimé Césaire, *Discours sur le colonialism*
1951	Third Battle of Seoul	Nirad C. Chaudhuri, *The Autobiography of an Unknown India*
		Johannesburg – *Drum* magazine begins publication
		J.L. Borges, "El escritor argentino y la tradición"
1951	London trams are retired	Cairo – *Al Akhbar* starts publication
	Beijing – Asia and Pacific Rim Peace Conference	Frantz Fanon, *Peau noire, masques blancs*
	Egyptian Revolution	Samuel Beckett, *Waiting for Godot*
		Ralph Ellison, *Invisible Man*
		Ralph de Boissière, *Crown Jewel*
		Andrée Chediz, *From Sleep Unbound*
		Mochtar Lubis, *A Road with No End*
		Amos Tutuola, *The Palm Wine Drinkard*
1953	Dublin – City boundaries expanded	Fidel Castro, "History will absolve me" speech
		George Lamming, *In the Castle of My Skin*
		Camara Laye, *The African Child*
		Roger Mais, *The Hills Were All Joyful Together*
		Alejo Carpentier, *Los pasos perdidos*
1954	Alexandria – Lavon Affair	Seoul – *Hankook Ilbo* newspaper begins publication
		Sahitya Akademi Award established
		Samira Azzam, *Little Things*
		Martin Carter, *Poems of Resistance*
		Driss Chraibi, *The Simple Past*
		Kamala Markandaya, *Nectar in a Sieve*
		Nicanor Parra, *Poems and Antipoems*
		Abd al Rahman Shasrawi, *The Earth*
1954–62	Algerian War of Independence	

Date	Urban Developments	Cultural and Literary Events
1955	Istanbul pogrom	Amrita Pritam, *Messages*
	Bandung – Afro-Asian Conference, Indonesia	Juan Rulfo, *Pedro Paramo*
	Legislative Assembly of the State of Singapore established	Saadi Youssef, *Songs Not for Others*
	Vietnam War begins	
1956	Johannesburg – Treason Trial begins	Octavio Mannoni, *Prospero and Caliban: The Psychology of Colonization*
	New York Coliseum opens	Congress of Black Writers and Artists
		George Padmore, *Pan Africanism or Communism?*
		Carlos Bulosan, *America is in the Heart*
		Mongo Beti, *The Poor Christ of Bomba*
		David Diop, *Hammer Blows*
		Faiz Ahmed Faiz, *Prison Thoughts*
		João Guimãres Rosa, *The Devil to Pay in the Backlands*
		Samuel Selvon, *The Lonely Londoners*
		Kwame Nkrumah, *Ghana: The Autobiography* of *Kwame Nkrumah*
		Octavio Paz, *Sunstone*
		Albert Memmi, *The Colonizer and the Colonized*
1956–57		Naguib Mahfouz, *The Cairo Trilogy*
1957	Johannesburg –Alexandra Bus Boycott	
	Accra – Black Star Gate completed	
1958	London bus strike	Chinua Achebe, *Things Fall Apart*
		Tashkent – Afro-Asian Writers' Conference
		Édouard Glissant, *The Ripening*
		N.V.M. González, *Bread of Salt*
		Ludu U Hla, *The Caged Ones*
1959	Beijing – Great Hall of the People opens	Qurratulain Hyder, *River of Fire*
	Cuba – overthrow of Batista regime; Fidel Castro assumes power	Es'kia Mphahlele, *Down Second Avenue*
		Lorraine Hansberry, *A Raisin in the Sun*
		Naguib Mahfouz, *Children of Gebelawi*

Date	Urban Developments	Cultural and Literary Events
1960–1969		
1960	Mimeo (DIY book production) revolution begins in North America (ca. 1960s to 1980s)	Wilson Harris, *Palace of the Peacock*
	Local Administration Law; Alexandria, Cairo receive governate status	Ousmane Sembene, *God's Bits of Wood*
	Belgian Congo achieves full independence	George Lamming, *The Pleasures of Exile*
	Mumbai – Bombay becomes capital of newly formed state, Maharashtra	
	Johannesburg – Sharpeville massacre	
1961	Cairo Tower built	Rajat Neogy founds *Transition Magazine: An International Review*
	London – Spy Trials	Nnamdi Azikiwe, *Zik: Selected Speeches*
	Johannesburg becomes part of the Republic of South Africa	Ernesto "Che" Guevara, *Guerrilla Warfare*
	Paris – last journey of the Orient Express	Adonis, *Songs of Muhyar the Damascene*
	Singapore – Bukit Ho Swee fire	Cyrpian Ekwensi, *Jagua Nana*
	Paris massacre	Attia Hosain, *Sunlight on a Broken Column*
		Cheikh Hamidou Kane, *Ambiguous Adventure*
		V.S. Naipaul, *A House for Mr. Biswas*
		Istanbul – *Hürriyet Daily News* begins publication
		Grand prix littéraire de l'Afrique noire is established; *Transition/Ch'indaba* is founded
		Paul Celan, "Der Meridian"
		Frantz Fanon, *Les damnés de la terre*
1962		Alan Hill at Heinemann initiates its African Writers Series (AWS)
		Mehdi Ben Barka, "Resolving the Ambiguities of National Sovereignty"
		Kenneth Kaunda, *Zambia Shall be Free*
		Patrice Lumumba, *Congo My Country*
		Albert Luthuli, *Let My People Go*

Date	Urban Developments	Cultural and Literary Events
		Carlos Fuentes, *The Death of Artemio Cruz* Alex La Guma, *A Walk in the Night* Carlos Martínez Moreno, *The Wall* Mario Vargas Llosa, *The Time of the Hero*
1963	Singapore merges with Federation of Malaya to form Malaysia Johannesburg – Rivonia Trial begins	São Paulo – *Notícias Populares* newspaper begins publication Julio Cortázar, *Hopscotch* Ghassan Kanafani, *Men in the Sun* Severo Sarduy, *Gestures* C.L.R. James, *Beyond a Boundary* Govan Mbeki, *South Africa: The Peasants' Revolt* Forugh Farrokhzad, *Another Birth*
1964	New York City – race riots in Harlem	José Craveirinha, *Xigubo* Martin Luther King Jr. (b. Jan. 15, 1929, d. Apr. 4, 1968), Nobel Peace Prize First conference on Commonwealth Literature, University of Leeds *Journal of Commonwealth Literature* founded
1965	New York City – Northeast Blackout Singapore and Malyasia sign separation agreement Parliament of Singapore established	Paul Scott, *The Raj Quartet* (1965–75) Nelson Mandela, *No Easy Walk to Freedom* Kwame Nkrumah, *Neo-Colonialism: The Last Stage of Imperialism* Michael Anthony, *The Year in San Fernando* Guillermo Cabrera Infante, *Three Trapped Tigers* Kamala Das, *Summer in Calcutta* Wole Soyinka, *The Road*
1966	Dublin – Garden of Remembrance opens	World Festival of Black Arts, Dakar Nikolai Konrad, *Zapad i Vostok* Miguel Ángel Asturias, *Men of Maize*
1966–76	Beijing – Cultural Revolution	
1967	Issue of the first Singapore Dollar Lagos State Government founded	Miguel Ángel Asturias (b. Oct. 19, 1899; d. June 9, 1974), Nobel Prize for Literature
1967–70	Nigerian Civil War	

Date	Urban Developments	Cultural and Literary Events
1968	Moscow – Red Square demonstration	Cairo – *Lotus: Afro-Asian Writings* begins publication
	Singapore – National Archives established	Booker Prize established
	Mexico City student protests; *Tlatelolco massacre*	Ayi Kwei Armah, *The Beautyful Ones Are Not Yet Born*
1969	Singapore – Race Riots	Samuel Beckett (b. Apr. 13, 1906; d. Dec. 22, 1989), Nobel Prize for Literature
	Chicago – Chicago Eight trial opens	Cairo International Book Fair founded
	Istanbul – Bloody Sunday	Neustadt Prize for Literature established
1970–1979		
1970	New York City – LGBT Pride March begins	Istanbul – *Türkiye* newspaper begins publication
		Toni Morrison, *The Bluest Eye*
1971	YTN Seoul Tower completed	Bai Xianyong, *Taipei People*
	United Arab Emirates founded	
	Manila – Plaza Miranda bombing	
1972	Lagos – Tafawa Balewa Square built	
	Britain imposes direct rule on Northern Ireland	
	Dublin – British Embassy in Merrion Square destroyed by protesters	
	Singapore – Merlion inaugurated	
1973	Singapore – Presidential Council for Minority Rights established	Patrick White (b. May 28, 1912; d. Sept. 30, 1990), Nobel Prize for Literature
		Amilcar Cabral, *Return of the Source*
		Mahasweta Devi, *Mother of 1084*
		First Paris Fashion Week held
		Eduardo Galeano, *The Open Veins of Latin America*
		Keiji Nakazawa, *Hadashi no Gen* (1973/1974)
1974		Nadine Gordimer wins Booker Prize for *The Conservationist*
		M. Gopalkirshna Adiga, *Song of the Earth and Other Poems*
		Emile Habiby, *The Secret Life of Saeed, the Ill-Fated Pessoptimist*
		Bessie Head, *A Question of Power*
		Daniel Moyano, *The Devil's Trill*
		Agostinho Neto, *Sacred Hope*

Date	Urban Developments	Cultural and Literary Events
		Augusto Roa Bastos, *I the Supreme* José Luandino Vieira, *The Real Life of Domingos Xavier* Adonis, *The Fixed and the Changing: A Study of Conformity and Originality in Arab Culture* Barry Feinberg, ed., *Poets to the People*
1975	Liberation of Saigon	Soyinka, *Death and the King's Horseman* Frankétienne, *Dézafi* Bharati Mukherjee, *Wife* Indira Sant, *The Snake-Skin and Other Poems* Antonio Skármeta, *I Dreamt the Snow Was Burning*
1976	Johannesburg – Soweto Uprising	Alex Haley, *Roots* Miguel de Cervantes Prize is established *Callaloo* journal established Jaranta Mahpatra, *A Pain of Rites* Manuel Puig, *The Kiss of the Spider Woman* Antonio Torres, *The Land* Soyinka, *Myth, Literature and the African World*
1977	Istanbul – Taksim Square massacre	São Paulo International Film Festival begins Bessie Head, *The Collector of Treasures* Lagos – National Arts Theatre built Elias Khoury, *Little Mountain* Clarice Lispector, *The Hour of the Star* Ngũgĩ wa Thiong'o, *Petals of Blood* Sergio Ramirez, *To Bury Our Fathers* Manuel Rui, *Yes Comrade!* Sydney Festival begins Samir Amin, *Imperialism and Unequal Development* Satjayit Ray, *Shatranj Ke Khilari*
1978	New York City – newspaper strikes	Johannesburg – *Staffrider* literary magazine begins publication Edward Said, *Orientalism* Noma Award for Publishing in Africa established

Date	Urban Developments	Cultural and Literary Events
		Dambudzo Marechera, *The House of Hunger*
		O.V. Viajayan, *Short Stories*
		Shanghai Translation Publishing House founded
1979	Singapore – National Courtesy Campaign	Istanbul – *Kadınca* magazine begins publication
		Cairo – *Egypt Today* magazine begins publication
		Kunapipi journal established
		Mariama Ba, *So Long a Letter*
		Buchi Emecheta, *The Joys of Motherhood*
		Nuruddin Farah, *Sweet and Sour Milk*
		Nadine Gordimer, *Burger's Daughter*
		Roy Heath, *The Armstrong Trilogy*
		Earl Lovelace, *The Dragon Can't Dance*
		Xi Xi, *My City: A Hong Kong Story*
		Pramoedya Ananta Toer, *Buru Quartet*
1980–1989		
1980	Seoul – Gwangju Massacre	J.M. Coetzee, *Waiting for the Barbarians*
	Johannesburg – Municipal Workers strike	Anita Desai, *Clear Light of Day*
		Pepetela, *Mayombe*
		Ricardo Piglia, *Artifical Respiration*
		Salman Rushdie, *Midnight's Children*
		Osvaldo Soriano, *A Funny Dirty Little War*
		Michael Thelwell, *The Harder They Come*
		Albert Wendt, *Leaves of the Banyan Tree*
		Johannesburg – Federated Union of Black Artists Academy established
		Johannesburg – Federated Union of Black Artists Academy established
1981	London – Brixton riots	Johannesburg – *The Sowetan* newspaper begins publication
		César Aira, *Ema, la cautiva*
		Salman Rushdie wins Booker Prize for *Midnight's Children*

Date	Urban Developments	Cultural and Literary Events
		Ariel Dorfman, *Widows* Mongane Wally Serote, *To Every Birth Its Blood* Aminata Sow Fall, *The Beggar's Strike* Malek Alloula, *The Colonial Harem* Benedict Anderson, *Imagined Communities: Reflections on the Origins and Spread of Nationalism* Édouard Glissant, *Caribbean Discourse*
1982	Mumbai – Great Bombay Textile Strike	Istanbul – Timas Publishing Group established International Istanbul Film Festival begins Octavio Paz wins Neustadt Prize Abdelwahab Elmessiri, ed., *The Palestinian Wedding* Gabriel García Márquez (b. Mar. 6, 1927; d. Apr. 17, 2014), Nobel Prize for Literature Thomas Keneally wins Booker Prize for *Schindler's Ark* Inaugural issue of the series *Subaltern Studies*, edited by Ranajit Guha Isabel Allende, *The House of the Spirits* Reinaldo Arenas, *Farewell to the Sea* Edward Kamau Brathwaite, *The Arrivants*
1983		J.M. Coetzee wins Booker Prize for *Life and Times of Michael K* Jamaica Kincaid, *Annie John* Njabulo Ndebele, *Fools and Other Stories* Grace Nichols, *i is a long memoried woman* Sony Labou Tansi, *The Antipeople* Luisa Valenzuela, *The Lizard's Tail* Nirmal Verma, *The Crows of Deliverance* Johannes Fabian, *Time and the Other* Abdelkébir Khatibi, *Maghreb pluriel*
1984	Municipality of Greater Istanbul established	*Wasafiri* journal established

Date	Urban Developments	Cultural and Literary Events
		Rigoberta Menchú, *I, Rigoberta Menchú: An Indian Woman in Guatemala*
		Miguel Bonasso, *Memory of Death*
		Maryse Condé, *Segu*
		Abdelrahman Munif, *City of Salt*
		Cristina Peri Rossi, *The Ship of Fools*
		Edward Kamau Brathwaite, *History of the Voice*
		Wiesław Myśliwski, *Kamień na kamieniu*
1985		Sydney – Granny Smith Festival begins
		Shanghai – *Wenhui Book Review* begins publication
		Keri Hulme wins Booker Prize for *The Bone People*
		Tahar Ben Jelloun, *The Sand Child*
		Assia Djebar, *Fantasia: An Algerian Cavalcade*
		García Márquez, *Love in the Time of Cholera*
		Nayantara Sahgal, *Rich Like Us*
		Ken Saro-Wiwa, *Sozaboy*
1986	Manila – People Power Revolution	Soyinka, Nobel Prize for Literature (b. July 13, 1934)
	Istanbul – Neve Shalom Synagogue massacre	Nuruddin Farah, *Maps*
		Waleed Khazindar, *Present Verbs*
		Hanif Kureishi, *My Beautiful Laundrette*
		Álvaro Mutis, *The Snow of the Admiral*
		Carly Phillips, *A State of Independence*
		Anton Shammas, *Arbasques*
		Derek Walcott, *Collected Poems*
		Partha Chatterjee, *Nationalist Thought and the Colonial World: A Derivative Discourse*
		Peter Hulme, *Colonial Encounters: Europe and the Native Caribbean, 1492–1797*
		Ngũgĩ wa Thiong'o, *Decolonising the Mind: The Politics of Language in African Literature*

Date	Urban Developments	Cultural and Literary Events
		Frederic Jameson, "Third World Literature in the Era of Multinational China"
1987	New York City – "Black Monday"	Commonwealth Writers' Prize is established
	Paris Arab World Institute inaugurated	New York City – *The New York Observer* begins publication
	Manila – Mendiola Massacre	Agha Shahid Ali, *The Half Inch Himalayas*
		Jesus Díaz, *The Initials of the Land*
		Daniel Maximin, *Soufrieres*
		Horacio Vazquez Rial, *Triste's History*
		Shrikant Verma, *Magadh*
		Benita Parry, "Problems in Current Theories of Colonial Discourse"
		Toni Morrison wins Pulitzer Prize for *Beloved*
1988	Accra Metropolitan Assembly founded	Naguib Mahfouz (b. Dec. 11, 1911; d. Aug 30, 2006), Nobel Prize for Literature
	New York City – Human Rights Watch headquartered in city	Peter Carey wins Booker Prize for *Oscar and Lucinda*
	Johannesburg – Bombing of Khotso House	Raja Rao wins Neustadt Prize
		Upamayu Chatterjee, *English, August*
		Prémio Camões is established
		Amit Chaudhuri, *Afternoon Raag*
		Michelle Cliff, *No Telephone to Heaven*
		Tsitsi Dangarembga, *Nervous Conditions*
		Amitav Ghosh, *The Shadow Lines*
		Suong Thu Huong, *Paradise of the Blind*
		Chenjerai Hove, *Bones*
		Tomás Eloy Martínez, *The Peron Novel*
		Salman Rushdie, *Satanic Verses*
		Bapsi Sidhwa, *Cracking India*
		Héctor Tizón, *The Man Who Came to a Village*
		Chandra Talpade Mohanty "Under Western Eyes: Feminist Scholarship and Colonial Discourse"

Date	Urban Developments	Cultural and Literary Events
		V.Y. Mudimbe, *The Invention of Africa: Gnosis, Philosophy, and the Order of Knowledge*
1989	Beijing – Tiananmen Square protests	Kazuo Ishiguro wins Booker Prize for *The Remains of the Day* Moscow Music Peace Festival Bill Ashcroft, Gareth Griffiths, and Helen Tiffin, *The Empire Writes Back* Nissim Ezekiel, *Collected Poems* Ngũgĩ wa Thiong'o, *Matigari* M.G. Vassanji, *The Gunny Sack* Jean Bernabe, Patrick Camouiseau, and Raphael Confiant, *In Praise of Creoleness* Pan African Writers' Association (PAWA) founded
1990–1999		
1990	Persian Gulf War	Octavio Paz (b. Mar. 31, 1914; d. Apr. 19, 1998), Nobel Prize for Literature Gayatri Spivak, *The Postcolonial Critic* Robert Young, *White Mythologies* Mia Couto, *Every Man is a Race* Abd al Wahhab Bayati, *Love Death and Exile* Terry Eagleton, Fredric Jameson, and Edward Said, *Nationalism, Colonialism and Literature* Orhan Pamuk, *The Black Book*
1991	Moscow – Soviet *coup d'état* attempt Johannesburg – Central Witwatersrand Metropolitan Chamber founded Seoul – Blue House (government residence) completed Delhi formally made into National Capital Territory Lagos – capital moved to Abuja	Cairo – *Al-Ahram Weekly* begins publication Nadine Gordimer (b. Nov. 20, 1923; d. July 13, 2014), Nobel Prize for Literature Ben Okri wins Booker Prize for *The Famished Road* Khalil Hawi, *From the Vineyards of Lebanon* Timothy Mo, *The Redundancy of Courage* Derek Walcott, *Omeros* Salman Rushdie, *Imaginary Homelands: Essays and Criticism*

Date	Urban Developments	Cultural and Literary Events
1992	Accra – Kwame Nkrumah Memorial Park dedicated	Moscow – *Moscow Times* newspaper begins publication Shanghai – *Shanghai Star* newspaper begins publication Derek Walcott (b. Jan. 23, 1930; d. Mar. 17, 2017), Nobel Prize for Literature Michael Ondaatje wins Booker Prize for *The English Patient* João Cabral de Melo Neto wins Neustadt Prize Ambai (C.S. Lakshmi), *The Purple Sea* Patrick Chamoiseau, *Texaco* Michael Ondaatje, *The English Patient* Aijaz Ahmad, *In Theory: Class, Nations, Literatures* Marie Louise Pratt, *Imperial Eyes: Travel Writing and Transculturation* Arturo Uslar Pietri, *The Creation of the New World* Roberto Schwarz, *Misplaced Ideas: Essays on Brazilian Culture*
1993	Moscow City Duma founded	Toni Morrison (b. Feb. 18, 1931; d. Aug. 5, 2019), Nobel Prize for Literature
	Formal end of apartheid in South Africa; anti-apartheid revolutionary, Nelson Mandela is President from 1994 to 1999	*Parlement international des écrivains* is founded
	Moscow designated capital of the Russian Federation	Roddy Doyle wins Booker Prize for *Paddy Clarke Ha Ha Ha* Salman Rushdie wins Booker of Bookers for *Midnight's Children* Edward Said, *Culture and Imperialism* Amin Maalouf, *The Rock of Tanios* Vikram Seth, *A Suitable Boy* Ivan Vladislavic, *The Folly*
1994	Johannesburg – Shell House Massacre	Muhammad al Maghut, *Joy Is Not My Profession* Chu T'ien-wen, *Notes of a Desolate Man* Shyam Selvadurai, *Funny Boy* Kamau Brathwaite wins Neustadt Prize

Date	Urban Developments	Cultural and Literary Events
		Homi K. Bhabha, *The Location of Culture*
1995	Bombay renamed Mumbai	José Saramago, *Blindness*
	Johannesburg – Greater Johannesburg Metropolitan Council founded	Seamus Heaney (b. Apr. 13, 1939; d. 30 Aug. 30, 2013), Nobel Prize for Literature
		Subcommandante Marcos, *Shadows of Tender Fury*
		A.K. Ramanuhan, *Collected Poems*
		Keki Daruwalla, *A Summer of Tigers*
		Declan Kiberd, *Inventing Ireland: The Literature of the Modern Nation*
		Nelson Mandela, *No Easy Walk to Freedom*
1996	Istanbul – United Nations Conference on Human Settlements held	Assia Djebar wins Neustadt Prize
	Delhi – Lajpat Nagar market blast	Rohinton Mistry, *Love and Longing in Bombay*
		Nizar Qabbani, *On Entering the Sea*
1997	Britain returns sovereignty of Hong Kong to China	Arundhati Roy wins Booker Prize for *The God of Small Things*
		Cairo – Aldiwan Arabic Language Center opens
		Jouvert, *Journal of Postcolonial Studies* (1997–2003)
		Vikram Chandra, *Love and Longing in Bombay*
		Arundhati Roy, *The God of Small Things*
		A. Sivanandan, *When Memory Dies*
1998	Sydney water crisis	Orhan Pamuk, *My Name is Red*
	Peace Agreement signed for Northern Ireland	Nuruddin Farah wins Neustadt Prize
1999	Istanbul bombings	J.M. Coetzee wins Booker Prize for *Disgrace*
		Shanghai – *Shanghai Daily* newspaper begins publication
2000–2009		
2000	Istanbul – city expands to include eight additional districts	Margaret Atwood wins Booker Prize for *The Blind Assassin*
	Manila – Rizal Day bombings	David Malouf wins Neustadt Prize
	Johannesburg – Metropolitan Municipality established	Caine Prize for African Writing: short story established

Date	Urban Developments	Cultural and Literary Events
	Moscow becomes part of the Central Federal District	Dublin Writers Festival begins
		Naiyer Masud, *Essence of Camphor* Marjane Satrapi, *Persepolis* Zadie Smith, *White Teeth* Manila – Green Papaya Art Projects founded V.S. Naipaul (b. Aug. 17, 1932; d. 11 Aug. 11, 2018), Nobel Prize for Literature
2001	Delhi – Indian Parliament attack	Peter Carey wins Booker Prize for *True History of the Kelly Gang*
	Dublin – Dublin Corporation renamed Dublin City Council	Franz Kafka Prize is established
	Terrorist attacks on US soil on September 11 sparks subsequent era of War on Terror	Roberto Bolaño, “El viaje de Álvaro Rousselot”
	Manila – EDSA Revolution Manila – EDSA III protest	
2002	Johannesburg – Soweto is incorporated into the city	Yann Martel wins Booker Prize for *Life of Pi* Álvaro Mutis wins Neustadt Prize São Paulo – Casa das Áfricas founded
2003	Moscow – Red Square bombing	J.M. Coetzee (b. Feb. 9, 1940), Nobel Prize for Literature
	US invasion of Iraq	David Damrosch, *What is World Literature?* Nairobi – *Kwani?* literary journal begins publication
2004	Sydney – Redfern riots	*Postcolonial Text* journal begins publication Cairo – *Al-masry Al-youm* newspaper begins publication Edward Said, *Humanism and Democratic Criticism*
2005	Sydney – Cronulla riots	Damon Galgut wins Regional Commonwealth Writers’ Best Book Prize John Banville wins Booker Prize for *The Sea* Man Booker International Prize established Chimamanda Ngozi Adichie wins Commonwealth Writers’ Best Book Prize

Date	Urban Developments	Cultural and Literary Events
		Ismail Kadare wins Man Booker Prize
2006		Ajay Navaria, *Pat˙ kathaaur anya Kahaniyam*
		Orhan Pamuk (b. June 7, 1952), Nobel Prize for Literature
		Lagos – Cassava Republic Press founded
		Claribel Alegria wins Neustadt Prize
		Kiran Desai wins Booker Prize for *The Inheritance of Loss*
		Ngozi Adichie, *Half a Yellow Sun*
		Mexico City – Centro Cultural Bella Epoca bookshop opens
		Kenya's first online Sheng Dictionary goes live
2007	San Francisco – Steve Jobs unveils the first iPhone	Sheldon Pollock, *The Language of the Gods in the World of Men*
	London – new Wembley Stadium completed	Doris Lessing (b. Oct. 27, 1919; d. Nov. 17, 2013), Nobel Prize for Literature
		Beijing – National Grand Theatre of China built
		Anne Enright wins Booker Prize for *The Gathering*
		Pascale Casanova, *The World Republic of Letters*
		Chinua Achebe wins Man Booker International Prize
2008	New York City – Times Square bombing	Junot Díaz wins Pulitzer Prize for Fiction
	Beijing Olympics India plants flag on moon for first time	Cairo – *Youm 7* newspaper starts publication
		Aravind Adiga wins Booker Prize for *The White Tiger*
		Patricia Grace wins Neustadt Prize
2009	Moscow – City of Capitals completed	Alice Munro wins Man Booker International Prize
	Istanbul – City districts increase from 32 to 39	Vivid Sydney festival
	Mass protests in Iran	Penguin African Writing Prize launched
		J.M. Coetzee, *Summertime*
2010– present		
2010	Rio de Janeiro – Brazil wins bid for 2016 summer Olympics	New York City – *Humans of New York* begins publication

Date	Urban Developments	Cultural and Literary Events
	The Arab Spring protests begin	UNESCO launches World Digital Library Global Initiative
	Earthquake in Haiti	Kiran Desai (India) wins Booker Prize for *The Inheritance of Loss*
	Student protest in Dublin	Daniyal Mueenuddin (Pakistan) wins Pulitzer Prize for Fiction
	Dubai – the Burj Khalifa, tallest man-made structure to date, is opened	Mario Vargas Llosa (b. Mar. 28, 1936), Nobel Prize for Literature
2011	Dublin – Occupy Dame Street begins	Arvind Krishna Mehrotra, *Songs of Kabir*
	Alexandria – Egyptian Revolution	Ahmet Hamdi Tanpinar Literature Museum Library opens in Istanbul, Turkey
	New York City – Occupy Wall Street begins	S. Anand, Srividya Natarajan, Durgabai Vyam, and Subhash Vyam, *Bhimayana*
2012	Istanbul – Museum of Innocence opens	Mo Yan (b. Feb. 17, 1955), Nobel Prize for Literature
		Rohinton Mistry wins Neustadt Prize
2013	Manila – Million People March	Windham Campbell Literary awards established
	South African President Nelson Mandela dies	
2014	Moscow – Peace Procession against war in Ukraine	Mia Couto wins Neustadt Prize
		Richard Flanagan wins Booker Prize for *The Narrow Road to the Deep North*
2015	Johannesburg – #FeesMustFall protest	
	New York City – Disability Pride Parade held	
2016		Istanbul – *Özgürlükçü Demokrasi* begins publication
2017	Istanbul – March for Justice	
2018		Edwidge Danticat wins Neustadt Prize
2019	Paris Notre-Dame de Paris fire	Kazuo Ishiguro wins Nobel Prize for Literature (b. November 1954)
2020	WHO declares COVID-19 as a pandemic on March 11	Ismail Kadare wins Neustadt Prize
	Minneapolis – killing of George Floyd on May 25 sparks worldwide demonstrations	
	Lagos – End SARS protests	

CHAPTER I

Introduction
World Literature, Cities, and Urban Imaginaries

Jini Kim Watson and Ato Quayson

City Worlds

Why has world literature been such a compelling framework for literary scholars to think through and against over the last decades? And what might a volume that examines the city's relationship to this field add to these debates? *The Cambridge Companion to the City in World Literature* contributes to this growing body of scholarship by foregrounding the key relationship of urbanism to world literature, a relationship that has not yet been adequately explored. Through a series of chapters spanning a number of metropolises across the globe, we address the way cities have given rise to aesthetic dispositions, acts of linguistic and cultural translation, topographic conceptualizations, global imaginaries, and narratives of self-fashioning that are central to understanding world literature and its debates. Deploying a wide variety of reading methods and textual objects, our contributors offer case studies from cities both well known in the world literary orbit and those less often anthologized: Beijing, Bombay/Mumbai, Dublin, Cairo, Istanbul, Johannesburg, Lagos, London, Mexico City, Moscow and St. Petersburg, New York, Paris, Singapore, Sydney, as well as (in Part I chapters) Chicago, Dubai, Manila, Seoul, and New Delhi. Our expansion of the typical nodes of world literary production activates not just a broader spatial imaginary or geographical reach for the field, but multiplies the historical and linguistic formations of potential literary world systems. Instead of offering a singular new theory of world literature to supersede previous ones, this volume aims to proliferate the "worldings" which urban literatures simultaneously invoke and create.[1] This introductory chapter will trace several of the most salient contributions to the field of world literature in order to position our volume's focus on city literature.

We start with two uncontroversial propositions about the appeal and prominence of world literature formulations. The first is that, at a very basic level, theories of world literature have sought to move beyond the boundedness of national literatures, challenging the way literary texts have typically been divided up and organized by both the modern university and publishing practices. Such theories emphatically contest the divisions of literary study into departments of English, French, German, and – for non-Western languages – the so-called "area studies" departments of Asian, African, or Latin American studies. The turn to world literature, in Emily Apter's phrase, is an "experiment in national sublation."[2] The burgeoning of critical interest in world literature approaches over the last twenty years or so is undoubtedly related to the rise of the post-Cold War era of globalization, understood as ushering in a new economic and cultural regime that supersedes national literatures.[3] But invocations of world literature formulations often refer back to two well-known nineteenth-century pronouncements on the subject. The first, by Johann Wolfgang von Goethe (1749–1832), enthusiastically announced an epoch of *Weltliteratur* beyond national literatures, while Karl Marx and Friedrich Engels famously wrote in *The Communist Manifesto* (1848) of the power of worldwide capitalism to break down national barriers: "National one-sidedness and narrow-mindedness become more and more impossible, and from the numerous national and local literatures, there arises a world literature."[4] In 1952, comparative philologist Erich Auerbach would write: "[N]ew outlooks on history and on reality have been revealed, and the view of the structure of inter-human processes has been enriched and renewed. We have participated – indeed, we are still participating – in a practical seminar on world history [....] In any event, our philological home is the earth: it can no longer be the nation."[5] For better or worse, Goethe, Marx, and Engels are frequently invoked as a kind of origin point for thinking about literary cultures beyond national boundaries, while Auerbach is taken to provide an important twentieth-century literary critical method for thinking beyond individual national literatures. Such approaches offer the substantive appeal of studying literature in a global frame and attending to its boundary-crossing, transnational, translational, cosmopolitan, worldly, or globalizing dimensions. To quote one influential definition from David Damrosch, world literature takes as its remit the sum of literary works that "circulate beyond their culture of origin, either in translation or in their original language."[6]

A second, and related, proposition is that the expansion of literary study from the nation to the world brings with it a theoretical concern for literary systematicity or *totality*. As Ben Etherington and Jarad Zimbler have noted, the concept of totality "brings to the fore the dynamic relationship between parts and whole: that is, the ways in which the interrelations and interactions of particulars cumulatively constitute a *single intelligible entity*."[7] Witness, then, the proliferation of studies that seek to model those "dynamic relationships" between part and whole at a world scale. The most cited of these is arguably Pascale Casanova's *The World Republic of Letters* (1999), which depicts a literary world system structured by its own internal laws. Centered on Paris, the "literary Greenwich meridian," this system comprises "dominant and dominated literary spaces" which jostle in a rivalrous contest of "literary geopolitics."[8] Relatedly, we have Franco Moretti's turn to "distant reading" as a necessary methodology for understanding the worldwide distribution of literary forms such as the novel; he explicitly theorizes such an approach in imitation of "world systems theory" – with its concern for the *longue durée* and changing relationships between core and periphery – formulated by economic historian Immanuel Wallerstein.[9] A variant of this interest in literary world systems, with more emphasis on a Trotskyian understanding of uneven development, occurs in the work of the Warwick Research Collective. In *Combined and Uneven Development* (2015), the group recasts world literature as that which registers the core–periphery unevenness of the world system resulting from modern capitalist globalization.[10] Joe Cleary has further contributed to these debates by interrogating the push and pull of great literary capital cities, showing how the rise of Dublin and New York effectively de-centers "the Anglophone world long dominated by London."[11] As he puts it, "the literary world was no longer a tale of two cities but of many."[12] Acknowledging literary world systems beyond the core capitalist countries, he also takes into consideration the important rise of Moscow as the center of an alternative Soviet world literary system, as does recent work by Rossen Djagalov, Amelia Glaser, and Steven S. Lee.[13]

What does a focus on cities and city literature add to these debates? Regarding our first proposition, we can immediately note that urban centers are typically highly networked at regional, national, and global scales. As Brigid Rooney puts it in this volume, "cities are simultaneously subnational, operating below nation at regional level, and supranational, transcending nation via city-to-city global circuits." Ananya Roy and Aihwa Ong note that by virtue of being "a milieu that is in constant formation, drawing on disparate connections, and subject to the play of national and global forces,"[14] cities readily epitomize the vibrant interactions and border-crossing cultural ecologies that have motivated a significant tributary of world literary studies. Indeed, the phenomenon of globalization has prominently been theorized through the "world" or "global" city by theorists including Saskia Sassen, Anthony D. King,

Doreen Massey, and Manuel Castells.[15] Yet these latter approaches have typically remained within the purview of social scientists and geographers, focusing on empirical questions of infrastructure, housing, transport, inequality, governance, and so on. Our volume, by contrast, proffers accounts of world-connecting circuitry that depends upon the complex dialectics of urban materialities and worldly imaginations.[16] Cities are therefore much more than nodes in the circuitry of global flows; they profoundly shape our understanding of the conditions of the global itself.

By foregrounding the linguistic, cultural, political, and economic commingling at the heart of urban world-making, the chapters in this volume demonstrate that cities are also central to our second proposition regarding totality, but that they exceed merely registering competitive flows of the global literary market (Casanova, Damrosch) or the uneven development of global capitalism (Warwick Research Collective). If geographers and urban sociologists have typically been concerned with the empirical aspects of the city, world literature theorists have sometimes disregarded the texture and materiality of the local for an emphasis on systematic models of global circulation and universality. In theories such as Casanova's, for example, cities function mainly as sites through which texts must pass in order to accrue literary value (and of course, the most influential publishing houses, such as Random House, Penguin, Knopf, Bloomsbury, Larousse, have been located in cities). Our point is, rather, that cities function as "switchboards" of cultural translation for local, regional, and transnational flows, and therefore provide an especially rich site for activating questions of part to whole, and local to global. We can unpack this idea in relation to the shift from what Raymond Williams memorably called "knowable communities" – or traditional village communities – to the unknowable spaces of the large metropolis.[17]

Most large urban centers, such as London, Paris, Lagos, Johannesburg, Mexico City, and Sydney, expanded through the accretion of hitherto disparate neighborhoods and districts. This uneven process of conurbation resulted in the impetus to tell stories about the people of the city since urban migrants and people from the assumed outskirts of the city were unknown to those at its business or political core, and were often as unfamiliar as people who had come from outside the relevant area entirely. The need for telling stories about strangers sometimes found peculiar outlets, such as the narratives of criminals made popular in the criminal portraits of London's Newgate Calendars in the eighteenth century.[18] The marriage notices and obituaries in papers such as Paris's *Gazette de France* (first issued in 1625), the *New-York Gazette* (first issued in 1725), London's *The Times* (first issued in 1785), Singapore's *The Straits Times* (first issued 1845) and Johannesburg's *The Sowetan* (first issued in 1981) served a similar purpose, while the Onitsha Market pamphlets that spoke of the knowledge required to survive Nigerian cities served a similar function (see Emmanuel N. Obiechina [1972], Stephanie Newell [2001] and Madhu Krishnan, this volume).[19] In their chapter for this volume, María Moreno Carranco and José Ruisánchez Serra tell us of the nineteenth-century *forastrero*'s (outsider's) gaze toward Mexico City, which was associated with the genre of the early travel guide and "attempted to portray the city, its attractions and amenities, for an imagined visitor." What we see in all these cases is the way urban narratives serve to make the *strange knowable* and, in turn, work to resolve the problem of the part to whole. Cities, each perceived as a potential "single intelligible entity",[20] constantly demand new theorizations of that totality and thus become engines of storytelling. Urban narratives therefore tend to produce imagined worlds – not on the national scale of imagined communities as described by Benedict Anderson in his classic book, *Imagined Communities*[21] – but rather on the smaller scale of evolving cities. Moreover, if cities have always been "principal sites for launching world-conjuring projects,"[22] conversely, urban experiences themselves have also been deeply shaped by a web of global processes including colonialism, capitalism, and migration that in their turn engender stories, desires, and counter-worldings.

To think about cities as contested sites for imagined communities or potential totalities raises a third and final proposition about world literary debates. This approach, we might say, is motivated by the desire to complicate the first two propositions through a postcolonial interrogation of what counts as world literary space in the first place, and to repoliticize what has often thought to be a depoliticizing theoretical framework. This branch of the field has therefore offered an ideal venue for thinking through the manifold cultural legacies of conquest, colonialism, and imperial domination. Scholars such as Amir Mufti, Francesca Orsini, and Baidik Battacharya, for example, focusing on British-South Asian literary relations, have shown the way that a notion of worldwide literary space emerged out of colonial and Orientalist philological study.[23] In *Forget English!*, Mufti reveals how Orientalist knowledge structures were the unacknowledged ground for the production of a world literary space, a space in which English would dominate as the global vernacular and "vanishing mediator."[24] Orisini, with reference to the specific locatedness of multilingual South Asian literatures, has rejected the notion of world literature "as a single global or transnational scale or a movement towards global integration," to instead emphasize the "many significant geographies" that "creatively manage, shift and combine scales.[25] A different tack of postcolonialist intervention into the world literary debates has been equally provocative. This strand is aptly described by Philip Holden as those that involve an "ethical value" or the attempt "to remake the world" (this volume), with Pheng Cheah's work being the most emblematic of this turn. In *What Is a World?* (2016), Cheah takes issue with circulation-based models of world literature for reducing literature to an effect of the global market, instead emphasizing literature's "worldly causality" and its potential for remaking the world.[26] For this task, he argues that postcolonial literatures from the Global South carry the capacity to craft "new stories of world-belonging" in the face of the "worldlessness" of global capital. J. Daniel Elam's work broadly echoes Cheah's rejection of the empiricism of much circulation-inspired world literature theory. In *World Literature for the Wretched of the Earth*, he takes South Asian anti-colonial literature from the 1920s and 1930s as exemplars of thinking that "attempt[s] to articulate a world that has yet to exist." Conceiving of the "world" as literature's *demand* rather than its external set of conditions, writings by M.K. Gandhi, B.R. Ambedkar and others help us conceive world literature less as "a list of texts" or institutional program and more as "a critical orientation toward a political and aesthetic world that may never be known in its totality."[27] Such approaches exceed established notions of world literary space by conceiving, as Jane Hiddlestone has observed in relation to Moroccan literary critic Abdelkébir Khatibi, "literary worldiness not as the result of a text's circulation but as a mode of thought."[28]

The chapters in this volume are largely written in the spirit of our third proposition about world literature: that it offers an arena in which the dominant notions of world literary space may be complicated by urban-based "significant geographies" (Orsini), such that the ongoing decolonization of literary cultures can be pursued. Chapters by Varma, Nerlekar, Krishnan, and Moreno Carranco and Ruisánchez Serra help to challenge narrow notions of world literature by engaging with the spatial, linguistic, and literary afterlives of imperial and colonial rule in London, Bombay/Mumbai, Lagos, and Mexico City. Other essays by Holden, Rooney, Watson, and Bush – on Singapore, Sydney, colonial/neocolonial cities, and Paris – offer new starting propositions for rethinking world literary space in ways that decenter European literary capitals. Together, our volume's chapters stress cities as vibrant cultural ecologies that are embedded in multiple scales and interlaced imperial histories; they are both the spatial *objects* of specific (imperial, capitalist, nationalist, or statist) worldings and *generative sites* for the critical counter-demand of world-making projects, in the sense invoked by Cheah and Elam. Several chapters also revise the well-known trope of "world capitals" to account for the fact that the largest and most vibrant metropolises are now located in the Global South.[29] The latter, moreover, are sites where the contradictory processes of modernity, coloniality, globalization, and neoliberalism are typically most acute, resulting in the most prescient cultural and political responses.[30] City literatures thus suture together the local and the global without smoothing away their contradictions, and call forth the problematic of totality or wholeness, while incessantly demanding alternative storytelling against imperial processes. To quote Roy and Ong again: "Worlding projects remap relationships of power at different scales and localities, but they seem to form a critical mass in urban centers, making cities both critical sites in which to inquire into worlding projects, as well as the ongoing result and target of specific worldings."[31]

One of our central arguments in this volume is that the city tends to be the favored scalar unit for multiple world-making projects both below and above the nation-state scale. Cities are thus simultaneously sites where "global designs" touch down,[32] and matrices of possibility, where connectivity, reinvention, and self-translation also occur. As such, *The Cambridge Companion to the City in World Literature* is less interested in "conceptualizing the entire sphere of literary activity"[33] and more interested in *proliferating* literary formulations around the possibilities, genealogies, and coordinates through which worlds can be imagined and constructed. The chapters presented here help us ask: What emerges if we go beyond the notion that cities are paradigmatic sites for analyzing intercultural mixing and literary vibrancy, and instead claim that city literatures are productive of new methods for thinking through the relationship of local to global, of part to whole, of comparativity, of movement and stasis, or of nation, time, and translation? The chapters that follow offer multiple approaches to urban allegories, cosmopolitan imaginaries, and migrant itineraries in order to theorize a range of relationships between the local and the global, the regional and national, and everything in between. Consequently, if theories of world literature tend to vie with each other to produce a single master theory, the seventeen chapters of this volume reject the field's will-to-totality and instead offer contributions that do not cohere into a smooth version of the globe or an agglomeration of regional literatures that add up to a whole. Rather, different chapters offer competing versions of worldliness that may be untranslatable and incompatible with others.

Itineraries

Part I, Critical Approaches, will provide introductory overviews of the city in world literature through three different lenses: the skyscraper and urban poetics; the legacies and literary aesthetics of the divided Manichean city; and literary mapping. Martin's chapter on "Chicago Schools" delineates the way in which the skyscraper has functioned as a transnational figure of both modernity and exclusion, tracing its transformation from early twentieth-century Chicago to the Burj Kalifa in twenty-first-century Dubai. Watson's chapter on "Writing the Manichean City" excavates the anti-colonial literary energies that arise from within the partitioned spaces of colonial and neocolonial cities, and shows how such texts then travel via unexpected routes and temporalities across Asia, Africa, and Latin America. "The Urban Itinerary and the City Map" by Tally explores the tensions inherent to literary cartographies that necessarily involve both a subjective perspective and abstract mapping. Each of the framing chapters addresses multiple cities in a comparative mode through world literary examples.

In Part II, rather than base our choice of cities on the notion of "coverage" (which would be impossible), we have selected some sites for their obvious importance for literary writing and circulation (London, Paris, New York, Mumbai, Johannesburg, Beijing), and others that especially lend themselves to examinations of urban and literary "worlding," that is, cities that have functioned as distinct crossroads and which evince the intermingling of cultures, peoples, and imperial processes (Singapore, Istanbul, Lagos). Our goal in each chapter is not an overview of all the literature that pertains to that city, but rather to pinpoint particular facets of the urban that have been essential to the production of literary worlds – whether that be reckoning with the city's particular "world-conjuring project," the experiences of migrant and other communities, the role of the city as a node in a regional "world," or the multilayered transformation from colonial to global metropolis. In lieu of a list of discrete chapter descriptions we instead offer the following keywords which may function as nodal points or suggested itineraries for reading between and across the chapters.

Scale demands we attune our senses to different aesthetic dimensions of urban worlding, from the distinct neighborhoods of Johannesburg or New York (Jones, Quayson) and the specific architectural forms of the skyscraper (Martin), Cairo's balconies, rooftops and *hara* (Naga) to the multiscalar mental mappings that guide the subject through city spaces

(Tally). While cities are obviously key circuitry for global **networks**, our contributors explore the way literary cities narrate cultural networks in multifarious ways; in one key we have the cultural mixing and imbricated language worlds of major port cities (Holden on Singapore, Nerlekar on Bombay/Mumbai, Krishnan on Lagos); in another, we have imperial and postcolonial cities that constellate diaspora with empire and nation (Varma on London, Bush on Paris), or cities that orient to "migrant elsewheres" such as Johannesburg's turn toward Bulawayo and Kigali (Jones). Despite the obvious spatiality of cities-as-worlds, **time and temporality** are equally central to many of our chapters, from the deep indigenous pasts that haunt the global connectivity of Sydney (Rooney), the enduring colonial spatial hierarchies of rising Asian cities (Watson), to the "stacked slices of time" that constitute Dublin (Morash). Relatedly, many of the cities here are depicted as **palimpsests** of multiple worlds: Mexico City is the "layered city," combining pre-Hispanic Altepetl with centuries as the capital of New Spain (Moreno Carranco and Ruisánchez Serra), while Mumbai retains imprints of the Mughals, the Portuguese, and the British (Nerlekar), and Cairo those of the tenth-century Fatimid dynasty (Naga).

Love and desire form another pair of keywords, whether pertaining to Cairo's cramped spaces of courtship (Naga), Istanbul as "the city the world desires" (Aynur), or New York as sublime "celestial city" and beacon of migrant self-fashioning (Quayson). Meanwhile, the city as an **imperial center** of gravity has long underwritten a plethora of world-making projects. These range from Moscow's imagined status as "a new Jerusalem" around which all provinces orbited (Lounsbery), to London as center of an imperial "exhibitionary complex" (Varma), back to Beijing and Istanbul as renowned pinnacles of architecture, literature, and civilization as well as political or religious power (Song, Aynur). Finally, a number of these chapters offer paradigms for thinking through the social worlds of today's **mega-cities**: Moreno Carranco and Ruisánchez Serra on Mexico City's boundlessness; Nerlekar on Mumbai's "congregation of the world's differences"; and Krishnan on the "extraversion" of Lagos's unmappable conurbation.

Let us conclude by returning to the question of totality, but less in terms of the totality of any ideal world literary system and rather as the unfinished project of urban literary energies. Writing of the spaces of Accra, Quayson has noted that urban phenomena are always connected to "other phenomena that may not appear in the first instance to be immediately related to it."[34] This analytical challenge demands a literary method which must "draw out the mediated relations between different aspects of a *potential totality*"[35] while historicizing those related phenomena. In her work on the industrial transformation of postwar Asian cities, Watson has similarly observed that there is "no unmediated, total view of all the processes and forces making up [Seoul's] new urban landscape"; nevertheless, "struggles over the creation of new urban and material spaces constitute the social, material, and ideological world that is imperfectly incorporated by fictional texts."[36] That literary forms take up a city's "potential totality" as their aesthetic remit informs, in very different ways, all the chapters in this volume, suggesting the way material and historical urban processes precipitate worldly imaginations. This notion also usefully connects our first two propositions on world literature (that it is boundary crossing and concerned with totalities) with the third (that it offers space to imagine other, decolonizing worlds). Put otherwise, if theories of world literature have often viewed cities simply as nodes which consecrate literary value or as indicators of uneven culltural capital our volume understands them as peculiarly concentrated sites where multiple – and often contradictory – temporal and spatial processes of worlding interact with each other and generate important stories as they do so. The narratives of self-making and self-fashioning that one often finds in urban fictions are precisely the means by which city dwellers create a new urban spaces that are already palimpsests of multiple worldings.

Note on the Text

Because discourses relating to racial, national, ethnic, and indigenous identities are constantly changing, we have not attempted to standardize capitalization regarding such terms across the chapters. Instead, we have allowed individual authors to choose whether to capitalize them, which often varies depending on specific locations and histories.

Notes

1 "Worlding" invokes Martin Heidegger's influential notion of world and worlding, as discussed in his 1956 essay "The Origin of the Work of Art": "The *world worlds*, and is more fully in being than the tangible and perceptible realm in which we believe ourselves to be at home." See David Farrell Krell, ed., *Basic Writings* (New York: HarperCollins, 1977), 170. We are also influenced by Edward Said's key concept of the "wordliness" of textual production. See Said's *Orientalism* (New York: Pantheon, 1978); *The World, the Text and the Critic* (Cambridge, MA: Harvard University Press, 1983); and *Culture and Imperialism* (New York: Knopf, 1993).

2 Emily Apter, *Against World Literature: On the Politics of Untranslatability* (New York: Verso, 2013), 15.

3 On the era of globalization as a post-1989 vibrant "intellectual exchange alley" see Debjani Ganguly, *This Thing Called the World: The Contemporary Novel as Global Form* (Durham, NC: Duke University Press, 2016), 20.

4 Karl Marx and Friedrich Engels, "The Communist Manifesto," in Karl Marx, *Selected Writings*, Lawrence H. Simon, ed. (Indianapolis, IN: Hackett, 1994), 162. We should also note that the *Manifesto* itself was self-consciously conceived as a world literary text, declaring that it was to be immediately "published in the English, French, German, Italian, Flemish and Danish languages" (ibid., 158).

5 Erich Auerbach, "Philology and Weltliteratur," trans. Edward Said and M. Said, *The Centennial Review* 13, no. 1 (1969): 10–11; 17. First published 1952.

6 David Damrosch, *What is World Literature?* (Princeton, NJ: Princeton University Press, 2003), 5.

7 Ben Etherington and Jarad Zimbler, "Introduction" to *The Cambridge Companion to World Literature* (Cambridge: Cambridge University Press, 2018), 4 (emphasis added).

8 Pascale Casanova, *The World Republic of Letters*, trans. M.B. DeBevoise (Cambridge, MA: Harvard University Press, 2007), 83, 82.

9 See Franco Moretti, "Conjectures on World Literature," *New Left Review* 1 (2000); and *Graphs, Maps, Trees: Abstract Models for a Literary History* (New York: Vintage, 2007). For world-systems theory, see Wallerstein's *The Modern World-System* (New York: Academic Press, 1974).

10 Warwick Research Collective, *Combined and Uneven Development: Towards a New Theory of World-Literature* (Liverpool: Liverpool University Press, 2015).

11 Joe Cleary, *Modernism, Empire, World Literature* (Cambridge, New York: Cambridge University Press), 38.

12 Ibid.

13 See Rossen Djagalov, *From Internationalism to Postcolonialism: Literature and Cinema between the Second and Third Worlds* (Montreal: McGill-Queen's University Press, 2020); and Amelia Glaser and Steven S. Lee, eds., *Comintern Aesthetics* (Toronto: University of Toronto Press, 2020).

14 Ananya Roy and Aihwa Ong, eds., *Worlding Cities: Asian Experiments and the Art of Being Global* (Chichester: Wiley-Blackwell, 2011), 3.

15 See, for example, Saskia Sassen's *The Global City: New York, London, Tokyo* (Princeton, NJ: Princeton University Press, 2011); Anthony D. King, *Global Cities: Post-Imperialism and the Internationalization of London* (London: Routledge, 1990); Doreen B. Massey, *For Space* (London: Sage, 2005); and Manuel Castells, *Technopoles of the World: The Making of 21st Century Industrial Complexes* (Hoboken, NJ: Taylor and Francis, 2014).

16 The editors and a number of our contributors are indebted to the thinking of Marxist spatial theorist, Henri Lefebvre who, in *The Production of Space*, theorizes social space as simultaneously material, practical, ideological, and imaginative; *The Production of Space*, trans. Donald Nicholson-Smith ([1974] Malden, MA: Blackwell, 1991).

17 See Raymond Williams, *The Country and the City* (New York: Oxford University Press, 1973). See chapter 16 "Knowable Communities."
18 See Stephen K. Knight, *Crime Fiction Since 1800: Detection, Death, Diversity*, (London: Red Globe Press, 2010).
19 See Emmanuel N. Obiechina, *An African Popular Literature: A Study of Onitsha Market Pamphlets* (Cambridge: Cambridge University Press, 1973); and Stephanie Newell, *Ghanaian Popular Fiction: "Thrilling Discoveries in Conjugal Life" and Other Tales*, (Athens, OH: Ohio University Press, 2001).
20 Etherington and Zimbler, "Introduction", 4.
21 Benedict Anderson, *Imagined Communities: Reflections on the Origin and Spread of Nationalism* (London: Verson, 1983).
22 Roy and Ong, *Worlding Cities*, 1.
23 See Amir Mufti, *Forget English! Orientalisms and World Literature* (Cambridge, MA: Harvard University Press, 2016); Francesca Orsini, "Significant Geographies: Scale, Location, and Agency in World Literature," in Diana Roig-Sanz and Neus Rotger, eds., *Global Literary Studies: Key Concepts* (Berlin and Boston: De Gruyter, 2022), 113–136; Baidik Battacharya, *Postcolonial Writing in the Era of World Literature: Texts, Territories, Globalization* (London: Routledge, 2018).
24 Mufti, *Forget English!*, 16. Relatedly, Battacharya, focusing on the development of Anglophony, argues that, "The passage from 'literature' to 'world literature' in the nineteenth century [...] was mediated by colonial histories"; *Postcolonial Writing*, 8.
25 Orsini, "Significant Geographies," 133, 113. Another important strand of world literary debates has attended to the question of translation. See, for example, Emily Apter's attempt to "activate untranslatability as a theoretical fulcrum of comparative literature with bearing on approaches to world literature," *Against World Literature*, 3.
26 Pheng Cheah, *What Is a World? On Postcolonial Literature as World Literature* (Durham, NC: Duke University Press, 2016).
27 J. Daniel Elam, *World Literature for the Wretched of the Earth: Anticolonial Aesthetics, Postcolonial Politics* (New York: Fordham University Press, 2021), 17.
28 Jane Hiddlestone, "'Un Nouvel Internationalisme Littéraire'? Dreams and Delusions of 'World Literature' in Khatabi, Djaout, and Adimi," *PMLA* 137, no. 2 (2022): 390.
29 For an influential theorization of "world city," see Walter Benjamin, "Paris, Capital of the Nineteenth Century," in *The Arcades Project*, trans. Howard Eiland and Kevin McLaughlin (Cambridge, MA: Belknap Press of Harvard University, 1999), 3–26.
30 This line of thought follows from Jean and John Comaroff's *Theory from the South: or, How Euro-American is Evolving toward Africa* (Boulder, CO: Paradigm, 2012), in which they argue that cities in the Global South are taking the lead in providing formulas for understanding contemporary crises.
31 Roy and Ong, *Worlding Cities*, 12.

32 On imperialism as "global designs" see Walter Mignolo, *Local Histories/Global Designs: Coloniality, Subaltern Knowledge and Border Thinking* (Princeton, NJ: Princeton University Press, 2021).
33 Etherington and Zimbler, "Introduction," 2.
34 Ato Quayson, *Oxford Street, Accra: City Life and the Itineraries of Transnationalism* (Durham, NC: Duke University Press, 2014), 30.
35 Ibid., 31 (emphasis added).
36 Jini Kim Watson, *The New Asian City: Three-Dimensional Fictions of Space and Urban Form* (Minneapolis, MN: University of Minnesota Press, 2011), 15, 20.

PART I

Critical Approaches

CHAPTER 2

Chicago Schools

The Skyscraper in Translation

Reinhold Martin

Tall buildings – skyscrapers – are among capitalist globalization's most visible avatars, cities-within-a-city in which are crystallized the wealth and power of elites governing world affairs from conference rooms, executive suites, and penthouses far above the daily, precarious life of the street. Even so, the skyscraper appears in the annals of the long twentieth century as a less stable figure than we might think. To be precise, the gigantism measured by the term *globalization* and the historical processes it names find the skyscraper changing scale as it moves – miniaturizing, even as it reaches ever higher – as what was once a stage becomes more like a prop.[1] This shift in scale is registered in the margins of certain literary works as these works cross paths with theories and histories of the modern city. In the historical sequence we will reconstruct here, which moves from Lake Michigan to the Persian Gulf, the skyscraper is not self-evidently a poetic figure or symbol, nor is it manifestly background or setting; rather, the skyscraper and its world appear in motion, most tellingly just outside the frame, over the horizon – glimpsed, if at all, out of the corner of the eye.

All worlds are, to borrow from Nelson Goodman, made from others.[2] Hence the "world" in "world literature," which meets here the "world" in "world trade," may well denote more than cosmopolitan sensitivity to difference in translation, or even subaltern struggle mediated by language. Permanently under construction, this plural, ceaselessly adapted world also translates in the sense of moving physically from place to place, an active making and remaking that is discernible even in the most obdurate instruments of hegemonic univocality, like skyscrapers. As a spectral prop in globalization's great game, the skyscraper's material translations – its movements – put worlds into convulsive, kinetic contact, bringing their asymmetries into stark relief. Beginning but not ending in Chicago and guided by three novels, Frank Norris's *The Pit* (1902), Richard Wright's *Native Son* (1940), and Abdelrahman Munif's *Cities of Salt* (1984), we will follow the skyscraper through three such translations in space and time, as these are mediated by three commodities: wheat, news, and oil.

Wheat

Despite its popular origins in New York as a feat of engineering and real estate development, the modern skyscraper fully entered architectural discourse in Chicago, with the 1896 publication – in a literary monthly – of the Chicago architect Louis Sullivan's essay, "The Tall Office Building Artistically Considered," in which Sullivan popularized the organicist dictum, "*form ever follows function*."[3] What Sullivan meant by "function" had mostly to do with the technical requirements of offices, stacked one atop the other. But the forces of capital accumulation serviced by those offices were also visible much closer to the ground when, just a few years earlier, Chicago hosted the World's Columbian Exposition of 1893.

Located at the city's outskirts, the Exposition was many things: a Gilded Age monument to agricultural and industrial capitalism, a managerial Potemkin village, a laboratory for City Beautiful urbanism, and a prism of imperial conquest.[4] Not least, the Chicago Exposition also provided a setting for the Wisconsin historian Frederick Jackson Turner to announce the "closing" of the North American continental frontier, and with it, the dawning of a new age of accumulation to be built with labor and materials recirculated as intellectual and finance capital.[5] The White City, as the exhibition was popularly known for its staff plaster facades, reproduced this world in microcosm, with its Mines and Metals Building, its Agricultural Building, its Transportation Building, its Electricity Building, and more reflexively, its Manufactures and Liberal Arts building, where the imaginary of the frontier was commodified and reprocessed as culture. In William Cronon's account, the Fair was also a setting in which Midwestern wheat danced (as Marx said of commodities) onto the world market, accompanied by parade of regional-seeming characters: farmers, traders, and curious onlookers.[6] Although the Exposition's ornate beaux arts monuments turned their backs on the skyscrapers rapidly rising in Chicago's downtown Loop (the city's central business district), the products displayed at the Exposition were converted downtown into numbers bought and sold, a process that defined the material function of tall office buildings as calculating machines, or, as the New York architect Cass Gilbert later put it, "machine[s] that make the land pay."[7]

A decade into the twentieth century, the Exposition's lead planner, the architect Daniel Burnham, proposed a master plan for Chicago that moved the City Beautiful downtown. This was Chicago as Paris as Rome: a new kind of imperial city, laced with boulevards on which strode not conquering bourgeois legions, but "salaried masses" metonymized in the buildings in which they daily recalculated and redrew the symbolic frontiers of material accumulation.[8] Burnham was a leading member of the "Chicago School" of architects known principally for their technical innovations in the design of skyscrapers. By the time the Exposition opened, Burnham had designed, in partnership with John Wellborn Root, a number of the city's important "tall office buildings." Most of those were located within the Loop, at the center of which was the Board of Trade Building, designed by William W. Boyington. Upon its completion in 1885, the Board of Trade was the city's tallest structure, with its central clocktower rising to a height of 303 feet. The eclectic building's most distinguishing feature was, however, at its base: a grand, four-story high commodities trading hall. By 1865 the Chicago Board of Trade had become the site of the first formally recognized futures transactions, which the new building's great hall accommodated in three octagonal amphitheaters, or trading "pits," for wheat, corn, and provisions.[9] The largest of these, in which wheat futures were traded, gave the second volume of Frank Norris's incomplete *Epic of the Wheat* trilogy its title.

The Pit compresses a big bang's worth of circulatory energies into the Board of Trade's great hall and the offices that rose above it, only for these energies to dissipate, as the narrative progresses, into an entropic stillness captured in the novel's closing paragraphs. Headed to her Western exile, Laura Dearborn, the novel's spectator-protagonist, gazes back through the rear window of her carriage at "the Board of Trade Building, black, monolithic, crouching on its foundations like a monstrous sphinx with blind eyes, silent, grave."[10] Strictly speaking, Boyington's Board of Trade is not a Chicago School building if that moniker is taken, as it normally is, to refer to a matter-of-fact approach to skyscraper design developed in that city featuring steel frame construction wrapped in machine-cut stone or in factory-made brick and terra cotta, punctuated by wide, regular expanses of plate glass.[11] Rather for Norris and for the political economy of wheat that by then extended from Omaha to Odessa, the building was, like the pit it housed and the city around it, a stage on which a world-historical drama replayed daily, from early morning to late afternoon, Chicago time.

Establishing this air of performance in the novel's opening pages, Norris assembles his characters in the lobby of a monument of more proper Chicago School vintage: the multipurpose Auditorium Building designed by Sullivan and his partner Dankmar Adler, through which passed a veritable genealogy of the skyscraper. Among the apprentices in the Adler and Sullivan office who worked on the Auditorium was Frank Lloyd Wright, who, in the twilight of his career, would unveil to great fanfare a 528-story "Mile-High Skyscraper" for a hypothetical site in Chicago as a memorial to Sullivan. Some decades later still, Wright's unbuilt project would, in turn, provide a precedent for the 110-story Sears Tower, designed by the Chicago office of Skidmore, Owings & Merrill, which took over the title of "world's tallest building" from New York's World Trade Center in 1973.

Back in the Auditorium lobby around 1900, Norris introduces various personages drawn from Chicago's investor classes – speculators on the future price of wheat and other staples grown in the American Midwest. Self-consciously and not a little righteously, Norris portrays these denizens of the Board of Trade's wheat pit, along with their employers, their patrons, and their families, as half-blind agents of the great, presumptively natural law of profit and loss, whereby prosperity for some results in despair for others. Among the investors, this hydraulics follows rhythms of supply and demand that stretched from the Midwestern plains to the villages of Eastern Europe, as American speculators squeezed profits from the bread that fed Europe's reserve armies of peasant labor. Among the producers and consumers of the wheat, those rhythms, bound to ecological vicissitudes, are mediated in the pit by price manipulations like the "corner" on July wheat attempted by Norris's two-dimensional anti-hero, Curtis Jadwin.

Chicago's wheat pit was a geometrical place, a sunken octagon onto which streamed morning sunlight through the row of tall windows on the building's eastern edge. A world populated in the novel by figures cut out from available archetypes, the pit-as-metonym reproduced the Hegelian struggle for recognition, reprocessed through Darwin, as a matter of escape from the day-to-day financial maelstrom into the more remote banking offices and brokerages in the skies around La Salle Street, which terminated in the Board of Trade Building. Among the surrounding structures was Burnham's Rookery where, in the novel, the offices of Samuel Gretry, Jadwin's confidant, broker, and co-conspirator, are located. The novel's cadence reproduces this geography, to which Norris adds a palatial house on Lincoln Park where Laura, descended from pre-industrial New England and now married to Jadwin, occupies a suffocatingly pretentious interior that appears insulated from the pit's furies, but is ultimately subject to the "wheat's" thoroughly naturalized wrath.[12] The enigmatic sphinx – the Board of Trade – disappears over the horizon as she, with Jadwin, concedes defeat.

News

The social relations mediating these dynamics became the focus of a second Chicago School that arose during the first decades of the twentieth century, made up primarily of sociologists at the University of Chicago. This "school" construed the life of the metropolis as an ecosystem that could be mapped spatially and conceptualized by terms like "human ecology." Working alongside reformers such as Jane Addams, the sociologist Robert Park, his colleague Ernest Burgess, and others saw Chicago's sociospatial relations crystallized into neighborhoods arranged in concentric zones of urban growth, like the rings of a tree.[13] The Chicago sociologists placed a special emphasis on the ethnic and racial communities that formed in these zones and on their means of communication, mapping the patterns of life in particular cities and particular neighborhoods as expressions of a natural-cultural ecology.

Exemplary in this regard was Park's 1925 essay, "The Natural History of the Newspaper." By "natural history" Park meant a Darwinian story of struggle and survival that treated newspapers as organisms within an evolving human ecology that had yet to be studied "as the biologists have studied, for example, the potato bug."[14] Park's history crescendos toward the emergence of a "yellow press," which as he saw it replaced the intimacies of country life, still available to distinct groups in urban enclaves reading in different languages, with dramatic, daily stories of vice, crime, and muckraking for the masses that aroused the passions and conformed to type: "love and romance for the women; sport and politics for the men."[15]

Race, too, was naturalized as a feature of the metropolitan ecosystems studied by the Chicago sociologists. Park, who had once written speeches for Booker T. Washington, regarded racial inequality as a quasi-evolutionary phenomenon to be overcome with time as groups "assimilated" – a favored term of his – in urban centers. Among this Chicago School's most important empirical contributions were studies of racial segregation, notably in the work of two African American sociologists, St. Clair Drake and Horace Cayton, who dedicated *Black Metropolis*, their landmark 1945 study of Chicago's South Side, to the memory of Robert E. Park.[16]

Introducing Drake and Cayton's study, the novelist Richard Wright linked *Black Metropolis* in passing to another, more ephemeral Chicago School of writers and poets as diverse as Carl Sandburg, James T. Farrell, and Theodore Dreiser, in which Wright could well have included himself. As he explained to readers of *Black Metropolis*, adopting the harsh sociological language of his subject:

> If, in reading my novel, *Native Son*, you doubted the reality of Bigger Thomas, then examine the delinquency rates cited in this book; if, in reading my autobiography, *Black Boy*, you doubted the picture of family life shown there, then study the figures on family disorganization given here. *Black Metropolis* describes the processes that mold Negro life as we know it today, processes that make the majority of Negroes on Chicago's South Side sixth-graders, processes that make 65 percent of all Negroes on Chicago's South Side earn their living by manual labor.[17]

When skyscrapers appear at all in *Black Metropolis*, which applies Chicago School methods to that city's "Black Belt" and its core, Bronzeville, it is mainly as distant silhouettes in the downtown Loop, all but inaccessible to the Black inhabitants of the South Side "ghetto." These same skyscrapers also loom in the distant background of Wright's 1940 novel, *Native Son*, but not, as in Norris (or even more starkly in Ayn Rand's *The Fountainhead*, 1943), as near-parodic symbols rising from the Promethean forges of white male virility. Instead, in Wright, as in Drake and Cayton, the skyscraper appears as a kind of stylus that draws the color line.

In *Black Metropolis*, the skyscraper-as-stylus appears by proxy in two forms. First, via the labor of Black men and women operating Chicago's elevators, whose vocation Drake and Cayton chart and tabulate along with others – from service workers to clerks – in a statistical portrait of the racialized "job ceilings" demarcating Bronzeville's class structure. Unskilled manual labor and service work made up a disproportionate share of the jobs available to Black men in Chicago; skilled construction trades, like the ironworkers who built the city's skyscrapers and the unions that controlled the construction sites, excluded Black workers almost entirely. Among such sites was the new, still taller Board of Trade Building, designed by Daniel Burnham's legacy firm and completed in 1929. Although, as Adrienne Brown has shown, dissident Black intellectuals from W.E.B. Du Bois to James Weldon Johnson imaginatively appropriated the skyscraper as a figure of self-emancipation, Drake and Cayton's statistics remind us that the skyscrapers of the first, architectural Chicago School structurally excluded those Black men and women who were not operating their elevators or servicing their offices.[18]

Second, a particular skyscraper appears indirectly in *Black Metropolis* in a lively section on the *Chicago Defender* written in the spirit of Park's "natural history." A weekly newspaper with a circulation of about 40,000 published by a Black Republican, Robert S. Abbott, the *Defender* espoused what Drake and Cayton call a "racial" rather than an "economic" radicalism capable, in one instance, of defending Chicago's white communists for their program of racial equality.[19] The sociologists emphasize the importance of such "Negro weeklies" in simultaneously "reporting news and stimulating race solidarity." Where "white dailies" such as the *Tribune* drew significant income from advertising, Black weeklies such as the *Defender* depended mainly on circulation. Hence, the paper "gives the public what it wants – in news and in attitude toward the white world." In turn, the *Defender*'s wide circulation made the paper an attractive venue for white advertisers seeking business on the South Side (the "Black Belt"), to the extent that, as Drake and Cayton report, three-quarters of the *Defender*'s advertising revenue came from whites.[20]

Two decades earlier, the headquarters of the Chicago *Tribune* had been the subject of an architectural design competition that inventoried virtually all of the possibilities available for the design of skyscrapers at the time. Consequently, the resulting Tribune Tower, a neo-Gothic spire designed by John Mead Howells and Raymond Hood, was only one among dozens of possible Tribune Towers that circulated in print among cosmopolitan observers in the northern transatlantic. Standing out was, for example, the Austrian architect Adolf Loos's entry, which proposed a tower in the form of a single Doric column – a Dadaistic parody that took the problem of inventing new symbols to an absurdly logical conclusion. Others used the competition to showcase functionalist or expressionist designs that they had been unable to realize in Europe.[21] Seen from a later vantage point, the most salient feature of this vanguardist *salon des refusés* was its near-universal attempt to make the skyscraper advertise its relevance, like a newspaper. By the early 1920s, as architects and urbanists sought an expressive language adequate to forces like those swirling in Chicago's pit from which modernity's arithmetic seemed to spring, the skyscraper became a symbol that built the "job ceilings" and other structural barriers recorded by *Black Metropolis*, one floor atop the next.

But if newspapers such as the *Tribune* and their skyscrapers remain in the background of Drake and Cayton's study, they draw the color line more brightly in Wright's *Native Son*. Bigger Thomas, a young Black man from Chicago's South Side, has accidentally killed the daughter of the white real estate developer and philanthropist, Henry Dalton, who has employed him out of charity. On the run, Bigger reads of his fate in the newspapers that map, Chicago School-style, the block-by-block progress of organized white vigilantes in concentric rings that converge on the geographic center of Drake and Cayton's Bronzeville. The first of the newspaper headlines that caption Bigger's fate implicates the young woman's communist companion on whom Bigger has tried to cast suspicion; a second implicates the "Red" further as Bigger prepares his escape. But it is ultimately a group of newspapermen assembled in the Dalton mansion whose discovery of incriminating evidence prompts Bigger to flee: "The papers ought to be full of him now. It did not seem strange that they should be, for all his life he had felt that things had been happening to him that should have gone into them."[22]

The first paper Bigger reads is the *Tribune*, which has not yet caught up with his unfolding flight. Having killed again, and more deliberately this time, Bigger seeks refuge in the South Side's abandoned buildings, guided by headlines that seem to be closing in on him. No longer recognizing himself in their grotesque portrayals, Bigger learns that he has been discovered, but also that the white dailies have converted Mary Dalton's death into an imagined rape. The vigilantes had raided the one-room apartment he shares with his mother and two siblings, of which the paper reports: "A curious sidelight was revealed today when it became known that the apartment building in which the Negro killer lived is owned and managed by a sub-firm of the Dalton Real Estate Company."[23] The map tightens; Bigger is caught. The *Tribune* now describes him as a bestial, "brutish" figure who "gives the impression of possessing abnormal physical strength," but who nevertheless faints when brought before the mob for an extrajudicial inquest.[24] Later, Bigger learns from the headlines that he has confessed and later still, he reads in the *Tribune* that the courtroom in which he will be tried will be cordoned off by the Illinois National Guard. According to Wright, many of these newspaper items are, in fact, "rewrites of news stories from the *Chicago Tribune*."[25] Reading *Native Son* through them therefore relocates Wright's novel within the "natural history" of the *Tribune*, if only by way of dialectical artifice, to secure the novel's deeper kinship with the *Defender*: life in the Black Belt as seen from a skyscraper, a distorting mirror that maps the enemy's movements.

For Bigger, map and territory converge in a prison cell, through the window of which he is barely able to glimpse the "tips of sun-drenched buildings in the Loop." Boris Max, Bigger's sympathetic communist lawyer, attempts to console his condemned client by reinscribing the skyscraper into a history of collective striving: "Those buildings sprang up out of the hearts of men, Bigger. Men like you. Men kept hungry, kept needing, and those buildings kept growing and unfolding. You once told me that you wanted to do a lot of things. Well, that's the feeling that keeps those buildings in their places." The problem, says Max, is that "A few men are squeezing those buildings tightly in their hands. The buildings can't unfold, can't feed the dreams men have, men like you .... The men on the inside of those buildings have begun to doubt, just as you did. They don't believe any more. They don't feel it's their world."[26]

This is the skyscraper's ultimate worldlessness, its intractable exteriority, recognized now, in Max's wishful story of awakening, even by office workers as they "go in the streets and they stand outside of those buildings and look and wonder."[27] That wonder, converted to despair in Bigger's prison cell, is at the unfolding of someone else's world and the collapse of one's own.

Oil

That same exteriority keeps the skyscraper on the move, just beyond the frame, peeking above the shifting frontier. Only a decade separated the design of Chicago's Tribune Tower and the signing of a concession agreement between the California Standard Arabian Oil Company (later, Aramco) and Abdul Aziz (Ibn Saud), ruler of the new Kingdom of Saudi Arabia. In his 1927 epic, *Oil!*, Upton Sinclair had already documented the Californian ecopolitics that lay behind this transaction, in which the frontiers of accumulation went deeper underground while also doubling back, eastward toward the Gulf. But it would not be until 1984, with the publication of the first volume of Abdelrahman Munif's *Cities of Salt* quintet, that the other side of the oil encounter would yield what Amitav Ghosh has described as a paradigmatic work of "petrofiction."[28]

Skyscrapers as such are nowhere to be seen in *Cities of Salt*, the eponymous title of which was given by the first volume's English translator, Peter Theroux, as a substitute for the more enigmatic "wilderness" (recast by Rob Nixon as "bewilderment," which we can distinguish from Wright's "wonder") signified by the novel's Arabic title, *'al-Tih*.[29] That is, *Cities of Salt* describes disoriented life on someone else's frontier. Like the wheat in Chicago's pit, the oil itself remains offstage, underground, inaccessible to literary representation. In its place is a world in motion, of semi-nomadic Bedouins displaced from their water-rich oasis to become migrant workers, of American prospectors and their Marsh Arab guides, probing and surveying the desert, of "maddened machines" leveling groaning, wailing trees, and eventually of Harran, a bustling refinery port run by nicknamed Americans enclaved in their replica suburb, and built by the displaced Bedouins who have been consigned to the makeshift huts of what is perhaps the Gulf's first labor camp, as their emir, relocated from tent to palace, plays with his new telescope and bemusedly tunes a radio.[30]

Tariq Ali has paraphrased Munif, who spent a career in the Middle Eastern oil industry, explaining that "[c]ities of salt means cities that offer no sustainable existence. When the waters come in, the first waves will dissolve the salt and reduce these great glass cities to dust."[31] The cycle's fictional Harran evokes most transparently the Saudi port of Dhahran, where Aramco, later Saudi Aramco, moved its headquarters in 1952 from a New York high-rise to a low-slung corporate campus. Arguably, however, the Gulf's paradigmatic "city of salt" was soon to be Dubai, a few hundred miles down the coast.

At the time Munif wrote, the tallest building in the Gulf was Dubai's forty-story World Trade Center, designed by the British architect John Harris and completed in 1979.[32] Harris was also that city's first master planner, hired by the ruling Sheikh Rashid bin Saeed Al Maktoum in 1959 to map Dubai's fragmented enclaves and guide the future growth of a coastal settlement that had yet to see paved roads, running water, or a utilities network. Oil was not discovered in Dubai until 1966, following which Harris designed a second master plan for bridging the wide creek that divided the town, and establishing distinct residential, commercial, industrial, and institutional zones and a major port. The second Harris plan envisioned what was still essentially a mirage punctuated by urban landmarks, the most distinctive of which became the World Trade Center tower, which joined dozens of other such complexes worldwide that paid tribute to – but also joined forces with – the towering symbol of "world trade" that had been completed in New York just a few years earlier, in 1972.[33]

Unlike New York's still-functionalist Twin Towers, however, Dubai's garish skyscrapers are not readily susceptible to the naturalizing optics of a latter-day Chicago School. This remains true for the first, architectural version, which treated buildings as naturally growing technological organisms, or the second, sociological one, which considered the modern city as a concentrically evolving human ecosystem. If anything, Dubai's tall buildings only begin to make sense when refracted through a third Chicago School, of economic theory dedicated to the promulgation of markets liberated – seemingly – from the regulatory apparatus of a state to which the zoning codes limiting the growth of Chicago's tall buildings still belonged.

In a nod to the leading figure of the American school of neoliberal economic thought headquartered at the University of Chicago, Mike Davis cheekily called twenty-first century Dubai "Milton Friedman's beach club."[34] Although, as Davis says, that city has "achieved what American reactionaries only dream of – an oasis of free enterprise without income taxes, trade unions, or opposition parties," what Davis calls the "feudal absolutism" of the ruling Maktoum dynasty decked out as "the last word in enlightened corporate administration" belies some of the more common assumptions about neoliberal planning – or the lack thereof – pertaining to the built environment.[35] As the Harris master plan and its successors suggest, the city's archipelago of deregulated enclaves was the product of careful planning intended to attract foreign capital, overseen by a real estate and construction industry controlled almost entirely by the dynastic families that govern the emirate. Dubai's "planned suburban growth" of the 1980s saw the establishment of Sheikh Zayed Road as the axial corridor around which a new, towering business district would form, and, in a bid to prioritize flexibility above all else, in 1995 the city adopted a "structural plan" that affirmed the deregulated urban enclave as the primary unit of planned growth. In that sense, the seeming arbitrariness of urban development in Dubai was built-in by design, as witnessed by the ease with which the "structural plan's" nominal height limit of thirty stories along Sheikh Zayed Road, which sought implicitly to preserve the vertical preeminence of the World Trade Center, was promptly transgressed by the fifty-story Burj Al Arab Hotel in 1999, which was in turn eclipsed by Hazel Wong's twinned, fifty-one-story Emirates Towers the following year.[36]

Dubai has never been as rich in fossil capital as its neighbor, Abu Dhabi, and an important aim of the planned deregulation was to ease the conversion of oil and gas profits into real estate. An apotheosis of this long-term strategy was the Burj Khalifa, a 163-story tower that upon completion claimed the designation of tallest building in the world. The Burj Khalifa's developer, Emaar Properties, is one of three major real estate and construction firms controlled in whole or in part by Dubai's Maktoum family. The other two are Dubai Holding, developers of luxury resorts, and Nakheel Properties, developers of the hallucinatory, palm-shaped artificial islands that reverse Munif's formula: rather than a city dissolving like salt into the Gulf, a city of luxury sandcastles emerging from the Gulf like so many patterned salt crystals. Impressed by the Kuala Lumpur City Centre anchored by the Petronas Towers, Emaar hired that project's master planner to repeat the exploit in Dubai's central business district. With shades of the Chicago Tribune Tower, the firm held an international competition for the design of a mixed-use commercial and residential complex to be anchored by what was then called the Burj Dubai. Closing the historical circle, the Chicago office of Skidmore, Owings & Merrill, designers of the Sears Tower, won the competition with a proposal that adapted the bundled tube design of Sears with distinct echoes of Frank Lloyd Wright's Mile-High Skyscraper, now configured as a desert flower: Chicago on the Gulf.[37]

Coda: Guests

Explaining the choice of Chicago to accompany New York and Los Angeles in her study of America's "global cities" as command centers of financial capitalism, the urban historian Janet Abu-Lughod pointed out that what Chicago lacked in corporate headquarters it made up in world trade. Specifically, Abu-Lughod noted the presence of the Chicago Mercantile Exchange, or MERC, which by 1969 had eclipsed the Board of Trade as a leader in the global futures market. By the early 1970s, with the end of the Bretton Woods monetary regime, the MERC had become home to the International Monetary Market, which by 1991 was trading $50 trillion worth of currency futures, or forty times the value of equities on the New York Stock Exchange. Run, as Abu-Lughod reports, by former students of Milton Friedman, the MERC thus came to signify the vast distance separating the "global" beneficiaries of such trade from the "have-nots."[38] Among the latter were those residents of Black Metropolis descended from Bigger Thomas who, as Abu-Lughod shows with a vivid series of maps in the manner of the Chicago sociologists, remained cut off from the prosperity of the financial markets, in segregated neighborhoods on the South Side and elsewhere.[39]

When the 2008 financial crisis threatened the Burj Dubai project, Sheikh Khalifa bin Zayed Al Nahyan, president of the United Arab Emirates and emir of oil-rich Abu Dhabi, made the necessary funds available. Completed in 2010, the building, duly renamed in his honor, was thus confirmed as a work of petro-architecture: a brazenly strident retort to the melancholy petrofiction of writers such as Munif. The Burj Khalifa was, like so many buildings of its type, a token to be traded as symbolic capital. A few years earlier, that first arrival of American petroleum speculators in the Gulf so vividly chronicled by Munif recurred, when the Chicago MERC, as a subsidiary of the CME Group – the world's largest derivatives exchange – became a partner in the new Dubai Mercantile Exchange (DME), holder of the benchmark Oman Crude Oil Futures Contract. In 2007, the DME opened its trading floor – a computerized descendant of Chicago's pit – in the Gate Building of the Dubai International Financial Center, a bloated triumphal arch redolent of the Chicago fair's City Beautiful, on axis with Emirates Towers and Dubai's World Trade Center.

These buildings were built by migrant labor – "guest workers," or, as Deepak Unnikrishnan named them in 2017, *Temporary People* – mostly from South Asia, and mostly under the notorious "kafala" system that entails virtual indenture to their employer-sponsor. Unnikrishnan opens his collection of stories, poems, and fables dedicated to these workers, who "disappear after their respective buildings are made," with a fragment that ends like this: "If you are outside, and there are buildings nearby, ghosts may already be falling, may even have landed on your person."[40] The fantastically real urban imaginaries thus recorded, of these living, dying ghosts and of their unwitting passers-by, are related to, but not identical with, Richard Wright's ambivalent "wonder," or Abdelrahman Munif's "bewilderment" at modernity's disjunctive convulsions. What for Wright was an uneven encounter between two groups and for Munif an uneven encounter between two worlds has become a splintered city-world populated by an anxiously raucous multitude of eternal visitors. Just offstage, out of view but implacably present, are the skyscrapers these visitors have built, moved from here to there by history's hand like pieces on a board game: a stage made of wheat and oil with props made of sand and steel.

Notes

1 Literary forms matched to this scale shift are explored in Andreas Huyssen, *Miniature Metropolis: Literature in the Age of Photography and Film* (Cambridge, MA: Harvard University Press, 2015).

2 Nelson Goodman, *Ways of Worldmaking* (Indianapolis, IN: Hackett Publishing Co., 1978), 6ff.

3 Louis Sullivan, "The Tall Office Building Artistically Considered," *Lippincott's Monthly Magazine* (March 1896), 408. Italics in original.

4 Alan Trachtenberg, *The Incorporation of America: Culture and Society in the Gilded Age* (New York: Hill and Wang, 1982); Robert W. Rydell, *All the World's a Fair: Visions of Empire at the American International Expositions, 1876–1916* (Chicago: University of Chicago Press, 1984); and Tony Bennett, "The Exhibitionary Complex," *New Formations* 4 (Spring 1988): 73–102.

5 Frederick Jackson Turner, "The Significance of the Frontier in American History," in *Report of the American Historical Association for the Year 1893* (Washington, DC: United States Government Printing Office, 1894), 199–227.

6 William Cronon, *Nature's Metropolis: Chicago and the Great West* (New York: W. W. Norton & Co., 1991).

7 Cass Gilbert, "The Financial Importance of Rapid Building," *Engineering Record* 41, no. 26 (June 30, 1900): 624.

8 Siegfried Kracauer, *The Salaried Masses: Duty and Distinction in Weimar Germany*, trans. Quintin Hoare (New York: Verso, 1998).

9 Gretta Tritch Roman, "The Reach of the Pit: Negotiating the Multiple Spheres of the Chicago Board of Trade Building in the Late Nineteenth Century," unpublished PhD thesis, Pennsylvania State University (2015), 383.

10 Frank Norris, *The Pit: A Story of Chicago* ([1902] New York: Penguin Books, 1994), 369.

11 For example, Carl W. Condit, *The Chicago School of Architecture: A History of Commercial and Public Building in the Chicago Area, 1875–1925* (Chicago: University of Chicago Press, 1998). As Tritch Roman points out, the historiography has since been revised in, for example, Daniel Bluestone, *Constructing Chicago* (New Haven, CT: Yale University Press, 1991); Robert Bruegmann, *The Architects and the City: Holabird & Roche of Chicago, 1880–1918* (Chicago: University of Chicago Press, 1997); and Joanna Merwood-Salisbury, *Chicago 1890: The Skyscraper and the Modern City* (Chicago: University of Chicago Press, 2009).

12 On literary naturalism and naturalization in *The Pit* see Walter Benn Michaels, *The Gold Standard and the Logic of Naturalism: American Literature at the Turn of the Century* (Berkeley, CA: University of California Press, 1987), 72–73.

13 See for example, Martin Bulmer, *The Chicago School of Sociology: Institutionalization, Diversity, and the Rise of Sociological Research* (Chicago: University of Chicago Press, 1984); Andrew Abbott, *Department and Discipline: Chicago Sociology at One Hundred* (Chicago: University of Chicago Press, 1999); and Edward Shils, "The Sociology of Robert E. Park," *The American Sociologist* 7, no. 4 (Winter 1996): 88–106.

14 Robert E. Park, "The Natural History of the Newspaper," in Park and Ernest W. Burgess, *The City: Suggestions for Investigation of Human Behavior in the Urban Environment* (Chicago: University of Chicago Press, 1925), 97.

15 Ibid., 95.

16 St. Clair Drake and Horace R. Cayton, *Black Metropolis: A Study of Negro Life in a Northern City* ([1945] Chicago: University of Chicago Press, 2015).

17 Richard Wright, "Introduction" to Drake and Cayton, *Black Metropolis*, lxii.

18 Adrienne R. Brown, *The Black Skyscraper: Architecture and the Perception of Race* (Baltimore, MD: Johns Hopkins University Press, 2017).

19 Drake and Cayton, *Black Metropolis*, 401.

20 Ibid., 411.

21 Manfredo Tafuri, "The Disenchanted Mountain: The Skyscraper and the City," in Giorgio Ciucci, Francesco Dal Co, Mario Manieri-Elia, and Manfredo Tafuri, eds., *The American City: From the Civil War to the New Deal*, trans. Barbara Luigia La Penta (Cambridge, MA: MIT Press, 1979), 390–421.

22 Richard Wright, *Native Son* ([1940] New York: HarperCollins, 1993), 222.

23 Ibid., 256.

24 Ibid., 279–280.

25 Wright, "How Bigger Was Born," in ibid., 455.

26 Ibid., 426–427 (Ellipsis in original).

27 Ibid., 427.

28 Amitav Ghosh, "Petrofiction: The Oil Encounter and the Novel," *The New Republic*, March 2, 1992, 29–34.

29 Rob Nixon, *Slow Violence and the Environmentalism of the Poor* (Cambridge, MA: Harvard University Press, 2011), 90.

30 Abdelrahman Munif, *Cities of Salt*, trans. Peter Theroux ([1984] New York: Vintage International, 1989).

31 Tariq Ali, "A Patriarch of Arab Literature," *Counterpunch* (February 1, 2004), www.counterpunch.org/2004/02/01/a-patriarch-of-arab-literature/.

32 Yasser Elsheshtawy, *Dubai: Behind an Urban Spectacle* (New York: Routledge, 2010), 155.

33 Ibid., 108–109.

34 Mike Davis, "Sand, Fear, and Money in Dubai," in Davis and Daniel Bertrand Monk, eds., *Evil Paradises: Dreamworlds of Neoliberalism* (New York: New Press, 2007), 60.

35 Ibid., 60–61.

36 Elsheshtawy, *Dubai*, 111–116; on Burj Al Arab, 137–139; 156; on the Emirates Towers, 156–157. On enclaves more generally, see Stephen Graham and Simon Marvin, *Splintering Urbanism: Networked Infrastructures, Technological Mobilities and the Urban Condition* (New York: Routledge, 2001). See also Kishwar Rizvi, "Freehold/Freedom: Ex-urban Existence in the UAE," in Reinhold Martin and Claire Zimmerman, eds., *Architecture against Democracy: Histories of the Nationalist International* (Minneapolis, MN: University of Minnesota Press, forthcoming).

37 Elsheshtawy, *Dubai*, 158–164.

38 Janet L. Abu-Lughod, *New York, Chicago, Los Angeles: America's Global Cities* (Minneapolis, MN: University of Minnesota Press, 1999), 327–329.

39 Ibid., 329–345.

40 Deepak Unnikrishnan, *Temporary People* (New York: Restless Books, 2017), 3.

CHAPTER 3

Writing the Manichean City from Colonial to Global Metropolis

Jini Kim Watson

The Manichean City

Frantz Fanon opens his manifesto of anti-colonial liberation, *The Wretched of the Earth* (*Les Damnés de la Terre*, 1961), famously written in the midst of the Algerian war of independence, with a thick description of colonial Algiers. The city is a "compartmentalized world" that is both particular and universal:

> The colonial world is a world divided in two. The dividing line, the border, is represented by the barracks and the police stations [....] The "native" section is not complementary to the European sector. The two confront each other, but not in the service of a higher unity [....] The colonist's sector is a sector built to last, all stone and steel. It's a sector of lights and paved roads, where the trash cans constantly overflow with strange and wonderful garbage, undreamed-of leftovers [....]
>
> The colonized's sector, or at least the "native" quarters, the shanty town, the Medina, the reservation, is a disreputable place inhabited by disreputable people [....] It's a world with no space, people are piled one on top of the other, the shacks squeezed tightly together. The colonized's sector is a famished sector, hungry for bread, meat, shoes, coal, and light.[1]

Against a long history that figures the city as a space of freedom from the backwardness of agrarian life[2] – or at least a site of exchange and intermingling – the urban spaces invoked in *The Wretched of the Earth* are anything but liberatory. The city's two sectors are unnaturally severed, segregated, and contradictory. With the well-built settler zones of "stone and steel" and disappearing garbage on the one hand, and the shanty town "hungry for bread, meat, shoes, coal, and light" on the other, the colonial city is defined by a fundamental duality, or Manicheanism, whereby the physical division of the city reflects and sustains the apartheid structure of colonial society. Anchored by grand colonial buildings, barracks, and police stations, colonial capitals and administrative cities have often functioned as both symbols of the colonial system and the means by which its hierarchical social order is put into practice. Importing urban forms, social practices, and settler populations from the imperial metropolis, such cities also attract native rural migrants – typically displaced by colonial land policies – from across the colonized territory; their labor is, in turn, often put toward colonial wealth extraction. As I've argued in more detail elsewhere, the colonial city thus functions as a crucial node in the *production and reproduction* of the imperial system itself, effectively "worlding" disjunctive populations and geographies into a new relation.[3]

This chapter argues that alongside the better-known literary and urban histories that emerge from cities of the Global North – London, New York, or Paris – the colonial (and postcolonial) city's contradictory, antagonistic spaces are constitutive of both modern urban experience and world literature. In what follows, I use Fanon's Manichean city as a starting point to think through this foundational aspect of modern urbanism along two axes. First, I argue that global structures of imperialism and exploitation are made tangible through the spaces of the (post)colonial city. In contrast to Europe's scandalous wealth and "towers of opulence," which obscure the fact they were "built with the sweat and corpses of blacks, Arabs and Indians and Asians,"[4] the very disjunctiveness of colonial urban forms is key for perceiving, analyzing, and indicting the colonial system. As Fanon puts it, "colonialism, as we have seen, is precisely the organization of a Manichean world, of a compartmentalized world."[5] If the essence of the colonial system is most clearly grasped in its spatial manifestation, the divided city is crucial for incubating anti-colonialist struggles and imagining paths toward decolonization. The colonial city is thus at once colonial policy, urban reality, and a translatable, ontological predicament that demands to be overturned through worldwide anti-colonial struggle, whether in Algiers, Sharpeville, Delhi, or Saigon.

Second, I argue that seeing the city as a site of contestation and anti-colonial desires allows us to rethink the role of the urban in world literature studies. In conceptions of the latter, the imperial city, or "metropolitan" space more generally – and note the symptomatic conflation of "Europe" with "the metropole" – is often the assumed node through which literary works must travel in order to gain recognition *as* world literature. Think of Pascale Casanova's influential account of "world literary space" centered around Paris, the "Greenwich meridian of literature."[6] For Casanova, the operations of world literature are visible precisely in "the turn to Paris" by those from the literary "provinces" of Ireland, Portugal, Yugoslavia, and beyond.[7] In other words, literature becomes world literature by passing through the metropolitan capital. Meanwhile, the emphasis on uneven capitalist development and world systems theories, as seen in work by Franco Moretti and the Warwick Research Collective, relies on the positing of a core, periphery, and semiperiphery. For the Warwick research group, uneven development – their ground for thinking world literature – is understood as analogous to a worldwide story of urbanization and rural underdevelopment: "If urbanization [...] is clearly part of the story, what happens in the countryside as a result is equally so."[8] The story of city and country stand in for the story of global uneven development, and the urban-rural divide is valuable insofar as it "registers" uneven capitalist modernization.[9] In contrast to models that assume the city as either a node that endows literary value (Casanova) or as what reveals uneven capitalist processes (Warwick), this chapter views the (post)colonial city as a crucible in which the critical energies of decolonization emerge, take literary expression, and circulate in new ways. As we shall see, the very translatability of the Manichean city form prompts networks of literary travel that do not always reroute through the imperial cities of the Global North nor merely confirm a story of peripheral development. Instead, they enable horizontal connections between Asia, Africa, and Latin America via a modality, to borrow from J. Daniel Elam, we may call "world literature for the wretched of the earth."[10]

This chapter addresses the antagonistic spaces of three Asian cities from three different moments in history, which may be loosely categorized as colonial, post- or neocolonial, and neoliberal. The cities and texts chosen are not intended to be globally representative or to produce another, rival systematization of world literature. Rather, Manila, Seoul, and Gurgaon/New Delhi appear as rich but idiosyncratic sites for understanding the literary impulse toward decolonizing our urban worlds. The three texts are: José Rizal's 1887 classic anti-colonial novel of the Philippines, *Noli Me Tangere*; Kim Chi-ha's 1970 savage poetic satire of South Korea's neocolonial dictatorship, *Five Bandits* (*Ojŏk*) and Aravind Adiga's darkly humorous 2008 account of India's multinational financial and technology hub in *The White Tiger*. Despite each being written in different languages – Spanish, Korean, and English, respectively – all three texts employ an urban aesthetic to make visible ongoing imperial hierarchies at the same time as they conjure oppositional imaginaries at local, regional, and global scales.

José Rizal and Colonial Worlding in the Spanish Philippines

Fanon's depiction of French-controlled Algiers was, of course, not the first to examine the hierarchical and contradictory nature of colonial space. José Rizal's 1887 *Noli Me Tangere* (Latin for "touch me not") is known as the novel that launched the (short-lived) Philippine revolution against the Spanish. Rizal's fate – he faced the firing squad in 1896 – has cemented the book's legacy as *the* novel of the country's nascent revolutionary nationalism, written by its most famous martyr; the book is now required reading in schools across the Philippines.[11] The great anti-colonial novel is frequently understood to be paradigmatically translational and transnational. The mixed-race Rizal was a native speaker of Tagalog and fluent in several European languages; his "novelistic translations of Philippine realities" effectively transferred "local meaning and realities from the Tagalog language and the Philippines' Hispanicised culture to the idioms of the Spanish cosmopolitan tongue in particular, and to nineteenth-century European culture in general."[12] The novel has since been translated at least six times into English, into Tagalog at least three times, as well as into Indonesian, French, Dutch, German, and Italian. But if the *Noli* readily offers itself up to established conceptions of boundary-crossing world literature, we must also understand it as a great urban novel. The *Noli*'s critique of Spanish rule and the Philippine "friarocracy"[13] hinges on its portrayal of a matrix of interlocking urban, town, and rural spaces, which each play a crucial role in the worlding of imperial structures and practices.

The novel begins with the return of its hero, Crisóstomas Ibarra, to Manila after seven years in Europe, enabling us to see the colonial capital through our mixed-race, hybrid, Europeanized protagonist. The bulk of the story, however, takes place in the fictional San Diego, a provincial town where Ibarra and his friend, the wealthy Captain Tiago, have homes; the town is also the site of Ibarra's father's unjust imprisonment and death (during Ibarra's absence) and of a dramatic attack on the army barracks. Finally, there are the outskirts of San Diego, where the poorest peasants reside, and the forests where outcast "bandits" gather forces against the town's contemptible friars and Civil Guards. In contrast to the stark dualism of Fanon's Algiers, the *Noli* is carefully structured through a system of interconnecting spatial tendrils that hierarchically order the social world from Europe to San Diego's outskirts. We can thus think in terms of a sort of geographic "chain of being" connecting Europe/Spain/Madrid with the Philippines/Manila, the provinces/San Diego, and everything beyond. The *Noli* worlds Europe and Asia into complex, hierarchal relation.

Let us look more closely at the novel's depiction of Manila. The *Noli* memorably opens with a dinner party at the Manila residence of Captain Tiago, who is himself initially absent. Allowing the house and its motley crew of guests to welcome the reader, Rizal – with characteristic irony – depicts colonial society as hybrid, bustling, and opportunistic. Thus, "[t]he news [of Tiago's party] surged like a jolt of electricity among the parasites, spongers, and freeloaders that God, in his infinite goodness, has so lovingly multiplied in Manila."[14] Even Binondo Creek, on which Tiago's mansion is built, serves the "multiple roles of bathhouse, sewer, laundry, fishing hole, thoroughfare, and even drinking water, if that serves the Chinese seller."[15] Manila is both cosmopolitan marketplace and unruly multiplicity, exuding a vibrant energy our returning hero Ibarra initially relishes.

> Ibarra's coach drove on through the liveliest section of the outskirts of Manila [....] The energy that surged all around him, the comings and goings of so many coaches trying to escape, carts, carriages, Europeans, Chinese, natives, each in his distinctive dress, women selling fruit, merchants, the naked freight-handlers, the food stands, inns, restaurants, shops, even carts pulled by impassive and indifferent carabao, who rather than simply dragging cargo behind them seemed to be entertaining themselves by also discussing philosophy, everything, the noise, the bustle in the fullness of the sun, an odd type of smell, the many colors, it all awakened in him an entire world of dormant memories.[16]

In this description, the *Noli* seems to accord with many accounts of the metropolis in late nineteenth- and early twentieth-century modern literature, which figure the city as an effervescent, shifting place of encounter and speed.[17] Appropriately, its diverse contents are described in a breathless itinerary: "women," "merchants," "freight-handlers," "foodstands," "inns," "carts" and "carabao" crowd each other in the city and on the page. By contrast, the memory that Ibarra involuntarily calls up a moment later is one of intense colonial violence. Recalling the sight of a team of laboring convicts doing road repairs, Ibarra describes prisoners bound in iron chains, "tied two-by-two, burned by the sun, united by the heat and their exhaustion, lashed and beaten by another prisoner who must have gotten consolation from his power to mistreat the others."[18] "Etched on his imagination" is the image of a dead prisoner on the road, as "two others quietly prepared a cane stretcher, without anger, pain or impatience the way natives are thought to be."[19] Rizal's Manila is one in which the cosmopolitan "bustle in the fullness of the sun" jostles with a darker, material truth: the spectacular, Foucauldian cruelty of prison gang labor, built on racial assumptions about "the way natives are thought to be."[20] The perspective structuring our narrator's experience is both that of the native and the European, and it is able, therefore, to acknowledge the fundamental spatial discrepancy of the city: bustling markets, commerce, and modern cultural forms coexist with the violent means by which the native territory is to be disciplined and controlled. As Nezar AlSayyad notes, "colonial cities, more than other cities, serve as expressions of dominance."[21]

If Manila is vividly depicted as both modern and brutal, it is San Diego where Rizal's critique of Spanish colonial rule takes more granular form and which leads, eventually, to Ibarra's own enlightened mestizo subjectivity. The literary focus on San Diego accords with Rizal's special indictment on the colony's layer of provincial petty officials and friars, under only nominal supervision of Manila.[22] Moreover, as Epifianio San Juan puts it, San Diego is "not merely a stage backdrop but an organically interwoven property of the milieu which determines the moral quality of the behaviour of the major characters."[23] In other words, the fictional town is populated by the *types* necessary to maintain the colony's functions: the corrupt priests, the power-hungry mayor, the cruel Civil Guard, the sadistic army ensign, and the pretentious upper layer of Europeanized Filipinos, while the town's native population – emblematized by the tragic figure of the widow Sisa – struggles to survive under the twin tyrannies of the friars and the military. At the same time, San Diego's streets, barracks, churches, and cockfighting pits are the narrative means by which different sectors of colonial society come into contact and drive the plot forward. San Diego is thus the spatial tissue connecting the different worlds of colonial Philippine society: its spaces are traversed by every class and race, from his Excellency, the Captain-General – who visits during the town's festival and complains of "the burden we [Spaniards] carry on our shoulders here in the Philippines"[24] – to the Hispanicized elite who carry with them authority, fashion, and goods from Manila and Europe, down to the oppressed outcasts who plot Ibarra's downfall. Both the *Noli*'s novelistic reality and its anti-colonial moral force, therefore, are predicated on the way it makes visible the circuits of imperial power emanating from Madrid, and flowing unevenly through Manila's and San Diego's sociospatial hierarchies.

Paradoxically, it is San Diego's very generalizability – it is interchangeable with any other provincial town – that creates the possibilities for new forms of imagined collectivities. Using the *Noli* as one of his primary examples, Benedict Anderson has famously argued that the form of the novel, those "one day bestsellers,"[25] is key for expressing the modern consciousness of the nation. Commenting on the opening scene of the novel we examined above, Anderson points out the way Rizal's depiction of "hundreds of unnamed people, who do not know each other, in quite different parts of Manila, in a particular month of a particular decade, immediately conjures up the imagined community."[26] Drawing also from early Mexican and Indonesian novels, Anderson further theorizes that, "Here [...] we are in a world of plurals: shops, offices, kampungs [Malay villages], and gas lamps," such that the hero of these fictions is typically juxtaposed against "a socioscape described in careful, *general*, detail."[27] We should note, however, that the stable, generalized socioscape that allows fiction to "seep quietly and continuously into reality, creating that remarkable confidence of community in anonymity which is the hallmark of modern nations"[28] is typically an *urban* one. That is, if the city or town is expressive of colonial worlding, its literary representations are simultaneously material for newly imaginable, anti-colonial national communities.

Rizal's *Noli* and the Philippine revolution would, of course, reverberate across Asia, inspiring nationalist struggles in other sites. But scholars such as Paula C. Park have more recently attended to Rizal's work by placing it within the intercolonial networks of the Spanish empire and the field of "Global Hispanaphone Studies."[29] For centuries, the transpacific Manila-Acapulco galleon trade (1565–1815) constituted a material, maritime link between the Philippines and Mexico that bypassed the colonial metropole of Spain. Park argues that although Rizal is thought of as an exemplary "global" figure because of his mixed ancestry and multilingualism, his writing also specifically invokes the "Philippines' past intercolonial link to Latin America."[30] Moreover, recalling that the Spanish imported their planning blueprints from Latin America as the Philippines had "no urban legacy prior to Spanish conquest,"[31] the spatial organization of the Spanish Philippines connects the archipelago to imperial practices in Spanish America. The unexpected legacies of this link emerge in the publication history of a 1976 edition of the *Noli* by Biblioteca Ayacucho in Caracas, Venezuela, the first Spanish American edition of the novel. In a preface by the Mexican philosopher Leopoldo Zea, Rizal is figured as "hombre puenta entre nuestra América y el Asia and el Africa."[32] By invoking this "bridge between our America and Asia and Africa," Zea renders Rizal a "precursor to liberation movements in the twentieth century" and to the "vision of an alliance between Latin America, Asia, and Africa."[33] The *Noli*'s status as "world literature," therefore, is not simply gained by its travels and translations through European networks of literary space. Reverberating through time across different cities of the Global South, the novel's anti-colonial energies radiate from Manila to Caracas, gesturing toward possible transcontinental political communities of the postcolonial era.

Kim Chi-ha and the Architecture of Neocolonialism

If Rizal's novel foregrounded the role of an urban literary imaginary in critiquing the Spanish colonial regime, what role do depictions of the contested city play as we move to the postcolonial era? As urban historians have well noted, the segregated spaces of the colonial city typically persist into the era of nominal national independence.[34] Further, the era of decolonization of Asia and Africa brought with it not just a grappling with colonial residues and afterlives, but a new world order shaped by Cold War polarities, US global dominance, and neocolonial economic restructuring, of which Fanon had so presciently written.[35] In this section I turn to Kim Chi-ha, the dissident poet who faced the wrath of the South Korean military dictatorship under General Park Chung Hee (in power 1961–79). Most famously, his long narrative poem of 1970, *Five Bandits* (*Ojŏk*), uses the city of Seoul as a canvas for decrying the abuses of the US-backed neocolonial regime. The poem would result in his imprisonment, torture, and very public trial.[36]

In *Five Bandits*, we again encounter the motif of the perceptually discrepant or Manichean city, familiar to us from Fanon. Yet rather than the foreign colonial rulers in their settler town, the neocolonial elite now occupy the city's spacious mansions, halls of power, and golf courses, while the urban poor eke out a living in the city's slums. The poem opens with a grotesque description of Seoul:

> Once, five thieves were living in the heart of Seoul, the capital city.
> To the South, you see, turds went bobbing down the Han River,
> which is nothing but sewage, with Dongbinggo-dong high beside it[37]
> to the North, its treeless hills bare as a chicken's bald ass,
> [...]
> and in the space between South and North, packed tight, tight, tight,
>   shacks are clustered,
> clustered like crab shells, clustered like snot, and above them soar
> Jangchung-dong and Yaksu-dong, where shacks are demolished
>   helter-skelter to erect majestic gates.
> Those gateways, soaring high as they please, gaudily glittering,
> lead to magnificent, luxurious palaces full of flowers.[38]

Even before the appearance of the five bandits themselves – General Park's five closest cronies – the poem presents a material and social geography of the capital, where squatter settlements in the hills "cluster like crab shells" and slum clearance projects violently replace them with "luxurious palaces" for the elite. Employing a bawdy idiom combining myth, satire, and poetic traditions of the Korean folk opera *pansori*, Kim's description nevertheless concretely refers to the urban transformations of Seoul's postwar decades. Following the end of Japanese colonial rule (1910–45), hundreds of thousands of Koreans returned to the capital from other Japanese territories. Just a few years later, the devastation of the Korean war (1950–53) resulted in massive numbers of refugees settling in Seoul after fleeing violence in the North; up to one-third of the city was transformed into squatter settlements. Beginning in the 1960s, the city's slum clearance projects inaugurated a new, painful chapter. Rapid industrialization went hand in hand with the breakneck construction of (often shoddily built) massive tower blocks, frequently displacing the poorest even further from the city center.[39]

Although its opening indexes this painful urban transformation, the poem is best known for its ribald parodies of General Park and the country's corrupt rulers. Kim provides a devastating caricature of the "ConglomerApe," the leader of one of the large *chaebol* (conglomerate) companies that dominate Korea's economy, who "gulps down bank money replenished by tax funds, money borrowed from overseas, plus every kind of privileged concession."[40] The "AssemblyMutt" (*kukhoi ŭi wŏn*) and "TopCivilSerpent" (*kogŭp kongmuwŏn*) spout revolutionary slogans while enriching themselves, and the "General-in-Chimp" (*jangsŏng*) "fills the sacks of rice destined for his troops with sand, after taking the rice and reselling it."[41] The figure of "HighMinisCur" (*jangch'aguan*) explicitly acknowledges the neocolonial relationship with Japan, which the US helped repurpose into regional economic motor and anti-communist bulwark for the region: "Export even though people starve [....] Use the bones of those who've died of hunger to build a bridge to Japan; let's go over and greet their gods! (*kamisama bae'alhajat!*)"[42] Yet, after describing these five corrupt personages of the dictatorship, the poem follows the police chief and his mistaken arrest of a poor street peddler, Kkwesu, who leads the officer to the mansion of the five thieves. The police chief is instantly seduced by the opulence he finds, rendered in a fantastical mix of architectural styles:

> To keep the lawns from freezing, underground heating's installed; to keep the carp from broiling, the ponds are air conditioned;
> to protect the birds from the cold, the bird cages are equipped with heaters; to keep the dog food from spoiling, each kennel has a fridge;
> a Korean tiled roof perches lightly on top of a Western-style marble house, the pillars are Corinthian, the crossbeams Ionian.[43]

The depravity of the ruling elite is here viscerally rendered in architectural form via the ridiculous luxury of the mansion and its non-sensical amenities. And while the police chief may be confused about who to arrest, the architecture itself insists on speaking the truth: "the latticework of the sliding doors [is] designed to form the [Chinese] character for thief."[44] Thus, although *Five Bandits* provides scathing parodies of General Park's administration, it is just as interested in performing a material inspection of the urban and architectural forms of neocolonial dictatorship. Updating the trope of the divided, compartmentalized city for a new age, the poem condenses in literary form the new material and social arrangements that follow formal colonization. To quote Fanon again, this is a period in which nominal independence "merely corresponds to a transfer of power previously held by foreigners."[45]

If Kim's Seoul makes visible the revived and renewed imperial power relations structuring the postcolonial Korean peninsula, it is also a text that travels in unexpected, lateral directions. In 1976, celebrated Kenyan dissident writer, Ngũgĩ wa Thiongo, began his essay "Africa and Asia: The History That Refuses to be Silenced" by quoting Kim's poem at length. Ngũgĩ had encountered an English translation of Kim's work in *The Cry of the People and Other Poems* (issued by Tokyo's Autumn Press in 1975), a volume published in the midst of the international "free Kim Chi-ha" campaign. Ngũgĩ credits Kim's work with poetically articulating the third of three general stages of imperialism – neocolonial comprador capitalism – which follows the first two stages of slavery and classic colonialism. "That is why," Ngũgĩ remarks, "the Korean people's struggle for democracy and unity is the struggle of *all* oppressed peoples."[46] At the same time, Kim's work was circulating in Afro-Asian literary networks that had been made possible by the Afro-Asian Writers' Bureau, founded in 1957, an organization directly inspired by the historic 1955 Afro-Asian Bandung Conference in Indonesia.[47] The organization's journal, *Lotus*, issued trilingually in English, French, and Arabic, was published first from Cairo, then Beirut and Tunis.[48] In 1975, it awarded Kim, alongside writers including Chinua Achebe and Faiz Ahmad Faiz, the prestigious Lotus Prize. Echoing the *Noli*'s career in Latin America, Kim's work invokes an Afro-Asian solidarity that unexpectedly links postcolonial Asia with Africa and the Middle East. (Kim himself would cite Frantz Fanon in his 1976 trial in another linking of the two continents.)[49] I want to suggest that Kim's *Five Bandits* resonates with broader decolonization struggles precisely because of the translatability of both its neocolonial political and urban forms. That Kim's poetry was subsequently seized by the repressive Kenyan government makes visible another instance of the subversive circulation of "world literature for the wretched of the earth."

Millennium City and its Discontents

Aravind Adiga's 2008 novel, *The White Tiger*, reveals a third permutation of the literary career of the compartmentalized city. This time, we are presented with the postcolonial city turned global hub of capital and consumption under conditions of twenty-first century neoliberalism. Like Rizal's *Noli*, the novel is structured as a spatial journey, but this time the reverse journey from the remote rural hinterland to the teeming capital city of Delhi. We follow our narrator and protagonist Balram Halwai from Laxmangargh, a small village in Rajasthan, northeast India – located in the "Darkness" according to our narrator – to the shiny malls, hotels, and apartment complexes of Gurgaon, "the most American part" of Delhi,[50] where Balram works as a driver for the wealthy Mr. Ashok. Known as India's "millennium city" and sprouting up in a manner of decades since the 1990s, Gurgaon emblematizes the country's "embrace of global capital flows." By 2015 it boasted forty-three malls, numerous golf courses, five-star hotels, biotech special economic zones, and over a hundred Fortune 500 companies.[51]

Much of the drama of the novel occurs while Balram drives Mr. Ashok and his American-born wife Pinky Madam around the city. As they sit in their immaculate, air-conditioned Honda City, Balram describes how, "with their tinted windows up," the rich move through the city like "dark eggs down the roads of Delhi."[52] Meanwhile, the city's poor exist in the literal margins of the city:

> Dim streetlights were glowing down onto the pavement on either side of the traffic; and in that orange-hued half-light, I could see multitudes of small, thin, grimy people squatting, waiting for a bus to take them somewhere, or with nowhere to go and about to unfurl a mattress and sleep right there. These poor bastards had come from the darkness to Delhi to find some light—but they were still in the darkness [....] We were like two separate cities—inside and outside the dark egg.[53]

Imagining his own late father among the pavement-dwellers, Balram finds himself, as Toral Gajarawala has noted, "left out of the middle class aspiration that globalisation has fed the urbanites."[54] This is an unfreedom that emphatically supersedes the terms of decolonization. As our narrator scathingly remarks near the beginning of his tale, "in 1947 the British left, but only a moron would think that we became free then."[55] One of the novel's primary tropes, therefore, is the persistent spatial and social apartheid of the city, understood as both colonial residue and neoliberal innovation.

We see such a logic condensed in the "gigantic apartment building" where Mr. Ashok and Pinky Madam live. Their residence is part of the "Buckingham Towers" complex, next door to "Windsor Manor" and part of a district of gated communities, "all shiny and new and with nice big English names."[56] From here, Balram regularly drives Pinky Madam to shopping malls modeled on those air-conditioned temples to American consumer culture. Despite the prohibition on servants entering the privileged sanctum of the mall, Balram manages one day to sneak past the guard:

> I was conscious of a perfume in the air, of golden light, of cool, air-conditioned air, of people in T-shirts and jeans who were eyeing me strangely. I saw an elevator going up and down that seemed made of pure golden glass. I saw shops with walls of glass, and huge photos of handsome European men and women hanging on each wall. If only the other drivers could see me now![57]

Reminiscent of the luxury that overwhelms the police chief upon arriving at the bandits' mansion in Kim's poem, the mall projects a seductive fantasy world of glass and "golden light," and is populated by the idealized visages of European fashion models. It epitomizes the "global lifestyle and new architecture of neoliberal accumulation"[58] that Gurgaon represents, while deliberately excluding the vast majority of Delhi's inhabitants.

Adiga's novel makes use of another of the motifs of urban literature we saw earlier, whereby the city "determines the moral quality of the behavior of the major characters."[59] Balram, nicknamed "Country Mouse" by the other drivers in the servants' compound, is the archetypal country bumpkin: his geographic journey to the urban center is simultaneously one of personal self-fashioning as he sheds his village naivety and remakes himself as a city dweller. Yet this moral journey is a decidedly doubled one. On the one hand, his induction into the city involves documenting and decrying the injustices of the "two separate cities," as we saw above, partly echoing the projects of Fanon, Rizal, and Kim. On the other hand, Balram readily acculturates to urban ways. He partakes of alcohol, pursues a blonde-haired prostitute, and learns of the many ways that drivers can cheat their masters. He gradually formulates his own version of justice, one that is both retributive and specifically neoliberal: he murders his boss and steals a large sum of intended bribe money to fund his own start-up company.

It is at this moral juncture of the novel that the city itself enters the debate. While waiting at a stop signal, the paan-chewing driver of a neighboring car spits out two "vivid puddle[s] of expectorate [which] splashed on the hot midday road and festered there like a living thing."[60] With their dialogue arranged in two columns on the page, the two puddles of phlegm proceed to debate the pros and cons of Balram's murder plan with statements such as, "Mr. Ashok does not hit you or spit on you," and "Mr. Ashok made you take the blame when his wife killed that child on the road."[61] Balram will ultimately follow the advice of the right-hand puddle: he kills his master with a broken Johnny Walker whisky bottle, and escapes to Bangalore where he launches a successful car service business transporting call center workers who serve global tech companies. This is one version – albeit violent and harrowing – of the big city dream come true. Its realization follows from Balram's blunt philosophical observation on the nature of neoliberal India: "in the old days there were one thousand castes and destinies in India. These days, there are just two castes: Men with Big Bellies, and Men with Small Bellies."[62] Nevertheless, several passages note an undercurrent of political organizing in the margins of the city. Balram hears rumors of Naxals (Maoist insurgents) and sees people in discussion "under trees, shrines, intersections, on benches, squinting at newspapers, holy books, journals, Communist Party pamphlets."[63] Balram misreads, or perhaps misinterprets, the city's signs as speaking only to individual action. His rebellion is to happen on the scale of one servant and one master, and the moral journey of the novel ends when Balram himself makes it into the caste of "Men with Big Bellies."

Let me now argue for the way *The White Tiger* again complicates the centering of Euro-American cities by models of world literature. There are at least two ways to read the question of literary circulation in relation to the novel: one external to and one internal to the text. On the external level, Adiga's Anglophone novel was the winner of the Man Booker Prize in 2008, assuring it would be widely read in metropolitan space. Published by a subsidiary of the massive New York publisher Simon & Schuster, it received rave reviews in major newspapers from the US, the UK, Australia, Russia, China, and India. At the novel's internal level, however, it is formally structured as a series of letters, written by Balram (we assume in Hindi since he admits his English is poor) and addressed to His Excellency Wen Jiabao, then premier of China, in Beijing. The latter is addressed alternatively as "Mr Premier" or as "Mr. Jiabao" (incorrectly, since Wen is the surname). With more than a hint of Scheherazade's 1,001 nights, the novel comprises seven letters, or chapters, titled "The First Night," "The Second Night," and so on. But instead of staving off death as in the Arabian Nights tale, each of *The White Tiger*'s evenings brings us closer to the eventual murder of Mr. Ashok and Balram's reincarnation as successful Bangalore entrepreneur. In fact, the literary model explicitly credited is the American entrepreneurial self-help book, although *The White Tiger* claims also to supersede "those American books." Rather, it is a story of "how entrepreneurship is born, nurtured, and developed in this glorious twenty-first century of man. The century, more specifically, of the yellow and brown man."[64]

Contra the *actual* circulation of the novel in metropolitan literary circles, *The White Tiger* is formally staged as a private correspondence between an Indian entrepreneur in Bangalore (the "brown" man) and the Chinese premier in Beijing (the "yellow"), in a language of the Global South, Hindi, which only one of them can read. Its somewhat illogical literary premise short-circuits the literary networks that pass through London, Paris, and New York as it imagines – if only within the novel's fictional world – a horizontal literary connection between "the yellow and the brown man" appropriate to the era of globalizing Asia. To be sure, this is no militant gesture, nor is it a Zea- or Ngũgĩ-like gesture of transcontinental solidarity. It invokes instead a common connection born of Global South aspirations to upward mobility. As Balram ironically explains in his first letter, the world has moved emphatically beyond European domination by "our erstwhile master, the white-skinned man."[65] And yet, recalling via Fanon that "the Manicheanism that first governed colonial society is maintained intact during the period of decolonization,"[66] we see how such spatial antagonisms linger on, even in our apparently globalizing era.

In this chapter, I have argued for attention to the enduring social and material structures of the Manichean (post)colonial city as a way to rethink the role of the city in conceptions of world literary space. As we see in the works of Rizal, Kim, and Adiga, discrepant urban forms make visible the enduring dominant forces of imperialism and capital accumulation. For that very reason, cities such as Manila, Seoul, and New Delhi are sites of critique, satire, and alternative decolonizing imaginaries that themselves may travel to other cities of the Global South. Departing from standard genealogies of world literature as a single worldwide literary culture that originates in nineteenth-century Europe and gradually admits newcomers, this chapter posits alternative circuits of cultural exchange that arise precisely out of the vexed spaces and critical energies of the Manichean city.

Notes

1 Frantz Fanon, *The Wretched of the Earth*, trans. Richard Philcox (New York: Grove, 2004), 3–4.
2 See, for example, the classic book by urban historian Lewis Mumford, *The Culture of Cities* (New York: Harcourt Brace, 1938).
3 For more on colonial cities, see chapter 1 of my book, *The New Asian City: Three-Dimensional Fictions of Space and Urban Form* (Minneapolis, MN: University of Minnesota Press, 2011).
4 Fanon, *Wretched of the Earth*, 58, 53.
5 Ibid., 43.
6 Pascale Casanova, *The World Republic of Letters*, trans. M.B. DeBevoise (Cambridge, MA: Harvard University Press, 2004), 95.
7 Ibid.
8 Warwick Research Collective, *Combined and Uneven Development: Toward a New Theory of World-Literature* (Liverpool: Liverpool University Press, 2015), 13. See also Franco Moretti, "Conjectures on World Literature," *New Left Review* 1 (2000): 54–68.
9 Ibid., 20.
10 See J. Daniel Elam, *World Literature for the Wretched of the Earth: Anticolonial Aesthetics, Postcolonial Politics* (New York: Fordham University Press, 2021).
11 Paradoxically, this founding nationalist text is now typically read in translation rather than the Spanish original. For this analysis, I rely on the 2006 English translation by Harold Augenbraum.
12 J. Neil C. Garcia, *The Postcolonial Perverse: Critiques of Contemporary Philippine Culture* (Manila: University of the Philippines Press, 2014), vol. 2, 45.
13 José Rizal, *Noli Me Tangere (Touch Me Not)*, trans. Harold Augenbraum (New York: Penguin, 2006), "Introduction" by Harold Augenbraum, xiv.
14 Ibid., 5.
15 Ibid., 5–6.
16 Ibid., 52.
17 For example, see Stephen Kern, *The Culture of Time and Space: 1880–1918* (Cambridge, MA: Harvard University Press, 1983).
18 Rizal, *Noli Me Tangere*, 52.
19 Ibid., 53.
20 See Michel Foucault, *Discipline and Punish: The Birth of the Prison* (New York: Vintage, 1995).
21 Nezar AlSayyad, ed., "Urbanism and the Dominance Equation: Reflections on Colonialism and National Identity," in *Forms of Dominance: On the Architecture and Urbanism of the Colonial Enterprise* (Aldershot: Averbury, 1992), 5.
22 Ignacio Tofiño-Quesada, "José Rizal's Ghost," *Anclajes* 5 (2001): 96.
23 Epifanio San Juan, "Towards Rizal: An Interpretation of Noli Me Tangere and El Filibusterismo," *Solidarity* 5, no. 12 (1970): 13.
24 Rizal, *Noli Me Tangere*, 246.

25 Benedict Anderson, *Imagined Communities: Reflections on the Origin and Spread of Nationalism* (London: Verso, 1983), 35.
26 Ibid., 27 (emphasis in original).
27 Ibid., 32.
28 Ibid., 36.
29 Paula C. Park, "Transpacific Intercoloniality: Rethinking the Globality of Philippine Literature in Spanish," *Journal of Spanish Cultural Studies* 20, no. 1–2 (2019): 84.
30 Ibid., 86.
31 AlSayyad, "Urbanism," 7.
32 Leopoldo Zea quoted in Park, "Transpacific Intercoloniality," 83.
33 Park, "Transpacific Intercoloniality," 92.
34 See Anthony King, *Urbanism, Colonialism and the World Economy: Cultural and Spatial Foundations of the World Urban System* (London: Routledge, 1990).
35 See Fanon, *Wretched of the Earth*, "The Trials and Tribulations of Nationalist Consciousness."
36 For more on Kim's trial, see Youngju Ryu, *Writers of the Winter Republic: Literature and Resistance in Park Chung Hee's Korea* (Honolulu, HI: University of Hawai'i Press, 2015).
37 The suffix *-dong* in Korean is equivalent to an administrative district or neighborhood.
38 Kim Chi-ha, "Five Bandits," trans. Brother Anthony of Taizé, *Manoa* 27, no. 2 (2015): 94–95. For the Korean original, I have consulted the bilingual edition: *Ojŏk/Five Thieves*, trans. James Han and Kim Won-chung (Seoul: Tapke, 2001).
39 See Joochul Kim and Sang-Cheul Choe, *Seoul: The Making of a Metropolis* (Chichester: Wiley, 1997).
40 Kim, "Five Bandits," 96.
41 Ibid., 97.
42 Ibid.
43 Ibid., 101.
44 Ibid., 102.
45 Fanon, *Wretched of the Earth*, 104.
46 Ibid., 124 (emphasis added).
47 The institution has received much recent scholarly attention in relation to a South–South sphere of literary circulation, in particular by Hala Halim, Duncan Yoon, Rossen Djagalov, and Monica Popescu.
48 Hala Halim, "Lotus, the Afro-Asian Nexus, and Global South Comparativism," *Comparative Studies of South Asia, Africa and the Middle East* 32, no. 3 (2012): 566.
49 Ryu, *Winter Republic*, 57.
50 Aravind Adiga, *The White Tiger: A Novel* (New York: Free Press, 2008), 101.
51 Thomas Cowan, "Fragmented Citizenships in Gurgaon," *Economic & Political Weekly* (June 27, 2015), 64.
52 Adiga, *White Tiger*, 112.
53 Ibid., 116.

54 Toral Gajarawala, "The Last and the First," *Economic & Political Weekly*, (December 12, 2009), 22.
55 Adiga, *White Tiger*, 18.
56 Ibid., 107.
57 Ibid., 127–128.
58 Namita Dharia, "Artefacts and Artifices of the Global: Practices of US Architects in India's National Capital Region," *The Global South* 8, no. 2 (2014): 55.
59 San Juan, "Towards Rizal," 13.
60 Adiga, *White Tiger*, 209.
61 Ibid., 210.
62 Ibid., 54.
63 Ibid., 189.
64 Ibid., 4.
65 Ibid.
66 Fanon, *Wretched of the Earth*, 14.

CHAPTER 4

The Urban Itinerary and the City Map

The Experience of Metropolitan Space

Robert T. Tally Jr.

In Italo Calvino's *Invisible Cities*, the narrator (Marco Polo) speaks of Esmeralda, "city of water," in which "a network of canals and a network of streets span and intersect each other." He then explains:

> To go from one place to another you have always the choice between land and boat: and the shortest distance between two points in Esmeralda is not a straight line but a zigzag that ramifies in tortuous optional routes, the ways that open to each passerby are never two, but many, and they increase further for those who alternate a stretch by boat with one on dry land.[1]

As Calvino puts it, the inhabitants of this city are "spared the boredom of following the same streets each day" and "enjoy every day the pleasure of a new itinerary to reach the same places." He then adds that the more "adventurous" inhabitants, including "cats, thieves, [and] illicit lovers," will move along "discontinuous ways," such as "dropping from a rooftop to a balcony" or "crossing the city's compactness pierced by the spokes of underground passages."[2] In this unique urban landscape, as in cities everywhere, there are many ways to get around.

The description of Esmeralda's spaces evokes the wondrous, mysterious, or magical, like those of many of the other "cities" in Calvino's novel, yet the focus here on multiple and changing itineraries is well suited for a more general discussion of the "culture of cities," as it were. For the individual inhabitant of a city, the experience of its spaces is likely to be most vivid in the ways in which one moves through them. The trajectories from Point A to Point B offer a number of distinctive vistas onto the urban landscape, and the fact that such trajectories are numerous compounds this proliferation of views almost exponentially. Even the most straightforwardly purposive individuals will find their paths strewn with all manner of possibilities and confundities, and the variety of identifiable routes themselves form a complex and dynamic web or network of spatial practices. With those travelers who are less utilitarian or pragmatic, such as Charles Baudelaire's infamous *flâneur* (or *flâneuse*, as I discuss below), the effect of moving along these itineraries evoke a sort of polysensorial phantasmagoria, which may well merit the metaphor used by Baudelaire himself, who compared the *flâneur* to "a kaleidoscope equipped with consciousness."[3] The joys of walking in the city are manifold, but it is also the case that such situations and circumstances can occasion, cause, or amplify feelings of danger, disorientation, and displacement. Indeed, precisely for these reasons, among others, the urban *Wandersmänner* may wish to reach for a map.

A map, in this case, refers not so much to the physical document to be found in guidebooks or tourist brochures, a graphic depiction of the city's spaces laid out as if seen from high above. In many places that cater to tourists, travelers, and visitors, actual maps in the form of spatial diagrams are found on signs or posters, which in turn aid the user in navigating the real geospaces abstractly projected upon the map's figured surface. Such *actual* maps may also be very useful, but I am thinking especially of the ways in which individuals in cities form their own *virtual*, imaginary, or mental maps, which become abstract models for use in navigating the material spaces and places encountered "on the ground." The point of view of the individual subject walking in the city is thus supplemented by a more abstract or projective perspective afforded by the imagination via a sort of mental cartography.

This is not to say, however, that a map will solve the problems encountered by the spatially bewildered denizen of the city. Such urban *bewilderment* would appear paradoxical, for the "wilderness" one finds oneself situated within is precisely that "civilization" against which the wild is normally defined. A map is supposed to make these spaces more practically legible, organizing them into a strictly rational system, such as a grid, that tames their wilder characteristics. Yet maps are not always reliable guides, even when they are technically "accurate," whatever that means. Although the idea of "accurate maps" may be widely understood, in theory and perhaps also in practice such accuracy may be difficult to determine, given that what would count as accuracy varies according to the uses for which it was designed and the experience of the users. Because maps are by their very nature figural, thus defined by the dilemma of representation, "there can be no true maps," as Fredric Jameson has put it.[4]

Maps can often be confusing even when they are deemed accurate. As Alberto Toscano and Jeff Kinkle have pointed out in *Cartographies of the Absolute*, "one of the first products of a genuine striving for orientation is disorientation, as proximal coordinates come to be troubled by wide, and at times overwhelming vistas."[5] While pragmatic, the abstraction of maps can be alienating in its own right. In some cases, the map may not coincide with the mental maps one had already formed, leading to greater confusion. All maps are abstractions, of course, but certain maps more than others will serve intended or unintended ideological purposes. In creating a map, as with creating a story, the cartographer will necessarily choose elements to be included and consider those that are better left out. No map, not even the fabled Imperial Map from Jorge Luis Borges's celebrated fragment "On Exactitude in Science" (i.e., a map that is coextensive with the territory it purports to represent), is ever going to be a total and complete, identical representation of the space it purports to display. The principle and practice of selection will usually be based on the perceived uses to which the map will be put.

Indeed, in *Invisible Cities*, just after mentioning the well-nigh infinite varieties of potential itineraries in the "city of water," Calvino's narrator introduces the figure of the map, which he deems necessary for the proper understanding of Esmeralda's urban spaces, even as he emphasizes the apparent impossibility of representing these vicissitudinous trajectories in any meaningfully cartographic form. As he puts it,

> A map of Esmeralda should include, marked in different colored inks, all these routes, solid and liquid, evident and hidden. It is more difficult to fix on the map the routes of swallows, who cut the air over the roofs, dropping long invisible parabolas with the still wings, darting to gulp a mosquito, spiraling upward, grazing a pinnacle, dominating from every point of their airy paths all the points of the city.[6]

Esmeralda's civic spaces thus not only blend terrestrial and aquatic (as well as visible and invisible) pathways, but also disclose a heterotopian amalgam of constructed and natural worlds. That the unmappable errancy of the swallows can imply the dominance of "all the points of the city" suggests the crises of both knowledge and power implicit in our ability to move about and to map the city. So it goes in the "invisible city" of Esmeralda, as it does in the vibrant, ecstatic, and vexed experience of cities more generally.

As cultural critics have observed, the experience of the city presents distinctive problems, both for navigation and for representation. In his classic 1903 essay, "The Metropolis and Mental Life," Georg Simmel asserted that "the psychological basis of the metropolitan type of individuality consists in the *intensification of nervous stimulation* which results from the swift and uninterrupted change of outer and inner stimuli."[7] For Simmel, the individual moving through a metropolitan space is confronted by a sensual bombardment; this is already disorienting in itself, even before one examines the prospect of losing one's way within that domain. Of course, this "intensification of nervous stimulation" is also among the more desirable aspects of city life, and the polysensory delirium of a vibrant and heterogeneous urban setting can just as easily enchant the individual with its delights as be a cause for alarm. For example, in a lovely passage in which he describes people walking along Oxford Street in Accra, Ghana, Ato Quayson mentions "the bemusement and otherwise irritated hurrying-to-get-somewhere-yet-being-constantly-interrupted quality of walking," a brilliantly described form of urban experience that is further compounded by "a dimension of distractedness" even as, in its own cacophonous auditory maelstrom, "the street demands attention in a way that does not allow zoning out its ambient sounds."[8] The dangers of "zoning out" such sounds are real, given the traffic and other hazards one faces in moving along busy streets in major commercial districts. For a critic less attuned to the welcome vitality and polyphonic discourse of the metropolitan setting, these aspects of being situated and moving within urban space might be figured as infernal, a great Mephistophelean pandemonium from which the pure of heart may wish to escape. But Quayson notes that "Oxford Street proffers *a form of sensorial totality* that is only unpleasant if you go against the flow of its multimodal sensory offerings."[9]

The rhetorical figure of "flow," as in Calvino's "city of water," is particularly apt for understanding the experience of the individual subject in the city, but so is the concept of "totality." For one situated in the midst of these multifarious social and sensual flows, one who is plunged *in medias res*, the exhilaration is palpable, and this need not be formulated in strictly binary terms – or, worse, in ethical evaluations – of good or bad, liberatory or repressive, and so forth. Similarly and notwithstanding the potential for hegemonic or ideological distortions, there is a need for some sense of totality, which may require at least provisionally something like a bird's-eye view or an abstract model, which is to say, a map. Such a map can help to give form to these flows in ways that make them and our experience within them both comprehensible and meaningful, and this strikes me as also being essential to the experience of the city. The urban itinerary and the city map go hand in hand.

In *The Image of the City*, Kevin Lynch describes the conjoined problematic of subjective navigation of urban space and its seemingly objective representation in a map-like form in terms of what he calls "wayfinding" and "imageability." That is, the inhabitants of a city need to be able to find their way around its spaces, but in order to do so, they must be able to form mental maps to aid them in navigating. From the perspective of urban planning, Lynch's goal would be to have clear landmarks, natural or otherwise, by which the individual subjects moving about the city could find their way easily, allowing them to quickly form mental maps representing the urban space that would facilitate its traversal. The lack of such landmarks, and thus of the raw material for one's mental map, results not only in making it more difficult to move purposively about the city but also in a more general sense of anxiety and alienation. As Jameson succinctly summarizes Lynch's argument in this respect,

> the alienated city is above all a space in which people are unable to map (in their minds) either their own positions or the urban totality in which they find themselves [....] Disalienation in the traditional city, then, involves the practical reconquest sense of place and the construction or reconstruction of an articulated ensemble which can be retained in memory and which the individual subject can map and remap along the moments of mobile, alternative trajectories.[10]

The city's imageability, then, is related to this need for a sort of imaginative cartography, but precisely in order to facilitate *itineraries*.

These problems of wayfinding and imageability would arise and persist in even relatively small cities, presumably, but it is clear that both the growth of metropolitan areas and the increasing complexity of the societies characterized by a burgeoning urbanization exacerbate the orientational and representational dilemmas. The problem is not only *spatial*, strictly speaking, but also *epistemic*, insofar as one cannot really "know" the city one is inhabiting without being able, in some manner, to "map" it in useful ways. In *The Country and the City*, Raymond Williams connects the theory of the novel to the social spaces depicted in them when discussing the idea of "knowable communities," which in nineteenth-century English literature and culture become more difficult to create and represent amid the radical transformations of society in that epoch. As he puts it, "[t]he growth of towns and especially of cities and a metropolis; the increasing division and complexity of labour; the altered and critical relations between and within social classes: in changes like these any assumption of a knowable community – a whole community, wholly knowable – became harder and harder to sustain."[11]

Part of this transformation, which then requires different modes of representation or mapping to make possible effective ways of knowing, consists in the vast multiplication and confusion of ways of moving around the social space. For example, in her analysis of Herman Melville's fiction and the urban form of nineteenth-century New York, Wyn Kelley notes the historical development away from the older "Walking City," in which an observant pedestrian "can master his urban environment in a day's walk," to something more confusing, "a dense maze where he may get lost."[12] "The Walking City of Knickerbocker New York, as cultural construction, provided the urbane spectator with an ideal terrain," writes Kelley, before describing the ways that

> [u]nprecedented growth, deepening class divisions, rising land values, the flight of the wealthy from the urban center, the tearing up and rebuilding of the streets, the pressure of immigration, all made the old city unrecognizable. In its place evolved a changing urban structure, one difficult to navigate or to comprehend—one that writers, artists, and city dwellers described as a labyrinth. Getting through that labyrinth became a new challenge in urban life and literature.[13]

In such a case, something like Lynch's vision of a city's imageability takes on additional urgency. As Jonathan Arac put it, in his analysis of "the shaping of social motion" in nineteenth-century literature, "the chaos of urban experience fostered a wish for a clarifying overview."[14] This, in turn, leads to the development of new narrative techniques aimed at capturing and "knowing" the social scene more effectively, but it also suggests the ways in which a form of *mapping* is required for the successful wayfinding and movement of those engaged in urban itineraries, as well as to those writing about the experience.

How we imagine the spaces we inhabit and move within has real effects on the "reality" of those spaces. As Edward Soja has noted, the distinction between "real" and "imagined" spaces often breaks down in practice, as the "real-and-imagined" places constitute the spatial framework by which we experience the world.[15] Such experience combines elements of the subjective and the objective, which is also to say, it combines our own peculiar perspective on things with our sense of a vaster reality or totality beyond our immediate ken. These in turn have correspondences with the spatiotemporal distinctions between the figures and practices associated with the itinerary and the map.

Using slightly different terminology, linguists Charlotte Linde and William Labov have shown how our very ways of speaking about space and place indicate different modes of imagining, perceiving, and navigating spaces. In "Spatial Networks as a Site for the Study of Language and Thought," Linde and Labov distinguish between the *tour* and the *map*, which are more or less analogous to the itinerary and the map as discussed by other theorists.[16] The *tour* would establish a sort of spatiotemporal narrative structure; that is, the verbal representation of the space implies a subject who moves through space in a certain sequential or diachronic order, such that it involves something like syntax. The *map*, by contrast, posits a synoptic or synchronic spatial matrix in which everything is laid out at once; all places are present simultaneously. Linde and Labov find examples of this sort of thinking about space in the ways that residents of New York describe their apartments. Some speak of these places in such a way as to offer a virtual tour of the apartment (e.g., "you enter the kitchen and then you find a dining room to the left"), thus essentially narrating a spatial story of the environment for the auditor or reader. Far rarer, according to Linde and Labov, were the New Yorkers who would use a more map-like discourse, with its presumably objective depiction of the apartment's layout (e.g., "there is a dining room east of the kitchen"). For these linguists, the preference for the *tour* over the *map* reflects the ways in which "cognitive inputs" (the knowledge of the *space*, in this case) are transformed into grammatical and syntagmatic structures that become in effect temporal, at least with respect to the ways in which we represent our knowledge and experience of space in language. To take it a step beyond Linde and Labov's more strictly linguistic arguments, we might say the speaking subjects *make sense of* space by transforming it into a narrative structure. To know a place is to tell a story.[17]

Storytelling partakes of both modes, and one might characterize this distinction in terms of narrative techniques that emphasize the tour- or itinerary-like flow of a subject's movements in space *versus* a more descriptive or static, map-like sketch of the space's features or contours.[18] Narratologist David Herman in *Story Logic* invokes Linde and Labov's work in examining the narrative technique employed by Ernest Hemingway in this passage from *A Moveable Feast*:

> After you came out of the Luxembourg [Gardens], you could walk down the narrow rue Férou to the Place St.-Suplice and there were still no restaurants, only the quiet square with its benches and trees. [...] From this square, you could not go further toward the river without passing shops selling fruits, vegetables, wines, or bakery and pastry shops. But by choosing your way carefully you could work to your right around the grey and white stone church and reach the rue de l'Odéon and turn up to your right toward Sylvia Beach's bookshop and on your way you did not pass too many places where things to eat were sold.[19]

Herman notes that "Hemingway's use of landmarks [...] help readers map his progress through subregions within the city of Paris," and the mention of distinctive toponyms "lend a sense of authenticity and credibility to the account." Notwithstanding the map-like notations, however, Herman observes that "the dominant mode of spatial reference" involves this tour-like trajectory. "With the help of the second-person narration," writes Herman, "the passage works to position the reader in the spatiotemporal coordinates that define the protagonist-narrator's changing vantage-point on the storyworld."[20] In sum, Herman concludes, "the passage takes the reader on a *tour* through the streets of Paris, rather than encoding spatial representations that take the form of an aerial *map*, a static view of the city from above."[21]

By contrast, consider this scene from William Faulkner's 1948 novel, *Intruder in the Dust*, in which a character surveys the geographical terrain of a section of the fictional Yoknapatawpha County, Mississippi:

> he seemed to see his whole native land, his home [...] unfolding beneath him like a map in one slow soundless explosion: to the east ridge on green ridges tumbling away toward Alabama and to the west and south the checkered fields and the woods flowing on into the blue and gauzed horizon beyond which lay at last like a cloud the long wall of the levee and the great River itself flowing not merely from the north but out of the North.[22]

Marie-Laure Ryan cites this passage as an examples of "map strategy in narrative fiction," pointing out that the character's position on crest of a ridge "detaches him from the landscape and provides a substitute for the bird's-eye point of view of maps." As Ryan et al. affirm, "[t]he map-like perspective is reinforced by the absolute directional terms of east, west, and south," such that the reader "can not only locate the elements of the landscape with respect to each other but also situate them with the real-world geography."[23] It is true, Yoknapatawpha County – which provides the primary locale for the "storyworld" in many of Faulkner's writings – is, strictly speaking, a fictional place, but the direct references to Alabama and "the North" (in which the capital letter "N" designates a political and cultural reality that supplements the merely directional sign) place the reader within a "real-world" setting almost as much as Hemingway's pedestrian-in-Paris formulation.[24] Here the reader is invited to apprehend the place almost all at once, whereas Hemingway's readers were guided through the streets nearly step by step. However, Faulkner's metaphor of the "tumbling away" of the ridges and the "flow" of the woods (not to mention, presumably, the actually fluvial river) suggests a temporal element in which both the reader and the land itself are caught up, much as Hemingway's narrative tour had to include map-like place names as points of reference. Even map-like narrative may include tour-like narration, and vice versa.

Linde and Labov's distinction between the tour and the map shows the degree to which the spatial and the temporal registers necessarily overlap in our apprehension of the spaces we inhabit and our ways of representing them. But this also might be said to indicate the degree to which the dichotomy breaks down, as a kind of spatiotemporality must be acknowledged as lying at the heart of all touring and mapping. That is, the apparently dynamic movement of the tour and the static description of the map present something of a false binary, since in reality both features are present in both our personal experience and in any given narrative that attempts to give form to such experience. The subject's movement through space and among places and his or her perceptions of them presupposes, and is informed by, a more abstract or theoretical vision of a non-subjective or supra-subjective image: an abstract, imaginary, or bird's-eye perspective that brings order and a sense of objectivity to the limited point of view of the itinerant subject. The difference between the tour and the map ought not be viewed as a diametrical opposition, but rather as complementary and cooperative. The distinction is therefore still valuable, as it illuminates two fundamental aspects of the spatial imagination, which in the older discourse of philosophy might simply be transcoded as subjective and objective, and yet we find that the two registers cannot long be held separate, as each infuses the other and makes knowledge, and perhaps more importantly narrative, possible.

Michel de Certeau, in examining what he refers to as "spatial stories," highlights the distinction between different sensory registers along these lines, as he distinguishes between "either *seeing* (the knowledge of an order of places) or *going* (spatializing actions)."[25] These correspond to the difference between a map and a tour, and Certeau then uses this dichotomy to inform another, as he develops a more elaborate analysis of the opposition between the map and the itinerary. In this vision, the map is conceived of as "a plane projection [of] totalizing observations," while the itinerary represents "a discursive series of operations," and Certeau sees these as two distinctive "symbolic and anthropological languages of space." He adds that these represent "[t]wo poles of experience" and that, "in passing from 'ordinary' culture to scientific discourse, one passes from one pole to the other."[26] However, Certeau also insists upon a more political or even moral character associated with these two poles. In his formulation, the "ordinary" culture is somehow more liberatory and worthy of our admiration than scientific discourse, which he finds repressive, as he makes clearer in his famous discussion of "walking in the city" in *The Practice of Everyday Life*.

There Certeau sharply distinguishes between two perspectives from which to view as well as experience or even, in a more abstract sense, actively shape urban space. Unsurprisingly these perspectives align closely with the distinction between the itinerary and the map. Certeau contrasts the perspective of the pedestrian walking along the city streets with that of a "voyeur" who gazes upon the city's spaces from some lofty vantage point. Writing in the 1970s just as the World Trade Center's towers had recently opened and when they represented the world's tallest buildings, Certeau opposes the pedestrian's street-level experience with the point of view afforded by standing upon the observation deck of the World Trade Center, from which on a clear day one could see most of the city of New York as well as surrounding areas. Certeau maintains that such a perspective removes one from that city, and he writes, "to be lifted to the summit of the World Trade Center is to be lifted out of the city's grasp." Comparing the view to "an Icarus flying above these waters," Certeau claims that a person becomes a voyeur, attempting to "read" the city from a distance, or worse, "to be a solar Eye, looking down like a god. The exaltation of the scopic and gnostic drive: the fiction of knowledge is related to this lust to be a viewpoint and nothing more."[27] The image of the city from this perspective is "the analogue of the facsimile produced, through a projection that is a way of keeping aloof, by the space planner urbanist, city planner or cartographer."[28]

Certeau contrasts this perspective to that of the "ordinary practitioners of the city" who are on the street below, whom he calls: "walkers, *Wandersmänner*, whose bodies follow the thicks and thins of an urban 'text' they write without being able to read it." Alluding to Michel Foucault's examination in *Discipline and Punish* of the Panopticon as a model of modern disciplinary power and knowledge formation, Certeau imagines these streetwalkers as forces of resistance, inasmuch as they attempt to locate "the practices that are foreign to the 'geometrical' or 'geographical' space of the visual, panoptic, or theoretical constructions."[29] The "speech acts" of pedestrians are spatial practices, "tricky and stubborn procedures that elude discipline," which turn out to *write* the city in what Certeau names "the long poem of walking," which

> manipulates spatial organizations, no matter how panoptic they may be: it is neither foreign to them (it can take place only within them) nor in conformity with them (it does not receive its identity from them). It creates shadows and ambiguities within them. It inserts its multitudinous references and citation into them (social models, cultural mores, personal factors). Within them it is itself the effect of successive encounters and occasions that constantly alter it.[30]

As if to emphasize the impossibility of positively localizing the *flâneur* in the geometric or panoptic space of a map-like order, Certeau insists that "to walk is to lack a place."[31] And yet, walking is an inherently topophrenic activity, as it would be hard to imagine urban pedestrians who are not aware of their place and the variety of spatial arrays within which they move.

One might note that, in addition to the linguistic or grammatical "gendering" of terms such as *flâneurs* and *Wandersmänner*, there are clearly key differences in the way that "streetwalkers" are understood when the gender of the itinerant subject changes.[32] It is no mere accident, after all, that the term "streetwalker" is used as a synonym for "prostitute," and along those lines the surveillance, regulation, and even criminalization of women's movements about an urban landscape have developed historically in ways that help to establish and reinforce relations of power, serving patriarchal or otherwise sexist ends. As Rebecca Solnit has pointed out, "Women have been routinely punished and intimidated for attempting that most simple of freedoms, taking a walk, because their walking and indeed their very beings have been construed as inevitably, continually sexual in those societies concerned with controlling women's sexuality."[33] Far from embodying the freedom to write "the long poem of walking" and thereby to "elude discipline," as Certeau would have it, women who wished to walk the streets have often been perceived as being thoroughly reckless or, more likely, sexually deviant and immoral. Needless to say, alas, some of that opprobrium with respect to women on the street lingers still in many cities and cultures.

For example, Walter Benjamin, whose influential analyses of Baudelaire have helped make the *flâneur* such a salient figure for modern cultural studies, maintains his own strictly gendered vision. In *The Arcades Project*, there are numerous references to prostitutes and prostitution, but at no point is the *flâneuse* offered as a representative type or transgressive subject. According to Benjamin, the sex worker (a term Benjamin does not use, of course) "does not sell her labor power," but rather her job "entails the fiction she sells her powers of pleasure," and thus becomes "a precursor to commodity capitalism," but he effectively denies that prostitution counts as "work": "[t]he closer work comes to prostitution, the more tempting it is to conceive of prostitution as work – something that has been customary in the argot of whores for a long time now."[34] Whereas Benjamin along with most of his readers could identify with the *flâneur*, he rhetorically and ideologically tends to position himself at a distance from, or even athwart, the urban female "streetwalker," who tends to represent the predations of modern capitalist society in *The Arcades Project*.[35]

A more positive view can be found in Lauren Elkin's *Flâneuse: Women Walk the City in Paris, New York, Tokyo, Venice, and London*, which combines aspects of memoir, literary criticism, social history, and urban studies. As Elkin notes, while the term *flâneur* is well established, even today most French dictionaries do not include the word *flâneuse*.[36] Further, she notes that while "women in the street" have been historically seen as "most likely streetwalkers," no connection between the *flâneur* and the criminal "street prowler" is ever made. Moreover, Elkins points out, prostitutes, quite unlike *flâneurs*, rarely have anything like free range over the city streets, but are almost always limited to carefully demarcated zones (e.g., red-light districts), officially or otherwise.[37] Notwithstanding these prejudices, Elkin discovers a lost history of the *flâneuse*, revealing a vibrant, dynamic, and multifaceted tale of women's urban itineraries and *flâneries*, which had been hidden in part by the very male gaze that has objectified women in the first place. The *flâneuse* cannot maintain relative invisibility, a privilege enjoyed by "the man of the crowd" in most instances, precisely because crowds of men will undoubtedly be eyeing her. Elkin cites Virginia Woolf's notion of "street haunting," from a 1927 essay of that title, to indicate "a freedom for women on the streets of the city to come and go as they please, on foot," and the implied reference to ghosts cannot be merely coincidental. Elkin states that "street haunting" is "an attempt to claim an ungendered place in the city by walking through it."[38] Such a "claim" would involve an assertion of authority in its own right, to be able to map for oneself, and in some ways this invokes the liberatory function of mapping.

The exuberance of Certeau's vision of the transgressive streetwalker who subverts the totalizing gaze of the cartographic order of knowledge and power is compelling, but it also ignores the ways in which mapping can itself be understood as active spatial practice, rather than as a force to which one is subject. Even apart from revisionary mapping practices or counter-mapping, whereby subaltern groups reclaim and modify representation structures such as the official maps of a hegemonic power to their own ends, one must recognize the degree to which mapping is itself a potentially liberatory practice as well. A map of the prison is of supreme value to one who would escape, after all. Something like Jameson's concept of cognitive mapping, which draws upon Lynch's ideas while enlarging their scope to include all social and well as spatial disorientation, ultimately moving to the global scale of the late capitalist world system,[39] suggests some of the politically pertinent and valuable aspects of mapping, both for the person on the city street and for those elsewhere in the world. In the spaces of the cities and in the literature that represent them and our experiences in them, "we all necessarily *also* cognitively map our individual social relationship to local, national or international class realities."[40] Whether the aim is to represent an unrepresentable international social class, or, as Jameson's model makes clear, to situate one's position relative to others in a vast, seemingly unrepresentable social space, a cartographic project is required. In a more figurative sense, world literature also partakes in that project, projecting a larger system in which the various storylines elaborate themselves, unfolding, intersecting, and veering off in new, unforeseen directions.

Ultimately, the itinerary and the map fold into one another as the lines, produced by what Quayson refers to as "spatial traversal," or "the characters' movement from one spatial location to another," give shape not only to the experience of the city, but also to the city itself.[41] These itineraries, in the aggregate, may be said to weave together the warp and woof of the city, helping to produce its spaces even as the itineraries are themselves conditioned by them. The map offers a vision of this urban rhapsody,[42] figuring forth its many lines and threads in a manner consistent with the aims of the users of these places, who are also the makers thereof. The experience of metropolitan space emerges at the intersections and intertwinings of the urban itinerary and the city map, which in turn make possible the aesthetic and poetic representations that give this experience lasting significance.

Notes

1 Italo Calvino, *Invisible Cities*, trans. William Weaver (New York: Harcourt, 1974), 88.
2 Ibid., 88–89.
3 Charles Baudelaire, "The Painter of Modern Life," in *The Painter of Modern Life and Other Essays*, trans. and ed. Jonathan Mayne (London: Phaidon Press, 1964), 9. See also Lauren Elkin, *Flâneuse: Women Walk the City in Paris, New York, Tokyo, Venice, and London* (New York: Farrar, Strauss & Giroux, 2016).
4 Fredric Jameson, *Postmodernism, or, the Cultural Logic of Late Capitalism* (Durham, NC: Duke University Press, 1991), 52.
5 Alberto Toscano and Jeff Kinkle, *Cartographies of the Absolute* (Winchester: Zero Books, 2015).
6 Calvino, *Invisible Waters*, 89.
7 Georg Simmel, "The Metropolis and Mental Life," in *The Sociology of Georg Simmel*, trans. and ed. Kurt H. Wolff (New York: The Free Press, 1950), 409–410. Emphasis in original.
8 Ato Quayson, *Oxford Street, Accra: City Life and the Itineraries of Transnationalism* (Durham, NC: Duke University Press, 2014), 17.

9 Ibid., 17 (emphasis added). On polysensoriality and place, see Bertrand Westphal, *Geocriticism: Real and Fictional Spaces*, trans. Robert T. Tally Jr. (New York: Palgrave Macmillan, 2011), especially 131–136.
10 Jameson, *Postmodernism*, 51.
11 Raymond Williams, *The Country and the City* (Oxford: Oxford University Press, 1973), 165.
12 Wyn Kelley, *Melville's City: Literary and Urban Form in Nineteenth-Century New York* (Cambridge: Cambridge University Press, 1996), 69, 93.
13 Ibid., 94.
14 Jonathan Arac, *Commissioned Spirits: The Shaping of Social Motion in Dickens, Carlyle, Melville, and Hawthorne* (New York: Columbia University Press, 1989), 3.
15 See Edward W. Soja, *Thirdspace: Journeys to Los Angeles and Other Real-and-Imagined Places* (Oxford: Blackwell, 1996).
16 See Charlotte Linde and William Labov, "Spatial Networks as a Site for the Study of Language and Thought," *Language* 51, no. 4 (December 1975), 924–939.
17 As Peter Turchi has put it, "To ask for a map is to say, 'Tell me a story.'" See Turchi, *Maps of the Imagination: The Writer as Cartographer* (San Antonio, TX: Trinity University Press, 2004), 11.
18 See Georg Lukács, "Narrate or Describe?," in *Writer and Critic and Other Essays*, trans. and ed. Arthur D. Kahn (New York: Merlin Press, 1970), 110–148.
19 Ernest Hemingway, *A Moveable Feast: The Restored Edition,* Sean Hemingway, ed. (New York: Scribner Books, 2009), 65–66.
20 David Herman, *Story Logic: Problems and Possibilities of Narrative* (Lincoln, NE: University of Nebraska Press, 2004), 281. Herman quoted a somewhat longer selection from Hemingway's text (280–281).
21 Ibid., 281, emphasis added.
22 William Faulkner, *Intruder in the Dust* (New York: Vintage Books, 1994), 147–148.
23 Marie-Laure Ryan, Kenneth Foote, and Maoz Azaryahu, *Narrating Space/Spatializing Narrative: Where Narrative Theory and Geography Meet* (Columbus, OH: Ohio State University Press, 2016), 28.
24 Lennard Davis, in *Resisting Novels*, distinguishes between three types of place: the actual (such as the London of Dickens), the fictitious (say, George Eliot's Middlemarch, which is similar to parts of Great Britain but not localizable on a map), and the renamed (F. Scott Fitzgerald's East and West Egg, for instance, which mirror locales on New York's Long Island); Faulkner's Yoknapatawpha County, which is quite similar to Lafayette County, Mississippi, where he lived, partakes of both the fictitious and the renamed, in Davis's formulation. See Lennard Davis, *Resisting Novels: Ideology and Fiction* (London: Routledge, 2014), 55.
25 Michel de Certeau, *The Practice of Everyday Life*, trans. Steven Rendall (Berkeley, CA: University of California Press, 1984), 119.
26 Ibid.

27 Ibid., 92.
28 Ibid., 92–93.
29 Ibid., 93. See Michel Foucault, *Discipline and Punish: The Birth of the Prison*, trans. Alan Sheridan (New York: Vintage, 1977), especially 195–229.
30 Certeau, *Practice of Everyday Life*, 96, 101.
31 Ibid., 103.
32 See, e.g., *La Marcheuse*, a 2016 film (released in English with the title *She Walks*) about a prostitute living in Paris. As Dorothee Hou points out, "The film's title, 'la marcheuse' (the walker, or marcher), is a slang for streetwalkers in French. It also refers to second-rate ballet dancers who are on stage only to walk or march, a living prop of sorts." See Dorothee Hou, "From Rust Belt to Belleville: Two Recent Films on Chinese Migrant Sex Workers in Paris," in Melody Yunzi Li and Robert T. Tally Jr., eds., *Affective Geographies and Narratives of Chinese Diaspora* (New York: Palgrave Macmillan, forthcoming).
33 Rebecca Solnit, *Wanderlust: A History of Walking* (New York: Penguin, 2001), 233.
34 Walter Benjamin, *The Arcades Project*, trans. Howard Eiland and Kevin McLaughlin (Cambridge, MA: Harvard University Press, 2002), 348, 360. Needless to say, perhaps, that all prostitutes are women in Benjamin's work.
35 Take, for example, the following aphorism: "Love of the prostitute is the apotheosis of empathy with the commodity" (ibid., 511).
36 Elkin, Flâneuse, 7.
37 Ibid., 8–9.
38 Ibid., 13–14, 92, 288.
39 See, e.g., Jameson, *The Geopolitical Aesthetic: Space and Cinema in the World System* (Bloomington, IN and London: Indiana University Press and the British Film Institute, 1992).
40 Jameson, *Postmodernism*, 52.
41 Quayson, *Oxford Street, Accra*, 214–215.
42 From the Greek, *rhapsōidein*, to weave or to stitch together. In this sense, the literary cartography of the writer stitches together the disparate strands of spatial experience into a cognizable whole, like a completed story or a map.

PART II

Spotlight Literary Cities

CHAPTER 5

The Neighborhood and the Sweatshop

Immigrant and Diasporic Rites of Passage in the Literature of New York

Ato Quayson

> This is certainly the city for everyone being from somewhere else.
>
> –John Dos Passos, *Manhattan Transfer*

If, following Goethe and various other commentators on world literature, we take the world itself as defined by a temporal process of becoming, we ought to add that it is also to be understood as the product of the aesthetic practices that animate it. More importantly, with reference to cities, their literature inscribes the urban as the source and trigger of imaginative responses to space (in transport infrastructure, architecture, shops and pleasure, and urbanized green spaces) as well as to the social relations of which urban space is both a symptom and producer.[1] It is this combination of world-as-process-of-becoming yet also grounded in a set of spatial and social relations that connects urban literature to world literature. The challenge for us, however, is how to interpret urban literature as providing us with the analogues and refutations to the ways in which concepts such as world, globe, and planet have been historically interpreted, especially when we examine these with respect to the challenge to narrow conceptions of world literature posed by the work of immigrants, diasporics, postcolonials, and citizens of the Global South.[2] This chapter will lay out a potted account of the literature of New York and its relationship to world literature braiding two main themes: first will be that of New York as a center of self-invention, a place that was primarily commercial at its inception but progressively expanded to embrace diverse forms of ethnic, cultural, sexual, and urban interactions. And second will be to focus on the significance of neighborhoods and sweatshops as the spatial vectors through which immigrants and diasporics gain a sense of New York. Dos Passos's comment on the universal attraction of New York to people from elsewhere is definitive of the city. This will be reflected directly in the discussion here. The bulk of the chapter will be devoted to a close analysis of the chronotopes of the neighborhood and the sweatshop in Toni Morrison's *Jazz* (1992) and Melissa Rivero's *The Affairs of the Falcóns* (2019) respectively, as a means of grasping the relationship between the localized foci of individual mobility, identity, and alienation and the ways in which we might also discern these as key organizing principles of world literature.[3]

A central feature of the literature of New York is that the city has always been depicted as a place where people come to (re)invent themselves. This has obvious purchase with the many arrivals from both the United States and elsewhere that have settled in the city from the seventeenth century to recent times. The theme of self-invention also echoes in the related story of LGBT people and their literary expressions in New York. There is much in this literature that overlaps with that of migrant self-invention, to be found as much in James Baldwin's *Another Country* (1962) as in Edmund White's *City Boy* (2010) and Andrew Holleran's *Dancer from the Dance* (1978), along with the work of Truman Capote, Frank O'Hara, Allen Ginsburg, Audre Lorde, and Djuna Barnes, among many others. And Brian Silverman has written that "gay and lesbian culture is as much a part of New York's basic identity as yellow cabs, high-rises, and Broadway theatre."[4]

The city's avowed cosmopolitanism is defined by what historian Thomas Bender has described as its particular "political and cultural dialectic" that makes it part of American history but at the same time distinguishes it from all others.[5] A good literary example of this principle of exchange is to be found in Anne Nichols's *Abie's Irish Rose* (1924), a lighthearted depiction of the marriage between a Jewish boy and a Catholic Irish girl. As Eric Homberger notes, apart from the play being a commercial success of American culture, it is also "a prism in which powerful cultural forces – ethnic relations, the impact of mass migration, and the cross-generational complexities of assimilation – are refracted, exaggerated, and also unexpectedly clarified."[6] And yet cultural exchange and self-invention in New York is not always successful, as we discover in Chang-rae Lee's *Native Speaker* (1995), which through the genre of detective fiction depicts the difficulties of immigrant and first-generation Korean-Americans in their struggles to assimilate to American life. We find similar difficulties in Mohsin Hamid's *The Reluctant Fundamentalist* (2008), where the city's multicultural exchange mechanisms come under threat following the cataclysmic events of September 11, 2001, when difference becomes retranscribed as inherently dangerous and repugnant through the nativist and jingoistic discourses that become manifest in New York and elsewhere in America. The danger of nativist jingoism has often flared up in different historical periods in response to immigrant Irish, Italian, Jewish, Puerto Rican, and Dominican communities in New York.

***

The Lenape tribe are easy to forget in accounts of today's New York. But when Dutch colonists first settled Mannahatta (Manhattan's original name) in 1624 and renamed it New Amsterdam two years later, the Lenape tribe had lived there for centuries. Broadway was originally a trail carved by Mannahatta's native inhabitants that snaked through swamps and rocks throughout the length of Manhattan Island. While Broadway is today's metonym for New York's famous theater district, the road of the same name runs the entire length of Manhattan, roughly parallel to the Hudson River, and stretches from Bowling Green (home of the financial district's Charging Bull sculpture) at the south end to Inwood at the northern tip of the island. Today's Times Square was a forest with a beaver pond, and the site of the Jacob Javits Federal Building at Foley Square (south of Chinatown and east of Tribeca) was littered with oyster dunghills. East Village was marshy and under water until the beginning of the nineteenth century.

New York's changing landscape reflects not only the changes in commercial investment that the city is renowned for, but also the alteration in the number of immigrants at different stages of its evolution. From 1643–64 the Dutch allowed a group of Black Angolans to settle on what was later to become Washington Square Park, as a buffer between the Dutch, settled in the areas around Wall Street, and the native tribes with whom they were having regular battles. But from the early 1800s to 1825 Washington Square Park was used as a cemetery, with people that died from the city's various yellow fever epidemics interred there. The city also depended on slavery, with all the oppression that this entailed. In 1741, a series of arsons over several weeks resulted in the arrest and execution of thirty slaves, with the trial and conviction of another seventy. The African burial ground in today's financial district is a reminder of the extensive presence of slaves in the area.[7]

Elsewhere developments in the city also concealed a veritable palimpsest of different ethnic and cultural groups. When Frederick Law Olmsted and Calvert Vaux won the commission to design Central Park in 1857, residents of this 843-acre expanse of natural habitat had to be evicted, including the free Black residents of Seneca Village, who planted crops and cultivated pigs in the area. Immigration from the American South, China, and different parts of Europe throughout the nineteenth century would also completely change New York's demographic and social character, so that by 1890 William Dean Howells could observe in *A Hazard of New Fortunes*:

> The small eyes, the high cheeks, the broad noses, the puff lips, the bare, cue-filleted skulls, of Russians, Poles, Czechs, Chinese; the furtive glitter of Italians; the blonde dullness of Germans; the cold quiet of Scandinavians—fire under ice—were aspects that he identified, and that gave him abundant suggestion for the personal histories he constructed, and for the more public-spirited reveries in which he dealt with the future economy of our heterogeneous commonwealth [....] There were certain signs, certain facades, certain audacities of the prevailing hideousness that always amused him in that uproar to the eye which the strident forms and colors made.[8]

While the physiognomy and social typology of ethnic types Howells lays out here are objectionable and to be seriously contested, "the uproar to the eyes" and the "strident forms and colors" of New York are without a doubt a central part of how writers, denizens, and visitors to the city have come to understand it, for better or for worse.

On returning home from serving in the First World War in 1918, e. e. cummings writes about New York, invoking it as America's Celestial City:

> The tall, impossibly tall, city shouldering upward into hard sunlight leaned a little through the octaves of its parallel edges, leaningly strode upward into firm hard snowy sunlight; the noises of America nearingly throbbed with smokes and hurrying dots which are men and which are women and which are things new and curious and hard and strange and vibrant and immense, lifting with a great undulous stride firmly into immortal sunlight.[9]

The repeated phrasal structures ("tall, impossibly tall"), evocative neologisms ("leaningly," "nearingly"), and conjunctives ("and") in the passage register a sense of gushing admiration but also capture something of the multifarious effervescence of the city, something already noted in Howell's *A Hazard of New Fortunes*. As we shall see presently, the impression created by New York's tall buildings becomes a trope that defines the sensual impact its skyline has on various other people that encounter it.

A sudden self-consciousness about New York's uniqueness erupts from the middle of the nineteenth century, and is expressed in starkly bold terms. As E. Porter Belden put it in 1849, "North American barbarism was to give place to European refinement."[10] The idea that New York was enlivened by European influence was later driven by merchant industrialists such as the Vanderbilts, the Astors, and the Belmonts, who spent extraordinary amounts of money to build their mansions on Fifth Avenue and sought to establish their reputation as connoisseurs of the beaux arts. However, European influences on the city predated the industrialists' efforts by several decades through the large working-class immigrations from the continent that also took place. New York's population expanded from 123,706 in 1820 to 813,669 in 1860, roughly a quarter of whom were Irish-born. And by 1910, 40 percent of the population was foreign-born. The Irish, along with the large incoming population of Eastern European Jews fleeing Europe in the late nineteenth and early twentieth centuries, had to make do with highly straitened living conditions in the tenements of the notorious Five Points, the Bowery, and the area around what is today's Chinatown. Poverty and gang violence in the period were rife; some of it is captured in Herbert Ashbury's *Gangs of New York* (1927), which was later turned into an Oscar-winning film directed by Martin Scorsese in 2002. The contrasting facets of New York were in turns celebrated and critiqued by Edith Wharton, Henry James, Truman Capote, Michael Cahan, and the photographer Jacob Riis, among many others. Mark Twain's sly reference to the period as the "gilded age" in 1873 was designed to make the point that the city's splendid surface served to mask an underlying core of disturbing sociopolitical realities.[11] Whatever was European about New York was progressively translated into a hybrid American medium throughout the nineteenth century, so that the skyscraper and building booms at century's end were the products of local visions as much as of European styles and inspiration, and of foreign working-class labor. As Harlem was formally annexed by New York in 1873 and was increasingly settled by African American migrants from the South, and the modern-day five boroughs of New York were created with the consolidation of Brooklyn, Queens, Staten Island, the Bronx, and Manhattan in 1898, the range of opportunities for imagining the almost limitless possibilities for self-fashioning across the city's changing social landscape increased accordingly. The Rockefeller family's donation of $8,500,000 to purchase land along the East River for the United Nations headquarters in 1946 further sealed New York's reputation as a superlative world city of trade, tourism, and diplomacy, with culture and entertainment leavening the mix through the city's 144 museums, its array of Broadway theater offerings, film festivals, and wide diversity of culinary pleasures.

The metropolis also sometimes eludes the reach of realist representation, often stimulating formal and linguistic innovations that their authors hope might render literature adequate to the city's own restless capacity for reinvention. Isaac Asimov's *Robot* novels (1940–95) chronicle the surprising partnership between a New York city detective and a humanoid robot to solve a series of problems pitting Spacers and Earthmen, a thinly veiled reference to the hierarchical elite and ethnic forms of life that have always constituted the city's social fabric. Or Thomas M. Disch's *334* (1972), a candidly dystopian look at everyday life in New York in 2025. When Disch's novel was first published, its future-time projection must have appeared extremely distant. But by 2021, and the way in which the COVID-19 pandemic ravaged New York, it might be time to take another look at these dystopian visions. These science fiction novels, as well as literary works that specifically take New York's underground transport system for inspiration such as Colin McCann's *This Side of Brightness* (1998) and Felice Holman's *Slake's Limbo* (1974), also help to expand our sense of New York beyond the areas that are normally referred to in general literary representations of the city.

The Neighborhood: Harlem in Toni Morrison's *Jazz*

A neighborhood may be defined as a demarcated set of both residential and commercial buildings, with specific morphological features that anchor it, such as a corner grocery store, a butcher's shop, a park, a library, and perhaps a school as well as specific features of public transport. The range of architectural built-up features and the geographical size of a neighborhood are not as important as the fact that all its features come together to create a special sense of the neighborhood that may be distinctive from the sense generated by a different neighborhood, or indeed by the city in general. Essentially, the neighborhood is a chronotope. The term chronotope combines two words in Greek and simply means "space-time," and was adopted by Mikhail Bakhtin to explain the ways in which spatial and temporal indices came together in an expressive unity as a key aspect of the European novel.[12] And yet the ways in which spatial and temporal indices are configured also means that different chronotopes divulge different social relations. Fundamentally, a chronotope is primarily a means for displaying different kinds of human interaction and also the interaction of humans with their environment so that the chronotope's spatial and temporal indices also help to frame and indeed inflect the ways in which the interactions are to be perceived within literary or other artistic representation.

Typically, a change in geographical or spatial location in literature is not void of ethical significance. When there is a change in geographical locations, it is often to demarcate a shift in the ethical character of the different locations. This shift in ethical character of different spatial locations is most evident in works where there is also an implication of stark racial or class differences, or, indeed, of distinct spatial correlatives, as in the observation of the differences between rural settings and urban ones. Not unusually, the sharp change in settings also impose a challenge to the character's ethical sensibility and what choices they are able to make. Almost every New York literary text we can think of can be used to illustrate these chronotopes and the sense of altered responses to space. However, I am going to focus here mainly on Toni Morrison's *Jazz*, where the steep layers of nostalgia and disavowal for the characters that have migrated from the American South is combined with the sense of awe and dazzlement on the encounter with their neighborhood in Harlem, where the city becomes the site of both self-anchoring and alienation for the Black characters.

Originally a Dutch village named Haarlem in 1658, Harlem's history has been defined by a series of economic highs and troughs, with significant population changes accompanying each cycle. Predominantly settled by Italians and Jews throughout the nineteenth century, the area became the preferred location for the Great Migration from the American South in end of nineteenth and early decades of the twentieth century. A flowering of Black culture involving music, literature, and the arts took root in the 1920s and 1930s to give a new dimension to Harlem life. The Harlem Renaissance set out the terms of a new literary flowering in the context of the new socio-cultural forms that the Great Migration produced. And yet writers of the Harlem Renaissance such as Countee Cullen, Langston Hughes, Claude McKay, Carl Van Vechten, Jean Toomer, and others were not the only Black writers to take Harlem as an inspiration for their work. Ralph Ellison's *Invisible Man* (1952) and the several novels and short stories of James Baldwin have also creatively detailed the nature of Black life in Harlem. Also important have been the writings of Hispanic Americans that settled in East Harlem, also known as Spanish Harlem – a community made up of Puerto Rican, Dominican, Mexican, and Cuban immigrants that came to settle steadily from the 1940s onward. Piri Thomas's *Down These Mean Streets* (1967), part of the Nuyorican collective, provides a detailed street view of Spanish Harlem during the author's childhood and adolescence.

Toni Morrison's *Jazz* is an intricate story set in Harlem of the deteriorating relationship between Violet and her husband Joe, both immigrants from the American South escaping violence and the lack of opportunities in the postbellum period. There are many descriptions in the novel of the physical aspects of Harlem and the city, the houses where people live, and the relationships of gossip and small talk that they exchange with one another. The characters' foibles and peculiarities are set against the material aspects of the city, and we discover that their lives are a mixture of nostalgia and projections onto the cityscape. *Jazz* is also a historical novel, and provides sensual and psychological specificity to the lives of the many Black folk that migrated to Harlem and New York in their struggles to reinvent themselves:

> The wave of black people running away from want and violence crested in the 1870s; the '80s; the '90s but was a steady stream in 1906 when Joe and Violet joined it. Like the others, they were country people, but how soon country people forget. When they fall in love with a city, it is for forever, and it is like forever. As though there never was a time when they didn't love it. The minute they arrive at the train station or get off the ferry and glimpse the wide streets and the wasteful lamps lighting them, they know they were born for it. There, in a city, they are not so much new as themselves: their stronger, riskier selves. And in the beginning when they first arrive, and twenty years later when they and the City have grown up, they love that part of themselves so much they forget what loving other people was like – if they ever knew, that is.[13]
>
> [...]
>
> But I have seen the City do an unbelievable sky. Redcaps and dining-car attendants who wouldn't think of moving out of the City sometimes go on at great length about country skies they have seen from the windows of trains. But there is nothing to beat what the City can make of a night-sky. It can empty itself of surface, and more like the ocean than the ocean itself, of deep, starless. Close up on the top of buildings, near, nearer than the cap you are wearing, such a citysky presses and retreats, presses and retreats, making me think of the free but illegal love of sweethearts before it is discovered.[14]

In each instance the Black arrivants from the South find something of themselves already reflected in the city. The allure of their "stronger, riskier selves" is however so strong that it hampers their capacity to love others. This idea of the love of an incipient self that inextricably ties self-invention to solitude and loneliness defines Joe and Violet's responses to the city. And as we see in the second passage, both cityscape and skyscape interfuse with characters' thoughts and reflections of present and past. And so, we find ourselves asking: Does the city sky encapsulate a residue of the changeable skies of their Southern childhood or is it distinctly different from any other sky? The fact that the question cannot be answered with certainty suggests that in *Jazz* the Black characters' perceptions of New York are always tinged with some form of nostalgia.

Morrison's depiction of the effect of the skyline on the newly arrived Black characters in Harlem recalls Nick Carraway's viewpoint as he and Gatsby drive toward New York across the Queensboro Bridge in *The Great Gatsby*:

> Over the great bridge, with the sunlight through the girders making a constant flicker upon the moving cars, with the city rising up across the river in white heaps and sugar lumps all built with a wish out of non-olfactory money. The city seen from Queensboro Bridge is always the city seen for the first time, in its first wild promise of all the mystery and beauty in the world.[15]

Like *Jazz, The Great Gatsby* is set in the early twentieth century. Despite the differences in subject matter, one thing the two novels share in common is the effect that elevated structures such as skyscrapers and bridges have on the consciousness of the characters: in each instance the city's skyline generates the sense of an absolute and heady firstness of experience (even if it is not the first time), that is filled with the promise of mystery, beauty, and self-discovery. The effect of New York's architectural elevation is to force the eyes to be raised toward the sky, and by that form of proprioception, to conceptually reach beyond the boundary of the mundane toward something more sublime that ramifies both without and within the self. This is a distinctive part of the urban imaginary of New York. As Edward Soja defines it, the urban imaginary is "the mental or cognitive mapping of urban reality and the interpretative grids through which we think about, experience, evaluate, and decide to act in the places, spaces, and communities in which we live."[16] We might recall e. e. cummings's reference to New York as a Celestial City, noted earlier.

Violet has a miscarriage, and once it is confirmed that she can no longer have children she surrenders herself to issuing non-sequiturs and begins to talk exclusively to the parrots she has assembled in her hallway for companionship. But the non-sequiturs also have an objective correlative in the specific physicality of the urban landscape itself. For example, the sidewalk provides her with an opportunity to enter another reality:

> I call them cracks because that is what they were. Not openings or breaks, but dark fissures in the globe of light of the day. She wakes up in the morning and sees with perfect clarity a string of small, well-lit scenes. In each one something specific is being done: food things, work things; customers and acquaintances are encountered, places entered. But she does not see herself doing these things.
>
> She sees them being done. The globe of light holds and bathes each scene, and it can be assumed that at the curve where the light stops is a

> solid foundation. In truth, there is no foundation at all, but alleyways, crevices one steps across all the time. But the globe of light is imperfect too. Closely examined it shows seams, ill-glued cracks and weak spaces beyond which is anything. Anything at all. Sometimes when Violet isn't paying attention she stumbles onto these cracks, like the time when, instead of putting her left heel forward, she stepped back and folded her legs in order to sit in the street.[17]

It is perhaps salutary to note that the repetition of the word "globe" immediately imports echoes of Shakespearean drama and thus encourages the interpretation of Violet's condition by way of dramaturgical inflections. This is further emphasized in the fact she herself adopts a position of spectatorship regarding the scenes of everyday life that unfold before her. In the dramaturgical scenes laid out before her, hers is not the agency of a dramatic actor within the unfolding scenes of everyday life, but that of a spectator, almost distantiated and god-like. Crucially, also, the globe is both a globe and a dome of light, the two being interfused in the image of cracks emerging in the globe. And these cracks and crevices are the openings into another world, one that requires her total vigilance to prevent her from slipping into them. Sometimes she is not quite successful at keeping from slipping. The cracks and crevices are the interstitial spaces within which her actions are interpreted as completely normal by her (to sit down without preamble or ceremony in the middle of the street and take a rest because she suddenly feels tired; another time she actually lies right down in the middle of the street) and by the rest of the world as simply weird. In other words what we have, hinted at in the references to the cracks and crevices, is a series of perspectival modulations between the perceived physical and phenomenal world and that of another, yet inchoate and unclaimed one in her eyes. And it is the material form of the city itself, or in this case of Harlem, that frames these perspectival modulations for Violet and in turn, for the reader. The chronotopes of neighborhood and streetscape then enact a means by which nostalgia, self-invention, and utopia are merged in a deeply personal mode of crisis that cannot be fully resolved. This modality of loneliness that also reflects a sense of the cityscape is not exclusive to Violet alone, but also defines the relationships that other characters in the novel such as Joe, Dorcas, and Alice Manfred also have to the city.

What might be described as the encounter with the urban sublime as it is depicted in *Jazz* can be seen as a repeated theme in world literature, from Clarice Lispector to Dionne Brand, and Virginia Woolf and Italo Calvino to Naguib Mahfouz, among many others. The point of it is to grasp its evocation of wonder that is equally mixed with self-making and self-unraveling, especially as the self is shown as not being able to completely surrender emotional attachment to its past.

La Factoría in Melissa Rivero's *The Affairs of the Falcóns*

While Toni Morrison's *Jazz* gives us complex and evocative sensibilities of the Black folk that have migrated to New York from America's South, there is an entire literature of migration that speaks of poverty, extremely straitened material conditions, and also of the constant sense of not being able to fit in. Fear of the latter is often a factor of language, for it takes a long time for first-generation immigrants from someplace else to be able to fully assimilate to the speech forms of New York as place of sojourn. This theme is as evident in Henry Roth's *Call it Sleep* (1934) and Michael Gold's *Jews without Money* (1930) as it is in Kiran Desai's *The Inheritance of Loss* (2006) and Imbolo Mbue's *Behold the Dreamers* (2016). Published in 2019, Melissa Rivero's *The Affairs of the Falcóns* is one of a long line of novels that touches on these themes. The novel turns on the story of Ana Lucia Cardenas Rios and her relentless pursuit of the elusive American Dream. She has moved as an undocumented immigrant with her husband Lucho Falcón and their two children from Peru to live in Brooklyn, and works in a garment sweatshop.[18] The city itself is dissolved into a series of economic exigencies: working extra time at la factoría, the garment sweatshop; saving to move from the apartment they reluctantly share with a benefactor into a bigger place yet also frequently having to borrow from Mama, a loan shark in another part of Brooklyn to make ends meet; navigating the humiliation of having to sleep with Don Beto, Mama's creepy husband when she cannot get money from the loan shark herself; and worrying incessantly about whether she has been made pregnant by Don Beto. The novel shuttles between the space of their cramped shared home and that of la factoría, in each of which the bulk of the social interactions take place. Unlike what we saw in *Jazz*, in *The Affairs of the Falcóns* New York fades into the peripheral background, and it is rare that Ana has the luxury to dwell on any specific features of the city except functional ones such as public transport in her many spatial traversals to and from home and work, the home of the loan shark, and other places that she goes to out of necessity. For her there is none of the architectural sublime that we saw in the characters' encounter with the city in Morrison's novel. And yet, at the same time, Rivero's novel is redolent with thoughts of Peru. But whereas for Lucho, America is a land of complete humiliation and loss of masculinity, making him always eager to return to the land of his birth, to Ana Peru is the land of menace and danger and America the place of elusive promise.

Furthermore, even though both Ana and Lucho come from Peru, the fact of their different skin pigmentations (he is criollo and she is Black) means that they have different prospects in their country and that despite being undocumented migrants, the cosmopolitanism of New York holds more promise for her than for him:

> The promise of a better future, one she'd heard about in the classroom as a child, cut its way into the country. It was a future that was only possible with the blanching of brightly colored clothes, the fading of patterns that had been worn for centuries; in the undoing of braids and the disappearance of tongues for a single, dominant one. That was Peru's way forward. Lucho was criollo, already a harbinger of that future, with his light skin, his gray slacks, and that side part. He was already obsessed with the purity and preservation of the Spanish language. Why else would he spend hours reading the Spanish-language newspapers in New York, searching for, as he put it, the butchering of the mother tongue? That and his last name, so clearly not born of the land, could get him a job with relative ease, and therefore, he could debate the fairness of his compensation, the meddling of outsiders, and what could be done to preserve the house his father bought.
>
> She could not debate such things. In Lima, she was plainly a woman, dark-skinned at that, from some mountainous province, only a couple of decades left before she'd be considered too old to hire.[19]

Here we see how the braiding of gender and colorism leads to a definitive hierarchy in Peruvian society that renders Ana permanently inferior and Lucho unquestionably superior. New York and America free her from all that.

And yet being an undocumented alien institutes another kind of dread, namely, that absolute terror of being discovered and sent back home by immigration authorities. And it is precisely la factoría that functions as the focal point for this dread. Ana is obviously not the only one to be worried; everyone, including the supervisors, is mindful of the negative effects that an unannounced raid might have on the factory:

> George [the supervisor] was already on the fourth floor when they arrived. He held a rolled-up sheet of paper in one hand, which he used to shepherd the women inside. "Vamos, muchachas, adentro," he said. Minutes later, Olga [the supervisor's translator] took her place beside him like a sentinel. The bell rang, and the two began to make their way through the room. He tapped the paper into the palm of his hand as he stopped by each island. Olga translated. Since she'd been at la factoría, Ana had only seen this

> scenario play out three times: once, when George let go of some workers, then again when the boss was coming for a visit. The last time was after the raids in June, when immigration rushed into a nearby meat-packing plant, stuffed men into vans, and made them disappear. It was the same raid that had spooked Lucho's boss and prompted him to let him go.
>
> [....]
>
> Then they reached Ana's station, it was Olga who spoke. "Something happened with one of the girls," she said. Ana glanced at the other women, but their eyes were glued to the floor.[20]

Nilda, one of the younger and sassier workers among them, had the police called on her and her husband by a neighbor one night, when they were having a loud fight on account of an affair that Nilda was having. Matters quickly deteriorated from there, and Nilda was arrested and deported without her two young children. Her husband had papers, but she never got them. Ana's desire to make it in New York is balanced with the anxiety of one day being deported and separated from her own children, something that looms threateningly at the very end of the novel when another raid descends on the factory and all the women have to make a desperate run for it. Ana thinks of Nilda as she scrambles down the various flights of stairs through other jammed bodies heading outside to freedom. It is unclear at the very end whether she manages to indeed escape or is caught by the ICE officers, but her last thought is that whatever it takes, she will fly back to her children like Nilda did a few weeks earlier:

> Wherever they took her, wherever she might end up, she'd find her way back. Back to Victoria and Pedro. Back to Lucho. She'd run across the dirt, swim against the river if she needed to. Fly above whatever she couldn't force her way through. There was her mother's voice. "You'll have to do things for love," she said, all those years ago. It was the only way she'd learn to fly. No matter where they were or where she was, she'd make it back to them. She had to trust, finally. Trust that she could make it back to her flock. Back to los Falcon.[21]

The novel ends on this enigmatic note.

Apart from the fact that for the immigrant or diasporic, *this* place is always in some form of dialectical relation to *that place* and to an *elsewhere*, the dialectical relation may in certain instances produce breaches in the commonplace, an *unheimlich* of place, as it were. The *unheimlich* or unhomeliness of place is undergirded by the fraught dynamic of the links between ideas of the place of departure and that of arrival or sojourn that take as their theater the *mind of the beholder* (i.e., the immigrant or diasporic individual or community) in negotiating the present. It is evident that to Ana, the *unheimlich* of place is deeply entangled not just with a specific sense of physical location, but with the palpable danger of being separated from her children. And thus, the constant dread of the undocumented alien is for her coupled to her role as mother. While her assertion that she will go through any impediment and indeed fly like a bird if necessary to return to her children is clearly a strong assertion of her determination, it is also clear that for her the land of sojourn (i.e., New York) is the space where motherhood helps her enact a form of anchoring in place. And because she cannot see any fruition back in Peru, New York then becomes the only guarantee of wholeness, even under the infernal conditions of undocumented migration.

New York and World Literature

New York's Midtown is an area of the city that provides us with the literary city's monumental form, from the Candler Building in Times Square, which was built by Coca-Cola owner Asa Griggs Candler in 1914 and where Alfred A. Knopf had their first office, to the Scribner's Building on Fifth Avenue, the McGraw-Hill Building on West 42nd Street (birthplace of Marvel Comics in 1939), along with the New York Public Library on 5th Avenue and 42nd Street, and the iconic Empire State Building. Macmillan, Hachette, and Penguin Random House (where Toni Morrison worked as an editor from 1967 to 1983) all have their offices in Midtown.[22] And because this area has been at the epicenter of the American publishing world since the late nineteenth century, the hotels and hotel bars around the area are also rich with literary associations. Tennessee Williams lived and died in the Elysée on 54th Street, the bar of the St. Regis was a meeting place for many authors and publishers, and what was probably the best-known American literary salon of any period was the Alongquin Round Table, presided over by Dorothy Parker in the Oak Room of the Algonquin Hotel on 59th Street. The Oak Room was also a favored hangout of many journalists and theater reviewers, who relayed its witticisms to a wider public and thus helped to consolidate the image of New York as a city of writers. And throughout the 2000s the staff of the *New York Times Book Review* gathered regularly at Jimmy's Corner, "a scruffy, boxing-themed joint tucked into a wrinkle in Times Square's space-time continuum," according to Dwight Garner, editor of the *New York Times Book Review* at the time.[23] The literary monumentalism of Midtown Manhattan is also a mark of its cosmopolitan connection to world literature, given how many famous writers have been brought out by the main publishing houses to be found there. And yet, as we have noted, the city's vaunted cosmopolitanism is also the direct product of the eddies and flows of immigrants and diasporics from both within the United States and elsewhere. If New York is a city of literary monumentalism and of temporal becoming where people continually redefine themselves, it is so because no past is ever lost that is not also recreated in the consciousness of those that come to the city. It is their stories that illuminate the social infrastructure linking people to place, and from which we can derive the analogues for the entangled networks that are at the core of world literature.

Notes

1 This last point is central to contemporary spatial theory and has been prominently asserted by thinkers as diverse as Henri Lefebvre, David Harvey, Edward Soja, and Doreen Massey, among various others.

2 On this question, see especially Pheng Cheah's *What is World Literature?: On Postcolonial Literature as World Literature* (Durham, NC: Duke University Press, 2016); Eric Hayot, *On Literary Worlds* (Oxford: Oxford University Press, 2012); Joe Cleary, *Modernism, Empire, World Literature* (Cambridge: Cambridge University Press, 2022); and Franco Moretti, "Conjectures on World Literature," *New Left Review* 1 (2000): 54–68 and "More Conjectures," *New Left Review* 20 (2003): 73–81.

3 Toni Morrison, *Jazz* (London: Picador, 1992); and Melissa Rivero, *The Affairs of the Falcóns* (New York: Ecco, 2019).

4 Brian Silverman, *Frommer's New York City from $90 a Day* (Hoboken, NJ: John Wiley & Sons, 2005). The Frommer's Guide Books were started by the travel writer Arthur Frommer, then a resident of Brooklyn, in 1957, and have run to several editions.

5 Thomas Bender, "New York as a Center of Difference," in Bender, *The Unfinished City: New York and the Metropolitan Idea* (New York: New Press, 2002), 185–198.

6 Eric Homberger, "Immigrants, Politics, and the Popular Cultures of Tolerance," in Cyrus R.K. Patell and Bryan Waterman, *The Cambridge Companion to the Literature of New York* (New York: Cambridge University Press, 2010), 134.

7 See Peter Charles Hoffer, *The Great New York Conspiracy of 1741: Slavery, Crime, and Colonial Law* (Lawrence, KS: University of Kansas Press, 2003); and Jill Lepore, *New York Burning: Liberty, Slavery, and Conspiracy in Eighteenth-Century Manhattan* (New York: Knopf Doubleday, 2007).

8 William Dean Howells, *A Hazard of New Fortunes* ([1890]; New York: Penguin 2001), 163.

9 e.e. cummings, *The Enormous Room*, George J. Firmage, ed. (New York: Liverlight, 1978), 242.

10 E. Porter Belden, *New York: Past, Present, and Future* (New York: Putnam, 1849), 1.
11 Mark Twain and Charles Dudley Warner, *The Gilded Age: A Tale of Today*, 2nd ed. (New York: Penguin Classics, 2001).
12 Mikhail Bakhtin, "Forms of Time and of the Chronotope in the Novel," in Michael Holquist, ed., *The Dialogic Imagination: Four Essays* (Austin, TX: University of Texas Press, 1982), 84–258.
13 Morrison, *Jazz*, 33.
14 Ibid., 35.
15 F. Scott Fitzgerald, *The Great Gatsby* (Peterborough, ON: Broadview, 2007), 97.
16 Edward W. Soja, *Postmetropolis: Critical Studies of Cities and Regions* (Oxford: Blackwell, 2000), 324.
17 Morrison, *Jazz*, 23.
18 The Triangle Shirtwaist Factory fire is the most famous garment factory disaster in New York's history and it furnishes a whole series of insights about the place of indigent migrant labor, their terrible and exploitative working conditions, and the after-effects of the fire that killed 123 women and girls and 23 men. In many ways, all New York novels that have the sweatshop as part of their setting automatically invoke the Shirtwaist Factory. For historical accounts, see Leon Stein, *The Triangle Fire*, 2nd ed. (Boston, MA: Bedford/St. Martins, 2016) and Richard A. Greenwald, *The Triangle Fire: Protocols of Peace and Industrial Democracy in Progressive Era New York* (Philadelphia, PA: Temple University Press, 2005).
19 Rivero, *Falcóns*, 111–112.
20 Ibid., 132.
21 Ibid., 273.
22 Random House was originally founded in 1927 but was merged with Penguin in 2013 when Bertelsmann and Pearson amalgamated their respective trade publishing companies.
23 Dwight Garner, "A Critic's Tour of Literary Manhattan," *The New York Times* (December 14, 2012), www.nytimes.com/2012/12/16/travel/a-critics-tour-of-literary-manhattan.html.

CHAPTER 6

"The Whole World in Little"

London as the Capital of World Literature

Rashmi Varma

Although historically the world's literary capitals have not necessarily been the most dominant in the political and economic spheres, London stands out as an exception to that formulation within world literary studies.[1] For an extended period in the twentieth century, it was the world's most powerful city in terms of imperial and capital dominance, the center of world literary production, and an arbiter of literary value in the global Anglosphere. As it was for English writers a center through which Englishness was mediated as a cultural dominant as opposed to Welshness, Irishness, or Scottishness, so it was for writers from the empire's peripheries in the Caribbean, Africa, Southeast Asia, and South Asia, for whom London was the threshold where the peripheral and the dominant literatures of the world converged, albeit in unequal formations. To understand this phenomenon, Franco Moretti's theorization of world literature as "simultaneously one, and unequal," with "a core, and a periphery (and a semiperiphery) that are bound together in a relationship of growing inequality," provides an important entry into reading London as the capital of world literature.[2]

However, the fact that modernist English literature in the early twentieth century, which coincided with London's rising preeminence as an imperial city, was being challenged and transformed at its edges and margins by writers from the colonies meant that its position as a literary capital was less settled than usually assumed. Raymond Williams had pointed to the importance of "seeing the imperial and capitalist metropolis as a specific historical form" that "involves looking, from time to time, from outside the metropolis: from the deprived hinterlands, where different forces are moving, and from the poor world which has always been peripheral to the metropolitan systems."[3] Extending Williams's line of argument, Fredric Jameson has argued that colonialism entailed the relocation "elsewhere" of a key structural segment of the economic system.[4] This relocation, he argues, had distinct "representational effects" such that only a "fresh and unprecedented aesthetic response" comprised of "formal, structural and linguistic invention" could bring to light "the structural connections between [...] daily life in the metropolis and the absent space of the colony."[5] Jameson's foregrounding of the colonial world system comprising a center from where the periphery and its subjects are invisible but indispensable to the maintenance of power allows us to read London as a spatiotemporal disjuncture within world literature. Other readings of "postcolonial London" have likewise represented the city's imperial history as always complex and conflicted when pitted against the "totalizing and abstract concept of the 'colonial centre'."[6] In other words, the centrality of London in the world literary space of the twentieth century was relative, simultaneously reinforced and undermined by what it marginalized and excluded.

This chapter explores how the shifts in London's representational history are mapped and imagined in world literature, and how world literature is imagined in London. The chapter focalizes this discussion through two linked tropes – the city's "exhibitionary complex" and its "circulatory network." Tony Bennett's concept of the "exhibitionary complex," comprised of the "permanent display of power" as in the iconic British Museum as well as in the city's shopping arcades that are "places of pilgrimage to the fetish Commodity," defines it as a disciplinary nexus that deploys new technologies of vision to establish a "specular dominance over a totality" that in our context we could grasp as the world system in terms defined by Moretti.[7]

The exhibitionary complex was inextricably linked to the circulating network in the city: the spaces of the exhibitionary complex that lay claim to totality were also the spaces where the circulatory flows of people, commodities, and ideas collided, converged, and abstracted for display; the circulatory network consists of walking and transportation routes, particularly elements of it that go underground and connect the disparate and unequal parts of the city both horizontally and vertically. So when we read for the ways in which writers have mapped the city fictively through its circulatory network, we can read for the ways in which these networks reveal a dialectic of the seen and the unseen within London's exhibitionary complex.

Here the chapter seeks to extend Michel de Certeau's theorization of "walking in the city" as a potentially subversive everyday practice that allows those who live "down below" to resist the panoptic gaze of power above. It does so by focusing in particular on the modern systems of transportation that were revolutionizing both individual and collective experience of the city.[8] Thus although the London Underground that was inaugurated in 1863 played a crucial role in lending unity to the city's disparate parts, it also functioned, as Omaar Hena puts it, as an "unconscious strata of Englishness."[9]

Joining the invisible to the visible and the peripheral to the central, the circulatory network, this chapter suggests, embodies a spatialized dialectic that constitutes the literary geography of London as a world city.

"The Whole Empire in Little"

In the Prologue to Andrea Levy's novel *Small Island* (2004), the young Queenie, daughter of a provincial English butcher, recalls going to the British Empire Exhibition of 1924–25 held in Wembley Park, London:

> The year we went to the Empire Exhibition, the Great War was not long over but nearly forgotten. Even Father agreed that the Empire Exhibition sounded like it was worth a look. The King had described it as "the whole Empire in little". Mother thought that meant it was a miniature, like a toy railway or model village. Until someone told her that they'd seen the real lifesize Stephenson's Rocket on display. "It must be as big as the whole world," I said, which made everybody laugh.[10]

Queenie's memory of visiting the Exhibition prompts the question of whether imperial London contained the world in miniature or whether the city itself was a miniature version of the world. The Exhibition, set across many acres of land, contained pavilions representing the colonies under British dominion. It also provided the spectacle of "natives" of colonized lands in artificially created habitats of imported tropical trees and Oriental shrines that attempted to simulate actual worlds at the periphery of empire. It thus offered up the world and its things – commodities, artifacts, monuments, landscapes, and ways of life – as a spectacle for the enjoyment of the British public at home who could traverse the world virtually without physically leaving London.

But there was another writer whose representation of the Wembley Exhibition had presciently imagined the destruction of empire. Virginia Woolf in her essay "Thunder at Wembley" (1924) sounded a deeply critical and dissatisfied note about the Exhibition, unimpressed by the falsity and brittleness of the spectacle of imperial grandeur. Even so, the essay takes an unexpected turn when her wry observations are interrupted by a series of fevered premonitions in which:

> Dust swirls down the avenues, hisses and hurries like erected cobras round the corners. Pagodas are dissolving in dust. Ferro-concrete is fallible. Colonies are perishing and dispersing in a spray of inconceivable beauty and terror which some malignant power illuminates. Ash and violet are the colours of its decay. From every quarter human beings come flying [...] The Empire is perishing; the bands are playing; the Exhibition is in ruins.[11]

Woolf's essay opens up cracks in the wondrous displays of the Exhibition that sought to catalogue and condense the glories of empire. As Christina Britzolakis pointedly suggests, "the representational dilemma of imperial culture pointed out by Jameson – the structural dependency of the metropolitan centre on a colonial periphery [...] found a solution, of a kind, in the world's fairs" held in world capitals such as London.[12] The Exhibition embodied a time-space compression integral to the workings of colonial capitalism such that everyday life in the colonies represented through staged rituals of timeless tableau-like village scenes is intercepted by the hourly tolling of the Big Ben that reminded visitors of the temporal discipline required to participate in empire's spatialized spectacle. Further exacerbating the time-space compression, the Exhibition consisted of replicas of ancient monuments and dioramas that froze traditions in time placed next to objects of modern technology, producing the combined and uneven effects that configured and shaped London as a world city.[13]

Beyond the tenuously but carefully curated space of the Exhibition, however, the centers of ceremony and power were constantly under threat by, to use Ann McClintock's evocative phrase, "the impossible edges of modernity" that were the slums, the ghettos, and the brothels of the city.[14] Descriptions of the London poor in the East End borrowed key notions of social difference from the repertoire of colonial discourse such that, as Ian Baucom writes, the London poor came to function as "local allegories of the empire's distant 'savages'".[15] From parliamentary reports to urban censuses, colonial discourse drew an analogy between the savages on the edges and frontiers of the British Empire with those within it.[16] In this, "darkest" East End was pitted against the "blaze of light" that was the imperial capital.[17] So in an important sense, the empire's "impossible edges" were already "here" in London, even when its subjects were not citizens, yet.

If the Empire Exhibition displayed a phantasmagoria of commodities for the visual and material consumption of imperial citizens, Jean Rhys, the white Creole writer from Dominica who arrived in London in 1907 at the age of seventeen, presents the gendered body itself as the object of colonialist and capitalist exhibition and accumulation. Her novel *Voyage in the Dark* (1934) narrates the discrepant realities of London as an imperial city in which she intertwines the commoditized body of the novel's Creole working-class protagonist Anna Morgan, taking in the display of shops to fantasize about improving her prospects with affluent men, with a longer history of "exhibitions" that made a spectacle of black women such as Sara Baartman, the so-called "Hottentot Venus," in London and Paris in the nineteenth century. The exhibition of Baartman who had been transported from southern Africa had provoked both an abjection of the black female body as irreducibly other in its sexual pathology and rendered it as the site of racialized fantasies.

In Rhys's novel *Good Morning, Midnight* (1939), the protagonist Sasha Jensen has a nightmare in which she finds herself in a London Underground station that is festooned with placards bearing the sign of a finger pointing to the words "This Way to the Exhibition," their very multiplicity contributing to a sense of dizzying disorientation. Sasha finds herself frantically looking for the exit out of the station:

> There are passages to the right and passages to the left, but no exit sign. Everywhere the fingers point and the placards read: This Way to the Exhibition. I touch the shoulder of the man walking in front of me. I say: "I want the way out". But he points to the placards and his hand is made of steel [....] The steel finger points along a long stone passage. This Way – This Way – This Way to the Exhibition.[18]

Good Morning, Midnight is set around the 1937 International Exposition of Art and Technology in Modern Life in Paris that took place under the shadow of rising fascism and the impending doom of another world war. But this hallucinatory sequence in the London Underground conjoins the two exhibitions of London and Paris. The Exhibition consumes the entire space of her experience of the city, "making the time-space of the Exhibition seem total and inescapable."[19]

"Neither Forward Nor Backward"

If Rhys's modernist fictions registered a peripheral modernity that upturned the center, the Trinidadian writer Sam Selvon's novel *Lonely Londoners* (1956) stands at the helm of a new turn within London's world literary scape in which other Caribbean writers such as George Lamming and V.S. Naipaul would also set anchor. Discovering a community of fellow writers from the Caribbean, Selvon referred to London as "literary headquarters" where his writing life found a shape and a purpose.[20] Rendered in a vernacularized Creole English, the novel reprises the sense of alienation that the immigrant from the colony experiences in London. But the novel's use of social realism to depict the jagged and still thwarted possibilities of citizenship and belonging opened up by postwar postcolonial migration lends a unique insight into metropolitan space. The 1948 British Nationality Act had granted citizenship rights and the right to abode to all subjects of the British Empire. The Act in many ways was a response to the postwar labor shortages that were hampering the rebuilding of the British economy. But as the novel's characters take up rooms in dilapidated housing, flock to Employment Exchange offices, hustle to pay rent and buy decent clothes, and go "liming" in Hyde Park, they forge a floating community in a city that grows hostile to their presence. The popular media represented immigrants as flooding London's streets, and racial disturbances in the city became increasingly common occurrences, culminating in the 1958 Notting Hill riots sparked by a series of violent racial assaults. The Immigration Act of 1962 finally reversed the openness of the 1948 legislation.

But if the Underground is the site of a paranoid urbanism in Rhys's fiction, the circulatory network functions as a crucial map for Selvon's fictionalized London. *Lonely Londoners* opens with a scene set at the iconic Waterloo station that evokes T.S. Eliot's poetic rendering of London as "the unreal city" in *The Wasteland*. It is here focalized through the perspective of a working-class black immigrant:

> One grim winter evening, when it had a kind of unrealness about London, with a fog sleeping restlessly over the city and the lights showing in the blur as if is not London at all but some strange place on another planet Moses Aloetta hop on a number 46 bus at the corner of Chepstow Road and Westbourne Grove to go to Waterloo to meet a fellar who was coming from Trinidad on the boat-train.[21]

As the boat-train offloads migrants from islands in the Caribbean, it evokes in Moses "a feeling of homesickness [....] For the old Waterloo is a place of arrival and departure,"[22] a threshold between the state of being subjects and becoming citizens.

The scene is part of a long sequence crafted from the transportation networks that weave the city and the novel together. Even as newcomers like Galahad pretend to give the impression that they "hep, that they on the ball"[23] by not asking for directions, to know the city's real geography allows one to hustle one's way through it. Selvon's narrative of immigrant men moving about the city is briefly interrupted by Tanty's experience of traveling on the Underground. One of the few women characters in the novel, Tanty has been content to stay by Harrow Road where black and working-class people live in cold, ramshackle housing. But it "rankle Tanty that she never travel in tube or bus in London."[24] Determined to overcome this lack as a Londoner, Tanty sets out to find the entrance to the Underground, even as the very thought of "going under the ground in this train nearly make she turn back." Eventually, Tanty triumphs over her fears and makes her way into the city by public transport, an act that reinforces her resilience as well as underscores her right to the city as an immigrant woman.

Crossing the city on transport then is not just a journey across time and space, but is also one of self-discovery. Galahad, who in spite of his meagre circumstances thinks of himself as a king in London, is often struck by loneliness as he sees the world passing by the big clock in Piccadilly station "what does tell the time of places all over the world." Only "watching for Trinidad" seems impossible as "the island so damn small it only have a dot and the name."[25] Centralized clock time, controlled by the Greenwich Meridian in London, reinforces Trinidad's time as peripheral. In another scene set in Piccadilly station that has distinct Fanonian overtones, a little child holding on to their mother's hand points to Galahad and says "Mummy, look at that black man!"[26] When Galahad bends down to caress the child's cheek out of embarrassment, the child begins to cry. Thus even as the Underground network is a space of the commingling of differences of races, classes, genders, and geographies, it is also the space where Galahad's blackness becomes a marker of unassimilable difference. Ultimately, despite Moses and Galahad's lives circulating in constant motion alongside London's streets, tube lines, and bus routes, Selvon's novel strikes a melancholic note of being stuck in the same place, going "neither forward nor backward."[27]

If Selvon's novel invented a new cartography and language for the city's immigrant subjects, the writer Buchi Emecheta's journey from a newly independent Nigeria to London in the 1960s provides a stark counterpoint. Adopting the register of documentary realism, her autobiographical novel *Second-Class Citizen* (1974) narrates the life and experiences of twenty-one-year-old Adah's arrival to the city where she becomes the breadwinner for her ever-expanding family. Although the precarious and decrepit conditions in which the family finds itself point to the city's deeply structured inequalities, Adah's story is about achieving "citizenship" against all odds. Perhaps the first novel by a black Londoner that ostensibly takes on the discursive and legal meanings of citizenship as both a sense of belonging as well as indicative of a legal right to the city, Adah's narrative is attuned to the "second-class" status afforded to black people in 1960s London and also the opportunities afforded there to overcome that status.

Like writers before her, Emecheta deploys the trope of circulation to represent possibilities of belonging in the city. On Adah's first day to work she takes to the Underground, and glimpses hope as she "saw beauty on the faces of her fellow passengers and heard beautiful sounds from the churning groans of the speeding underground train."[28] Thus, where Rhys's protagonist experienced the Underground as a nightmare of alienation, Adah glimpses the future here as one of an emergence into belonging, a passage into dignity and freedom: "On her way home on the platform at Finchley tube station, it seemed to her ears and mind that the train that curled gracefully into view was singing with her. Sharing her happiness and optimism."[29] The Underground makes it possible for her to crawl out of the tunnel into being "a first-class citizen for the part of the day when she worked in a clean, centrally-heated library."[30]

It is important to remember that Emecheta is the first major black woman writer whose works take London to be an indispensable point of reference in narratives of selfhood and citizenship. Her work straddles both the despair of Rhys's London and the comic vision of Selvon in which London is, for all its exclusions and deprivations, a city where the world finds its way in through the tracks of migration and circulation. Against the purported comfort of home, kinship, and ethnicity, Adah forges her own community with people across races, and it is London's circulatory networks that enable her to do that.

"Smoking Cities"

The publication of Hanif Kureishi's novel *The Buddha of Suburbia* (1990) constitutes yet another turning point in London's career as a city in world literature. Like the author himself, the protagonist of Kureishi's novel, seventeen-year old Karim, is British-born, the child of an immigrant. But as for the writers that preceded him, the circulatory network of the city is key to Kureishi's exploration of both the aesthetic and political possibilities of remaking the self in the face of an existential and social restlessness and conflict amid the social and political turmoil of the late 1960s and 1970s. In his script directions for the film *Sammy and Rosie Get Laid*, as the characters of Danny and Rafi walk down an Underground tunnel, Kureishi wrote of "the tunnel" as evoking "a superb sensation [...] of endless walking in both directions."[31] Set in the 1970s, *The Buddha of Suburbia* is a coming-of-age story of Karim that parallels London's indomitable spirit in a decade of growing disorientation and exhaustion of the political and cultural projects of liberation as the Thatcher era comes into view. The novel provides a searing account of radical London's decline in the 1970s when the city is literally "ripped apart" with strikes and marches against rising unemployment and housing shortages that brought to the surface simmering contradictions of class, race, and gender. Margaret Thatcher's tenure as Britain's Prime Minister from 1979 to 1990 left its mark on the capital city when she dissolved the Greater London Council, the socialist Labour-dominated local government. Although this was a move that was seen by her supporters as her attempt to control and manage the chaos of the city, it was an integral part of the larger agenda of the neoliberal assault on grassroots democracy and social welfare.

For the young Karim, travel into the city from the suburbs (a "leaving place"), where many working-class and middle-class people had retreated to escape proximity to the city's black migrants, is a move against "dullness" as much as it is a flight into temptation.[32] Although the commuter train from the suburbs reveals views of the "slums of Herne Hill and Brixton" and of "rows of disintegrating Victorian houses" with gardens "full of rusting junk,"[33] Karim is hooked to the London that is also a city of books, record shops, and of a rebellious counter-culture as embodied by his cousin Jamila and her brand of feminist and socialist politics. However, arrival in the city leaves Karim directionless, not entirely unlike his black immigrant predecessors. The novel ends on the day in which Thatcher is elected, just before we learn that Karim does not show up to oppose the National Front (NF) in a demonstration in Southall, a densely immigrant area in west London. On April 23, 1979, the far-right white supremacist NF met in Southall to provoke and intimidate the area's black and Asian residents. Thousands of protesters showed up and confronted the police who were protecting the NF's right to assemble. Hundreds were injured and many arrested in the ensuing violence. The protests brought together Asian and black residents of Southall alongside members of the Anti-Nazi League, reflecting a broad coalition of anti-racists in London. In the novel we learn that although Karim had grown up taking the train from the suburb of Bromley to London, he does not take it to Southall.

Although not British-born like Kureishi, Salman Rushdie has also been an important chronicler of black London in an era in which "black" still served as a broad political identity challenging racism in all spheres of British life. While his novel *The Satanic Verses* (1988) is often read as "the paradigmatic text of postcolonial London" in its depiction of "a city visible but unseen" which is the city of its migrants, it is in his novel *Shame* (1983) that Rushdie offers the Underground as the scene of violence and conflicted identity in multicultural London where the ghosts of the colonial past have not been laid to rest.[34] The narrator writes of the spectral presence in his imagination of a young "Asian" girl who is attacked by a group of teenage white boys on a late-night Underground train. Disturbingly, the assault, instead of filling her with rage, imbues her with a deep sense of shame. As he looks at "smoking cities" on his television screen in London, where he sees "groups of young people running through the streets, the shame burning on their brows and setting fire to shops, police shields, cars," the narrator notes that these youths give vent to the humiliation of an entire Asian community by rioting.[35] This leads him to imagine an alternative ending to the scene in the Underground:

> what would have happened if such a fury could have been released in that girl on her underground train—how she would have thrashed the white kids within an inch of their lives, breaking arms legs noses balls, without knowing whence the violence came, without seeing how she, so slight a figure, could command such awesome strength.[36]

As this passage demonstrates, the Underground functions as the repressed Unconscious of the city where racial barriers and gendered prohibitions find their most grotesque articulation, unleashing the violence that lies buried beneath the veneer of cosmopolitan citizenship and worldly belonging. Like Rushdie's other London novels, the city's racialized sensorium finds its sharpest manifestations in the peripheral and underground spaces of the city.

"History's Bubbles"

In his poem "Yobbos!" from the collection *Look We Have Coming to Dover* (2007) that interprets British metropolitan culture through the experiences of a working-class Punjabi British poet, Daljit Nagra reprises the Underground as a site where repression is unleashed as racialized violence. The poem opens with an epigraph of a Pears soap advertisement from *McLure's Magazine* in 1899: "The first step towards lightening THE WHITE MAN'S burden is through teaching the virtues of cleanliness."[37] Nagra's framing of a poem about a racist encounter in the London Underground with a reference to soap recalls the exhibitionary complex of the imperial city in which advertisements for commodities such as soap articulated racial and class anxieties about contamination. Pears company in fact had devoted an entire pavilion at the Empire Exhibition of 1924 to its cleaning products. In this poem, the space of the Underground, with its compressed proximity to different bodies and the dangerous intermingling of their sweaty odors and surfaces, makes the narrator foam at the mouth. This theme of the Underground as the site of contamination is also reprised in the Malawian writer Jack Mapanje's poem "Travelling In London Tubes," where a sneeze reveals "how much / charcoal was in your nose / eyes lungs / travelling in those lovely tubes."[38]

In an ironic twist, Rushdie's white teenage boys attacking an Asian girl in the Underground resurface in Nagra's poem as men who make the Asian male narrator the object of racial harassment. They mock him for reading Paul Muldoon on the train, the contemporary Irish poet. They are of course oblivious to the solidarities forged at the edges of white Englishness with the city's non-white others. So deprived are the "yobs" of cultural knowledge that they assume he must be reading "Paki shit," until one of them exclaims "Well mate, this Paki's more British than that inde / cipherable, impossibly untranslatable / sod of a Paddy." Paki is still a term of abuse for Asians, but race is complicated as the Irish poet is rendered as "sod of a Paddy."[39] Hena suggests that Nagra's poem "points to the ways colonial discourse othered the Celtic periphery and Asian subcontinent alike, making manifest how nineteenth-century imperial epistemologies of race subtend the moment of cross-cultural encounter in global London."[40] As both Muldoon and Nagra are "sozzled" together as "right savages," it is the space of the Underground where the repressed histories of the imperial capital bubble up to the surface.

Departing from the optimistic vision of her first novel *White Teeth* (2000) that reposed faith in the enduring promise of multicultural London at the turn of the twenty-first century through its comic portraits of mixed-race neighborhoods and families, Zadie Smith's *NW* (2012) presents a more attenuated sense of the city's possibilities in a world marred with increasing hostility to migrants and racialized others. While the novel's plot is structured around the various paths taken by its young protagonists who grow up in a housing estate in northwest London, the London Underground and the circulatory network it is embedded in is rendered once again as the space of danger and violence. The murder of Felix, a young black man, occurs after a chance encounter on the Underground. Earlier, traveling to Oxford Street in the iconic center of the city, Felix had stared at a map of the Underground, noting that "it did not express his reality. The center was not 'Oxford Circus' but the bright lights of Kilburn High Road."[41] In Smith's rendering, the view of London as the city of grand monuments and arcades that have been centers of global power is of necessity now reconstituted by the peripheral locations such as Kilburn where writers like her have been formed as Londoners.

In the Underground, when a pregnant white woman asks Felix to ask his "friend" to make space for her to sit in the carriage, Felix obliges with an appeal to their common "blud" solidarity. In response, the man explodes with hostility and queries the concept of "blud": "Who you calling blud? I ain't your blud?"[42] As he exits the train, two men follow Felix onto the platform and into his neighborhood where they deliver "a firm punch" that kills him.[43] This random but murderous encounter that is first unleashed in the Underground suggests the destabilization of the contours of racial solidarity and the blurring of the lines of racial divides. Felix's empathy for the white woman encourages so much rage in the young black men that they actually murder him.

Recreating London

If Smith's vision of London is of a violent metropolis struggling to come to terms with a buried but still iridescent racialized colonial trauma that becomes manifest in the peripheral and Underground zones of the city, more recent works such as Balli Kaur Jaswal's *Erotic Stories for Punjabi Widows* (2017) and Bernadine Evaristo's *Girl Woman Other* (2019) present the city's resilience in the face of both personal and public crises of the current moment in London's history, one that is marked by the conjuncture of a series of financial meltdowns and renewed racialized and gendered anxieties in the aftermath of Brexit (the UK's withdrawal from the European Union). In *Erotic Stories*, the young protagonist Nikki travels from north London to teach creative writing to Punjabi widows in Southall with its large concentration of South Asian migrants, an area that was shunned by Karim in Kureishi's *The Buddha of Suburbia*. The ghost of Rushdie's unknown Asian girl in the Underground seems to reappear and haunt Jaswal's narrative of gendered repression and rising religious fundamentalism in the city. It is here, amid the backdrop of killings of young women by an increasingly retrograde immigrant patriarchy that projects the honor of its women as a shield against racism, that the novel narrates an optimistic tale of conservative Punjabi widows crossing barriers of shame and space in the city to write their own stories about it.

In Evaristo's Booker Prize-winning novel, *Girl, Woman Other*, we get vignettes of the lives of twelve women across ages and spaces. But the stories that are set in London are stories that expand the limits of the city. From Carole, who grew up on a housing estate in edgy Peckham with her Nigerian parents and becomes a City banker, to Amma Bonsu who after decades of struggle finally launches a successful black feminist play in London's iconic National Theatre, the city's circulatory network plays a key role in staging the characters' experience of the city and its shaping of their subjectivities. While still pregnant with racialized and gendered tensions, the Underground also leads these women out into the light of the city where they can embrace its opportunities and possibilities. In a final scene reprising that other great novel of London, Virginia Woolf's *Mrs Dalloway* (1924), all the characters come together, from different parts of the city, to celebrate Amma's success at the theater that overlooks the River Thames, the ultimate sign of the city's embeddedness in circulatory networks that go back several hundred years. Here the dazzling array of differences of class, age, race, and sexuality offers a stark contrast to Mrs. Dalloway's party that had brought together the elite political classes of imperial London nearly a century before.

Re-Worlding London

If the very constitution of world literature is predicated on the translation and circulation of literary texts, the two tropes of the exhibitionary complex and the circulatory networks have been consistently subjected to interrogation and disruption by the writers considered here. The exhibitionary complex reveals both the symbolic power of the imperial city but also its brittleness, just as the focus on the London Underground reveals the many layers of the city that are not visible. Ultimately, both the exhibition and the Underground are sites of intensified social and material contradictions that the writers mine to reimagine the literary geography of London in the world and the world in London. But the Underground is also part of wider intersecting circulatory networks – both in the train lines that meet and diverge, but also in the city's streets, its walking paths, and bus routes, and the traffic on the river that divides the city into north and south. It is here that writers from the world's peripheries, as also from within the invisible and submerged terrains of London itself, are engaged in remaking London as the capital of world literature.

Notes

Many thanks to Ato Quayson and Jini Kim Watson for their sharp feedback on earlier versions of this chapter.

1 See Pascale Casanova, "Literature as a World," *New Left Review* 31 (Jan/Feb 2005): 71–90.
2 Franco Moretti, "Conjectures on World Literature," in Christopher Prendergast, ed., *Debating World Literature* (London: Verso, 2004), 148–162, 149–50.
3 Raymond Williams, *The Politics of Modernism: Against the New Conformists* (New York: Verso, 1989), 47.
4 Fredric Jameson, *The Modernist Papers* (New York: Verso, 2007), 150–151.
5 Ibid., 157.

6 See John McLeod, *Postcolonial London: Rewriting the Metropolis* (London: Routledge, 2004), 5. See also John Clement Ball, *Imagining London: Postcolonial Fiction and the Transnational Metropolis* (Toronto: University of Toronto Press, 2004) and Sukhdev Sandhu, *London Calling: How Black and Asian Writers Imagined a City* (New York: HarperCollins, 2003).

7 Tony Bennett, "The Exhibitionary Complex," *New Formations* 4 (Spring 1988): 73–102.

8 Michel de Certeau, *The Practice of Everyday Life*, trans. Stephen F. Rendall (Berkeley, CA: University of California Press, 1984), 93.

9 Omaar Hena, *Global Anglophone Poetry: Literary Form and Social Critique in Walcott, Muldoon, de Kok, and Nagra* (London: Palgrave Macmillan, 2015).

10 Andrea Levy, *Small Island* (London: Review, 2004), 2.

11 Virginia Woolf, *The Essays of Virginia Woolf*, Andrew McNeillie, ed. (San Diego, CA: Harcourt, 1986–88), 410–411.

12 Christina Britzolakis, "'This Way to the Exhibition': Genealogies of Urban Spectacle in Jean Rhys's Interwar fiction," *Textual Practice* 21, no. 3 (2007): 457–482, 466.

13 For a theory of world literature that reads it as the literature of the capitalist world system, see Warwick Research Collective, *Combined and Uneven Development: Towards a New Theory of World-Literature* (Liverpool: Liverpool University Press, 2015).

14 Anne McClintock, *Imperial Leather: Race, Gender and Sexuality in the Colonial Context* (London: Routledge), 72.

15 Ian Baucom, *Out of Place* (Princeton, NJ: Princeton University Press), 57.

16 McClintock, *Imperial Leather*, 46.

17 Raymond Williams, *The Country and the City* ([1973] London: The Hogarth Press, 1985), 229.

18 Jean Rhys, *Good Morning Midnight* (London: Penguin, 2000), 12.

19 Britzolakis, "This Way," 475.

20 Sam Selvon, *The Lonely Londoners* (London: Penguin, 2006), "Introduction" by Susheila Nasta, x.

21 Ibid., 1.

22 Ibid., 4.

23 Ibid., 19.

24 Ibid., 68.

25 Ibid., 72, 80.

26 Ibid., 76. In his book *Black Skin, White Masks*, the Martinican theorist of revolutionary anti-colonialism Frantz Fanon recounts being accosted in France with a child's cry, "Maman, look, a Negro; I'm scared!" (Frantz Fanon, *Black Skin, White Masks* (London: Penguin Classics, 2019), 91). This becomes the moment in which he experiences his black body as being the object of white gaze in a colonial society.

27 Selvon, Lonely Londoners, 124.

28 Buchi Emecheta, *Second Class Citizen* (London: Penguin Classics, 2021), 47.

29 Ibid., 86.

30 Ibid., 43.
31 Hanif Kureishi, *Sammy and Rosie Get Laid; The Script and the Diary (i.e. Some Time with Stephen)* (London: Faber, 1988), 18–19, quoted in Sandhu, *London Calling*, 248–249.
32 Hanif Kureishi, *The Buddha of Suburbia* (London: Faber, 1990), 117.
33 Ibid.
34 Caroline Herbert, "Postcolonial Cities" in Kevin R. McNamara, ed., *The Cambridge Companion to the City in Literature* (Cambridge: Cambridge University Press, 2014), 200–215, 203.
35 Salman Rushdie, *Shame* (New York: Vintage, 1995), 117.
36 Ibid., 117.
37 Daljit Nagra, *Look We Have Coming to Dover!* (London: Faber and Faber, 2007), 11.
38 Jack Mapanje, *Of Chameleons and Gods* (London: Heinemann, 1981), 35–36.
39 Hena, *Global Anglophone Poetry*, 134.
40 Ibid., 121–154.
41 Zadie Smith, *NW* (London: Penguin, 2012), 163.
42 Ibid., 165–166.
43 Ibid., 169.

CHAPTER 7

Unworlding Paris

Flânerie *and Epistemic Encounters from Baudelaire to Gauz*

Ruth Bush

A chapter on "world literature in Paris" or "Paris in world literature" is both an ambitious and hackneyed prospect. Connections between urban space and literary production in French cities have been excavated at least as far back as the thirteenth century.[1] The French capital has long sustained nuanced historical and theoretical discussions as "the capital of modernity" in the nineteenth and early twentieth centuries.[2] In world literature, one of the most influential theoretical arguments remains Pascale Casanova's claim that Paris has been the centrifugal "capital" of a World Republic of Letters from which archetypal ideas of the literary avant-garde, modernist invention, and cosmopolitan sensibility have emerged.[3] A number of critics have challenged or nuanced Casanova's model. This scholarship signals the homogenizing tendency of this account of Paris; the resistance of multilingual realities to a model of vernacular nationalism that links language to nationhood (a model set out in influential terms by German philosopher Johann Gottfried Herder in the late eighteenth century); Casanova's limited engagement with low- and middle-brow genres of writing; and the institutional positioning of Casanova's work in French and in English translation.[4] Nonetheless, accounts of Paris as an exemplary or exceptional literary hub continue to be reproduced in symbolic and material terms. The relative autonomy of this literary field – to use Bourdieu's terms – is inflected by France's economic, political, and military ties with formerly colonized regions of the world. The country's relationship with its overseas departments and territories, as well as its "post-migratory" population, inform everyday social dynamics characterized by recurrent issues of colonial memory, restitution, violence, epistemic injustice, and structural inequality.[5] In the literary realm, the reproduction of Francocentrism operates through the consecrating mechanisms of global publishing circuits, francophone literary prize culture, French legislation which protects the rights of booksellers and the price of books (witnessed in protectionist measures adopted during the COVID-19 pandemic), and linguistic influence perpetuated through the Académie Française and the Organisation de la Francophonie.[6]

The present chapter seeks to avoid rehashing reductive models of Parisian centrality or simply summarizing important critiques of universalism that have characterized debates in world literature and polemical political debates over the state of French Republicanism. It acknowledges and moves beyond universalizing, singular, or celebratory tendencies of Paris-centric theories of world literature and critical accounts of French national literary history.[7] The discussion explores the social dynamics identified above by reading literary forms of urban affect, epistemic encounter, and intimacy found in three novels of migration to Paris. These novels by Cheikh Hamidou Kane, Mbella Sonne Dipoko and Gauz reinvent and recycle familiar Parisian tropes, in particular the *flâneur* and his leisured navigation of the city. The writing tackles themes of alienation, *ennui*, and freedom in relation to racialized, masculine experience (interracial friendships as well as forms of discrimination in housing and employment) of the city. In contrasting ways, these African-centered narratives of Paris "unworld" the city space by giving literary form to social and epistemic encounters that disrupt resilient critical claims to aesthetic or epistemic universalism. In each case, the specter of the *flâneur* (often a student, or someone associated with the rich history of African students in twentieth-century Paris) is expanded through formal devices. These encounters are compressed into specific everyday spaces (the apartment; the department store; the café; a boat on the Seine) and delineated narrative temporalities (use of the diary form; coming-of-age narrative; "a few nights and days") which evoke recurrent tensions between the abstract "universal" promise of freedom and everyday experiences of racism and coloniality.[8] My discussion speaks to a contemporary sociopolitical context in the French public sphere where decolonial thought remains subject to intense public and media scrutiny.[9] It does so by examining the formal expression of epistemic fault lines and intimacies that characterize the production and circulation of knowledge in the city.

The Parisian *flâneur* – a free-wheeling wanderer, observer, and reporter of city life has dominated critical discourse on the literary expression of the relationship between urban space, time, and the formation of individual subjectivity since the mid-nineteenth century. Walter Benjamin's description of the *flâneur* as he "who goes botanizing on the asphalt" is intrinsically connected to Parisian urban cultures of dandyism, loitering, leisure, and shopping.[10] The figure's appeal and transnational resonance has also been connected latterly to both ideas of cosmopolitan freedoms, and the restrictions on human movement and border-crossing which characterize post-colonial immigration policies in western Europe.[11] Kane, Dipoko, and Gauz bring new global dimensions to this character-type that Benjamin situated squarely within the logic of capitalism. While Kane's classic *L'Aventure ambiguë* (Ambiguous Adventure, 1961) provides a semi-autobiographical poetic meditation on the spiritual loss encountered by his fragile protagonist Samba Diallo, Dipoko's *A Few Nights and Days* (1966) self-reflexively depicts a knowing protagonist, Doumbe, who navigates racialized city spaces through his sexual relationships and frustrated attempts to write it all down. More recently, Gauz's celebrated novel, *Debout payé* (Standing Heavy, 2014) offers a formally experimental and satirical reworking of the migrant-*flâneur* figure operating as *chômeur* and *débrouillard*.[12] This novel describes the tense social realities of security and surveillance in a post-9/11 Parisian world, giving a singular glimpse of the political economy of that space shortly before the Charlie Hebdo and Bataclan terrorist acts of 2015. Unlike the dandyish Parisian *flâneur*, African migrant *chômeurs* or *débrouillards* improvise to survive, and sometimes thrive, in the French capital. Ato Quayson, building on Rem Koolhaas's architectural analysis of Lagos, theorizes the inventiveness that obtains in African urban contexts of free time. According to Quayson, free time is the phenomenological dimension of an informal economy, leading to the impulse to recycle and transform the self/objects/space.[13] Subjects are forced to do something within contexts of frayed infrastructure – which, I want to suggest, include precarious, temporary spaces occupied by migrant-*flâneurs* in the metropole.

Parisian Modernity and Exilic Unworlding

It is a truism to state that Paris was a crucible for influential ideas of Western modernity in the nineteenth century. As fictionalized in the vast cycles of Balzac's *Comédie Humaine* and Zola's *Rougon-Macquart*, city dwellers grappled with social inequalities and opportunities offered by a city in the midst of urban transformation underpinned by colonial expansion. Following the Revolutions of 1848, Hausmann's bold architectural projects created grand avenues and neo-baroque apartment buildings to meet the political and social challenges of the Second Empire. The introduction of electric lighting, public transport infrastructure, and growth of a bourgeois consumer culture were offset by the physical violence of this period of the city's history, marked by the suppression of the Paris Commune in 1871, rural-urban migration, and visibility of extreme poverty. Against this context, the *flâneur* emerged in literary expression, sauntering through the city's streets and new shopping arcades. He (this normative gendering has been widely discussed elsewhere, notably in Polo B. Moji's fascinating recent study of AfroFrench flâneuse narratives) embodied new ways of navigating and looking at the contradictory juxtapositions of urban life.[14] Such ocular posturing was at odds with speed of social transformation underway and forms of direct political action. Susan Buck-Morss notes that "even when an author expressed sympathy for the new urban destitute, it was of a sort peculiar to modern perception. It evoked emotion without providing the knowledge that could change the situation."[15] Elsewhere, David Harvey notes that the "thousand uprooted lives," identified by Baudelaire as the obverse side to the new urban high life of modernity enjoyed by *flâneurs*, cannot be ignored.[16] Baudelaire's *Tableaux parisiens* are littered with examples of the discord between rapid urban development and individual subjective experiences, mediated through poetic form. The speaker in "Le Cygne" (The Swan) laments, "Paris is changing, but nothing in my melancholy / Has changed ! New palaces, scaffolds, and blocks." The poem's speaker draws a series of comparisons to explore themes of loss, exile, and freedom. An anonymous "négresse, amaigrie et phtisique" (starved and phthisic Black woman) stands in the mud, "Searching with wild eyes / For the absent coconut palms of superb Africa / Beyond the immense wall of fog."[17] Here the woman's inability to see is linked to her bodily decrepitude. She remains a hazy object rather than speaking subject of her experience. Exilic loss is deftly evoked across the poem's sequence of images despite the evident difference between the structural and affective experience of exile and migration, and that of a melancholic wanderer witnessing the changing urban landscape.[18] Paris is a location for the literary expression of class politics, but where the creative mystique and attraction of *flânerie* – with its incentive to wander off, be spontaneous, and express individual freedom amid material constraints – is also constantly at risk of submerging structurally uneven political, economic, and epistemic contexts of exile. As Buck-Morss notes, Walter Benjamin, writing between two world wars, uses his reading of Baudelaire and discussion of *flânerie* in *The Arcades Project* to navigate this larger sense of powerlessness, itself "the problem of the politically committed, bourgeois writer and intellectual of his own time."[19]

A sizable corpus of twentieth- and early twenty-first-century literature explores migration to Paris. The city was a privileged site of literary encounter in the interwar period, from exiled Latin American writers of what would become magical realism to the Black internationalism of négritude poets.[20] It was also a crucible for anti-colonial thought and action. Scholars have explored African writers' decentering of travel writing as a genre and their formal capacity to express collective, political and individual, psychological dimensions of "Black France."[21] Several of the so-called first wave of African novels written in the post-Second World War period deal with the experience of students traveling to the metropole.[22] They express formative moments of "coming of age" in the French capital, and the kind of contradictions and epistemic tensions that this experience exposed in the midst of the formal process of decolonization.

Samba Diallo, the protagonist of Cheikh Hamidou Kane's poetic *récit*, *L'Aventure ambiguë*, arrives in Paris to study philosophy following his Islamic education and study in the colonial school system in Senegal. He has been compelled to do so by family obligation in the context of colonial inequalities. He is haunted by the earlier journey of the Fou, a former *tirailleur sénégalais* whose Beckettian monologues express the psychological effects of his wartime experience in the French metropole. One such monologue recalls the pounding of shoes on asphalt – a distorted echo of Benjamin's description of the entranced *flâneur* who "goes botanizing on the asphalt." The Fou recoils from hard urban surfaces. Their sound resonates with his sense of dehumanized isolation:

> The asphalt [...] My gaze traversed the entire extent of what lay before me, and I saw no limit to the stony surface [....] I had not seen one single human foot since I disembarked. All along the asphalt, the tide of shells ran level with it [....] The bare and echoing shell of the stone turned the street into a basin of granite.[23]

In direct echo, Samba Diallo's descent of the Boulevard St Michel is characterized by a densely poetic, breathless, expression of alienation as he views his surroundings. He struggles to concentrate and to absorb or process in any meaningful sense what is before him; "A firm-spun thread of clear thought was filtering with some difficulty through the heavy down of his sensations."[24] Sensory excess stifles the ability to think. The figurative trope of light cannot penetrate the thick layer – not of fog, as for Baudelaire's "négresse," but of his own phenomenological experience. As he states, "One meets objects of flesh in them, as well as objects of metal [....] Time is obstructed by their mechanical jumble. One does not perceive the background of time, and its slow current."[25] This marks a contrast to earlier scenes in the novel of his spiritual plenitude and transcendence during Islamic prayer. Those scenes are characterized by vivid descriptions of color and sensation. As for Rilke's *Malte Laurids Brigge* (who Kane cites directly in the same passage), urban life is disorienting. The experience of sensory immersion in bustling streets leads to psychological disturbance.[26] For Kane this inner fracture is a consequence of epistemic violence under a colonial education system.

Critics have dwelled on the form of Kane's writing: the use of poetic diction, the transformation of his personal diary into this *récit*, and the text's relationship to European modernist aesthetics. Despite the literary genealogy of Parisian *flânerie* and introspection to which Kane alludes in the Boulevard Saint Michel scene and the Fou's monologue, several less-discussed passages express Samba Diallo's alienation through dialogue and are set in confined spaces. Samba Diallo's conversations with friend and fellow student, Lucienne, occur in cafés, her family's bourgeois apartment, and while rowing in a boat on the Seine. The conversations pit Samba's religious faith and interest in European philosophical thought against political ideas of the period (French communism in particular). In one example, Samba recalls his former happiness and sense of spiritual fulfillment. He disregards not only the landscape in Paris, but landscape *per se* – the mere "décor" in which his essential, happy experience of immateriality has become entangled:

> "I should so much like to know whether I have only dreamed that happiness I remember, or whether it existed."
> "I won't laugh. What happiness?"
> "The scene ['décor'] is the same. It has to do with the same house, hemmed in by a sky more or less blue, a countryside more or less animated, water running, trees growing, men and animals living there. The scene is the same, I still recognize it."
> She sat up straight and rested her elbow on the edge of the boat.
> "What happiness?" she asked again.
> "Lucienne, that scene, it is a sham! Behind it, there is something a thousand times more beautiful, a thousand times more true! But I can no longer find that world's pathway."[27]

Samba's loss of religious transcendence is described as an inability to conjure the world in the terms of his childhood. Less an exercise in "world-making," this passage relates a beleaguered inner state; a disoriented "unworlding." Faced with Lucienne's commitment to the Communist Party, the world of material things (whether the proletarian revolution, the natural world, or the cars and roads of Paris) is an irrelevance. He has been unworlded – where world is taken to mean "that world" of happiness which is reached (rather than *made*) along the path of prayer – through his experiences in the physical spaces of the French capital and exposure to epistemic conventions of the French education system at school in Senegal and at university in Paris.

This discussion of Samba Diallo as a migrant-*flâneur* may appear to concur with Franco Moretti's evolutionary model for the "rise of the novel" that foregrounds the melding of "local materials" with "foreign forms."[28] However, I read these three novels' expression of epistemic fault lines in relation to broader debates concerning knowledge production.

"To hell with Geography and the Sorbonne": Knowing the City in *A Few Nights and Days*

Kane's novel sets out alternative temporalities to the capitalist materialism encountered by Samba Diallo while studying Western philosophy in Paris. It exposes the limits of what Pheng Cheah describes as normative world-making in theories of world literature by staging the protagonist's inability to reach the world as he once knew it.[29] In contrast, Dipoko's novel, *A Few Nights and Days*, depicts a law student bibliophile protagonist, Doumbe, who is resolutely in control of the cityscape he navigates after being sent by his father to "learn all the books."[30] As the quotation in the heading of this section indicates, Dipoko's protagonist consigns the symbolic prestige of Parisian university education "to hell."[31] Instead, his knowledge of and in the city is expressed through his *flânerie*, his engagement with other characters, and the self-reflexive, repeated, ultimately dissatisfying, attempt to write creatively. For Doumbe, "the world is a hard world. The world isn't tender."[32] He struggles to engage with his studies, and although he yearns to "invent events in the workshop of the imagination," he ultimately feels compelled to write about actual events he has lived through his relationships with people he has met in the city.[33] He recounts his relationships with three women: Thérèse, a white, French, nineteen-year-old geography student who commits suicide at the dénouement; Bibi; and Ndome, a Cameroonian woman student who is engaged to another man and remains critical of Doumbe's engagement to Thérèse.

A Few Nights and Days offers a singular narrative insight into Doumbe's navigation of Parisian urban geography (in particular the fifth and thirteenth *arrondissements*). Rather than reading Dipoko's text primarily as an account of interracial relationships (as critics have done to date), I want to suggest that this novel offers a cartwheeling account of epistemic intimacy and urban affect in the French capital. It offers reflection on desire, violence, and freedom experienced in student bedrooms, cafés, and bourgeois apartments. Written by an anglophone Cameroonian, it does not sit easily within national or linguistic categories frequently used to label African literatures. Dipoko has been described by some as a French African writer, despite writing in English, while in Cameroon he was at times ostracized from anglophone Cameroonian identification because he was from the Mungo ethnic group, the bulk of whose members are located in Francophone Cameroon.[34] Dipoko built his literary reputation while in France during the early 1960s, writing for journals such as *Black Orpheus*, *Transition*, and *Présence Africaine*. His first novel, *A Few Nights and Days*, was almost rejected by Heinemann African Series because of its erotic content, deemed unAfrican in relation to other novels from the continent. Paul Theroux noted in his 1966 review: "It is not only a feminine novel written by a man, it is also a novel with a country; that is, France. An African novel about France? No. A French novel about France by a man who writes like a European woman."[35] Any close engagement with the novel – in particular its more misogynistic passages[36] – reveals the limitation of this evaluation, not least its reductive assumptions about gendered identity and literary form.

As an aspiring writer, Doumbe lays claims to Paris's privileged reputation for generating forms of cosmopolitan community and a masculine reimagining of the world. He describes Parisian café conversations with his communist student friend, Laurent, as synecdochic of a mode of thinking about the world:

> Paris. It wasn't only books. It was also dreams of a better world. That was one of the things that made us feel important in spite of our problems and difficulties. Meeting people from different parts of the world, talking to them. One lived and hoped. One hated and loved. Moments of courage and then of despair; days of loneliness until someone's daughter brought her body and sometimes her heart as well.[37]

Elsewhere, this description of the city is connected to his attempts to write: "That was Paris. A writer lives the city, feels it, observes it as he observes himself, lives his life, feeling."[38] Such anecdotal echoing of the position of a *flâneur* is part of Doumbe's attempts not only to understand himself, but also to document his sense of being understood and misunderstood by others.

Doumbe's account of his relationship with Thérèse recasts reductive perceptions of Africa in the metropolitan imagination and skewers Thérèse's epistemophilic impulses. These reported dialogues take place in private domestic settings, allowing Dipoko to reframe the city's associations with romantic love through his protagonist's childhood memories:

> I talked to her of the Africa of my childhood and she simply liked it. I told her the story of Mboke and Ewudu. She loved it; she said it was like a novel. She liked to hear me talk of Africa.
>
> [...]
>
> Being a geography student she would have talked to me about the regions of Europe; about the rivers, for example. But I didn't even encourage her. I didn't care for any river but the Mungo River in Cameroon, and about that I talked. The seasons – the dry season and the rainy season. The canoe-men and their women. My childhood by that river. River of desire. River of love-songs sung by the canoe-men and their women. Welcoming river.[39]

The lack of reciprocity in the exchange is reinforced by the first-person narrative structure. Where Lucienne and Samba Diallo grapple with ideas about God while floating down the Seine, Doumbe and Thérèse's transactional communication here displaces the Seine's romantic resonance by foregrounding that of the Mungo River.

Doumbe's attempts at writing in order to process or generate an image of his experience in Paris are alert to the class dynamics and "hard" materiality of this world. He describes visiting Thérèse's parents' apartment (a scene which echoes Samba Diallo's meeting with Lucienne's parents):

> There was a piano, glistening symbol of Western bourgeois culture. The furniture was antique. I have never been particularly interested in old European furniture. I know practically nothing about it; so it would be very difficult to describe the sitting-room in detail. The upholstery was rich and grimly showy. Two paintings of landscapes hung on the walls. They were huge paintings. They looked to me like shadows in pine woods with a sad, cloudy sky brooding in perspective. I am not sure by whom the paintings were. I didn't get near enough to them for me to read the signatures and I'm not good at detecting the styles of the various masters. I am convinced those paintings were masterpieces by the mere fact that they were in Monsieur Vaele's sitting-room. With a firm in the Ivory Coast and an office in Paris and more funds possibly invested elsewhere, Monsieur Vaele was a rich man. He could afford to buy masterpieces.[40]

The narrative voice here weaves between assumption and consumption; between inference and projection; between disregard for "old European furniture" that lies beyond his frame of knowledge, and the competing urge to provide a description: to reproduce this room on the page and in the mind of the reader. The ekphrasis evokes melancholy emphasized by a chain of negative sentence structures implying uncertainty and distance. It forms a connecting thread to the underlying economic structures which, in Doumbe's reading/writing of the Parisian sitting room, connect the bourgeois furnishings to Monsieur Vaele's transnational business dealings and wealth derived through France's colonial past and present. The relative stasis of Dipoko's novel of student *flânerie* meanders between Parisian myths and material realities, puncturing the hypocrisy of metropolitan "civility" through this introspective narrative voice.

Debout payé and the Forms of City Observation

As I have argued so far, transnational perspectives of the migrant-*flâneur* "unworld" the city's private and public spaces by exposing epistemic fault lines. The places and people of Paris are observed in ways that project ambivalence about urban experience, the city's claims to aesthetic exceptionalism, and its social, racialized inequalities. Gauz's 2014 novel *Debout payé* offers a further account of the city's capacity to make and unmake its human inhabitants, and their corresponding ability to represent the city to themselves.[41] The novel is structured chronologically through the interwoven lives of three contrasting migrant characters: Ferdinand, who arrived in France in the 1960s and has managed to build up a security business which employs African *sans-papiers* (a term that designates people without official residence papers); Ossiri, a science teacher in a private Lycée from Abidjan who travels to France in search of adventure, and despite his mother's experience of life in Paris, where she was friends with Ferdinand; and Kassoum, who comes from a slum area of Abidjan, traveled slowly to Paris, and gradually finds a new understanding of himself and of France when he becomes friends with Ossiri. The chapters describing each character's trajectory and employment as a security guard at the Grands Moulins in Austerlitz are interspersed with chapters formed of brief, often comic, anecdotes and aphorisms based implicitly on the observations of a security guard working at Camaïeu-Bastille (a clothing store) and Sephora-Champs Elysées (a chain store selling make-up and beauty products). In a further nod to the *flâneur*, the fragmentary structure of these chapters is indicative of the unstable, momentary temporality of urban life, as well as the attempt to observe, understand, and record shopping as a quintessential urban leisure activity.

Temporal jumps and kinetic contrasts animate the novel: from the three "ages" of Ferdinand, Ossiri, and Kassoum, including their respective journeys from Abidjan to Paris and from Parisian *banlieue* to the MECI (*Maison des étudiants de Côte d'Ivoire*), to the static perspective of the security guard. Gauz's text draws explicit attention to the lived experiences of *les sans-papiers* in the city through two key events: the 1974 crisis which brought about change in legislation and created the category of "*sans-papiers*," thereby imposing new restrictions on migrants from former colonies; and the 1996 occupation by and eviction of *les sans-papiers* from the Eglise Saint-Bernard-de-la-Chapelle in the Goutte d'or neighborhood of Paris's eighteenth *arrondissement*. These episodes explore state violence and drive the novel's satirical riposte to the tightening of European immigration laws. Further to these political contexts, I want to consider here the novel's expression of two key examples of everyday intimacy in Paris: the student residence and the security guard's gaze. These scenes speak to broader concerns in world literature, namely the making and unmaking of epistemic worlds through literary form in contexts of structural inequality.

The first of these examples is the MECI. Described as "cet incroyable taudis" (this incredible hovel),[42] the student residence on the Boulevard Vincent Auriol in the 13th *arrondissement* is a generative site for Ferdinand's pre-1974 generation. This generation benefited from what the novel terms the "golden age" of student mobility between France and newly independent countries in sub-Saharan Africa. The MECI is a place for rhetorical posturing and for mimicking the radical stances of an earlier generation of anti-colonial student activists, many of whom were themselves writers, loosely amalgamated under the banner of négritude, connected to the journal *Présence Africaine* and influential *Fédération des étudiants d'Afrique noire en France*. For Ossiri and Kassoum, however, and the later generation of *sans-papiers*, the MECI is no longer home to students. It offers a fragile roof and overcrowded floorspace for mostly male inhabitants who are engaged in forms of precarious, casualized labor, or unemployed (*au chômage*). The latter term is shorthand for unemployment subsidy paid by the state, but has broader etymological resonance with immobility, inactivity, stagnation and stasis linked to lack of opportunity to work, and to suspension of work for civic and religious holidays. When Ferdinand initially lives at the MECI, alongside his student cousin, André, following his arrival in France, he is struck by the illusion and reality of student life. The MECI is the site for gatherings of French African students from across Paris to discuss the infamously tearful reaction of President Bokassa (of Central African Republic) to the death of Georges Pompidou. Rather than meaningful political dialogue or pan-African solidarity, however, Gauz's satire pinpoints intellectual posturing via the linguistic gatekeeping of these students. They argue about commas, imagine they are Léopold Sédar Senghor, or obsess on the correct pronunciation of spoken French.

Ossiri comes to the MECI while working as a security guard. As a middle-class science teacher, a "good little civil servant" in Côte d'Ivoire, his trajectory is not that of an economic migrant, but one who feels the pull of the metropole and lure of adventure involuntarily.[43] He describes Paris via his relocation from the *banlieue* of Mée-sur-Seine ("a kind of 'non-town,' an administrative enclave on a map, a demarcated zone in the immense protean urban jungle with Paris as the distant centre"[44]). His move to the MECI inserts him into this "distant centre" via the economic deprivation of a specific *banlieue* location. Kassoum's experience of the MECI is that of a former slum dweller in Abidjan. He is at ease with the social strategies needed to negotiate hierarchies, hostilities, and solidarities in this space. His 16 m^2 room is shared with at least four other adults and "seemed like a palace to him" in comparison to Le Colosse slum in Abidjan. He is nonetheless acutely aware of the MECI's ghettoizing effects. In the closing section of the novel, Gauz redeploys the gestures of *flânerie*, in a contrasting description of the MECI's inhabitants' social and physical immobility. He draws first on the lexicon of enslavement:

> They stayed among themselves, shut in the hold of their own destitution, incapable of a simple walk in the fresh air on the deck of their galley. No wall, no jailer held them back physically.

Kassoum's decision to follow Ossiri and walk out into the city in this final section is presented as a liberation and form of transcendence of this inertia. It is compounded by a form of cosmopolitan self-awareness : "Ossiri showed him how the simple fact of having travelled made him rich." This is further qualified by a chiastic moral, flattening any hierarchy of urban experience, that Kassoum is "better than people in Colosse because they will never see Paris. Better than people in Paris because they will never see Colosse."[45] Together, Kassoum and Ossiri walk and look at the sky while walking down the Boulevard de l'Hôpital toward the Seine:

> Kassoum felt a bit ridiculous standing on the pavement like that, his head tilted up, scrutinizing a cloudless blue sky [....] In Abidjan the sky was never blue. It was always full of great herds of cloud [....] This clear azure vault above Austerlitz station, this deep blue scarred by white smoke trails of long-haul flights.[46]

Kassoum's revelation, directly preceding the eviction of the MECI residents, is that of a transcendent state inspired by Ossiri's guided walks across the city. It is connected to memories of Abidjan's humid climate and his formative experiences in the Colosse slum, as well as awareness of constant transport mobility in and above Paris.

The second key site of intimacy with broader implications for the world literary form of this novel is the cabin occupied by Ossiri and Kassoum during their shifts as security guards at the defunct Grands Moulins de Paris factory, which resurfaces as a motif for industrial decline throughout each section of the text. These Moulins were used to process wheat grown under French neocolonial agricultural policy in West Africa. They are overshadowed by a Western Union advertising hoarding that invites passers-by to "send some money back home," and which Ossiri memorably deconstructs from his vantage point in the cabin. Kassoum watches the 9/11 terrorist attacks in New York unfold on his portable mini-television within this space. He is captivated by the spectacular images seen through amateur cameras "*en mondovision*" (in world coverage).[47] The contrast is drawn between his Parisian status quo/immobility and the sudden, scarcely imaginable, ambush of United States and New York. The irruptive potential is filtered via Kassoum's gaze on the screen and then a shift of scale through Ossiri's analysis which signals the local consequences of this global event (namely an imminent loss of employment due to tightening of control around security, war, and forms of xenophobia). The future, he suggests, will be "the era of paranoia, the time of constant security measures. From this point on, the world will no longer look the same."[48] An impression of relative freedom inspired by the city, despite disparities in wealth and access to housing and employment, is undercut by the anticipated *visible* effects of these macropolitical events. Thus the eviction of all residents from the MECI that follows is not widely reported in the press, despite precedents such as the Saint-Bernard-de-la-Chapelle evictions of *les sans-papiers*. There are, after all, now "more spectacular things in current national and international news."[49]

Kassoum's final job before obtaining his coveted *carte de séjour* (residence permit) is as a security guard working on the door of an anonymous company. From within another box, "lit with white neon,"[50] he watches the security arch as employees put their bags through the metal detector. Read in the wake of the Charlie Hebdo attacks in 2015 which included the death of the building's security guard, the description is particularly poignant. Like a designer desk, Kassoum has become part of the expendable interior design of the contemporary office environment, governed by strict protocol: "An interactive element of the décor." Unlike the imaginative leaps of the department store security guard, captured through the interspersed anecdotal vignettes, "there is no place for personal initiatives and zeal."[51] Gauz's security guard is part of the infrastructure of contemporary office life in the French capital, dehumanized and reduced to his function within performative responses to perceived threats of terrorism, despite his individual situation beyond the regulatory bureaucratic systems of the French state. In such contexts of physical enclosure and surveillance in the workplace, *flânerie*'s promise of freedom is more of an illusion than ever. As Kassoum notes, he will leave this job as soon as he has his *carte de séjour*. Through its formal innovation, *Debout payé* bridges the experience of an African student "elite" to the precarity of the *sans-papiers*, embedded within Paris's urban cultures of shopping, luxury goods, and security. In each instance, as evoked by Gauz's descriptions and use of humor, these cultures rely on modes of observation and spectacle which operate in both covert and ostentatious ways, and remain embedded in socioeconomic hierarchies and discriminatory practices. The form of the novel nonetheless centers imaginative agency within structurally unequal contexts. It offers reflection on urban surveillance culture as integral to forms of social control by the state and by private companies, while playing throughout – via the satirical gaze of the security guard – with racialized typologies in contemporary French society.

Conclusion

Paris operates in world literature in ways which are embedded in the city's literary legacies as well as its acutely unequal everyday social contexts. This chapter has delved into francophone and anglophone literary representations of sensory engagement with urban phenomena; the self-sustaining artifice of commodity culture; and intersectional experiences of the city. Ultimately I suggest reading this city unexceptionally. It is a site of plural epistemic and aesthetic encounters amply expressed through the literary forms of migrant-*flânerie*. The "unworlding" gaze of Kane's protagonist positions Paris as a resiliently peripheral, though psychologically violent, counterpoint to his spiritual world. Dipoko's defiantly introspective narrative uses its characters' affective lives in the city's private spaces to highlight racialized and gendered urban experience. Lastly, Gauz's multigenerational tale of migrant subjectivity signals the city's many spatial and temporal scales. Its humor riffs on the theme of economic inequality, while foreclosing any reductive hierarchy between the transformative potential of Paris and Abidjan. My readings are a brief reminder of the limitations of francocentric structural models of Paris in world literature. Alert to the material contexts that inflect these texts' form, this chapter invites further analysis of the literary expression of intimacy in the city, characterized by desire and violence.

Notes

1 Sarah Kay, Terence Cave, and Malcom Bowie, *A Short History of French Literature* (Oxford: Oxford University Press, 2006), 16.
2 Walter Benjamin, *The Arcades Project* (Cambridge, MA: Belknap Press, 1999); David Harvey, *Paris: Capital of Modernity* (New York: Routledge, 2006).
3 Pascale Casanova, *The World Republic of Letters*, trans. M.B. DeBevoise (Cambridge, MA; London: Harvard University Press, 2004).
4 Christopher Prendergast, ed. *Debating World Literature* (London: Verso, 2004); Alexander Beecroft, *An Ecology of World Literature: From Antiquity to*

the Present Day (London and New York: Verso, 2015); Ruth Bush, *Publishing Africa in French: Literary Institutions and Decolonization 1945–1967* (Liverpool: Liverpool University Press, 2016); Tobias Warner, *The Tongue-Tied Imagination: Decolonizing Literary Modernity in Senegal* (New York: Fordham University Press, 2019); Gisèle Sapiro and Delia Ungureanu, "Pascale Casanova's World of Letters and Its Legacies," *Journal of World Literature* 5, no. 2 (2020): 159–168; Stefan Helgesson, *Decolonisations of Literature. Critical Practice in Africa and Brazil after 1945* (Liverpool: Liverpool University Press, forthcoming).

5 Kathryn Kleppinger and Laura Reeck, eds., *Post-Migratory Cultures in Postcolonial France* (Liverpool: Liverpool University Press, 2018), 2–6; Etienne Achille and Lydie Moudileno, *Mythologies postcoloniales: Pour une décolonisation du quotidien* (Paris: Editions Champion, 2018); Etienne Achille, Charles Forsdick, and Lydie Moudileno, eds., *Postcolonial Realms of Memory: Sites and Symbols in Modern France* (Liverpool: Liverpool University Press, 2020); Mame-Fatou Niang, *Identités françaises: Banlieues, féminités et universalisme* (Leiden: Brill Rodopi, 2020); Fanny Pigeaud and Ndongo Samba Sylla, *Africa's Last Colonial Currency: The CFA Franc Story*, trans. Thomas Fazi (London: Pluto Press, 2020); Felwine Sarr and Bénédicte Savoy, "The Restitution of African Cultural Heritage: Toward a New Relational Ethics," trans. Drew S. Burk (French Ministry of Culture, 2018).

6 Claire Ducournau, *La fabrique des classiques africains: écrivains d'Afrique subsaharienne* (Paris: CNRS Éditions, 2017).

7 Anne-Marie Thiesse, *La fabrique de l'écrivain national: entre littérature et politique* (Paris: Gallimard, 2019).

8 Etienne Achille and Lydie Moudileno, *Mythologies postcoloniales. Pour une décolonisation du quotidien* (Paris: Éditions Champion, 2018); Mame-Fatou Niang, *Identités françaises: Banlieues, féminités et universalisme* (Leiden: Brill Rodopi, 2020).

9 See, for example, the work of the "*Observatoire du décolonialisme*" collective.

10 Benjamin, *Arcades*; Beatrice Hanssen, *Walter Benjamin and the Arcades Project*, Walter Benjamin Studies Series (London: Continuum, 2006); Susan Buck-Morss, *The Dialectics of Seeing: Walter Benjamin and the Arcades Project*, Studies in Contemporary German Social Thought (Cambridge, MA: MIT Press, 1989).

11 Dominic Thomas, *Black France: Colonialism, Immigration, and Transnationalism* (Bloomington, IN: Indiana University Press, 2007).

12 These terms are maintained in French as their cultural resonances defy easy translation. Approximate translations are as follows: *flâneur* (a wanderer or lounger, with connotation of leisure and idleness); *chômeur* (an unemployed person); *débrouillard* (a resourceful, wily person).

13 Ato Quayson, *Oxford Street, Accra: City Life and the Itineraries of Transnationalism* (Durham, NC: Duke University Press, 2014), 244.

14 Polo B. Moji, *Gender and the Spatiality of Blackness in Contemporary AfroFrench Narratives* (New York: Routledge, 2022). See also: Janet Wolff, "The Invisible

Flâneuse: Women and the Literature of Modernity," in *Feminine Sentences: Essays on Women and Culture* (Berkeley: University of California Press, 1990); Rita Felski, *The Gender of Modernity* (Cambridge, MA: Harvard University Press, 1995); Catherine Nesci, *Le flâneur et les flâneuses: Les femmes et la ville à l'époque romantique* (Grenoble: Ellug, 2007).

15 Susan Buck-Morss, "The Flaneur, the Sandwichman and the Whore: The Politics of Loitering," *New German Critique* 39 (Autumn 1986): 110.

16 Harvey, *Paris*, 15.

17 Charles Baudelaire, "Le Cygne," in *Les Fleurs du Mal*, Graham Chesters, ed. (London: Bristol Classical Press, 1995), 86–88. My translation.

18 On Baudelaire's gendered use of irony, contestation, and critique, see Debarati Sanyal, *The Violence of Modernity: Baudelaire, Irony, and the Politics of Form* (Baltimore, MD: Johns Hopkins University Press, 2006), 13.

19 Buck-Morss, "Politics of Loitering," 111.

20 Jason Weiss, *The Lights of Home. A Century of Latin American Writers in Paris* (New York: Routledge, 2003); Brent Hayes Edwards, *The Practice of Diaspora. Literature, Translation and the Rise of Black Internationalism* (Cambridge, MA: Harvard University Press, 2003).

21 Thomas, *Black France*; Bennetta Jules-Rosette, *Black Paris: The African Writers' Landscape* (Urbana, IL: University of Illinois Press, 2000).

22 Ní Loingsigh Aedín, *Postcolonial Eyes: Intercontinental Travel in Francophone African Literature* (Liverpool: Liverpool University Press, 2009).

23 Cheikh Hamidou Kane, *L'Aventure ambigüe* ([1961] Paris: Juillard, 2003), 10–18, 103; Kane, *Ambiguous Adventure*, trans. Katherine Woods (London: Heinemann, 1972), 91.

24 Kane, *L'Aventure*, 140; Kane, *Adventure*, 128.

25 Ibid.

26 Riesz, János, "L'intertexte des Cahiers de Malte Laurids Brigge de Rainer Maria Rilke dans L'Aventure ambiguë de Cheikh H. Kane: pour une compréhension désenclavée du roman africain," in Ibrahima Diagne and Hans-Jürgen Lüsebrink, eds., *L'Intertextualité dans les littératures sénégalaises: réseaux, réécritures, palimpsestes* (Paris: L'Harmattan, 2019) 33–55.

27 Kane, *L'Aventure*, 157; Kane, *Adventure*, 144.

28 Franco Moretti, "Conjectures on World Literature," *New Left Review* (Jan–Feb 2000): 54–68.

29 Pheng Cheah, *What Is a World? On Postcolonial Literature as World Literature* (Durham, NC: Duke University Press, 2016), 5 and 191.

30 Dipoko, *Few Nights*, 38.

31 Mbella Sonne Dipoko, *A Few Nights and Days* (Cambridge: Proquest LLC, 1970), 55.

32 Ibid., 18.

33 Ibid., 24.

34 Joyce Ashuntantang, *Landscaping Postcoloniality. The Dissemination of Cameroon Anglophone Literature* (Bamenda: Langaa Research & Publishing, 2009), 136.

35 Paul Theroux, cited in Dibussi Tande, "In Memoriam: Mbella Sonne Dipoko – The Bard Who Dared To Be Different," *Palapala Magazine*, www.dibussi.com/2009/12/in-memoriam-mbella-sonne-dipoko.html.
36 See, for example, Dipoko, *Few Nights*, 17 on sexual consent.
37 Ibid., 14.
38 Ibid., 126.
39 Ibid., 4.
40 Ibid., 47–48.
41 The English translation by Frank Wynne, *Standing Heavy*, was published in 2022 by MacLehose Press. All translations here are my own.
42 Gauz, *Debout payé* (Paris: Le Nouvel Attila, 2014), 55, 136.
43 Ibid., 123.
44 Ibid., 127.
45 Ibid., 189.
46 Ibid., 189–190.
47 Ibid., 173.
48 Ibid., 185.
49 Ibid., 196.
50 Ibid., 199.
51 Ibid., 201.

CHAPTER 8

Sketching the City with Words

Istanbul Through Time in Turkish Literary Texts

Hatice Aynur

A Treasury of Worldly Beauties

Geology and geography underpin the significance of Istanbul. The city straddles the boundary between the European and Asian tectonic plates, thus occupying a central location between Europe to the west and north, and the lands far beyond Anatolia to the north, east, and south. Istanbul has been a complex tapestry of interwoven themes for many centuries – a kaleidoscopic patchwork, a city of contrasts – and we are not lost for ways to explore the city and its denizens of times past. The rich, literary culture of the Ottomans, a tradition that carried through into the current, republican era, serves admirably as a temporal conveyance.

As far back as the tenth century, Konstantinos of Rhodes, a Byzantine poet, described then Constantinople as "the city the world desires." Equivalently, Geoffroi de Villehardouin (d. ca. 1213), a knight in the Crusades, wrote "for they never thought there could be in all the world so rich a city."[1] These are early examples of the unique role that Istanbul played in Western and later Arab and Ottoman-Turkish perceptions, an example of the Arab view of Istanbul expressed by al-Harawi (d. 1215), "Constantinople is a city even greater than its reputation."[2] People of those times reflected this role by representing Istanbul as somehow larger than life, with parallels in the great mythopoeic cities of world culture such as Rome, Jerusalem, Athens, Babylon, Troy, London, and Paris.

Until the 1520s many Ottoman texts describe the construction of Hagia Sophia, the City Wall, the Hippodrome, the district of Galata, and the beauty of the mosques as a whole urban experience.[3] These texts also characterize the affluent population, the flora, the city's topography, its palaces, the Turkish baths, the market, and the beauty of the buildings and architecture.[4] But the city has always been far more than simply a large and complex conurbation. Istanbul is a city of the mind, an imaginary space that spurred writers and poets to document it in Turkish literature[5] and in the Greek, Armenian, Arabic, Hebrew, Bulgarian, Serbian and Albanian languages[6] too. However, Ottoman-Turkish literature alone portrays the rich and heterogeneous imagery of Istanbul in a variety of genres, including poems, plays, chronicles, memoirs, and novels, and this chapter explores that literary tradition by means of selected works ranging from the Ottoman conquest of the city in 1453 to the early nineteenth century. It then looks beyond that time toward the growth of a burgeoning print culture which incorporated new literary forms such as novels, plays, and short stories.

Early Ottoman Writings on Istanbul

Our first work of interest is a treatise on *Risâle-i Evsâf-ı İstanbul* (The Qualities of Istanbul), which comprises a description of the natural beauty, historical buildings, and monuments of the city. It was initially written in 1524 by Ottoman bureaucrat and intellectual Latifi (d. 1582), who revised the work subsequently, adding a new introduction.[7] He presented the work to Murad III in 1574, and its subject and genre are unique. It conveys all the knowledge an educated Ottoman would have possessed about Istanbul in 1524, and his descriptions show Istanbul to be the capital of the empire, describing the way in which it turned into an Islamic city and hinting at a perception of Istanbul from the eyes of the author himself as well as his contemporaries.

Each subject the author narrates, and the points to which he draws attention, amount to a composition drawing on previous texts, themes, narratives, and perceptions. In fact, only Tahtakale and Tophane districts, which he describes in the sixth chapter, are absent from other, earlier texts, and this indicates how those areas became living spaces for Ottoman literates at a relatively later date.

A second example is a work by poet Zaifi (d. after 1557).[8] Written in 1543, in prosimetrum (a combination of prose and verse), the poem speaks of the district of Fatih along with Hagia Sophia, the harbor, Galata, Eyüp, an area known as Çekmece, and the Mehmed II Complex (a mosque, mausoleum, madrasa, hospice and hospital, soup kitchen, baths). The vocabulary he uses is common to other poetic works, and is full of metaphor, allusion, and imagery. Consider the following extract:

> Upon entering through the gates of the city, he saw wondrous palaces, rooftops reaching the sky and marvelous pavilions that stretched up from the ground to the highest point in the sky. There were bazaars everywhere, each shop possessing unique signage. The small shops exhibited gems such as

> garnets and rubies. In this crowded city of great darkness, where there is a treasure of valuable gems and a feast of various foods, where people from many different nationalities gather, in this capital city of fair sultans, there are seven hills.[9]

Zaifi principally emphasizes the city's richness, indicating the many shops, the abundance of valuable goods and gems in these shops, the fashionable and expensive clothing that people wore, the glory of the Mehmed II Complex, and the quality of the materials used. He also depicts the populace, in which there were four different sects and seventy-two spoken languages. Notably, on the one hand, Zaifi speaks of the diverse beauty of the city while, on the other, he complains about losing his father's inheritance when attempting to do business. This gives us an understanding of the experience of trying to conduct business in Istanbul prior to 1543. As indicated above, these literary works describe and imply the immense contrasts and contradictions to be found in Istanbul at that time; a city of dreams and yet a place too of poverty, loss, disillusionment, and defeat.

A third example, also from the 1500s, is a romance written by Fikri Çelebi, which conveys the perception of Hagia Sophia in the minds of the local population.[10] He also talks of the crowd in the mosques, the many domes and their height, the area of Yedikule (the Theodosius Walls area), the city walls, the towers, and the people guarding those towers. He describes the Topkapı Palace, the Hippodrome, the gardens in the square and the beautiful people who roamed these gardens; but in focusing on Hagia Sophia, he elevates its importance above all the mosques he has visited. Praising its architecture, he also explains the symbols attributed to this mosque in the era, stating "if a poor person cannot make pilgrimage to the Ka'ba [Mecca], he can come here and this will be accepted as his pilgrimage."[11]

The descriptions of Istanbul in Ottoman-Turkish literature were every bit as symbolic and metaphorical as they were evidential of the physical place itself. Indeed, these authors depicted the city as a place of longing and desire, disappointment and evil. That is, while the rich beauty and diversity of this place formed a backdrop for the equally rich and beautiful people of those times, with all the intrigue and power-games that accompany the ruling classes, such a backdrop also threw human failures and disappointments into sharp relief. Poets and writers who were unable to realize their expectations and desires took a critical perspective of the city, especially of its people, and a good example can be found in two poems by Gelibolulu Ali, who died in 1600.[12]

In the first poem, he speaks of Istanbul's populace – in colloquial parlance, these are "savvy" people – and calls Istanbul "the mother of the world."[13] As with other authors, Ali describes the richness of Istanbul – the ships at the harbor, the sense of joy, and the precious stones in the bazaar – but he also writes of a group of elite people among whom he enjoyed a favorable position:

In this city, savants, virtuous men, poets, there are many
In this city abundant with the virtuous and skilled, there are as many minds as the sea
As the world's sultan rides his horse and goes to the Friday prayer
The city becomes a source of beauty and life for those who know how to see
For the ships that depart from the Mediterranean and Black sea
Look to the harbour as the grandest haven
A flood of people can be seen from all the streets of the bazaar
Enthusiastic and lively is the city centre and its sea
Although the smart goldsmith said that here is the Kapalıçarşı [Grand Bazaar],
Flooded with an ocean of pearls, silver and precious gems.[14]

While we have yet to determine the year in which this work was penned, it is clear that the writer's expectations were fulfilled, yet in the second example (written in 1596) we find that Ali is unemployed and has become pessimistic. He had not received favorable responses to his applications for appointment, and so his words reflect a despondent state of mind. Ali uses a repetitive rhyme positively in conveying the affluence of Istanbul, but negatively in this later text, in which he speaks of famine, poverty, the plague, and other diseases. He also points out the absence of competent doctors in the hospitals to treat people; how cruelty brings tears; how there is no hope of justice for the common people:

Istanbul's wine feasts have remained empty and without hors d'oeuvres
As the sinners are plenty
The lack of food and goods killed all its people
Objects of all kinds are rare, but Istanbul's plague exists widely
[…]
It does not matter if you spend all your income on these people, it has no value, no gratefulness
Promises are lies in Istanbul, the ungrateful are numerous[15]

Veysi (d. 1627–28), a contemporary of Ali, also criticizes Istanbul's elites, addressing the people of Istanbul directly in the first verse of a poem later named by scribes as "Veysi's Qasida," where he admonishes that God could one day suddenly destroy them out of anger:

> Behold, the people of Istanbul, think deeply and you will see
> One day, unexpectedly you will be annihilated, as God is angry

In the seventeenth verse he says:

> The cruelty and evil of Istanbul has exceeded the limits
> For, I fear unexpected damnation is near[16]

In sixty-seven couplets, Veysi covers issues such as injustice in Istanbul, the ill will, the illiterate and incompetent leaders, bribery, and so on, reminding the people of Istanbul how the tribes of the past strayed onto the wrong path only to suffer God's wrath.

As we move forward through time, we should also consider at this point Evliya Çelebi (d. after 1687) who dedicated the first book of his unique ten-volume, *Seyahatname* (the Book of Travels) entirely to Istanbul.[17] He describes a multitude of urban elements such as the shops and guilds, the mosques, baths, and fountains, the villages on the shore of the Golden Horn, and the Bosphorus. Evliya's descriptions of Istanbul are detailed and thorough. In essence, he wrote an encyclopedia of Istanbul, and we can still see today, three centuries later, traces of the things he described. For example, Evliya wrote about the coffee shops in an area called Eminönü that would grind coffee for the entire city, and specifically a street called "Tahmis," which means "a place that sells roasted and ground coffee." Today, Kurukahveci Mehmet Efendi (also the name of a famous brand of coffee) is located on that very street, and has enjoyed long queues of customers since the 1800s.

Risale-i Garibe is a similar text that was probably written in the late seventeenth century, although the author's identity is unknown. This work presents a detailed panorama of the Istanbul of the period, some details of which only residents would have understood, and criticizes immigrants to the city and the *nouveau riche*. This allows us to deduce the behavior that was acceptable in the late-seventeenth-century urbanite, and the way in which the elites were expected to comport themselves in the Ottoman capital.[18] For example:

> [I]n Eyüp, during the Feast of Sacrifice, there are ravens tearing to pieces the meat distributed, those singers who learned melody from the gipsies of Eyüp, those who hope to cure from the Balat Jews, those who paint the internal surfaces of their boats with stars for lechery, those who get on the ferry from the Ahırkapı and smoke their tobacco before they pass the Sinan Paşa Mansion, the muleteers at the Çatladıkapı (the hooves of whose beasts of burden have been ruined by very heavy loads), the greengrocers at Kumkapı that wear cassocks closed up until their necks because they fear

> the superintendents, [....] the devil's clowns and town criers on behalf of those who have decided to marry, go first to Avratpazarı, then roam around Çukur Hamam and Hazret-i Ayyub four times in order to apprise people of the impending marriage and to invite them; they say "I invite you to the wedding: may the wedding be as crowded as the entertainment venues."[19]

From this quote we can glean information on various ways of behaving indecorously in the different quarters of Istanbul, although limitations of space restrict us to examining only a few here. First, although condemnation for greed was universal, only in Istanbul would a person be one of the "ravens" of Eyüp. Second, it is inappropriate to learn to sing a song from the "gipsies of Eyüp" and then to visit the Jewish doctors in Balat hoping for a cure – this shows that Istanbul was segregated religiously and ethnically. Third, do not light your pipe immediately on boarding a boat! (To do so was seen as a breach of etiquette.)

Along with these works, the poems of Nedim, who was killed during the Patrona Uprising in 1730 in Istanbul, hold a very special and important place in Turkish literature. His poetry portrays the entertainments in the palaces and gardens, the illuminated boats and fireworks, the tulips and musical instruments, and the joyous life of the upper classes, as well as the lives of the ordinary denizens of Istanbul.[20]

The following couplets are from his best-known eulogy of Istanbul, the image of Istanbul that it evoked having become part of the collective memory since the first Turkish poems, but with fresh, new expression. This elevates the poem above all other Istanbul-related poems in the canon:

Istanbul is a unique pearl between two seas
It would only be right to measure it with the sun that enlightens the earth

Istanbul is the centre of blessings in its essence
It is a garden of Irem (a garden in Heaven) of which the roses are fame, honour and noblesse[21]

We can see from Nedim's poems, and the works of contemporary and later poets, that they regarded Istanbul as the very center of poetry. Notably, however, the poet Ruhi, whose identity is uncertain but who hailed from Burgaz in modern-day Bulgaria, paints a different image.[22] Taking a ship southward to Istanbul via the Bosphorus, and thus approaching the city from the Black Sea, he lists the common features of the districts around the Bosphorus, from Rumelia to the Anatolian Lighthouse, which developed as residential areas in those years, and speaks of the beauty of the mosques and of preparations for wedding festivities. An educated Ottoman traveling from a rural area in the 1720s, Ruhi conveys how provincial travelers would have seen the city and notes the areas that tourists still favor in current times. Indeed, the images he renders reflect the admiration such travelers felt for the cityscape:

> Long time ago entered my heart
> The eagerness to desire Istanbul
> [...]
> It is such a city that beautifies one's heart, so elegant
> In the world there is nothing similar[23]

The View of Visitors

Moving from the views of native inhabitants of the city, we can also examine the perspective of travelers from the Arabian provinces of the Ottoman Empire in the late sixteenth and early seventeenth centuries, when the city had become their political and administrative capital. These travelers' Arabic texts – which comprise travelogues, short stories (*maqamas*), poetry, and letter exchanges relating to visiting the city for study, to arrange affairs, or to settle permanently – refer to natives of Istanbul as "Rumis."[24] Literary perceptions in these texts differed from those describing pre-1516 Ottoman Istanbul and pre-1453 Byzantine Constantinople, and different authors had their own views of the city.

An example is Badr al-Din al-Ghazzi (d. 1577) from Damascus, who visited Istanbul in 1530 in order to secure a scholarly position, which required him to approach court authorities. Ghazzi was interested primarily in the transformation and development that Istanbul underwent under Ottoman rule, and he particularly praised the building activities of Mehmed II the Conqueror (d. 1481). His description of Istanbul starts with a eulogy:

> The biggest city freed by the hand of justice from moral destruction. How often did an extraordinarily great king of the past court her and offer the choicest dowry? She guarded herself as rigorously as possible until the right one came, who was announced in a message that needed long interpretation: the late martyr Mehmed Khan. Her stubbornness dwindled so that she bowed her neck.[25]

Above all, Ghazzi was keen to meet colleagues in Istanbul, which he did on many occasions, and he points out that the city attracted many Muslim scholars, who were descended from the Arabs, the Rum, and the Adjam (Persians). In the meantime, Ghazzi's case stagnated for many months, partly because the administration was preoccupied by a great feast in celebration of the circumcision of the Sultan's son. This delay significantly affected Ghazzi's attitude toward Istanbul.

Consider now Muhammad Kibrit from Medina, who regarded himself as a literary expert. He sought a patron among the grandees of the capital in 1630, but their lack of taste and learning denied him traction, and he was unhappy about the many charlatans. He describes seeing people from Jerusalem, Damascus, and other places, whose "turbans like castles" and "sleeves like saddlebags" made it hard for potential patrons to discern the true intellectual. He also felt that his failure lay in his decision to come to the city, rather than in those who did not grant him support, seeing that the putative benefits of his visit were only transitive pleasures that time would eventually erase. For him, Istanbul was a "theatre where the devastating effects of time can be observed."[26]

These travel narratives confirm our leitmotif of Istanbul as a reflection of the observer's self or psyche. We should therefore regard these texts as documents of the self that cast personal observations and messages in the form of travel narratives. That is, while authors such as Kibrit took a pessimistic view, Sufis saw it as a place of moral temptation par excellence, while ambassadors were impressed by the imperial splendor of the Ottoman capital, riches that were unsurpassed in their era.

A Modern City – Modern Ottoman Literature

Moving from those earlier times to the beginning of the nineteenth century, we see that the vast changes that occurred in the Ottoman Empire during, essentially, its final hundred years greatly influenced the cultural and literary spectrum of Turkish literature.

From a hundred printing houses publishing Turkish literary works in the nineteenth century, seventy-four were located in Istanbul, and of the ten authors producing the most fiction in this period, eight were born in Istanbul.[27] These statistics show the central role that Istanbul played in the production of modern Ottoman literature, in both physical production (i.e. printing) and the production of themes and metaphors. Indeed, strong parallels lie between the formation of modern Ottoman literature and the evolution of modern Istanbul.[28]

As with authors past, the writers of this era documented new locations in the city, linking these to the spirit of the metropolis. Namık Kemal's (d. 1888) novel *İntibah* (*The Awakening*, 1876) presents the area of Çamlıca as a metaphor for passion in Istanbul – a locale where people gather and encounters intensify; as nature blooms in the spring in Çamlıca, so too do carnal thoughts: "Some of our gentlemen attempt to hit on the ladies they come across here and there."[29]

The most prolific writer of the late nineteenth century, Ahmed Midhat (d. 1913), depicts the city geographically as a conjunction of two continents and seas, and thus a point of encounter between people from various continents and regions – a universal exhibition of humanity. Midhat thus regards Istanbul as a valuable source for anthropology, as illustrated by the rendering of carnivals in his writing:

> The clothing and outfits create the impression of a perpetual state of carnival in our city. Carnival is here. The attendees are dressed flamboyantly, and the colours of every flag-waving nation can be seen in front of the ballrooms.[30]

Moving forward again to the cusp of the twentieth century, the poem "*Sis*" ("Fog," dated March 3, 1902) by Tevfik Fikret portrays the city in a markedly different fashion. The fog over the Bosphorus in Spring is famous, but Fikret uses it metaphorically to replace Istanbul as an object of aesthetic enjoyment with an Istanbul that is the embodiment of degradation. The clarity of Istanbul that is to be found in the city (as described by other authors) and which reveals its beauty before our eyes, disappears as the fog envelopes the metropolis. This blurs the boundaries of objects and landscapes, obscuring one's views, and the degradation represented by the fog is Istanbul's quintessence rather than a meteorological aspect (our leitmotif again). Behind apparent "splendour" and "pomposity" lie "tragedies," "deaths," and "injustices,"[31] which Fikret recounts through a series of potent, mysoginistic images of the city:

> Istanbul as an "untouched widowed woman of a thousand man", is like "the dirtiest women" who use their friendliness to deceive men; she is the "whore of the world", the prostitute of the universe. The theme of womanhood is intermingled with dirtiness and Istanbul is pure dirt: "Always filthiness of hypocrisy, filthiness of jealousy, and that of expediency".[32]

Moving forward, the degradation of Istanbul in the First World War was a topic of many novels such as Refik Halid Karay's (d. 1965) *İstanbul'un Bir Yüzü* (*One Side of Istanbul, 1920*) and Ercüment Ekrem Talu's (d. 1956) *Gün Batarken* (*At Dusk*, 1922), which geographically divides the Istanbul of the armistice period into two parts: the concentrated degradation in Beyoğlu contrasted with the location of dignity in the historical peninsula and fictitious neighborhood of Estekzade.

Istanbul in the Early Republican Era

Inevitably, we arrive at the dawn of the republican era, with its wealth of twentieth-century authors, and again our leitmotif is in plain sight. An example is Zeynep Uysal, who summarized matters in suggesting that a perception of the city as both an Elysian and a catastrophic place can be understood as a metaphor for the writer's inner world.[33] She explored the works of Yahya Kemal Beyatlı (d. 1958), Ahmet Hamdi Tanpınar (d. 1962), İlhan Berk (d. 2008), Sait Faik Abasıyanık (d. 1954), and the contemporary writer Orhan Pamuk (b. 1952).

In essence, and as we have seen in the works of earlier authors and poets, the issue is not what the city actually is but what the people perceive it to be. It seems, however, that Istanbul writers have transformed the city since the 1920s into an alien enemy, and this appears to be linked to the construction of a national identity catalyzed by the advent of the republican era – it seems that the new *locus amoenus*, the Elysian place, is now Ankara, which became the capital city of the newly established Republic of Turkey in 1923.[34]

The most striking example of the alienation of Istanbul, of its transformation into an object of hatred, is to be found in the novel *Sodom ve Gomore* [Sodom and Gomorrah] (1928) by Yakup Kadri Karaosmanoğlu (d. 1974).[35] He recounts the dirty, depraved, and degenerate Istanbul, telling a story of moral breakdown and compradors that evokes the principal motifs of the story of Sodom and Gomorrah from the Old Testament.

Another leading writer and poet, Ahmet Hamdi Tanpınar, stated:

> For our generation, Istanbul is now a very different place from that of our grandfathers, or even of our fathers. In our imagination, it does not appear swathed in silver and gold robes of honour, nor do we see it set in a religious framework. Rather, its name is illumined for us by the memories and longings evoked by our own spiritual state.[36]

Indeed, Orhan Pamuk believes that Tanpınar and his mentor and former teacher, Yahya Kemal, were drawn into a feeling of loss, sadness, and melancholy at the fringes of the city, and that this was with a political purpose. That is:

> They were picking their way through the ruins, looking for signs of a new Turkish state, a new Turkish nationalism: The Ottoman Empire might have fallen, but the Turkish people had made it great (like the state, the twowere happy to forget the Greeks, the Armenians, the Jews, the Kurds, and many other minorities), and they wanted to show that though suffused in melancholy they were still standing tall.[37]

Pamuk also suggests that Yahya Kemal and Tanpınar constructed their literary identities by searching for and discovering the beauty and features that would enable the past, gathered from the outskirts of the city of the present, to be brought back to life, with the aim of rendering a component of the new national identity.

Tanpınar argues in the "Istanbul" chapter of *Beş Şehir* (*Five Cities*) that the character of the city was changed completely by the transforming aspects of civilization and the loss of many aspects of its identity – the former music, community life, and habits disappeared. Instead, Tanpınar imagines another, new lifestyle rather than a revitalization of the past:

> I turned my eyes to the crowd around me: they, too, resembled the last remnants of a dream.
>
> No, Istanbul needs a new life, new festivals, new diversions, a new historical time. From now on, it is a city that earns its bread by the sweat of its brow, and everything must be arranged accordingly.[38]

As with Yahya Kemal, Tanpınar described the relationship he established with the city in his essays on Istanbul, but the intricacy and ambivalence of this relationship are best presented in his novel *Huzur* (*Tranquility*, 1949).[39] In a manner that is redolent of the works of centuries past, it presents numerous faces and aspects of Istanbul – the city appears before us as both a carrier of the culture, time, and history, and a representation of existence and being a fragmented subject; in both ways the individual incarnate.

İlhan Berk is another poet who describes the city viewed by Tanpınar's protagonist Mümtaz, who gathers memories from these scenes; however, he is much less an outsider than Tanpınar, and Berk's stance is distinct from that of Kemal and Tanpınar.[40] The latter two prefer to turn their gaze toward a "Turkifiying" Istanbul, as Pamuk emphasized, but there is no explicit focus on cosmopolitanism, disappearing cultures, or lifestyles, apart from the coverage of Muslim culture. In contrast, Berk views the areas of Galata and Pera – where he finds non-Muslim people living in poverty, a community of nomads, and homeless people – and Byzantium, rather than trace remains of the Ottomans.

Berk also depicts a "leaden" city in his early poems. The city that bears traces of the poet's socialist-realist approach is overcast and dark, much like the city's outskirts in Tanpınar's works, but Berk's place is not actually on the fringes of the metropolis.[41] Berk also differs from Tanpınar in that the latter draws the reader toward static places, such as a museum, whereas Berk's location has movement and vitality. It elicits a desire for power, which is a clear facet of the works of centuries past; witness the disappointment of Gelibolulu Ali in the late 1500s. Hunger, desolation, untidiness, loneliness, evil, hatred, disease, and captivity are agglomerated, one after the other in Berk's Istanbul, and the feeling that emanates from the poem is "leaden":

Now you are in Istanbul, the city of leaden domes
The rustle of running clouds in the air

[…]

This city is ready to die of lust, not love
City of young whores, dead sultans and diseased […] disgraceful Istanbul![42]

Note, however, that while Berk's poem pursues the lost and the forgotten, as did Kemal and Tanpınar, it seems that anger and irony shapes his writing, rather than the melancholy of the latter two poets.

Pamuk also suggests that four "melancholic writers" painted modern Istanbul as possessing a downcast, dispirited quality: Abdülhak Şinasi Hisar (the Bosphorus memoirist, d. 1963), Reşat Ekrem Koçu (writer of the unfinished *Istanbul Encyclopaedia*, d. 1975), Yahya Kemal (the greatest and most influential poet of Istanbul, who published his work throughout his life but refused to do so in book form), and Tanpınar. In Pamuk's opinion, they brought an awareness of the beginning of a new era for Turkey with the fall of the empire: "[T]hese four melancholic writers drew their strength from the tensions between the past and the present, or between what Westerners like to call East and West; they are the ones who taught me how to reconcile my love for modern art and western literature with the culture of the city in which I live."[43]

Sait Faik, famous for his stories, also writes of those at the city's edge, more perhaps of those lost and swallowed up in its chaos. However, with the gradual loss of hope and *joie de vivre*, his characters make one feel that Istanbul has now become a city that gives pain, in which it is impossible to live.

Faik's corpus of stories is composed of the moments, scenes, and the city's inhabitants; most of all, the ordinary people who are stuck within and oppressed by the city. The issues that matter to them influence the protagonists' entire perspective, and the *Lüzumsuz Adam* (Useless Man) story is a good example of the character's relationship with the city being one of panic and a search for refuge. Alluding to the serried ranks of buildings, the rows of people in this city pain the narrator, yet his small neighborhood represents shelter for him where he interacts with the same people without conflict.

Epilogue: Orhan Pamuk's Istanbul

Thus, from there, we must weave in and tie the final thread in the tapestry presented herein: Orhan Pamuk, born and raised in Istanbul, for whom the city forms an indispensable part in almost all his writings. An example is *Kara Kitap* (Black Book), which *casts* Istanbul as a unique literary hero, and was written long before his *Istanbul: Memories and the City*. He presents non-contiguous images of the city in *Istanbul*, ranging from the geographical to the autobiographical, learning, as he walks its streets, to read and rewrite the many facets of the metropolis.

Yet uncomfortable duplicities abound for him. Identification with Atatürk's Republic with Europe on the one hand and the deeply-rooted Ottoman past on the other causes Turks to live the characteristic East–West cultural blend while affiliating to neither. Orhan Pamuk sees "the grand polyglot, multicultural Istanbul of the imperial age"[44] as having descended to the state of a monochrome, monotonous, monolingual town, in which he wrestles with the questionable representations of European travelers and Turkish writers, and the context their views lend to his perception of things. The blackened ruins of old wooden mansions draw forth his view, as do the dark back streets and the conflagration of ships burning on the Bosphorus, yet "afternoons in spring when the sun suddenly comes out full strength"[45] repel him.

He also discusses extensively the work of writers who spent time in Istanbul, including French and Turkish authors, revealing the influence they had on him and his view of the city from childhood onward. His accounts of European visions of the city are also beautiful and fascinating – an account that takes in Flaubert, Nerval, and Gautier, along with Gide and Brodsky, and the works of natives such as Tanpınar and Kemal.

Istanbul as the cultural heart of the Ottoman Empire and Modern Turkey was always ten times larger than any other city in the Ottoman Empire and the Republic of Turkey. Yet Istanbul is not the only great city of the world that fiction, poetry, and the literary modes of old have documented and reflected to such extent. Many great cities have hosted a juxtaposition of stark contrasts or have enjoyed strong romantic associations, while others have been equivalent loci of cosmopolitan influences.

Nevertheless, there appears to be an element that transcends these comparisons when we look to Istanbul. Is it, perhaps, because Constantine's city became the center of the Ottoman Empire, or can we identify a much deeper theme in the works of Ottoman-Turkish authors down through time? It seems that a clue might be found in the strong association those works present between aspects of the city, be they municipal, geographical, or societal, and the way in which citizens and travelers viewed their lives. There appears to be an element of each author's psyche enfolded within the writings of Latifi and Zaifi, through those of Ali and Veysi, and thence to the works of Kibrit, Berk, and Pamuk. Their words suggest that, unlike with other great cities of the world, one's perception of Istanbul is rooted somewhere within one's soul.

Taking that as a guide, we can ask if this will always be true: will scribes of millennia to come present reflections for the reader that continue the reflections of the authors of the past? Moreover, Istanbul will inevitably continue to develop and evolve over time, so will authors of the future extend in kind these metaphors for the soul?

Notes

1 See Mustafa Avcı, "Istanbul of the Orientalists," *History of Istanbul from Antiquity to XXIst Century*, vol. 7, *Literature, Arts and Education*, https://istanbultarihi.ist/624-istanbul-of-the-orientalists. This article also provides information on the Orientalists' Istanbul.

2 Nadia Maria el-Cheikh, *Byzantium Viewed by the Arabs* (Cambridge, MA: Harvard Center of Middle Eastern Studies, 2004), 204. This book is a principal source for the Arabic-Islamic view of Byzantium Constantinople.

3 The Istanbul theme in indigenous writings and translated into Ottoman texts prior to the conquest are generally from Arabic sources. For the mythical lores about Istanbul in earlier Ottoman texts, see Stefanos Yerasimos, *La fondation de Constantinople et de Sainte-Sophie: dans les traditions turques* (Istanbul: Institut Français d'Études Anatoliennes d'Istanbul, 1990).

4 For literary representations of Istanbul for earlier texts, see Hatice Aynur, "Istanbul in Divan Poetry," in Markus Köhbach, Gisela Procházka-Eisl, and Claudia Römer, eds., *Acta Viennensia Ottomanica, Akten des 13. CIEPO-Symposiums (Comité International des Études Pré-Ottomanes et Ottomanes) vom 21. bis 25* (September 1998) (Vienna: Institute for Oriental Studies, 1999), 43–50.

5 See Hatice Aynur's article for main texts and authors/poets, and for secondary sources on perception and images, and the representation of Istanbul in Ottoman texts until the nineteenth century: "Portraying The City with Words: Istanbul in Ottoman Literary Texts," *History of Istanbul*, https://istanbultarihi.ist/609-potraying-the-city-with-words-istanbul-in-ottoman-literary-texts.

6 See Johann Strauss's well-summarized article regarding how Istanbul was represented in various alphabets in Turkish and various languages (Armenian, Greek, Hebrew, Bulgarian, Albanian and Serbian) in the Ottoman period: "Other Literatures in Ottoman Istanbul," *History of Istanbul*, https://istanbultarihi.ist/622-other-literatures-in-ottoman-istanbul.

7 Abdüllatif Çelebi Latifî, *Evsaf-ı İstanbul*, Nermin Suner, ed. (Istanbul: Istanbul Fetih Cemiyeti, 1977).

8 Vildan Serdaroğlu Coşkun, *Sergüzeştüm Güzel Hikâyetdür: Za'îfî'nin Sergüzeştnâme'si*, rev. 2nd ed. (Istanbul: İSAM, 2013).

9 Ibid., 176–177.

10 Ali Emre Özyıldırım, *Mâşî-zâde Fikrî Çelebi ve Ebkâr-ı Efkâr'ı: On Altıncı Yüzyıldan Sıradışı Bir Aşk Hikâyesi* (Istanbul: Dergah Yayınları, 2017).
11 Ibid., 378.
12 For Ali's life and works see Cornell H. Fleischer, *Bureaucrat and Intellectual in the Ottoman Empire: The Historian Mustafa Ali (1541–1600)* (Princeton, NJ: Princeton University, 1986).
13 Gelibolulu Mustafa Âlî, *Divan: İnceleme, Tenkitli Metin*, İ. Hakkı Aksoyak, ed. (Cambridge, MA: Harvard University, Department of Near Eastern Languages and Civilizations, 2006), vol. I, 309/couplet 1–2.
14 Ibid., 309/couplet 9–13.
15 Ibid., vol. III, 14–16.
16 For analysis of Veysi's poem, see Günay Kut, "Veysî'nin Divanında Bulunmayan Bir Kasidesi Üzerine," *Yazmalar Arasında: Eski Türk Edebiyatı Araştırmaları*, 1 (2005): 41–48.
17 For Evliya Çelebi and his *Book of Travels* see: Robert Dankoff, *An Ottoman Mentality: The World of Evliya Çelebi* (Leiden: E. J. Brill, 2004).
18 Saygın Salgırlı, "Manners and Identity in Late Seventeenth Century Istanbul," unpublished Masters thesis, Sabancı University (2003).
19 Hayati Develi, "İstanbula Dair Risale-i Garibe," *İstanbul Araştırmaları*, no. 1 (1997): 103–104, 117–18.
20 To track the changes and transformation in Istanbul in the eighteenth century, see Shrine Hamadeh, *The City's Pleasures: Istanbul in the Eighteenth Century* (Seattle, WA: University of Washington Press, 2008).
21 Muhsin Macit, ed. *Nedîm Divânı* (Ankara: Kültür Bakanlığı, 1992), 92.
22 Orhan Aydoğdu, "İstanbul Hakkında Bilinmeyen Bir Mesnevi: İstanbulnâme," *Turkish Studies* 4, no. 7 (2009): 158–186.
23 Ibid., 164.
24 See Ralf Elger, "Istanbul in Early Modern Muslim Arabic Literature," *History of Istanbul*, https://istanbultarihi.ist/626-istanbul-in-early-modern-muslim-arabic-literature; this is an excellent source of writing by travelers from Arabian provinces.
25 Ibid.
26 Ibid.
27 Günil Özlem Ayaydın Cebe, "19. Yüzyılda Osmanlı Toplumu ve Basılı Türkçe Edebiyat: Etkileşimler, Değişimler, Çeşitlilik," unpublished PhD. thesis, Bilkent University (2009), 300, 376.
28 This part of the chapter draws greatly from Fatih Altuğ's brilliant article, "Istanbul in Modern Ottoman Literature: 1870–1923," *History of Istanbul*, 2021, https://istanbultarihi.ist/611-istanbul-in-modern-ottoman-literature-1870-1923.
29 Namık Kemal, *İntibah*, Mehmet Emin Ağar, ed. (Istanbul: Enderun Kitabevi, 1996), 11.
30 Ibid.
31 Tevfik Fikret, "Sis," *Yeni Türk Edebiyatı Metinleri: Şiir (1860-1923)*, İnci Enginün and Zeynep Kerman, eds., (Istanbul: Dergah Yayınları, 2011), vol. I, couplet 5–6.

32 Ibid., 248, couplet 9, 12, 15. See Altuğ, "Istanbul in Modern Ottoman Literature."
33 This part of the chapter draws greatly on Zeynep Uysal's article, "Re-writing the City: Five Istanbuls from the Republican Era," *History of Istanbul*, https://istanbultarihi.ist/612-re-writing-the-city-five-istanbuls-from-the-republican-era.
34 Ibid.
35 Ibid.
36 Ahmet Hamdi Tanpınar, *Tanpınar's 'Five Cities'*, trans. Ruth Christie (London: Anthem Press, 2018), 117.
37 Orhan Pamuk, *İstanbul: Memories and the City*, trans. Maureen Freely (New York: First Vintage International Edition, 2006, e-book), 264.
38 Tanpınar, *Five Cities*, 131–132.
39 Uysal, "Re-writing the City."
40 Ibid.
41 Ibid.
42 Ibid.
43 Pamuk, *İstanbul: Memories*, 123.
44 Ibid., 403.
45 Ibid., 529.

CHAPTER 9

Romance and Liminal Space in the Twentieth-Century Cairo Novel

Noor Naga

In the study of world literature, Egypt, like many nations in the Global South, is often relegated to the category of the postcolonial, the Oriental, the marginal; that is to say, the binaries in which this inherently comparative discipline engages with the Egyptian canon is usually through either the perceived antagonism of East versus West or the perceived alliance of the South-to-South. What these methods often overlook is the potential centrality of Egypt in its own right, as the site of a long tradition of textual production, literary pioneering, and intellectual influence within the Arab world.[1] As many critics have pointed out, for most of the twentieth century, to speak of the Arabic novel was to speak of the Egyptian novel de facto. And to speak of the Egyptian novel often meant speaking – if not *of* Cairo then – from Cairo or through Cairo; even works that were set elsewhere in the country were often written from the vantage point of the capital. The first Arabic work of fiction to be considered a novel is generally agreed to be Muhammed Husayn Haykal's *Zaynab* (1914), which follows two braided plot lines: of Zaynab, the peasant girl, who is married to a man she doesn't love and dies of tuberculosis; and of Hamid, the landowner's son (and author's surrogate), who returns to the countryside from studying in the capital only to find himself rebuffed by both his cousin and Zaynab. Following several awkward and half-hearted attempts at courtship, the novel ends with his disappearance (suggesting suicide) shortly after he returns to Cairo.

In the novel, idyllic pastoral scenes in the countryside are contrasted with the soulless grind of Cairo, where Hamid spends his days trapped between four walls and buried in books. Ultimately his emotional unraveling is blamed on the European habits he acquired in the capital, of overphilosophizing love, which has placed him out of step with the marital traditions of the countryside. Throughout the novel, Cairo is positioned as central to the education, modernization, and acculturation of the bourgeoisie of his generation, but it is also responsible for Hamid's romantic despair and alienation from his fellow countrymen, symbolized by the *fellahin*. Despite being an educated landowner and international traveler (indeed *Zaynab* was written while the author studied in Paris), Haykal published under the pseudonym "Masri Fellah" ("An Egyptian Peasant")[2] in 1914, months shy of the First World War and five years before the 1919 uprisings against the British occupation of Egypt and Sudan. Fifteen years later, in the introduction to the third printing of the novel, he claims to have done so as a point of pride, to prove the beauty and capability of the average Egyptian. Haykal may very well have been the first to equate the *fellah* with an authentic, precolonial Egyptian character compared to the modern city dweller who is corrupted by contact with Europe – but it has since become a common trope.

Because the birth of the Egyptian novel came so late in the Arabic literary tradition and coincided so closely with the country's independence from the British, it is no surprise that questions of national identity and authenticity are an overlying preoccupation. What is perhaps surprising is the extent to which these questions are enacted in the arena of courtship and marriage. Because of how strictly the division between public and private space is maintained in Cairo – through social policing more than, or at least in addition to, actual law enforcement – romance has always been a fraught endeavor. Even today, to stroll along the Nile corniche at sunset or evening is enough to convince any newcomer that Cairo – with its population of over ten million – is a city of lovers. The sheer number of couples walking arm in arm or huddled together on a bench overlooking the water can only be explained with a plea to the overpopulation, rampant makeshift urbanization, and ruthless erosion of public space over the last several decades. This chapter will explore possibilities for desire through liminal spaces in a select survey of (mostly) twentieth-century Cairene novels: Tawfiq al-Hakim's *Return of the Spirit* (1933), Naguib Mahfouz's *Midaq Alley* (1947), Latifa al-Zayyat's *The Open Door* (1960), Enayat al-Zayyat's *Love and Silence* (1963), Gamal al-Ghitani's *The Zaafarani Files* (1976), Abdel Hakeem Qassem's *An Attempt to Get Out* (1987), and Alaa al-Aswany's *The Yacoubian Building* (2002).

On Balconies

Tawfiq al-Hakim's *Return of the Spirit* (1933) is many prototypes rolled into one: the political novel – insofar as it is a call to national unity and a celebration of the Egyptian spirit – ultimately culminating in the 1919 revolution against British occupation; the family novel insofar as the main characters are largely blood relatives in a single household; and a romance insofar as everyone involved is searching for love, with the novel ultimately ending in marriage. With the exception of a few chapters in the rural countryside and in Damanhour, the novel is predominantly set in the neighborhood of al-Sayyida Zaynab in Cairo. More specifically, it is set on 35 Salama Street where Muhsin, a wealthy provincial boy, has been sent by his parents to attend secondary school and live with his three uncles, his aunt and a servant, in a small apartment where they sleep five males to a room. Published during the peak of the 1930s "marriage crisis,"[3] there is a concerted effort here to align the family to the nation.

The central drama revolves around Saniya, the girl next door whom most of the men fall in love with, as does their rival and neighbor, Mustafa. Ultimately, it is Mustafa, the wealthy inheritor of a famous textile firm in al-Mahalla al-Kubra, who wins Saniya's heart – and disappoints Muhsin's aunt Zanuba, who had been trying to seduce Mustafa for nearly a year. Spatially speaking, what is most striking about the novel's depiction of Cairo is the closeness of the characters' range of mobility, the restrictedness, and even naïvety of their romantic fantasies. While the characters do occasionally venture out to different districts of the capital – to buy love charms from a sheikh in al-Muski, visit a dentist on Abd al-Aziz street, or attend university in Giza, for example – most of their time is spent squashed at home or at the coffeehouse across the street trying either to spy on their beloved or to attract his/her attention. One potential explanation for this cramped approach to space is al-Hakim's background in theater which lends even his prose an entertaining melodrama and humor (occasionally bordering on slapstick, as when a leg of goose is thrown out of a window)[4] that has been much commented on.

A romance set in a culture where public space is so limited and so drastically segregated by gender poses an artistic challenge for any author – especially if the love lines are going to become triangular or quadrangular. Where can all these couples meet? If the encounter is going to be plausible, the answer in many twentieth-century Cairene novels has been *liminal space.* In order to preserve the prestige of their heroines in particular, balconies (and to a lesser extent rooftops) where the rules of social presentation can be innocently bent become crucial arenas for the accidental display of female beauty. In *Return of the Spirit,* they perform a double function: first, allowing women who would otherwise be publicly shrouded in a *melaya laff* (wrap sheet) and face veil in 1918 to appear in more revealing attire since they are technically at home – though also above street level, elevated from the masses as if on stage. Here they can be visible safely on their own turf, without the supervision of family members or servants, and ostensibly unaware of the strangers' gaze. Second, balconies provide a vantage point from which these women can also evaluate potential suitors and initiate contact. Not all pedestrians are equal from above. The balcony is a place for women to exercise romantic agency by choosing when, how, and before whom to appear.

In *Return of the Spirit*, Saniya's balcony is in the old Islamic style of a *mashrabiya*, with oriole windows enclosed by wooden latticework, which residents could open if they wanted to be visible to the street – while the building next door where Mustafa lives features more European, open balconies. Across from 35 Salama Street is the *ahwa* in which men from the neighborhood (and some less reputable women) idle away the hours of the day and have little to entertain them save glimpses from the private theater of the residences. Muhsin's forty-year-old aunt Zanuba and his seventeen-year-old neighbor Saniya seize every opportunity for exhibitionism, preparing to appear on their respective balconies as if at a soiree in dazzling dresses, noisily banging open the windows to announce themselves.[5] Of course, from this point of elevation the women are also in a strategic position to observe the men below, who preen and perform in their own fashion, ordering drinks loudly and twirling their waxed moustaches, often to comical effect. In the theater of desire, the balcony is equally for actors and audience.

When after weeks of trying to catch Mustafa's eye from her balcony, Saniya eventually succeeds, he smiles, and this is enough to confirm their place as the novel's darlings. Zanuba, who had been spying on both of them from between the gaps of her own closed shutters, throws a tantrum and sends an anonymous letter to Saniya's father claiming that "letters and signals pass nonstop between the balcony and the coffeehouse" in an attempt to besmirch her rival.[6] Though an exaggeration, her charge is indicative of the balcony's potential as a medium for courtship and/or licentiousness. In the novel, real love letters are routinely intercepted by family members, and even when they reach their intended recipient, there is often some deception or confusion about who has penned them. Banned from opening her own balcony windows now that suspicions have been raised about her and Mustafa, Saniya conveniently discovers that, although they each live in adjacent buildings, his own balcony, which had been hitherto neglected, is immediately across from her bedroom window. Thus their affair continues to develop through midnight rendezvous across the gap between their buildings.

While the balcony was once integral for facilitating chance encounters between strangers across the public–private divide, it has since become a laden architectural trope in the Egyptian imaginary due to its popularity as a suicide method – and cover-up for murder.[7] As Egyptian architecture moved away from the traditional Islamic *mashrabiya* to the modern European-style balconies that were open to the sky and street, it has become common to hear of people – women in particular – jumping off them. "The house I remembered was very high with wide wooden balconies. My mother jumped from one of those balconies, landing on the one below," wrote Sonallah Ibrahim in his novel *That Smell* (1966), which may be the very first fictional account of an attempted suicide by balcony in the Egyptian novel.[8] The indifference with which Ibrahim's Camusian protagonist recounts the episode indicates, among other things, its commonness in Cairo even at the time. In 1977, during the funeral procession of Abdel Halim Hafez – the heartthrob and famous singer of romantic and nationalist songs – there were many documented cases of women committing suicide – at least four of them by jumping from their balconies. After suffering clinical depression and schizophrenia, and surviving several suicide attempts, the communist and feminist poet Arwa Saleh jumped to her death from her tenth-floor balcony in 1997. Several months previously she had published a memoir of her experience in the student movement of the 1970s, *The Premature*, which has since become a cult classic. Her death has been fictionalized in numerous Cairene novels including Ahdaf Soueif's, *The Map of Love* (1999), Radwa Ashour's *Release* (2008), and Youssef Rakha's *The Crocodiles* (2013).

In a culture that is both highly circumspect about romantic desire and overprotective of its women, the literary trope of love at first sight – through a window frame, across a rooftop, or over the wall of a balcony – is even evident in feminist novels of the 1960s, many of which are even more claustrophobic than *Return of the Spirit*. Their female protagonists are often naïve and homebound, permitted limited outdoor excursions in which they are often also chaperoned or surveilled by male figures in their lives – brothers and fathers and cousins and drivers. If they do venture into society, it is often through the legitimatizing pursuit of education or work, and rarely with the same freedom of movement enjoyed by male characters. In contrast, their love interests are often activists or revolutionaries who demonstrate on the streets, fight in the Egyptian army, or publish political writing that lands them in prison. As a consequence of this claustrophobia, there is often an incestuous quality to the romance, wherein the heroine is pursued by virtue of proximity to neighbors and relatives, and suffers an acute myopia when it comes to imagining other romantic possibilities.

Perhaps the most celebrated of these novels is Latifa al-Zayyat's *The Open Door* (1960), which follows the coming of age of the middle-class protagonist Layla over a period of ten years, as she navigates the advances of various men, including her cousin Isam whose family lives on the floor above, her philosophy professor, and her brother's friend Hussein in the army, with whom she eventually elopes. In this novel, it is the roof of the building, rather than Layla's balcony, which is the liminal space most accessible to her and which witnesses many of the novel's pivotal scenes of romantic and marital engagement. In her essay "About 'The Open Door,'" the novel's translator, Marilyn Booth, contemplates the extent to which this trope is autobiographically inspired. She describes the rooftops of al-Zayyat's childhood homes in the Delta as "sites of desire, refuges, places of imagined freedom from the constraints of a socialized existence."[9] The novel opens up on February 21, 1946, a day of anti-British demonstrations, and ends with the Suez Crisis of 1956, during which the statue of Ferdinand de Lesseps was demolished by angry mobs in Port Said. Throughout these ten years, political events reach Layla exclusively through the reports of the men around her. In one of the rare scenes in which she participates in a student demonstration, she does so by accident, after being swept up by the crowd around her and "[finding] herself in the street." Despite the innocence and involuntariness of her political involvement, "she kept moving forward but she felt the eyes follow her with unabated pressure, as if they were aimed at the back of her neck."[10] This, of course, turns out to be her father, coincidentally on the street at that moment (there are many such coincidences in the novel), and results in a violent beating at home.

In a novel that is meant to be a political and feminist bildungsroman, Latifa al-Zayyat deals with this spatial confinement and political passivity by treating Layla as a surrogate for the capital. The fact that Cairo (*al-Qahira*) and Egypt (*Misr*) are both feminine nouns in Arabic (and *al-Qahira* is even colloquially called *Misr*) facilitates this interchangeability, as evident in the scene from *The Open Door* which depicts the Cairo Fire of January 26, 1952 when over 700 buildings downtown were destroyed in a series of anti-British riots. Predictably, news of the fire reaches Layla at home through her brother, rather than through any immediate experience, and the timing coincides with a personal blow: the discovery that her cousin Isam, who lives upstairs and who she'd been in a secret relationship with for months, has been sleeping with the maid. "The word 'betrayal' torched through Layla's ears. Fire – it enveloped the city, choked the city! Fire, choking her! She jumped to her feet and tore from the room, from the apartment, out, onto the stairs – up, up to the fire."[11] The ambiguity of the pronouns in this excerpt creates a parallel between Layla's pain and the capital, a common pathetic fallacy that plagues many mid-century Egyptian narratives.

Another feminist novel set in Cairo that is often spoken of in the same breath as *The Open Door* – due to the similarity in themes and the shared last name of the authors which mistakenly suggests blood relation – is *al-Hob wal-samt* (*Love and Silence*) by Enayat al-Zayyat. This novel, which was published posthumously in 1967, four years after the suicide of its author, was popularized by Iman Mersal's 2019 work *Fi athar Enayat al-Zayyat* (*In the Wake of Enayat al-Zayyat*). If the middle-class protagonist Layla from *The Open Door* was sheltered and naïve, Naglaa – the wealthy French-educated protagonist of *Love and Silence* – is practically infantilized. Unlike the apartments where the characters from *The Open Door* or *Return of the Spirit* reside, Naglaa's family owns a suburban villa with a private garden. But even in this more expansive residence, Naglaa's existence is reduced to a particular corner of her bedroom where she often sits alone looking out the window or finding society in the furniture. "Between me and these objects are bonds of friendship and love, more so than between my father or mother," she says of her possessions. "I miss them when I'm away, for they often chatter their stories at me. We are friends and they speak to me in their language – the language of things."[12] Where Layla at least had school friends and entertained a string of potential suitors, Naglaa is far less socially dynamic, having just one best friend and one love interest (and one sibling whose death is announced on the very first page). The combination of her acute loneliness, boredom, and grief culminates in an existential crisis that is heavily gendered.

Naglaa does eventually find ways to leave home unchaperoned. After campaigning for her father's permission, she secures a job working at a newspaper which allows her some financial independence. Her forays into the city are accompanied by an acute body-awareness and discomfort, however. She often feels that her femininity outs her in public spaces, announcing her presence too loudly to the men on the street.[13] "If only I could be decomposed into invisible atoms with freedom of movement," she complains, elsewhere wishing she were a cloud or a spring breeze, or a drop of river water.[14] She intentionally chooses clothes in dull, faded colors so as not to attract attention, and strives to blend in as much as possible. Despite this, at the newspaper she meets the activist-writer Ahmed Ibrahim, with whom she falls in love. As the poor son of a *fellah*, he is quickly positioned as a political authority and revolutionary idealist, compared to the French-educated, landowning, city-dwelling Naglaa, who is so oblivious, he calls her a "tourist" and a "criminal" for being uninterested in the plight of her 22 million compatriots.[15] He begins to accompany her on dates, which quickly become crash courses in the rising grievances of the working class against the nation's elite – including the monarchy whose incompetence, greed, corruption, and sycophancy toward the British had resulted in a crackdown against dissenters, in the form of censorship and political persecution. Once again, our jejune heroine is entirely reliant on her male lover to guide her – physically and ideologically – out of her private world and into the stratified streets of a Cairo on the brink of transformation. Like *Return of the Spirit* and *The Open Door*, *Love and Silence* ends on the deus ex machina of another uprising – the revolution of 1952, which reaches Naglaa over the wall of her villa garden, via the calls of newspaper sellers, after the death of her lover.

On the Hara

As the critic Hassan Youssef charmingly puts it, "most of Naguib Mahfouz's literary works are set in Cairo, in the old city specifically, in the Gamaliyya neighborhood even more specifically – in the alley to be exact."[16] Indeed, if there is any single chronotope that has dominated Cairene literature, it's the *hara*[17] as imagined by Mahfouz, over a career that spans seven decades and thirty-five novels. Mahfouz was born on December 11, 1911 in the *hara* of Darb Qirmiz in the Gamaliyya quarter of Old Cairo. The first novels of his realist period are set explicitly in Gamaliyya, including notable works such as his *Midaq Alley* (1947)[18] and his magnum opus, *The Cairo Trilogy* (1956–57). Even his later works such as *Children of the Alley* (1959) (sometimes titled *Children of Gebelawi* in translation) are clearly evocative of the neighborhood where Mahfouz spent his first twelve years of life. The Gamaliyya district was first settled after the Fatimid invasion of AD 969 and became the heart of the Fatimid dynasty when, four years later, the fourth caliph al-Muizz li-Din Allah moved into one of two palace complexes there.[19] The Fatimids founded Cairo as the capital of their dynasty, naming it *Qahirat al-Muizz* ("*al-Muizz*'s Victory") or simply, al-Qahira, from which we get the modern name, Cairo. Gamaliyya has seen many conquerors since, including the Ayyubids, the Ottomans, and the Mamluks, whose architecture is most visible in the present day. It remains the largest concentration of Islamic monuments in the world, and, in terms of Cairene novels, you couldn't hope for a more central setting or one with such historical pizzazz.

"My nostalgia for the alley is a nostalgia for authenticity," Mahfouz tells Gamal al-Ghitani, a fellow writer and resident of the Gamaliyya quarter in *Naguib Mahfouz yatathakkar* (*Naguib Mahfouz Remembers*, 1980).[20] He describes the alleys of his childhood as being extremely diverse, containing all levels of Egyptian society from the wealthiest patrons to the poorest peddlers – a reality that was no longer the case by the time al-Ghitani was born in 1945.[21] According to Mahfouz, the 1930s saw an exodus of upper- and middle-class residents from Gamaliyya to newer developments in Abbasiyya, which left the alleys to gain new associations of poverty, seediness, and repression – a metamorphoses that he dramatizes in *The Cairo Trilogy* which is set between 1917 and 1944. Despite these negative connotations, the mid-century alley is also often associated with tradition and old-world values. Like the mythology surrounding the countryside, it is often described as outside of time, sheltered from the march of modernity and Western contact and encapsulating a quintessentially Egyptian experience. As many critics have argued, Mahfouz treats the *hara* as a microcosm of Cairo – a small stage on which to represent the larger social, political, and ideological debates of the moment. "Although Midaq Alley lives in almost complete isolation from all surrounding activity, it clamors with a distinctive and personal life of its own. Fundamentally and basically, its roots connect with life as a whole and yet, at the same time, it retains a number of the secrets of a world now past," wrote Mahfouz on the opening page of *Midaq Alley* (1947).[22] This novel, which is set during the Second World War, when Cairo was teaming with 140,000 allied soldiers, subjects the sleepy, dead-end alley in Gamaliyya to a wave of colonial modernity that threatens to destroy those who cannot adapt fast enough to it.

The novel begins in Kirsha's café with the entrance of an elderly poet who had entertained the customers of the café with his recitations for twenty years. On this particular night, however, Kirsha is having a radio installed that will effectively replace him, and we learn that this café in Midaq Alley represents the last source of the poet's livelihood since all others had already discontinued his services. "Everything has changed!" Kirsha insists angrily when the old man attempts to defend the eternal appeal of his craft, and shortly afterwards, the poet leaves the café and the pages of the novel for good.[23] This is only the beginning of a series of literal and metaphorical character deaths, including Sheikh Darwish's demotion as a teacher and his subsequent mental breakdown in the face of reforms to the education system, and ending with the murder of Abbas – the *hara*'s greatest advocate and lover – at the hands of British soldiers. The only ones in the alley who profit are those who lean into various trades of the flesh: Hamida, the novel's vain orphan heroine, who dreams of material wealth to pull her out of the wretchedness of the alley and ultimately ends up prostituting herself to the British soldiers; Hussein Kirsha, who similarly despises the alley and attempts to get out by working in a British Army

Camp; Umm Hamida, the alley's matchmaker who successfully sells her wealthy fifty-year-old landlady to a man nearly half her age for a lifetime of rent exemption; Zaita, who cripples healthy men for a living to make them more successful beggars on the street; and Dr. Booshy, the quack dentist who, with the aid of Zaita, fills his patients' mouths with teeth stolen from corpses. The onslaught of colonial modernity forces every resident of the *hara* to make ideological choices with polarizing financial consequences, all of which are revealed by the end of the novel.

One quality that stands out in Mahfouz's treatment of the mid-century *hara* is the entanglement and interdependence of its residents – most of whom are too poor to practice the gender segregation of previous generations or higher classes. "The passage of the harah is not thought of as a street," wrote the anthropologist Nawal El Messiri Nadim, who in 1973 conducted her field research in Sokkareya, the titular alley for Mahfouz's *Sugar Street* in al-Darb al-Ahmar, a neighboring district to Gamaliyya; "it is an extension of the house and forms an integral part of the home."[24] Through observing the relations between the sexes in this working-class community, Nadim argues that the alley is private domain: it was acceptable for men to wear pajamas and women their house *gala-beyyas* within the alley, but when leaving it they changed into their outdoor clothes (for the women this often still meant wearing a *melaya laff* in 1973).[25] The high density of residents living in extremely close proximity and without enough indoor space meant that latrines were often shared, and many activities such as cooking and washing clothes had to take place in doorways and stairwells or in the space of the alley itself. Privacy was simply not possible.

"Here, if you wear rags it makes no difference for people know who you are," an elderly woman of Sokkareya explained to Nadim.[26] A success or scandal in one family was a communal event, exactly like a wedding or funeral, and in such cases the moral standing of the individual was measured directly by the rate of attendance and involvement from the *hara* as a whole. The pressure of communal judgment was exacerbated by the interdependence of the residents on each other. Failure to meet the demands of a *gamia*, an informal money lending system, for example, meant the individual could no longer be trusted by anyone in the *hara*.[27] Similarly, when the trousseau of a bride appeared, it would be ceremoniously carried in under the watchful eyes of the neighbors who considered it their duty to monitor the value of goods, ensuring her family had done right by her.[28] In the absence of police interference, the community was responsible for resolving conflicts between even residents of the same household.

A woman could ask for the intercession of the *hara* if her husband was stingy with her allowance, for example. In contrast, if the husband was generous or the family was prospering, this could be easily measured by the frequency of animals slaughtered in plain sight and prepared for the family meals.

In such a high surveillance space as the *hara*, there are no secrets – particularly none of a sexual or romantic nature. Everyone in Midaq Alley is aware of Kirsha's hashish addiction and homosexual activities, as well as the fact that his youngest daughter had eloped with a man from Bulaq and ended up in prison. They discover that Husniyya beats her husband Jaada with a slipper and that Salim Alwan's "bowl of cooked green wheat, mixed with pieces of pigeon meat and ground nutmeg" which he has for lunch every day is an aphrodisiac.[29] "Ask anyone in Midaq Alley, they all know," Abbas tells Hamida about the sincerity of his love for her, using the collective knowledge of the *hara* as a point of persuasion – a tactic that would have been disastrous in other middle- or upper-class urban settings.[30] By the end of the novel, even Zaita and Dr. Booshy's grave-robbing schemes have been exposed. Many critics have pointed out the role of gossip as both a punitive measure to enforce the social values of the alley and an oral archive for the dramas of a marginalized community who are otherwise overlooked in the grander political narratives of the time. Indeed the notorious gossip, Umm Hamida, is described as both a "herald and a historian of bad news," but her position as a busybody makes her a valuable matchmaker in the community.[31] Mahfouz's privileging of interpersonal, largely intersexual, "news" over national and global events is just one of the ways he argues for the *hara* as a metaphor.

On the Rooftop

Since Mahfouz popularized the use of the *hara* as microcosm for Cairene society, many writers have adapted the trope to various ends. As Yasmin Ramadan argues, Gamal al-Ghitani diverges from Mahfouz in making the alley a fantastic space in his novel *The Zaafarani Files* (1976) (in Arabic: *Events from the Zaafarani Alley*).[32] Al-Ghitani, who lived in Gamaliyya from 1945 to the 1970s, long after the Egyptian alley had become a space of smothering closeness and squalor, depicts the extraordinary events that besiege the inhabitants of the fictional Zaafarani alley when one resident, Sheikh Atiya, curses its men with impotence. There is an attempt to portray this alley in Gamaliyya as point zero for a global sexual epidemic fueled by the esoteric extremist ideologies that the sheikh puts forth in his vaguely political and expanding manifesto – thus making the alley a center not only of Cairo or Egypt but of the world. Al-Ghitani begins with the familiar only to quickly transform the alley into a space that is not only mystical but tyrannically and senselessly so. Samia Mehrez, the renowned scholar of literary Cairo, has argued that other fictional spins on the *hara* have included its vertical reimagining as a *imara*, or apartment building, as in Sonallah Ibrahim's *Zaat* (1992), Alaa al-Aswany's blockbuster *The Yacoubian Building* (2002), or Mohammed Tawfiq's *Murder in the Tower of Happiness* (2003). She argues that, as Cairo underwent the rapid physical expansion and spontaneous urbanization of the 1960s and 1970s, the use of the *hara* as a metaphor for the city or nation gradually became replaced by the *imara* which, "reflects the deconstruction of these relations at the economic and social levels" and more accurately represents the capital's new character of fragmentation.[33]

The Yacoubian Building describes these transformations on the titular building's usage from its first construction downtown in the mid-1930s as a luxury residence for "ministers, land-owning bashas, foreign manufacturers, and two Jewish millionaires"[34] to its co-optation by officers of various ranks after the revolution of 1952, which resulted in an exodus of Jews and foreigners from Egypt. Al-Aswany describes how the officers' wives began to use the small iron storage rooms on the building roof – one of which was assigned to each apartment – to house stewards, cooks, and maids, or to raise animals. Anwar Sadat's Open Door policies in the 1970s brought yet another wave of new occupants to the building – and more crucially to the rooms on the rooftop which were now rented out cheaply to working-class families:

> The final outcome was the growth of a new community on the roof that was entirely independent of the rest of the building. Some of the newcomers rented two rooms next to one another and made a small residence out of them with all utilities (latrine and washroom), while others, the poorest, collaborated to create a shared latrine for every three or four rooms, the roof community thus coming to resemble any other popular community in Egypt. The children run around all over the roof barefoot and half naked and the women spend the day cooking, holding gossip sessions in the sun, and, frequently, quarreling.[35]

The congregation of this working-class community in crowded rooms that are each 2 m^2, forcing them to share much of the remaining rooftop space, is reminiscent of the mid-century *hara*'s spatial conditions. Even after the official occupants of the building have accepted this makeshift neighborhood on their rooftop, it remains a contested space subject to its own policing, as evidenced when the Christian shirt-maker Malak tries to rent a room for commercial purposes. "Listen, sonny boy," says the thuggish driver, Ali after he has seen Malak's rental contract, "This roof is for respectable folk. You can't just turn up here in your own sweet time and open a shop, with workers and customers looking at the ladies going in and out."[36] Even in such close quarters, there are rules of propriety and male–female relations that its residents defend vigorously, even though sex "in which the people of the roof revel" is a pleasure they discuss openly and frankly.[37] Meanwhile, the proximity of much wealthier residents on the floors below allows for a cast of novel characters that is much more demographically diverse and socially representative – in many ways much closer to Mahfouz's *hara* at the turn of the century.

Another novel that explores more intimately the experience of one rooftop resident is Abdel Hakim Qasem's *Muhawala lil-khuruj* (*An Attempt to Get Out*, 1980), set in 1966 Cairo, at a time when rapid overpopulation, urbanization, and unemployment meant the promise of Gamal Abdel Nasser's socialist policies could no longer be economically sustained. This, combined with extreme restrictions on travel and migration, left many Egyptian youths feeling trapped. Hakim, the protagonist and narrator, is a prime example of this, along with his brother and his best friend Salah. As an unemployed Europhile from a small village near the city of Tanta, roughly 90 km north of Cairo, Hakim harbors escapist fantasies that are thwarted at every turn by his poverty and provincialism. In Tanta, he and Salah called the cafés by the names of capital cities around the world, so they could phone each other up and say glamorously, "I'll be waiting for you in Paris."[38] They kept up torturous correspondences with all kinds of European women they'd never met, exchanging photos, letters, and postcards, staying up all night with the dictionary in hand, begging these women to visit Egypt, which none of them ever did.[39] When Hakim moves to Cairo, he ends up renting a single room on the rooftop of a building downtown, which he shares with his brother who financially supports them both. This same brother, it should be noted, was denied a scholarship abroad after refusing to take the physical examination out of shame at the state of his underclothes, which he would have had to expose.[40]

Predictably, the Cairo of *An Attempt to Get Out* is brutal at best, but becomes only more dystopic as the novel progresses. The novel opens with the exhilarating news that Hakim will be introduced by his French tutor to a group of Swiss tourists visiting Egypt for a week – an opportunity Hakim lunges at. He accompanies them on a bus ride to the Saqqara necropolis, where he becomes enchanted by the aloof, smoking Elsbeth, whom he invites to visit his own village even before he has learned her name. "We're poor, backwards [...] but you'll find it nice. Egypt isn't Cairo, it's the countryside," he tells her, in an appeal to the centrality and national authenticity of the *fellahin* – himself included.[41] From the beginning, Elsbeth's disparaging comments about the poverty, squalor, and filth around her cause these qualities to become highlighted for Hakim in a way that he feels equally ashamed by and responsible for explaining. "I looked where she was looking," he says, "The houses were crowded together, dilapidated and disgusting. The people were sick, working diligently like an army of ants. I felt embarrassed and degraded."[42] In the face of Elsbeth's ignorance, racism, and elitism, he alternates between apology and defensiveness, all the while lusting after her and the access she represents to a world beyond the confines of the Egyptian border.

In an attempt to impress her, he takes on the role of an unpaid tour guide, accompanying her to the bustling market of al-Moski, al-Hussein Mosque, the Delta Barrage, and even his village where the simplicity and hospitality of people touches Elsbeth and endears him to her. Upon their return, however, Cairo, which they felt to be suffocating before they left, grows more nightmarishly so as they attempt to find ways to be alone. The fact that she shares a hotel room with her sister and he shares a permanent room with his brother means they are forced to find creative solutions for privacy in public or semi-public spaces – an experience that will be familiar to Egyptian lovers across the generations. Even today in the capital, which is far less conservative than smaller cities or the countryside, living alone and unmarried away from one's family is uncommon and suspect behavior. The city is crawling with surveillance. Officers, government informers, security guards, and ordinary laymen practice social policing on an informal basis, as when a taxi driver who takes them to the Nile Casino suspects that Elsbeth may be a prostitute, and threatens to abandon them in the middle of the road. Although generally protected by her foreignness and wealth, Elsbeth is in the company of a man who is obviously poor and provincial, and Cairo is a city that has always punished these qualities.

On their final night, they try to take a boat ride together but the boatman is watching them. They attempt to kiss under the darkness of a tree on the corniche, but hear the boots of strangers approaching, so that they are forced to spring apart, at which point even Elsbeth becomes frustrated. "My God, horrible. I've never seen a city like this," she remarks, "Eyes, eyes, in every corner. They stare at you. They never leave you alone."[43] They go up the Cairo Tower for a last glimpse of the city, but even here on the balcony that wraps around the observation deck, an employee leaps from the shadows to make his presence known. In a desperate last attempt, Hakim takes Elsbeth up to his room on the rooftop which he had elsewhere described as "a real hell, white-walled, without windows, and only missing a green bee buzzing in the silence to make it a real grave."[44] But even here they have no privacy since the roof is full of other tenants they can hear moving threateningly just outside the door. They sit nervously in the cramped space which contains two beds and a single chair before ultimately leaving without fulfilling their desire, at which point Elsbeth becomes almost mad with exasperation. She asks him repeatedly why he stays in this country, as though it were a prison of his own making that he could walk out of any time. "It's my country, Elsbeth," he says weakly, to which she replies, "It's horrible, this country of yours. Horrible."[45] Soon after, she is gone.

Conclusion

Much has changed since Muhammed Husayn Haykal's depiction of Cairo as a corrupting force on the character of the "authentic" *fellah*, at least insofar as the Egyptian novel has come to value a form of urban nationalism that did not previously exist. In the canon – as in the capital – however, liminal space remains prime real estate in the economy of desire. For those in Cairo who are unwilling or unable to marry at a conventional age, traditional values and familial structures, combined with a culture of surveillance and patriarchy, create a thorny romantic landscape. All of this is exacerbated by neoliberal policies that stretch the preexistent wealth gap, as well as the increased privatization, militarization, and monetization of public space. Today there is hardly a patch of grass that doesn't require an entrance fee, and the result is a truly desperate and predatory relationship between citizens and the city – particularly if they are looking for intimacy. While the earliest Egyptian novels were marked by innocence, sentimentality, and patriotic fervor, often set retrospectively on the precipice of some national uprising, fiction of the last two decades has been far less idealistic.

Rather than gazing backward at moments of political triumph, many writers today are following the trajectory of the capital into darker and more defeatist futures. The twenty-first century has ushered in a wave of dystopic fiction, most notably Ahmed Khaled Towfik's *Utopia* (2008), Mohamed Rabie's *Otared* (2014), and Youssef Rakha's *Paulo* (2016), all of which depict the city as a hellscape of violent and sexual perversions. The young male protagonist in each of these novels is sadistic, misogynist, and murderous – but hardly exceptional. In these imagined Cairos, romance has been blindfolded and executed a long time ago. Violence toward women is gratuitous, even creative, and sex an expression of rage, hatred, and boredom. The protagonist of Rakha's *Paulo,* who mutilates his lover's corpse in perhaps one of the most tender of the novel's scenes, finds himself asking: "Why was Cairo always in league with these things that happened to me?"[46] Why indeed? While the apocalyptic flavor of these novels is fairly contemporary, they have in common with their predecessors in the twentieth century a concern with the political that finds its most poignant expression in the arena of desire. They ask, for strangers in a city like Cairo, what kind of encounter is possible? If one is looking for love, just where does one look?

Notes

1 The decision to center the Egyptian canon for its own sake is inspired by May Hawas, *Politicising World Literature: Egypt, Between Pedagogy and the Public* (New York: Routledge, 2019).

2 Muhammad Husayn Haykal, *Zaynab* (Cairo: Mo'assaset Hindāwī lel-Ta'līm wal-Thaqāfa, 2012).

3 Hanan Kholoussy's research has shown that Egyptians throughout the twentieth century channeled anxieties about the nation's future into a perceived "marriage crisis," which spiked during moments of political uncertainty and waned in the optimistic periods of victory. After the Anglo-Egyptian treaty of 1936 which ushered in a new era of independence from the British, the former panic around a marriage crisis died down considerably, and after the revolution of 1952 against the pro-British monarchy, it had all but disappeared. For further reading, see Hanan Kholoussy, *For Better, For Worse: The Marriage Crisis That Made Modern Egypt* (Cairo: The American University in Cairo Press, 2010).

4 Tawfiq al-Hakim, *Return of the Spirit,* trans. William M. Hutchins and Russell Harris (London: Penguin Classics, 2019), 20.

5 Ibid., 254.

6 Ibid., 269.

7 In the mid-1970s, General Leithy Nassif, the Egyptian ambassador to Britain, and Ali Shafik, the famous arms dealer and secretary to the former Egyptian Vice President Abdel Hakim Amer, both fell from their balconies in what are believed to be state-sponsored murders. In 2001, the Cinderella of Egyptian cinema, Soad Hosny, also fell from her balcony shortly after beginning to write her memoirs, which were rumored to implicate several high-ranking government officials in a sex scandal. In 2007, the same fate awaited Ashraf Marwan, the billionaire and spy for the Israeli Mossad who was rumored to be a double agent serving Egypt. Curiously, all four of these figures fell from apartment complexes in London, not Cairo, but there is no doubt in the Egyptian imaginary that they were assassinations.

8 Sonallah Ibrahim, *That Smell and Notes from Prison*, trans. by Robyn Creswell (New York: New Directions, 2013), 61.
9 Latifa al-Zayyat, *The Open Door*, trans. Marilyn Booth (Cairo: Hoopoe, 2017), 363–364.
10 Ibid., 49.
11 Ibid., 151.
12 Enayat al-Zayyat, *al-Hob wal-samt* (Cairo: Dār al-Kitāb al-'Arabī lel-Tebā'a wal-Nashr, 1967), 71.
13 Ibid., 53–54.
14 Ibid., 135.
15 Ibid., 126–127.
16 Hassan Youssef, *Gamaliyyat al-makan: al-maqha 'end Naguib Mahfouz namuthajan* (Cairo: Burset al-Kotob lel-Nashr wal-Tawzī', 2013), 25.
17 In the medieval city, *hara* meant a quarter or district, often where houses were close together, whereas in the modern usage, it refers to a narrow street or alley.
18 Note that in *Midaq Alley*, the word translated as "alley" in the title is actually *zu'a'*, which refers to an alley narrower than a *hara*.
19 *Bayn al-Qasrayn*, literally "Between Two Palaces" is the plaza that separates these two Palace complexes, and this is the Arabic title of the first volume of Mahfouz's trilogy, often translated as *Palace Walk*.
20 Gamal al-Ghitani, *Naguib Mahfouz yatathakkar* (Beirut: Dar al-Masīrah, 1980), 70.
21 Ibid., 10–11.
22 Naguib Mahfouz, *Midaq Alley*, trans. Trevor Le Gassick (New York: Anchor Books), 1992.
23 Ibid., 9.
24 Nawal El Messiri Nadim, "The Relationship Between the Sexes in a Harah of Cairo," unpublished PhD thesis, Indiana University (1975), 70.
25 Ibid., 176–179.
26 Ibid., 68.
27 Ibid., 192.
28 Ibid., 124.
29 Mahfouz, *Midaq Alley*, 67.
30 Ibid., 84.
31 Ibid., 16.
32 Yasmine Ramadan, "Cairo: Urban Space, Surveillance and the State," in *Space in Modern Egyptian Fiction* (Edinburgh: Edinburgh University Press, 2021), 31–72.
33 Samia Mehrez, "From the Hara to the Imara," in *Egypt's Culture Wars: Politics and Practice* (London: Routledge, 2008), 146.
34 Alaa al-Aswany, *The Yacoubian Building*, trans. Humphrey Davies (New York: Harper Perrennial, 2007), 11.
35 Ibid., 14.
36 Ibid., 71.

37 Ibid., 14.
38 Abdel Hakim Qasem, *Muhawala lil-khuruj* (Cairo: al-Hay'a al-Masriyya al-ʿĀmma lel-Kitab, 1987), 104–105.
39 Ibid., 105.
40 Ibid., 88.
41 Ibid., 11.
42 Ibid., 10.
43 Ibid., 157.
44 Ibid., 8.
45 Ibid., 157.
46 Youssef Rakha, *Paulo* (Beirut: Dar al-Tanwīr lel-Tebāʿa wel-Nashr 2016), 73.

CHAPTER 10

Bombay/Mumbai and its Multilingual Literary Pathways to the World

Anjali Nerlekar

It is a tough job to write about Mumbai or the literature it has inspired over the years. In an interview about his writing that features Mumbai so centrally,[1] award-winning novelist Jerry Pinto says of the city: "It may be because it is the fountainhead of stories. It may be because the sea allows it to dream all the way to Africa and all the way to the South Pole. It may be the coast that brought the gifts of merchants and madmen and missionaries."[2] That Mumbai has also featured in the post-independence Bollywood films where the hero of the film arrives in the magical city, with hope and desire for a free and equitable world. And then there is the Bombay of Arun Kolatkar's *Kala Ghoda Poems*. In a famous poem from the book, Kolatkar's homeless drunk on the street, "the dingbat Demosthenes" shakes his fist against the global metropole of Mumbai and its neocolonialisms:

> Shit city, he thunders;
> the lion of Bombay thunders,
> Shit City!
>
> I shit on you.
> You were a group
> of seven shitty islands
>
> given in dowry
> to the Shit King of Ing
> to shit on
>
> —and now it's all
> one high-rise shit,
> waiting for God,
> to pull the flush.[3]

That is one drastic address to Mumbai, and it shines a light on the other side of this city of desires. How do we cover the long history and the staggering amount of representation that the city has received across cultural forms and mediums, but especially in literary texts where it shows so many mercurial aspects of urban life?

Mumbai has always been seen as the iconic urban space of colonial and postcolonial India, and it has inspired a stupefying amount of representation across all art forms and in literary texts. For the world beyond, it has been the port of entry and a gateway for both global trade and the global imagination. Mumbai as a location has been fought over and has changed hands throughout its history: from the Mughals initially granting the archipelago of seven villages to the Portuguese, who then handed it in dowry to the English king, Charles II in 1661; to the development of Mumbai (with massive land reclamation) as the foremost colonial space for the British in India; to the post-independence wrangling over the regional/linguistic/statist connections of the city in the *sathottari*[4] period (whether it belonged to the state of Gujarat or Maharashtra, or whether it should be a standalone city). It is frequently seen as a quintessentially colonial city, or a postcolonial city with visible colonial histories. During the colonial period, the British established a core British colonial space in the walled Fort area (today's South Mumbai) while the "Native Town" lay outside the walls of this secured imperial space. Dwivedi, Mehrotra and Mulla-Feroze note the "inherent polarity that had been established in the dual city pattern" of Mumbai since its colonial start as the key to its conflicted and complex postcolonial histories of difference, sectarianism, inequities, and polarities.[5]

As its history shows, Mumbai has never *not* been a cosmopolitan city in the world–even the first Marathi book on Mumbai by Govind Narayan lists in great detail how the world (from near and far) congregated in this urban location. After stating that the languages in Mumbai are innumerable and giving a long list of castes represented in Mumbai, the author states: "Moving on to other castes—Parsi, Mussalman, Moghul, Yahudi, Israeli, Bohra, Khoja, Memon, Arab, Kandhari; these are the castes identified by the eighteen different headdresses."[6] The city has always been a congregation of the world's differences. Or, as Rushdie's memorable hero in *The Moor's Last Sigh* states, "I, however, was raised neither as Catholic nor as Jew. I was both, and nothing: a jewholic-anonymous, a cathjew nut, a stewpot, a mongrel cur. I was—what's the word these days?—atomised. Yessir: a real Bombay mix."[7] Sunil Khilnani describes Mumbai as "permanently lodged in the popular imagination as a totem of modern India itself."[8] (137).

Therefore, the literary representations of Mumbai also present a landscape of diverse grounds: multilingual, multiethnic, stubbornly Marathi, globally connected, seemingly born British, home of communal riots, a megacity. Mumbai, like New York or Paris, has been central to the politics of modernity and the representations of modernism in the Indian cultural imagination, and there is an incalculable number of texts, films, art, and performative genres that map this city of dreams and nightmares. They sometimes split along the line of the colonial versus the postcolonial stories of Bombay; or along the crucial 1992 riots in the aftermath of the Babri Masjid destruction,[9] with literature configured as before and after this divide.[10] Ranjani Mazumdar contrasts the "city of debris" with the "city of spectacle"[11] (especially in Bombay films); while writers such as Raj Rao,[12] or more recently, Amruta Patil, through her graphic novels such as *Kari* (2008), present the queer Mumbai versus the heteronormative representations of the city.

The city has also undergone a contentious name change: in 1996 the right-wing political party, Shiv Sena, protested their way into changing the British name of Bombay to the Marathi name of Mumbai. When exploring Mumbai in world literature, therefore, we need to focus the discussion on which Mumbai is being referenced and in which kind of "world" it is being situated. Not only writers and poets but also scholars writing about Mumbai have each grappled with the problem of its intense and inherent globality and its resolute and intractable particularity. It is impossible to take a distant and all-emcompassing overview of all the ways in which Mumbai has figured in the literary and artistic imagination over the years.

In the idea of world literature as it currently stands, some of the landmark texts that have caught the attention of readers in the Global North and have presented the complex heterogeneity of Mumbai life are the works of Salman Rushdie, Vikram Chandra, Gregory Roberts, and Suketu Mehta (particularly his widely read *Maximum City* [2005]). Mumbai is a continuous presence in Rushdie's fiction, most prominently in *Midnight's Children* (1981), *The Satanic Verses* (1988), *The Moor's Last Sigh* (1995) and *The Ground Beneath Her Feet* (1999). In these novels, Bombay/Mumbai becomes the site on which the debates about the becoming of a nation, the postcolonial ravages of nationalism, the sectarian riots and violence, and the social and economic inequities are staged and decided. For example, *The Moor's Last Sigh* is the story of four generations of the Zogoiby family, but also one that transnationally references multiple other spaces and stories: the "moor" is the protagonist "Moraes," Shakespeare's Moor, Othello, and also King Boabdil, the last Moorish emperor of Granada. The separate sighs of these different Moors merge into a layered bemoaning for a lost tolerant and vibrant Bombay that Rushdie imagines to have existed before the 1992 riots and of the changing of the city's name. Gregory Roberts wrote another page-turner in *Shantaram: A Novel* (2004), a story of jail, the flight to Mumbai, and the experiences of slum dwellers, addicts, crime, and betrayal, the publication of which was soon followed by Vikram Chandra's 900-page *Sacred Games* (2006). This epic book taps into the genre of the Bombay noir to show the complex entanglements of the world of organized crime and political corruption in the story of the charismatic crime boss, Ganesh Gaitonde, and the upright police officer, Sartaj Singh. Through the tale of secrets, perfidy, and violent crimes, the underworld of Bombay and its pathways come into view in the novel. There is a heady swirl of stories, characters, and spaces in the novels of both Rushdie and Chandra, not unlike the crowded streets of Mumbai.

And yet, it is also true that Mumbai has been repeatedly recognized in the spaces of world literature through a very select and small range of texts, like the ones listed above. The divided nature of this dual city is reconfigured in the split manner in which only a particular kind of writing becomes legible in the larger world's gaze. David Damrosch points out the uneven nature of the selection of texts that are representative of world literature by categorizing the levels of visibility into the hypercanonical, the countercanonical and the shadow canonical:

> The hypercanon is populated by the older "major" authors who have held their own or even gained ground over the past twenty years. The countercanon is composed of the subaltern and "contestatory" voices of writers in languages less commonly taught and in minor literatures within great-power languages. Many, even most, of the old major authors coexist quite comfortably with these new arrivals to the neighborhood, very few of whom have yet accumulated anything like their fund of cultural capital [....] it is the old "minor" authors who fade increasingly into the background, becoming a sort of shadow canon that the older scholarly generation still knows (or, increasingly, remembers fondly from long-ago reading), but whom the younger generations of students and scholars encounter less and less.[13]

Of course, these are broad categories, and one can debate the boundaries of these classifications with the instances of Bombay texts. For instance, where would one place Pinto's novel, *Em and the Big Hoom*, that locates the city in a tiny flat in Bombay, among the lives of the Goan Catholic community with its multilingual footprint across English, Konkani, and Portuguese?[14] Or the writing by the Booker-Prize winner novelist, Anita Desai in *Baumgartner's Bombay* (1988) that denotes a lesser visible side of Bombay's literary connection to the world and shows the outsider's life of a German exile in Bombay ("Accepting but not accepted; that was the story of his life"[15])?

But if one were to paint in very broad strokes, then a persistent representation of Mumbai often encountered is that of the maximum city, after Mehta's highly popular and award-winning book. This book encapsulates the kind of Mumbai that appeared earlier in Rushdie's novels – excessive, rife with contradiction, teeming with crowds, buzzing, loud. This image is also connected with the global routes that connect this crowded postcolonial location with first world neocolonial and imperial politics.

As important as these texts are, they still form towering homes of the world literary neighborhood that Damrosch describes as changed but not substantially:

> The neighborhood is certainly looking different today than it did thirty and forty years ago—yet it's clear that the larger structure of the field doesn't look as different as one might have expected. A few new occupants enjoy the higher range, but most hover far below them, and there are few if any writers in a middle range.[16]

Therefore, I will instead train a multilingual gaze upon Mumbai to see what kinds of countercanons and shadow canons emerge into view.[17] This is not to reject the representations by Rushdie, Vikram Chandra, and others, but rather to complement that super-abundant presence of Mumbai in the world with literary representations of other experiences, spaces, and practices of living. This same world (that features a chaotic medley of people, lives, and experiences) becomes richer and fuller when viewed multilingually, within, say, the literatures of Marathi, Hindi, and English together, the three prominent literary spheres in Bombay. As Francesca Orsini notes:

> The publishing market and literary scholarship tell us that world literature is here, available to us at just a click away. But not only does the claim to systematic inclusion turn out to be a hollow one [...] similar "technologies of recognition" produce blindness to what is not immediately "there," breed supercilious disregard and misrecognition towards what does not match the tastes of so-called "world readers," marginalize translation, and deny the necessary learning of languages and the persistence of multilingualism in the age of "global English."[18]

While it is impossible to comprehensively reference all the linguistic and literary cultures in Mumbai, this chapter will attempt to move beyond the monological dominance of the anglophone to gesture toward the vast multitudes of literary approaches to the world in and about Bombay. One such Bombay that reaches outside and beyond is the *sathottari* period when the Beat-influenced generation of writers in English and Marathi created a modernist hub of little magazines and small presses with rebellious writing in English, Marathi, Hindi, and Gujarati, to name four prominent literary spheres in the city at that time. Several poets writing in these languages were variously influenced by the Beat poets (Allen Ginsberg and his fellow poets visited the city in 1962 and met some of the writers in the city), but also others who formed literary solidarities with the concrete poetry movement in Latin America and Europe (Arvind Krishna Mehrotra in English and R.K. Joshi in Marathi, to take just two examples), and yet others overtly referencing the French symbolists and Euro-American modernists (Dilip Chitre). In fact, in 1964, Dilip Chitre provided an initial impetus to the avant-garde sensibility in Marathi poetry through his translations of Ezra Pound, Rimbaud, Baudelaire, Rilke, and other modernists in Marathi in the journal *Satyakatha* that was published in Mumbai. This series of translations was much discussed in the 1960s, but it is crucial to note that one cannot trace a straightforward linear trajectory from Mumbai to the outside world even in these overt gestures to that world. There is a more complex citation and rejection of the European modernists, even if casually done, in the personal correspondence of the young Dilip Chitre and the young Arun Kolatkar (the letter is dated July 27, 1955, evening):

> Dear Arun,
> I received the translations of my poems. Even if Shapiro has left, one can see that the translations are good. I liked your own poem better [….]
> The Mumbai sky is soiled with clouds. I would appreciate the poetic line more, "The sky has melted into the waters of the Ganga,"[19] if some coarse sun were to randomly fling errant sunbeams around [….] My desire to seek your company is a thousand times more than the urgency I feel about the future of Marathi poetry. Therefore I say to hell with Rimbaud and Gauguin [….]
>
> Yours,
> Dilip[20]

Taken together with the actual translations of Rimbaud, this nonchalant setting aside of the French modernists indicates the complex world of Mumbai that was being constructed on the ground, even as it reached out to the world beyond the city.

Much has been written about the period of the *sathottari* (or the post-1960s) modern as well as modernist Bombay, and that period in the city's history, and its representations, have now become mythologized in contemporary works such as Jeet Thayil's *The Book of Chocolate Saints* (2017), where the novel presents fictionalized versions of Bombay poets Arun Kolatkar, Adil

Jussawalla, and others. This work, from the first generation of writers after independence in 1947, is the lived experience of the people who produce literature and art in the locations of the Global South. Not all their lives can be captured in the grid of world literature, neither do many of their voices find an ear on that world stage. These writers and poets repeatedly assert a *difference*, a belonging to their moment in time and space, that is not captured in the idea of world literature, a difference that is cosmopolitan and globally extensive, but in a way that escapes the distant, remote, "blue marble" view of the globe from above. Today, with the explosion of interest in this generation of writers from Bombay, this could be viewed as the countercanon – works that challenge not only the exclusivity of the hypervisible writers but also as texts that are increasingly themselves becoming canonical, and edging their way to the center of the anglophone and Marathi literary world's attention.

On the ground in Mumbai, life is and has always been multilingual and multiply anchored in diverse histories and geographies. A reading of literary representations of Mumbai has to grapple with this array of multilingual ways in which the urbanism of the location finds its voice. Therefore let's begin with some examples in Marathi, Hindi, Urdu, and English that reveal not only the multifariousness of Mumbai's connections to worldliness, but also the different worlds that are conjured up in each of them.

Mumbai's *duniya* in World Literature

First, let us look at the visionary Marathi poet of the *sathottari* period, activist, worker, widely loved by the working class and beyond, Narayan Surve. He writes about his millworker experience and the workers' strikes in the city in the poem, "*amuchi duniya*" ("Our world"):

> With rotten tatters on your body
>
> Your world is different
>   Our world is different
>
> African or Muslim
> South Asian, Burmese or from Siam
> Whoever unnamed still protests
> A salute to you from the Himalayas
> We don't seed wars
> We create Buddhas
> We work with our sweat
> To earn a living
>   Engulfed in the world's river
>   Our world is different.[21]

Referencing the socialist protest movements of the *sathottari* period in Mumbai (where left-wing union strikes and protests against the millowners merged with the mixed broader movement for a Marathi linguistic state of Maharashtra), Surve demarcates two separate "worlds" (*duniya*). Surve uses the Hindi/Urdu word, "*duniya*" rather than the more typical Marathi words "*jag*" or "*vishwa*." The Hindi/Urdu word references the lives of the Muslim workers from the Konkan who thronged in Bombay at that time, looking for work in the textile mills. The poem looks at the Mumbai streets with an awareness of world politics and the movements well beyond the city and the nation. Filmmaker and scholar, Arun Khopkar, who directed a film on Surve's life and works, compared Surve's revolutionary usage of the spoken language of the laboring class with that of Jacques Previn and Alexander Pushkin's work in their own languages.[22]

One can see a similar approach in another important Marathi text, *Mumbaichi Lavani* by the activist, union leader, and writer, Annabhau Sathe. This *lavani*, a folk cultural performative genre associated with the working classes, features a detailed naming and mapping of Mumbai's roads and neighborhoods, for example, even as it affirms its alignment with socialist politics and influence from Russia: in his listing of people and places in the *lavani*, Sathe also hails many groups of people, among them the Dalit federation and the socialists, and asks them to join the union workers' fight. This world of street protests and the texts that feature them are not restricted by national boundaries – it is a world of working-class solidarities and socialist vision.

The second evocation of the world is in the Urdu word "*jahan*," employed by the progressive Urdu poet and lyricist, Sahir Ludhianvi. The progressive writers movement was "an intellectual revolt against the outmoded past, the vitiated tendencies in contemporary thought and literature, the indifference of people to their human condition, against acquiescence to foreign rule, enslavement to practices," as Ahmed Ali, one of the founding members put it.[23] Establishing their identity with a manifesto drafted in London, this was a significant group of progressive Urdu writers living in Bombay and associated with the Hindi film world. Ludhianvi was a prolific poet and lyricist, and in a Raj Kapoor Hindi film from 1959, *Phir Subah Hogi* (*It Will Be Dawn Again*), he wrote a much loved and much quoted song:

Cheeno Arab hamara
Hindostan hamara
Rehene ko ghar nahin hai
Sara jahan hamara

(China and Arabia are ours
Hindostan is ours
No place to live in the city
The entire world is ours)[24]

Ludhianvi plays deftly with the ironies of "being at home in the world," as Manshita Dass notes:

> The song mocks the then Prime Minister Jawaharlal Nehru's vision of India's place in an international community through a witty parody of a well-known Urdu poem, "Tarana-e-Milli" ("Anthem of the Community," by the poet-philosopher Muhammad Iqbal), which envisions the nation of Islam in transnational terms. It deflates the grandiose cosmopolitanism of Iqbal's and Nehru's rhetoric through the trope of homelessness and plays on the contrast between the lofty idea of being at home in the world and the predicament of being literally homeless.[25]

This *jahan* or "world" stretches across a different trajectory from the *duniya* of the Bandung world evoked by Surve's poem, but both are equally entrenched in the Mumbai streets (in the film, the song shows homeless people sleeping in the streets of South Bombay). The grounded experience here is in being homeless in the inhospitable streets[26] and not, as Dass correctly points out, in being at home in the world.

One must note the word of caution raised by Jahan Ramazani in his latest book, where he deftly shows the transnational nature of seemingly local poetics. He evokes a similar semantics of "*jahan* / the world," that is also felicitously his own name:

> As someone whose given name, Jahan, is also a commonplace word in Persian for the "world," yet in English becomes a proper name only, I think we would do well to follow "Shahid," glorying in the untranslatable peculiarities and affordances of languages as illuminated by poetry, and at the same time embracing his suggestion that a language's signature capacities are often revealed in the interlingual junctures of translation.[27]

Indeed, as this chapter will also show, there are lines that run continuously from the narrowly specific locality out into the world, and one can never deny the global relations of any literary production. And yet, to come back to the affect of Narayan Surve's poem above, the impulse on the part of many writers from Mumbai is that the world out there does not "get" the *duniya* of these Mumbai workers and writers, that it does not understand their specific emplacement.

Yet another example can be found in the anglophone writing of Mumbai. As Adil Jussawalla, the poet who archived and documented the life of the city, stated in his introduction to his influential Penguin anthology, *New Writing in India* (1974):

> In the best Indian writing [...] [n]ot only is there an assured use of indigenous forms but the content is so very much the product of local stresses and strains, the dialectics of a particular socioeconomic situation, that the Western reader is more likely to be annoyed by a certain contrariness in the Indian's attitude to fundamental issues like war, sex and poverty, than be contemptuous of the similarities with his.[28]

This is no nativist assertion of a bounded "local" in the case of Adil Jussawalla, but an attempt by the poet and editor to more precisely demarcate the contemporary moment in his work. He does the same thing in his poetry: in "Missing Person," Jussawalla writes,

> We're the mix
> Marx never knew
> would make the best
> Communists. Also
>
> too fond was our hero of distinctions,
> [...]
> You see,
> we're *Das Capital*, a dried-up well
> And a big *Mein Kampf*. Also.[29]

That idea of "also," that one needs to add to any description of world literature, is where one needs to locate Mumbai writing and the writing about Mumbai. It is in that space of excess, of "more", but also of difference where one must seek out the unique character of Mumbai's spatiality.

Thus, the socialist connection, in a different guise, makes its presence felt in Bombay's English poetry too. This urge that Indian writers feel, to insist on difference amid the transnational connection – how can we acknowledge it in a theoretical framework that will be able to keep the world in view while remaining stubbornly sensitive to local perspectives? How then can we attend to this sense of being on the ground that the writers repeatedly assert, without denying their transnational echoes? The world is very much with us in Mumbai; any Mumbaikar will agree to that. But the global expansive model shows only some parts of this diverse space. Salman Rushdie is legible on the global level, for example, but Narayan Surve is not. This is the "provincial cosmopolitanism" that Swati Chattopadhyay talks about in *Unlearning the City*, the work of "resignif[ying] one's labor and one's body, without the desire or the luxury of decontextualizing oneself."[30] It is clear that flexible and tensile approaches to the heart of this city are required. The award-winning writers visible to the world – either because of their awards, or the genres of their work, or the affordances they provide for the theoretical practices of the West – are on the other side of the rebellious border crossings and world-making that one sees in the cultural and literary productions exemplified above.

A singularly vital view of Mumbai is provided by the Dalit writing of the post-independence period, much of which places the city at the center of its own resistant worldview. This literature articulates the oppressions inflicted by the caste-based society on the Dalits (variously termed in the past as "untouchables," "*harijans* (people of god)," "scheduled castes"). As Anupama Rao states, "Dalit emancipation was predicated on the existential, political, and ethical reordering of Indian society, but it also presupposed the imagination of the Dalit as a specific kind of political subject."[31] The city enabled such an imagining of the Dalit writerly self. As the Marathi poet Narayan Surve states in his poem "Mumbai," the story of Mumbai is his own biography (both as the Dalit and as a worker struggling in the city of the mill workers).[32] And as Vidyut Bhagwat notes with regards to Dalit presence in the city: "The dalit belongs to Bombay and Bombay belongs to the dalit. He is the anti-hero who strides on the metropolitan stage turned upside down."[33]

The Dalit writers repeatedly interpellate the world in their local imaginations. The very idea of the resistant nature of Dalit discourse is historically connected with the inspiration that the early leaders of Dalit literary activism in Marathi found in the Black Power movement of the United States and the history of African American writing that resisted ideologies dominant since the nineteenth century. Marathi Dalit poets and little magazine editors such as Raja Dhale wrote about the Black Panther movement in 1971, just a year before becoming involved in the creation of the Dalit Panthers with other poets such as Namdeo Dhasal and Arjun Dangle. African American histories and literary activism are the undercurrent below much of the Dalit writing of the *sathottari* in Mumbai and in India. That consciousness of a shared subalternity, if you will, underwrites the literary production of the time and in that sense, that part of world history is a spectral presence in Dalit Mumbai constructions in literature.[34]

Dhasal, "Man you should explode"

The Marathi poet Namdeo Dhasal has several books of poems mostly located in the geography of Mumbai. His first book of poems, *Golpitha* is located in the space near Dhor Chawl, the tenement area where Dhasal lived with his mother in Mumbai – a dangerous red-light district of violence, with commerce in bodies as well as goods. The book contains a well-known poem, "Man you should explode" where the poet lists the many things that need to be cleared out from Indian culture, history, urban living, and personal practices of daily living before there can be any talk of justice, fairness, and equality for Dalit lives:

> Man, you should explode
> Yourself to bits to start with
> Jive to a savage drum beat
> Smoke hash, smoke ganja
> [...]
> You should carry acid bulbs and such things on you
> You should be ready to carve out anyone's innards without batting an eyelid[35]

A large portion of the poem, right from its beginning, seems to be counter-intuitive in espousing violence, and hatred, and degradation. But among the list of debasing or dishonorable activities and institutions, Dhasal includes the authors of world literature:

> One should hurl grenades; one should drop hydrogen bombs to raze
> Literary societies, schools, colleges, hospitals, airports
> One should open the manholes of sewers and throw into them
> Plato, Eistein, Archimedes, Socrates,
> Marx, Ashoka, Hitler, Camus, Sartre, Kafka
> Baudelaire, Rimbaud, Ezra Pound, Hopkins, Goethe
> Dostoevsky, Mayakovsky, Maxim Gorky[36]

Of course, it is not that Dhasal the poet does not value, say, the work of Dostoevsky or Kafka or Gorky; he is not a nativist. In his essay on himself, the poet states, "I am here now only because my poetry has brought me up to this point in my life. The biggest influence on me has been that of major European poets."[37] But there is an attempt to harness that world to his locality, to his personal utterance in time and space such that his life and experience become decipherable in the depiction of the world. If they do not, then as Ludhianvi says in his popular film song, "*Yeh duniya agar mil bhi jaye toh kya hai*" ("Of what use is this world, even if one acquires it?"). Life in Mumbai's Golpitha district of prostitution and deprivation needs to become visible and comprehensible even when talking of world literature's totalities. Therefore, the poet's strategy is to summon up the literature of that larger world before wiping the slate clean and starting afresh. The European poets and the greats of Western and world literature might have shown him the method of articulating his deprivations, but in this poem, Dhasal wants to go beyond this and stake his ground in Golpitha in Mumbai:

Man, one should tear off all the pages of all the sacred books in the world
And give them to people for wiping shit off their arses when done[38]

In the end, one must descend from the heights of a Baudelaire or an Einstein to the material practicalities of negotiating a life in the scary spaces of Golpitha, represented here with the scatalogical images of "shit" and "arse."

After the fever has broken, and when the cycle of violence and oppressive acts has run its course, then,

Let all this grow into a tumour to fill up the universe, balloon up
And burst at a nameless time to shrink
After this all those who survive should stop robbing anyone or making others their slaves
[…]
To humanity itself, man should sing only the song of man.[39]

That is the utopian dream of the Dalit poet in Mumbai, almost voicing a John Lennon moment in dreaming of human connectivities. The poet then enacts the process of reaching the utopian futurity he imagines in Mumbai, which involves both a summoning and a rejection of the world's ways of being and writing.

It is impossible to cover the many ways in which Mumbai summons the world into its ambit. It occurs in graphic novels, such as Amruta Patil's *Kari* that brings Frieda Kahlo into the conversations of sexuality and gender in the city; or Gauri Deshpande's short stories and novellas where the women create global horizons for Marathi writing via their strategic use of English; or Ranjit Hoskote, who uses art and the sensuousness of music to weave the Cuban missile crisis and climate change into the contemporary Bombay world in *Jonahwhale* (2018); or Hemant Divate's Marathi book of poems, *Paranoia* (2020), which in its nightmarish description of the communal violence between Hindus and Muslims in Bombay, hails the world via its linguistic wordplay in Marathi.[40] Through such literary acts, diverse topographies and neighborhoods, lived practices, and affective universes become knowable, and each time a different city appears in view: the mill-workers' towns of Bhuleshwar, Girgaum, Nagpada, and Kamathipura in Surve's and Dhasal's poems; the tightly packed tenement housing of the chawls in working-class Mumbai in Kiran Nagarkar's novels such as *Ravan and Eddie* (1995); or the busy lanes of the Fort area in South Bombay's Kala Ghoda neighborhood of Arun Kolatkar's poems.

Mumbai here is the ground from which to imagine a world, and it is important to heed the materialities and the lived experiences of that ground from where such imaginings take flight. In a multilayered poem, "Old Men on a Bench," Jussawalla talks of the entanglements that become deeper with old age. The older men are chatting on a bench by the fishing dock in Bombay, imagining:

> [...] our children helpless in foreign cities –
> our excuse, through subterfuges of anger, to rattle
> agents, hurry the issue of visas – we speak,
> pressing another's hands should the need arise,
> counselling patience, as though drawing up plans for a building
> we're certain one day to share.[41]

The men look out to the ocean, toward those foreign worlds inhabited by their children, concerned about their well-being, *as if*, says the poet, they themselves would share the spaces of that world. As if, but not quite. The old men are rooted on that bench in Bombay and yet, as Jussawalla points out in another poem, "At night the sea's barely visible. / Beyond it other shorelines. / Beyond them fjords and galaxies."[42] Similarly Arundhati Subramanium, another poet who manages to articulate the diverse ways of being and belonging in Bombay, writes in "When Landscape Becomes Woman,"

> [...] a chink in the wall
> is all you need
> to tumble
> into a parallel universe.[43]

So much literature about Bombay/Mumbai walks that fine edge of being grounded in its time while simultaneously indicating the far-stretching worlds that lie just beyond the overt gaze.

Notes

1 Jerry Pinto, *Em and the Big Hoom: A Novel* (Penguin Books: New York, 2014).
2 "Words and the music of words are closest to my heart – Jerry Pinto" (September 2021), https://kitaab.org/2021/09/15/words-and-the-music-of-words-are-closest-to-my-heart-jerry-pinto-poet-author-translator/.
3 Arun Kolatkar, *Kala Ghoda Poems* (Mumbai: Pras Prakashan, 2004), 119.
4 *Sathottari* is a Marathi/Hindi term that indicates the period of post-1960. The use of this Marathi/Hindi word helps connect the multilingual tumult of the post-1960s in India to the global experience of the 1960s.
5 Sharada Dwivedi, Rahul Mehrotra, and Umaima Mulla-Feroze, *Bombay: The Cities Within* (Bombay: India Book House, 1995).
6 Govind Narayan, *Govind Narayan's Mumbai: An Urban Biography from 1863*, trans. Murali Ranganathan (London: Anthem Press, 2008), 52.

7 Salman Rushdie, *The Moor's Last Sigh* (New York: Pantheon, 1995), 104.
8 Sunil Khilnani, *The Idea of India* (New York: Farrar Straus Giroux, 1998) 137.
9 The destruction of the ancient mosque in Ayodhya in northern India set off the riots in Bombay in 1992–93.
10 See Rosella Ciocca, "From Nation to World: Bombay/Mumbai Fictions and the Urban Public Sphere," in R. Ciocca and N. Srivastava, eds., *Indian Literature in the World* (London: Palgrave Macmillan, 2017), 225.
11 Ranjani Mazumdar, *Bombay Cinema: An Archive of the City* (Minneapolis, MN: University of Minnesota Press, 2007).
12 See Rao's striking novel, *The Boyfriend* (New Delhi: Penguin, 2003) which presents a ground-level picture of an alternative queer mapping of Mumbai (where romance happens in the bathrooms near train stations and the supposedly safe spaces of the city are traced as hazardous), and where the self-aware protagonist explores the ways in which Mumbai spaces and identities meld into each other.
13 David Damrosch, "World Literature in a Postcanonical, Hypercanonical Age," in Haun Saussy, ed., *Comparative Literature in an Age of Globalization* (Baltimore, MD: Johns Hopkins University Press, 2006), 39–40.
14 Mumbai appears as a strangely manic space of psychological ups and downs in the Mumbai-Goan Portuguese/English/Marathi mixed space where the bipolar Em and her family reside.
15 Anita Desai, *Baumgartner's Bombay* (New York: A.A. Knopf, 1988), 20.
16 Damrosch, "World Literature," 48.
17 There is substantial literary scholarship on Mumbai. Some notable works are: Raj Rao, "Introduction; Bombay Poetry, Poems on Bombay City," *The Literary Endeavour* 8, no. 1–4 (1986): 1–20; Emma Bird, "'the things not in the picture': Bombay's poets and the re-representation of the city," *Journal of Postcolonial Writing* 53, no. 6 (2017): 644–658; Arun Khopkar, "Footloose and Fancy-Free in Bombay: A Partial View of the 1960s and 1970s," *Journal of Postcolonial Writing* 53, no. 1–2 (2017): 12–24; Ciocca, "From Nation to World"; Rashmi Varma, *The Postcolonial City and its Subjects: London, Narobi, Bombay, New York* (London: Routledge, 2012).
18 Francesca Orsini, "Present Absence: Book Circulation, Indian Vernaculars and World Literature in the Nineteenth Century," *Interventions* 22, no. 3 (2019): 326–327.
19 This is a famous line from a Marathi poem by the modern poet, B.S. Mardhekar (himself influenced by Eliot's modernism).
20 Dilip Chitre, unpublished correspondence. Published with permission from Vijaya Chitre.
21 Narayan Surve, *Surve: Narayan Surve Yanchi Samagra Kavita* (Mumbai: Popular Prakashan, 2011), 33–34. My translation.
22 Arun Khopkar, "Screening: Narayan Gangaram Surve, a short film by Arun Khopkar" (April 4, 2016), www.youtube.com/watch?v=deMMlO8eiio&ab_channel=icggoa.
23 Ahmed Ali, "The Progressive Writers Movement in its Historical Perspective," *Journal of South Asian Literature* 13, no.1–4 (1977–78): 91–97.

24 For various discussions of this song, see: A. Rajadhyaksha, "The Curious Case of Bombay's Hindi Cinema: The Career of Indigenous 'Exhibition' Capital," *Journal of Moving Image* (2006); P. Rag, "The Theme of Social and Political Consciousness as a Challenge for Indian Recorded Music," *Social Scientist* 32, no. 11/12 (2004): 84–93; Manshita Dass, "Cinetopia: Leftist Street Theatre and the Musical Production of the Metropolis in 1950s Bombay Cinema," *positions* 25, no. 1 (2017), 101–24, www.muse.jhu.edu/article/648452.

25 Ibid.

26 Mazumdar, "Introduction: Urban Allegory," in Bombay Cinema, xviii–xxxvii.

27 Jahan Ramazani, *Poetry in a Global Age* (Chicago: University of Chicago Press, 2020), 238.

28 Adil Jussawalla, *New Writing in India* (Harmondsworth, England: Penguin, 1974), 20.

29 Jussawalla, *Missing Person* (Bombay: Clearing House, 1976), 33.

30 Swati Chattopadhyay, *Unlearning the City: Infrastructure in a New Optical Field* (Minneapolis, MN: University of Minnesota Press, 2012), xxi.

31 Anupama Rao, *The Caste Question: Dalits and the Politics of Modern India* (Berkeley, CA: University of California Press, 2009), 1.

32 Surve, *Samagra Kavita*, 89–91.

33 Vidyut Bhagwat, "Bombay in Dalit Literature," in Sujata Patel and Alice Thornton, eds., *Bombay: Mosaic of Modern Culture* (Bombay: Oxford University Press, 1996), 121.

34 For more on Dalit Bombay, see the forthcoming book by Anupama Rao; Debjani Ganguly, *Caste and Dalit Lifeworlds: Postcolonial Perspectives* (New Delhi: Orient Blackswan, 2010); Juned Shaikh, *Outcaste Bombay: City Making and the Politics of the Poor* (Seattle, WA: University of Washington Press, 2021).

35 Dilip Chitre, ed. *Namdeo Dhasal: Poet of the Underworld* (Chennai: Navayana, 2007), 34.

36 Ibid., 35.

37 Ibid., "Namdeo on Namdeo," 167.

38 Ibid., 35.

39 Ibid., 36.

40 There is wordplay on the Marathi terms for the "world" ("*juhg*"), "battle" ("*jung*") and "rust" ("*ganj*") in the poem "*ganjat chalaloy*" ("I continue to rust"), where the poet states that he and the country are both rusting, as is the world. See Hemant Divate, *Paranoia* (Mumbai: Poetrywala, 2020), 26.

41 Adil Jussawalla, *Shorelines* (Mumbai: Poetrywala, 2019), "Old Men on a Bench," 15.

42 Ibid., "Shorelines," 4.

43 Arundhati Subramanium, "When Landscape Becomes Woman," *Usawa Literary Review* 1 (2018), www.usawa.in/poetry/three-poems-by-arundhati-subramaniam.html.

CHAPTER 11

At Home in the World

Singapore's Literary Translocality

Philip Holden

It is early June, 1995, in the Victoria Theatre in Singapore, next to Parliament House in the heart of the colonial governmental district that the new nation took over, separated by the Singapore River—now cleaned up, and emptied of commerce—from the skyscrapers of the financial district of Shenton Way. On stage, suit-clad yuppies who work across the river have migrated onto the stage and entered a new relationship with history. They are trapped in a set of framed glass spheres that look like a columbarium, or a series of prison cells, a hierarchical "network of pricks."[1] And as the play they appear in ends, the audience hears for the first time words that will become a canonical passage in Singapore literature:

> Nameless, sexless, rootless, homeless
> Everyone's a parent to the orphan
> Every god's a protector to the wanderer
> Every land and sky and water is home
> It's forever *Zaijian*, *Selamat Datang*, *Vanakkam*, Farewell
>
> I cannot tarry
> I must hurry
> The sea, the land, the sky is waiting
> The Market is calling me![2]

The final words of Kuo Pao Kun's play *Descendants of the Eunuch Admiral* build a number of historical and literary bridges. They place Singapore's present within a deep history, connecting the contemporary experiences of the city-state with the travels to the region of the Chinese Ming dynasty Admiral, Zheng He. This placemaking in turn generates productive metaphors. All who live in the city-state are engaged in acts of homemaking within ever-quickening flows of globalizing change, in which the communities of labor and of care dissolve and are remade. Leave-taking is done in Singapore's four official languages, through a multilingualism deeply intertwined with multiracialism, with the racial governmentality taken up from a century and a half of British colonialism and put to use by the nation-state after 1965. And yet the text moves beyond these confines: in 1995, it will be performed in both English and in Mandarin Chinese. Kuo leaves us with the spectacle of interpellation from a personified Market, but we are unsure what is calling us. Is it the Southeast Asian port city celebrated earlier in the play as a site of carnivalesque cultural exchange, or the marketplace that reduces its population to the status of *homo economicus*, a regulated colonial plural society that has, under post-independence neoliberal policies, become internalized in individual residents' selves and bodies?

This chapter uses the ending of Kuo's play as a touchstone to contemplate Singapore as a site of the production of world literature. We first explore the historical nature of the Southeast Asian port city, and literature's role in projects of translocal placemaking. As Clemens Greiner and Patrick Sakdapolrak have illustrated, translocality is a useful concept that problematizes the oppositional between global and the local by considering how senses of place are made though regional and connective imaginaries that dispense with "essentialising notions of spatially bounded territorial units."[3] We then turn to debates in world literature, and see how the tension between port and city, between structures of governance and flow, may question common formulations of Singapore literature, and of world literature as both a field and an ethical project. Returning to Singapore, the chapter examines a number of literary texts written over a span of seventy years as exercises in translocal self-fashioning in a linguistic environment where literary texts in a single language already incorporate immanent translation. Such texts, as much world literature does, enact ethical projects which are not simply critical but also foster the construction of communities, and in this process the marketplace of the port city offers both openings and constraints. The duality of the marketplace, indeed, provides a way of moving beyond readings of world literature in which close readings of a text's ethical efficacy co-exist uneasily with a simultaneous analysis of the determining power of neoliberal economic structures.

Port/City

Major Southeast Asian cities, Eric Tagliacozzo has argued, have a unique history.[4] Tagliacozzo draws on the work of Victor Lieberman and Anthony Reid,[5] placing European colonial intervention in the region within a much longer *durée* of trade flows and cultural networks over a millennium or more. Robert Redfield and Milton Singer's separation between two different cultural functions of cities – as a marketplace on the one hand, and religious, intellectual, and political center on the other – does not hold in the region, especially in maritime Southeast Asia.[6] Rather, Tagliacozzo argues, "since at least the first millennium C.E. [...] both the administrative and economic heart of many traditional Southeast Asian polities have been fused into one city."[7] This fusion persists today in regional port cities such as Manila, Jakarta (at least for the present moment), and Bangkok, that are also national capitals. These cities, in contrast to Asian capitals of polities such as Ming and Qing China, Mughal India, or Tokugawa Japan, were historically and continue to be bound to transnational networks of trade beyond the control of their political elites. This feature, Tagliacozzo notes, has had two consequences. First, urban elites have engaged in flexible exercises of self-fashioning, becoming politically and culturally nimble in order to survive. Second, a peculiar balance has existed between what Tagliacozzo identifies as "centrifugal politics and centripetal economics."[8] If the city as polis attempted to centralize and rationalize government, such efforts were undermined by the flows of a market dependent on the extraction of primary products outside its political domain.

Tagliacozzo's insights can readily be applied to Singapore today. Singapore is promoted as an "aspirational city" and a model for the "Global South,"[9] its changing urban landscape documented in diverse literary texts such as Goh Poh Seng's novel *If We Dream Too Long* (1972), Stella Kon's play *Emily of Emerald Hill* (1989, first staged 1984), and Suratman Markassan's novel *Penghulu yang hilang segala-galanya* (1998, translated as *Penghulu*, 2012). Unlike most of the conurbations that hope to follow in its developmental wake, it is also a geographically bounded city without an economic hinterland that is part of the same polity. Singapore's twentieth-century history severed it from the economic and political hinterlands of the periods of colonialism and decolonization (the British colony of the Straits Settlements within colonial Malaya, and then the nation-state of Malaysia), so that it entered a new engagement with the "fluid [...] hinterland" of the region.[10] The city has also now grown to encompass the island on which it is situated. In one of the texts we will discuss later, Han Suyin's novel ... *and the Rain my Drink* (1956), it is still possible to think of a division between city and country. The text begins with a map on which "Singapore City" is shaded at the southern tip of the island, marking a division still reflected in 1955 in the last colonial master plan.[11] By the 1960s, urban renewal conceptualized by a United Nations team plotted a reconfiguration of urban space. The historical city with its river was enfolded by new industrial areas and modernist housing estates, the latter now paradoxically considered the cultural "heartland" of the city-state.

Singapore has negotiated and survived the new international division of labor from the 1960s onwards through a series of becomings born from the regional past outlined above. In the twenty-first century, it embodies a crystallization of these historical trends, a city in which politics and commerce intertwine through neoliberal subjectification that draws on nationalism and other cultural resources. The city-state, as nationalist discourses of survival repeatedly emphasize, has little control over the web of economic networks in which it finds itself, and yet its political elites remain ever adaptive.

The Literary City in the World

Knowing this history enables us to rethink predominant concerns of literary scholarship concerning Singapore, which in turn parallel many of those emergent in world literature. Historians, sociologists, and anthropologists have frequently identified a tension within Singapore between city and port, between structure and flow. Much analysis of Singapore's colonial governance, as we have noted, has drawn on J.S. Furnivall's notion of the plural society as a governmental project, with racialized communities classified, solidified, and governed through community representatives, only meeting "in the market place, in buying and selling."[12] Memory of this governance is still embodied in central Singapore's cityscape, with the racialized heritage districts of Chinatown, Little India, and Malay Kampong Glam surrounding a commercial and administrative core still dotted with colonial-era edifices. This spatial logic of the city has also been internalized within individual subjectivities and condensed into individual bodies. As many commentators have noted, Singapore's particular model of multiracialism, based nominally on Chinese Malay Indian Other (CMIO) classification, extends the colonial plural society model into the nation-building projects of postcolonial governance. Race is assigned at birth and printed on citizen's identity cards: it determines the "mother tongue" a child learns at school, the monthly salary deductions made to ethnic self-help organizations, and in some circumstances eligibility to stand for political office. Recent efforts to allow individuals a limited capacity to change their race or adopt a hybrid identity have softened the edges of the system, but not fundamentally altered it.

Scholars, however, have also noted how such projects of urban governance are never fully realized, and are often undermined by flows of culture engendered by the port. The racial schema of the early colonial town planning in Singapore was opposed by an alternative cognitive mapping centered on the docks and their associated cosmopolitan "sailortown" of a world within the city.[13] The port engendered cultural crossings of language, dress, gesture, and consumption manifested in the unruly transgression of boundaries marked out by urban planning. Such conflicts might be over spaces – the public or private status of the covered five-foot way outside Singapore's shophouses[14] – or be concentrated into individual human bodies. Spatial mappings folded in on themselves. In the transition from colonial entrepôt to neoliberal city, the built environment was increasingly marked by modernist regulation, yet cultural crossings for all the inhabitants continued by passing through a different kind of portal, the gateways of the great amusement parks collectively known as the Worlds.[15] In the late twentieth century and the new millennium, such crossings have gained increasing visibility. Singapore's positioning of itself as a global city has resulted in the presence of "foreign talent," transnational professionals who come to call the city-state home, and who do not fit into the CMIO classification. Foreign labor, mostly construction and domestic workers from the region, supports Singapore's economy. Such migrants do not have the right to continue residence, yet their writing, mostly through translation into English, has become increasingly prominent over the last decade.

In literary studies in Singapore, most scholars have placed literary production on the side of the port rather than the city, embodying a destabilizing, critical fluidity that erodes the successive solidities of colonialism, the developmental state, and neoliberal governance.[16] Such critiques are insightful, but they are not the only way of placing literary texts within the global city. Literary texts in Singapore draw on the port and its mobility, but often do so to participate in projects of restructuring, self-fashioning, and placemaking.

The critical emplacement of literary texts in Singapore has parallels in the field of world literature. A decade ago, David Porter noted that in the rising field of world literature, scholars were using, often implicitly, a number of different and competing definitions of the field. For the purposes of this chapter, I will collapse Porter's five categories into three overlapping perspectives through which the field of world literature might be viewed. The first is aesthetic, in which texts are judged to be "significant masterpieces" worthy of critical attention.[17] Such attention is often phrased, however, not simply in terms of literary merit but in terms of a second perspective, ethical value. Peng Cheah's influential *What Is a World?* for instance, produces an implicit canon of "narrative literature from the postcolonial South that attempts to remake the world against capitalist globalization."[18] This ethical perspective often rubs up against a third view, an account of how the circulation of such texts is in itself exemplary of "a relationship of growing inequality" under capitalist globalization,[19] as evidenced in the work of Franco Moretti, the Warwick Research Collective, and, in a slightly different vein, Pascale Casanova.[20]

In discussions of world literature, scholars frequently elide a contradiction between the ethical efficacy of literary texts, expressed through close reading that focuses on the critical possibility of aesthetics, and sociohistorical attention to the inequalities of the neoliberal marketplace in which literary texts circulate. This contradiction is embodied in the critical work itself, in which accounts of how literary texts are inextricably part of the structures of capitalist globalization are followed by redemptive ethical/aesthetic readings that illustrate how these texts critique these structures. The literariness of the text, we are told, transforms and interrogates its contexts, whether this be through "a normative worldly force immanent to literature" that can "move human agents to worldly action,"[21] or the novel's creation of "various versions of possible worlds that sit apart from and partially free from the *actual* world out there,"[22] a "real world defamiliarised and transcended, while retaining its indelible imprint."[23] This moment of close reading summons a community of readers, interpellated by the use by Cheah, Debjani Ganguly, and others of the first-person plural "we." Such readers are bound not just by a shared experience, but also by a shared ethical project. "As *Saturday* opens," Sarah Brouillette writes of Ian McEwan's novel, "we meet Henry waking early in his posh London townhome."[24] "We see her passion for bones early in the novel," Ganguly notes of the characterization of Anil Tissera in Michael Ondaatje's *Anil's Ghost.*[25] This "we" shifts silently from a community of readers to a wider community who share a concern with the world. For Cheah, close reading Nuruddin Farah's *Gifts* suggests that "we emerge as self-determining agents and engage in reciprocal relations with others by telling stories."[26] Henry's celebration of peace in London within a larger context global violence, Brouillette notes, "depends upon a collective effort to keep at bay the things we tell ourselves we do not see."[27]

It might be easy to extend this critique, to wonder at the curious elision of the role played by British and American port cities of production in Cheah's analysis of novels by Timothy Mo, Amitav Ghosh, or Ninotchka Rosca as representations of a Global South, or to identify the "we" summoned in such critical works as a global class of "progressive neoliberals," in Nancy Fraser's terms.[28] Such a gesture, however, disregards aesthetics but leaves the binarism of structure and aesthetics in place. It is the argument of this chapter that we should not place city in opposition to port, structure in opposition to critical aesthetics. Rather we should see literary texts as engaged not simply in ethical critique but also in processes of local placemaking and subjectification that draw on the city's place in the region and the world. And it is with this insight that we return to the literature of the port city of Singapore.

Translocalism and Translation

Literary texts written and published in Singapore have historically been part of a number of overlapping worldings and their associated literary fields. English-language texts traditionally looked to London as colonial metropole, and then to Malaya and Malaysia as a cultural and economic hinterland. An initial generation of English-language writers, such as Goh Poh Seng and Lim Thean Soo, initially saw themselves as Malayan, not Singaporean writers. Later the Commonwealth became an important field, with figures such as poet Arthur Yap making connections through Leeds University in the United Kingdom, and, increasingly, regional links to Australia and Hong Kong, and this field was in turn superseded by a Southeast Asia in which English increasingly took on the role of a language of international communication. Chinese-language texts were connected to China and to other diasporic communities within the region. From the 1930s onwards, under the influence of intellectuals such as Yu Dafu, the now nation-states of Singapore and Malaysia were centers of Nanyang (South Seas) literary production. Connections with Taiwan deepened during the Cold War.[29] Singapore was also temporarily a key publishing center for texts in Malay, a "New York for the Malay-Indonesian intelligentsia,"[30] and part of the larger archipelagic imagination of Nusantara, or a Malay world preceding and, in its revival, potentially transcending the divisions of colonialism.[31] The port city was more peripheral to writing in Tamil, but nonetheless part of *Tamilakam*, a Tamil world centered on the Indian Ocean, and encompassing large diasporic populations in colonial trading cities such as Rangoon, Penang, Medan, and Singapore itself.[32]

Texts in different languages, however, did not simply remain part of separate linguistic wordings: they were influenced by particular community experiences in the port city. Before independence, Chinese-language texts drew on a heritage of social realism from China but gave it a particular nationalist and anti-colonial inflection in opposition to Japanese and British colonialism. Malay texts such as the short stories of Mohamed Latiff Mohamed elaborated indigeneity within modernity, even as the status of the Malay language changed from a lingua franca to a real and then only a nominal national language. Tamil texts engaged with the class positions of plantation laborers and railway workers, professions into which the majority of South Asian migrants were channeled. And yet, as with world literature, such texts in each language were written and read by literate elites, even if elements of these elites saw themselves as being in the vanguard of social reform.

The cultural mixing and hybridity of Southeast Asian port cities, Nurfadzilah Yahaya has argued, made simplistic nativist narratives less appealing to local elites,[33] encouraging them to enter into alternative projects of placemaking that involved a regional imagination. As Nicole CuUnjieng Aboitiz has shown of the Philippines, such projects often included projects of imaginative geography such as forms of pan-Asianism, as well as reworking of racial discourses in surprisingly complex ways,[34] with the Japanese people, as an example of successful Asian modernization, identified as sharing the Malay racial origin of the Filipino people.[35] Such imaginative work, indeed, might usefully be understood as translocal: a sense of place is manufactured by reference to communities and polities beyond the immediate boundaries of governance,[36] much as the trade of port cities was bound to surrounding resource-rich hinterlands beyond their control. Yahaya's study of the manner in which Arab elites in Singapore made use of the legal structures of British governance to solidify and claim leadership of an imagined community of Muslims illustrates the complexity of these projects. Indeed, her discussion of the way in which a "textual habitus engendered by the practice of writing constituted a world in the making by generating jurisdictions"[37] might be applied not simply to legal documents, but to literary texts. In this account, then, literary texts emerge as autoethnographies of translocal self-fashioning in the port city, mixing structure and flow, rather than simply embodying critique of structure.

A final point here concerns translation. In discussions of world literature, there has been substantial discussion of translated texts. In the aesthetic perspective that Porter first discusses, translation has been traditionally dismissed as unable to capture the cultural essence of the original, so that "translations are inevitably inferior to their originals."[38] Emily Apter extends this to Porter's third concern, commercial commodification embodying inequality, exploring "reflexive endorsement of cultural equivalence and substitutability, or toward the celebration of nationally and ethnically branded 'differences' that have been niche-marketed as commercialized 'identities.'"[39] Yet, in literary texts of Singapore, translation emerges as, in Rebecca Walkowitz's words, "the engine rather than the caboose of literary history,"[40] not from an engagement with the world, but through two forms of attention to a very specific place.

First, there is a sense in which literary texts in Singapore are always already translated. Most are written in a single literary language, with a single script, and yet bear within themselves the translated experiences of a multilingual world. In doing so, they deviate from canonical or classical precedents in their language. In an elaboration of a description originally made by Malaysian writer Ng Kim Chew, Chan Cheow Thia writes of Malaysian Chinese literature as a "literary Galápagos," a marginal and isolated environment which encourages the mutation and evolution of new forms in a "sui generis ecology."[41] The process of mutation, generated by the presence of other languages and their correspondence with objects, is at its core, literary, since it introduces a rupture in the process of representation in which language ceases to be transparent.

Second, texts that are then translated into other languages in the city-state, and read by Singapore residents who inhabit the same geographical, if not, linguistic space, are both familiar and unfamiliar. Rather than embodying untranslatability or, indeed, full transparency, they enact a particular politics of translation. Their readers perceive an environment that overlaps with the one that they know through literatures written in languages that they do read, and yet is not the same. If the translation of a Singapore text into another language (now frequently the dominant language of English) does result in what Lawrence Venuti terms domestication, it is also simultaneously, in its difference, "foreignizing," foregrounding cultural and linguistic difference as part of an ethical process of intercultural relation.[42] It is with this recognition that we turn to a series of literary texts of Singapore.

The City's Texts

The first text we consider is not habitually considered a Singaporean literary text. Its author, the impeccably cosmopolitan medical doctor Han Suyin, raised in Sichuan by her Chinese father and Belgian mother, lived in both Johor Baru, the Malayan and then Malaysian city immediately across the water from Singapore, and the city-state itself, from 1952 to 1964.[43] Her 1956 novel *… and the Rain my Drink* hovers between autobiography and fiction. Han's prefatory note makes the usual note of the fictionality of its characters but adds that an "[e]xception is made for the author, who insists on occasionally appearing in the chapters."[44] Han's novel is centrally concerned with the Malayan Emergency, the conflict between British, Commonwealth and then Malayan forces, and fighters allied to the Malayan Communist Party from 1948 onwards. Uniquely at the time, Han's bilingualism in Mandarin and English enables her to incorporate a variety of perspectives within an English-language text: members of the colonial security apparatus, compliant local elites, Marxist guerillas, and Chinese detainees in the New Villages that were set up as a strategy of counterinsurgency. Yet the acts of translation the text performs, and the identities it represents, are not simple ones. Discussing Han's first novel, *A Many-Splendoured Thing* (1952), set in Hong Kong and also drawing extensively on autobiographical material, Zhuang Chiyuan notes that it enacts linguistic and "cultural translation" from Chinese to English, incorporating both foreignization in the estranged use of language and domestication in the way that communism is explained through Christian values.[45] In ... *and the Rain my Drink* no simple unidirectional translation is possible. The hospital in Johor Baru that serves as a metonym for the colonial Malayan state is a "babel"[46] full of "soft cacophony,"[47] in which lay interpreters compete for the attention of professionals and colonial officials with limited ability to speak "vernacular languages."[48] From this babel, Han as narrator suggests, a new "pattern" of identity may emerge,[49] whether informed by the idea of a Malayan nation in which Singapore and the peninsula will be united politically, or expressed in larger translocal identities such as "we-Asians."[50]

In Han's narrative, Singapore emerges as both fluid and a nexus of political control. It is a place of economic production, "growing and pushing its [...] pseudopodiae of factory sites further towards the Causeway."[51] It is also a site of consumption, a place to buy dresses, hats, and sex, or visit the cinema, where "without money a man [is] nothing but labour."[52] From its port, political detainees are deported to China, while from Kallang airport elites jet off to Hong Kong and other regional centers. Singapore is a center of much tighter colonial governance and surveillance than Malaya, but it is also a center of underground resistance. Most memorably, in Han's novel, it is a place of elite self-fashioning – the site of Quovilla, the house of the Straits Chinese millionaire Quo Boon. In Quovilla compliant elites and colonial officials meet, mingle, dissimulate, and negotiate their relationship to each other. Two of Quo Boon's children, we learn, are allied to the insurgent Malayan Communist Party. If the hospital in Johor is a metonym for colonial government, Quovilla is a metonym for the new political order that will replace it, the "happy eunuchs who are bound to us," as one colonial officer remarks, "by their knowledge of English."[53]

Yet Quovilla serves a further metonymic function: it mimes the English-language literary text as a place both of domestication but also of potential foreignization, of openness to other languages. Writing of Han's developing creative project, Fiona Lee notes that she did not dismiss writing in English, but rather encouraged anglophone elites to realize their privileged position and to begin to "read the politics of language and race" under neocolonialism.[54] The imbrication of translation, opacity, and power in the text gesture in this direction.

In Kuo Pao Kun's play *Descendants of the Eunuch Admiral*, with which this chapter began, the eunuchs are no longer bound to British colonial interests. Originally a migrant to Singapore from China, Kuo had been involved in leftist Chinese-language theater in the late 1960s and 1970s, and was then detained without trial for over four years for alleged "subversion" and the spreading of "communist ideology."[55] After his release, Kuo developed a multilingual and allegorical theater practice over two decades before his untimely death in 2002. *Descendants* is often acknowledged as his most important work. In the play, the voice of Zheng He, the Ming dynasty eunuch sent from China with a flotilla of ships on voyages to Southeast Asia, South Asia, and beyond, is juxtaposed with the dreamlife of a contemporary Singaporean citizen, secure within an economic hierarchy that results from the violence of a spiritual rather than a physical castration. The rhythm of everyday contemporary life seems secure, but is undermined by the citizen's return to a "nightly unknown," in which apparent agency under neoliberalism is revealed to be subjection.[56] One night, the citizen dreams of being on the deck of Zheng He's flagship, "as if I was the commander. Yet I didn't have a clue where I was going."[57] There is no access to the lower decks, to the mechanisms of control: the neoliberal subject must perform life scripts in the cultural superstructure without any possibility of influencing the economic base. In an earlier passage, Kuo emphasizes that the roots of such violence to the self are complex: this is not simply something that a government does to a subject. Zheng He acquiesces to castration in order to benefit his family and to gain agency: "To live, I had to die; to act, I must submit."[58] The "climb" he made, the citizen speculates, "must have involved plenty of hard work – and often going against his own good conscience."[59]

Kuo does not, however, fetishize mobility: the spectacle of Singapore as a ship, sailing on through time, is as disconcerting as it is liberating. Rather, placemaking can be found in the processes of history that created Southeast Asia and Singapore as a city. In a 1997 report written by Kuo after a fellowship in Japan, the playwright reflected on the region's historical place as a "mediator for the major cultures and civilisations of the world," with influences from East Asia, South Asia, Europe, and the Middle East.[60] This history of mediation was also a history of ethical struggle for a better human society that drew on "deep-set emotional, rational, artistic, and spiritual habits, values and patterns" that economic affluence now threatened to erode.[61] *Descendants of the Eunuch Admiral*, several commentators have noticed, privileges the marketplace of the Southeast Asian port city as a place of cultural translation and exchange, of hospitality and "mutual respect."[62] What is less often noticed is that the city is not simply a place but a process of continual self- and communal reinvention. In their wanderings, Zheng He and his fleet come to a land in which an enlightened ruler has withdrawn from society and forbidden his descendants to succeed them: the country has become a "country of rulers, *negara raja-raja,* because all the people became their own rulers – *negara raja-raja.*"[63] Kuo here juxtaposes present politics to the past. When *Descendants* was performed, the memory of Singapore's Lee Kuan Yew stepping down as Prime Minister in 1990 was still fresh, as was the anticipation that his son, Lee Hsien Loong, would eventually succeed him as Prime Minister after a brief interregnum. The story of the *negara raja-raja* is revealed only to be a dream, and is followed by "a not-so-good dream – a dream in which he found that even the wise ruler had kept eunuchs."[64] The search for ethics in the present involves dreaming, but also ongoing struggles in which the legacy of the region's past as a center of cultural and linguistic translation is acknowledged and reworked in the present.

Such cultural and linguistic translation is more complexly embodied in texts written by Malay writers and carrying traces of Malay language. Article 152 of Singapore's constitution formally recognizes Malays as "the indigenous people of Singapore," even though the precise nature of Malay identity is complex.[65] The colonial history of the evolution of Singapore as a port city from the arrival in 1819 of East India Company adventurer Stamford Raffles and the 1824 Anglo-Dutch Treaty is also a history of Malay dispossession. Yet the Malay language has other resonances in Singapore. For an older generation in the port city, *pasar Melayu*, the Malay of the marketplace, was a lingua franca of both trade and affective ties. Furthermore, Singapore's original connection with Malaya and Malaysia has embedded Malay structurally in other ways. It is the national language, and the language of Singapore's national anthem, of military commands, and of the titles of public service awards. Malay's presence is thus a marker of an unfinished past in the present. Recent translations of Malay-language novelists such as Isa Kamari, Mohamed Latiff Mohamed, and Suratman

Markasan into English, along with translated poetry anthologies such as Annaliza Bakri's *Sikit-Sikit Lama-Lama Jadi Bukit* (2017) bring these histories into the present – stories of dispossession, catastrophe, and loss that serve as counternarratives to developmental stories of progress through hard work, industrialization, and economic growth. Malay authors writing in English use parallel foreignizing strategies. Alfian Sa'at's second poetry collection, *A History of Amnesia* (2001), presents the city-state of Singapore as a patient, born in 1965, suffering from a "history of amnesia of unknown onset and duration."[66] One element of Alfian's therapy is to expose the reader to the "white light of history,"[67] remembering both forgotten political actors from Singapore's independence struggle and also figures associated with Singapore from the medieval Malay narrative *Sulalat al-Salatin*. These figures, such as the strong man Badang or the young boy Hang Nadim, who is killed after saving Singapore because the Sultan fears he is too clever, are associated with particular parts of Singapore's topography: in Hang Nadim's case with Bukit Merah, or Red Hill, where he was murdered. These characters speak, as Badang says, in "a language not even my own,"[68] and their speech is foreignizing to both narrative and the everyday landscape that is marked with an overwritten Malay presence. Again, this is not an opposition here between fluidity and structure. Malay is the language of indigeneity and much of Singapore's topography, of its hills, rivers, and bays: it is firmly in place. It is also the language of the market, of trade, and of cultural interchange. In a recent essay Nazry Bahrawi has explored how what might seem simply regressive nostalgia for an imagined rural past in Malay writing is, in fact, a critique of "hyper-urbanism" in the present that emerges from an alternative conception of the modern that draws on indigeneity, "thirdwordliness," and a translocal connection with a region.[69]

Writing in Tamil, Singapore's fourth official language, is less well known to the majority of Singaporeans. A translated collection of stories, *The Goddess in the Living Room* (2014), by Latha (Krishnasamy Iyer Kanagalatha), illustrates translation's foreignizing potential when presented in English. As its title suggests, the stories in the collection often center on women, the domestic spaces in which they carry the burden of societal care, and their frequent experience of abuse and violence. They describe a cultural landscape through a lens that is unfamiliar to the majority of Singapore residents: ceremonies, festivals, contested rituals, and the microagressions that come with minoritization and racialization. Tamil as a language bridges elites, working classes, and migrant workers, and places them within a regional imagination that emerges from a different history, connecting to Sri Lanka as a source of migration, but also to Malaysian port cities such as Penang and to present-day Myanmar, from which many Indian residents were expelled after independence. Two stories, entitled "Alyssa" and "Alyssa Again" bookmark the collection: they describe a woman who spends her youth in rural Pulau Ubin, but then moves to a Housing Development Board flat on the main island of Singapore. After an accident that results in her arms being amputated at the elbow, and a divorce, she is forced to move to a one-room rental flat, the lowest rung of Singapore's public housing. Yet in her flat, she fills a tank with tropical fish, recalling the overnight fishing expeditions that she would go on with her grandfather, away from Singapore, and in particular a moment when she fell into the water, and he grabbed her and pulled her back. In her epiphany, the port comes alive within the city, the fish in the tank coming at her call and swimming "in a row near her mouth."[70]

Singapore's four official languages, of course, are not the only languages heard in the city. Chinese topolects such as Hokkien and Cantonese persist, and often enter other languages, as do other historically spoken languages such as Malayalam or Buginese. A variety of different linguistic practices are now brought together as Singlish, which has been codified as a "highly regulated and anxiously-kept-comprehensible" literary language in texts such as the 2012 edition of Ming Cher's novel *Spider Boys*,[71] or Cheryl Lu-Lien Tan's *Sarong Party Girls* (2016). Singapore has also seen, in the last decade, the publication of literary writing, mostly poetry, by migrant workers from the region who work in the city-state, either translated from languages such as Bengali, Bahasa Indonesia, Burmese or Filipino, or written in the original. Migrant poets have often been supported by Singaporean writers, editors, and publishers, and at times have also formed distinct, autonomous communities. Their writings do offer a genuine challenge, a further foreignization of the landscape of Singapore for Singaporean readers who encounter them largely in translation. And yet such writing does not simply offer subaltern experiences, a world literature from below. It, too, has become part of a series of structures of self-fashioning: festivals, competitions, and sites of pedagogy that are both expressive of communities and tied to the self-fashioning of liberal elites.[72]

Conclusion

Scholarship on Singapore in the humanities and social sciences frequently faces the problem of Singapore's exceptionalism: a city that became, in historian Edwin Lee's words, an "Unexpected Nation," an illiberal democracy, a postcolony whose per capita GDP vastly exceeds that of its former colonial power, with a cultural landscape marked by racial governmentality.[73] This very exceptionalism, however, makes the city a useful site through which to think through world literature, and particularly its ethical relationship to a global marketplace. In this account, Singapore emerges as a quintessential Southeast Asian port city, in which cultural, economic, and political precarity is matched by processes of localized and regional self-making that cannot appeal unproblematically to nativism. Literary texts in the port city may be usefully viewed not simply as critiques of structure, but as protean projects of self-making drawing on cultural artifacts and experiences that come to hand in the marketplace. Through self-fashioning in the marketplace, Kuo suggests, "the sea, the land, the sky" may become home.[74]

Notes

1 Kuo Pao Kun, *The Complete Works of Kuo Pao Kun. Vol. 4: Plays in English*, C.J.W-L. Wee, ed. (Singapore: World Scientific, 2012), 237.
2 Ibid., 253–254.
3 Clemens Greiner and Patrick Sakdapolrak, "Translocality: Concepts, Applications and Emerging Research Perspectives," *Geography Compass* 7, no. 5 (2013): 378.
4 Eric Tagliacozzo, "An Urban Ocean: Notes on the Historical Evolution of Coastal Cities in Greater Southeast Asia," *Journal of Urban History* 33, no. 6 (2007).
5 Victor Lieberman, *Strange Parallels: Southeast Asia in Global Context, c. 800–1830. Volume 1: Integration on the Mainland* (Cambridge: Cambridge University Press, 2003); Lieberman, *Strange Parallels: Southeast Asia in Global Context, c. 800–1830. Volume 2: Mainland Mirrors: Europe, Japan, China, South Asia, and the Islands* (Cambridge: Cambridge University Press, 2009); Anthony Reid, *Southeast Asia in the Age of Commerce, 1450–1680* (New Haven, CT: Yale University Press, 1988).
6 Robert Redfield and Milton B. Singer, "The Cultural Role of Cities," *Economic Development and Cultural Change* 3, no. 1 (1954): 53–73.
7 Tagliacozzo, "Urban Ocean," 914.
8 Ibid., 912.
9 Jini Kim Watson, "Aspirational City: Desiring Singapore and the Films of Tan Pin Pin," *Interventions* 18, no. 4 (2016): 543.
10 Tai-Yong Tan, "Port Cities and Hinterlands: A Comparative Study of Singapore and Calcutta," *Political Geography* 26, no. 7 (2007): 851.
11 C.J.W-L. Wee, *The Asian Modern: Culture, Capitalist Development, Singapore* (Hong Kong: Hong Kong University Press, 2007), 85.
12 J.S. Furnivall, "Some Problems of Tropical Economy," in Rita Hinden, ed., *Fabian Colonial Essays* (London: Allen and Unwin, 1945), 168.

13 Tim Bunnell, *From World City to the World in One City: Liverpool through Malay Lives* (Chichester: Wiley-Blackwell, 2016), 223.
14 Brenda S.A. Yeoh, *Contesting Space in Colonial Singapore: Power Relations and the Urban Built Environment* (Singapore: NUS Press, 2013).
15 Wong Yunn Chii and Tan Kar Lin, "Emergence of a Cosmopolitan Space for Culture and Consumption: The New World Amusement Park-Singapore (1923–70) in the Inter-War Years," *Inter-Asia Cultural Studies* 5, no. 2 (2004): 279–304; Philip Holden, "At Home in the Worlds: Community and Consumption in Urban Singapore" in Ryan Bishop, John Phillips, and Yeo Wei-Wei, eds., *Beyond Description: Singapore Space Historicity* (London: Routledge, 2004), 79–94.
16 See, for example, Holden, "Complicity and Resistance: English Studies and Cultural Capital in Colonial Singapore," *Kunapipi* 22, no. 1 (2000): 74–84; Joanne Leow, "'A Delicate Pellet of Dust': Dissident Flash Fictions from Contemporary Singapore," *Journal of Postcolonial Writing* 51, no. 6 (2015): 723–736; Gui Weihsin, "Public Transit and Urban Poetics: Singapore's Moving Words Poetry Project and Anthology," *Textual Practice* 35, no. 2 (2021): 227–245; and Watson, "Aspirational City."
17 David Porter, "The Crisis of Comparison and the World Literature Debates," *Profession* 1 (2011): 246.
18 Pheng Cheah, *What is a World? On Postcolonial Literature as World Literature* (Durham, NC: Duke University Press, 2016), 2.
19 Franco Moretti, "Conjectures on World Literature," *New Left Review* 1, no. 1 (2000): 56.
20 WReC (Warwick Research Collective), *Combined and Uneven Development: Towards a New Theory of World-Literature* (Liverpool: Liverpool University Press, 2016); Pascale Casanova, *The World Republic of Letters*, trans. M.B. DeBevoise (Cambridge, MA: Harvard University Press, 2004).
21 Cheah, *What is a World?* 5; 6.
22 Debjani Ganguly, *This Thing Called the World: The Contemporary Novel as Global Form* (Durham, NC: Duke University Press, 2016), 83.
23 WReC, *Combined and Uneven Development*, 92.
24 Sarah Brouillette, *Literature and the Creative Economy* (Stanford, CA: Stanford University Press, 2014), 177.
25 Ganguly, *This Thing*, 198.
26 Cheah, *What is a World?* 296.
27 Brouillette, *Creative Economy*, 181.
28 Johanna Brenner and Nancy Fraser, "What Is Progressive Neoliberalism? A Debate," *Dissent* 64, no. 2 (2017): 130.
29 Brian C. Bernards, *Writing the South Seas: Imagining the Nanyang in Chinese and Southeast Asian Postcolonial Literature* (Seattle, WA: University of Washington Press, 2015), 3–28; Kim Tong Tee, "Sinophone Malaysian Literature: An Overview" in Shu-Mei Shih et al., eds., *Sinophone Studies: A Critical Reader* (New York: Columbia University Press, 2013), 304–314; Chan Cheow Thia, *Malaysian Crossings: Place and Language in the Worlding of Modern Chinese Literature* (New York: Columbia University Press, 2022), 1–30.

30 Azhar Ibrahim, "Malay Literary Intelligentsia and Colonialism: A Stunted Discourse" in Alfian Sa'at, Faris Joraimi, and Sai Siew Min, eds., *Raffles Renounced: Towards a Merdeka History* (Singapore: Ethos, 2021), 151.
31 Hans-Dieter Evers, "Nusantara: History of a Concept," *Journal of the Malaysian Branch of the Royal Asiatic Society* 89, no. 1 (2016): 3–14; Ngoi Guat Peng, "Editorial Introduction: The Pluralistic Thoughts and Imagined Boundaries in Nusantara," *Inter-Asia Cultural Studies* 18, no. 3 (2017): 313–316.
32 Sunil Amrith, *Crossing the Bay of Bengal: The Furies of Nature and the Fortunes of Migrants* (Cambridge, MA: Harvard University Press, 2013), 179.
33 Nurfadzilah Yahaya, *Fluid Jurisdictions: Colonial Law and Arabs in Southeast Asia* (Ithaca, NY: Cornell University Press, 2020), 17.
34 Nicole CuUnjieng Aboitiz, *Asian Place, Filipino Nation: A Global Intellectual History of the Philippine Revolution, 1887–1912* (New York: Columbia University Press, 2020), 5.
35 Ibid., 154.
36 Greiner and Sakdapolrak, "Translocality," 373–384.
37 Yahaya, *Fluid Jurisdictions*, 16.
38 Susan Bassnett, ed., "Introduction: The Rocky Relationship Between Translation Studies and World Literature" in *Translation and World Literature* (London: Routledge, 2018), 3.
39 Emily S. Apter, *Against World Literature: On the Politics of Untranslatability* (London: Verso, 2013), 2.
40 Rebecca L. Walkowitz, *Born Translated: The Contemporary Novel in an Age of World Literature* (New York: Columbia University Press, 2015), 5.
41 Chan, *Malaysian Crossings*, 7.
42 Lawrence Venuti, *The Translator's Invisibility: A History of Translation*, 3rd ed. (London: Routledge, 2017), xvii.
43 Ina Zhang, "A Dissenting Voice: The Politics of Han Suyin's Literary Activities in Late Colonial and Postcolonial Malaya and Singapore," *Journal of Postcolonial Writing* 57, no. 2 (2021): 155–170.
44 Han Suyin, *... and the Rain My Drink* (London: Jonathan Cape, 1956), [6].
45 Zhuang Chiyuan, "Writer as Translator: Cultural Translation in Han Suyin's *A Many-Splendoured Thing*," *Journal of Postcolonial Writing* 57, no. 2 (2021): 207.
46 Han, *... and the Rain*, 37.
47 Ibid., 35.
48 Ibid., 36.
49 Ibid., 37.
50 Ibid., 252.
51 Ibid., 245.
52 Ibid., 242.
53 Ibid., 273–274.
54 Fiona Lee, "Neutralizing English: Han Suyin and the Language Politics of Third World Literature," *Journal of Postcolonial Writing* 57, no. 2 (2021): 238.
55 C.J.W-L. Wee, "Introduction: Art, Culture, Capitalist Development and Kuo Pao Kun," *Inter-Asia Cultural Studies* 21, no. 2 (2020): 184.

56 Kuo, *The Complete Works*, 235.
57 Ibid., 243.
58 Ibid., 247.
59 Ibid., 244.
60 Kuo Pao Kun and C.J.W-L. Wee, "Challenges to Asian Public Intellectuals," *Inter-Asia Cultural Studies* 21, no. 2 (2020): 208.
61 Ibid., 206.
62 Kuo, *The Complete Works*, 249.
63 Ibid., 251.
64 Ibid., 252.
65 An example of this is Halimah Yacob, who currently serves in the largely ceremonial role of President of Singapore. Halimah succeeded as the only candidate nominated in an electoral cycle reserved for Malay candidates despite having the designation "Indian" on her identity card. For a historical perspective on Malay identity in Singapore, see Syed Muhd Khairudin Aljunied, "Malay Identity in Postcolonial Singapore," in Maznah Mohamad and Syed Muhd Khairudin Aljunied, eds., *Melayu: The Politics, Poetics, and Paradoxes of Malayness* (Singapore: NUS Press, 2012), 145–167.
66 Alfian Sa'at, *A History of Amnesia* (Singapore: Ethos, 2001), [7].
67 Ibid., 53.
68 Ibid., 62.
69 Nazry Bahrawi, "Rindu Rustic: Singapore Nostalgias in Modern Malay Prose," *Journal of Intercultural Studies* 40, no. 4 (2019): 516.
70 Latha (Krishnasamy Iyer Kanagalatha), *The Goddess in the Living Room*, trans. Palaniappan Arumugum, Sulosana Karthigasu, Kavitha Karumbayeeram, Yamuna Murthi Raju, Ravi Shanker, and Kokilavani Silvarathi (Singapore: Epigram, 2014), 166.
71 Eunice Ying Ci Lim, "'Twice-Nationalized': The Expatriation and Repatriation of Ming Cher's Spider Boys," *Antipodes: A North American Journal of Australian Literature* 33, no. 2 (2019): 350.
72 Witness, for example, the annual Migrant Poetry Competition held in Singapore, or the 2018 and 2020 Global Migrant Festivals, both centered on Singapore. See Janice Tai, "Burgeoning Scene Blossoms into Migrant Literature Festival; About 200 Attend Inaugural Event Featuring Literary Works of Foreign Workers in S'pore," *Straits Times*, (December 23, 2019), www.straitstimes.com/singapore/inaugural-literature-festival-featuring-works-by-migrant-workers-held-at-the-national; Zakir Hossain Khokan, "Taking Down Borders: An Interview with Poet Zakir Hossain Khokan," interview by Theophilus Quek, *Asian Books Blog*, September 28, 2020, www.asianbooksblog.com/2020/09/taking-down-borders-interview-with-poet.html.
73 Edwin Lee, *Singapore: The Unexpected Nation* (Singapore: ISEAS, 2008).
74 Kuo, *The Complete Works*, 254.

CHAPTER 12

Imagining the Migrant in Twenty-First-Century Johannesburg

Megan Jones

Johannesburg has always been a city of migrants, drawing people and capital from across the globe when gold was discovered on the Witwatersrand in 1886, and it has been the dominant site of economic and cultural production in southern Africa ever since. Colonial and apartheid discourses of the city asserted worldliness by insisting on its Eurocentrism, but from its inception it has been physically and psychically shaped by African migrants.[1] The accepted narrative of white entrepreneurial presence in the city is contradicted by its reliance on black migrant labor from within South Africa and across the region, Mozambique, Botswana, Malawi, Lesotho, Zimbabwe, and Zambia.[2] By the start of the South African War in 1899, there were 100,000 African men working on the gold mines. Forms of social control exercised over black workers were unyielding; the movement of laborers was severely curtailed, and they were required to live in closed compounds on the mine premises.[3]

Colonial segregation of urban space formed the basis of a defining feature of apartheid – the migrant labor system. After gaining power in 1948, the National Party instituted legal measures that deprived black South Africans of land, culminating in the Bantu Homelands Citizens Act of 1970, which made them citizens of rural reserves or "homelands." Stripped of their South African citizenship, black people became migrants in their own country, working in "white" cities where they were subjected to pass laws and forcibly located in townships. Unlike internal migration, external migrants to Johannesburg were predominantly young and male until the 1990s, when the end of apartheid freed up national borders and the city became a hub for immigrants from all over Africa.[4] This chapter reads the afterlife of the migrant labor system alongside the multidirectional flow of people and goods between Johannesburg and the rest of the continent, registering the city's emplacement within a network of cities extending north.

The experiences of migration and black life in colonial and apartheid Johannesburg were captured across textual forms that asserted a right to the city. For example, Peter Abrahams's novel *Mine Boy* (1946) tracked the evolution of class consciousness through rural migrant Xuma; the pages of *Drum* magazine (1951–) vividly expressed the creolized spaces of Sophiatown; in the 1970s and 1980s the work of Black Consciousness poets such as Mongane Wally Serote and Sipho Sepamla positioned the township as the city's ontological center. The isolating consequences of apartheid meant that much of this literature was preoccupied with the national, but the late 1990s and early 2000s witnessed a transnational turn that revealed Johannesburg's enmeshment in continental and global geographies. The chapter takes the transnational moment at the cusp of the millennium as its starting point, considering migrant presences in Phaswane Mpe's now canonical novel, *Welcome to Our Hillbrow* (2001),[5] together with Ivan Vladislavic's *The Restless Supermarket*,[6] published the same year, and *The Exploded View* (2017).[7] The chapter explores how the spatial ambiguity of these earlier books cedes to a hardening of social and material difference in fictions produced after the xenophobic attacks of 2008. If Mpe's and Vladislavic's writing uses formal experimentation to convey urban multiplicities, Sue Nyathi's *The Gold-Diggers* (2018)[8] and Novuyo Rosa Tshuma's *Shadows* (2013)[9] draw on a realism that registers the claustrophobia and *immobility* of migrant experience. Johannesburg is to some extent decentered in the work of these two Zimbabwean writers, for whom the southern Zimbabwean city of Bulawayo is the nodal point of migrant identity. The challenge of generating a hospitable city is reflected in a second genre shift, this time toward the speculative. In Lauren Beukes's *Zoo City* (2010)[10] and Masande Ntshanga's *Triangulum* (2019)[11] the parameters of the real city become tenuous and are interpolated by depictions of alternate and future Johannesburgs oriented toward the continent and beyond.

The Indeterminate City

Migrant literatures map Johannesburg through close attention to specificity of place, particularly the inner-city neighborhood of Hillbrow, which is the setting of six of the works discussed here.[12] The area's dilapidated buildings are metaphorical of the shifting meaning of space and place in Johannesburg and South Africa more generally. Up until the mid-1980s, Hillbrow was a "whites only" area, a magnet for young people and European immigrants. A change in the political climate during the 1980s led to the "graying" of the inner city, and black families began to take advantage of a change in business and governmental attitudes toward spatial segregation. In the mid-1990s and early 2000s, as South Africa's borders opened, it became a gathering place for African immigrants seeking to gain a foothold in the continent's most industrialized city. The worlding of Hillbrow anticipated South Africa's increasingly transnational orientation, mirrored in literatures of the period.[13] Although external migration was not new to Johannesburg, the dismantling of apartheid meant that African migrants could be in the city in ways hitherto impossible. Mpe's paradigmatic *Welcome to Our Hillbrow* captures a Hillbrow imprinted by the patterns and pathways of multicultural histories: "Your first entry into Hillbrow was the culmination of many converging routes. You do not remember where the first route began. But you know all too well that the stories of migrants had a lot to do with its formation."[14] This emphasis on a city that looked to the global was matched by official discourses that, beginning in the 1990s, sought to position Johannesburg as a "world city."[15]

Welcome to Our Hillbrow begins with dizzying description of a walk through Hillbrow's streets by recent arrival, Refentše,

> If you are coming from the city centre, the best way to get to Cousin's place is by driving or by walking through Twist Street, a one-way street that takes you to the north of the city. You cross Wolmarans and there are three rather obscure streets, Kapteijn, Ockerse and Pietersen, before you drive or walk past Esselen, Kotze and Pretoria Streets.[16]

Mpe's impressionistic technique combines elements of the hyperreal with African orature to depict the disjointed and violent nature of life in inner-city Johannesburg. The vertiginous style disorients the reader, as the densely populated high-rise buildings of Hillbrow dwarf and disorient the street-level walker. His formal choices directly reflect the material disjunctures of the inner city, where the socioeconomic fractures that are apartheid's legacy are widening rather than diminishing. Although its two protagonists are local migrants – Refentše and Refilwe both move to the city from the rural Limpopo province – their narratives are intersected by the treatment of migrants from other parts of Africa. As Carrol Clarkson shows, the disintegration of community in Refentše's home village of Tiragalong is bound up with the fissured spaces of the city, and the ways in which Hillbrow is made unhomely and hostile to "foreigners."[17] Thus the ability, or failure, to instantiate meaningful communities in Hillbrow is evinced through the ties that bind rural South Africa not only to the cities but to a pan-African geography.

The book's defense of foreign migrants, or *Makwerekwere*, as they are pejoratively known, unsettles and expands prescribed notions of belonging in the city. It seeks to include not only migrants but also those living with HIV/AIDS, and xenophobic discourse renders the two synonymous: "AIDs's travel route into Johannesburg was through *Makwerekwere*; and Hillbrow was the sanctuary in which *Makwerekwere* basked."[18] Mpe's ethics of inclusion through pronouns has been noted by numerous commentators and is demonstrated by the "Our" in the book's title as well as the strategy of addressing the reader directly through the collective "You." For both Clarkson and Gugu Hlongwane, the mode of address indexes the gap between an imagined community and the absence of belonging and connection in Hillbrow.[19] Refentše reflects that the South African state's claim to human rights discourse is distinctly lacking in its treatment of migrants: "Ambiguities, paradoxes, ironies […] the stuff of our South African and *Makwerekwere* lives."[20] In fact, it is not the lives but the deaths of Refentše and Refilwe that draw together Hillbrow's fricative spatiality with the contradictions of migrant experience. Having discovered that his lover is sleeping with a mutual friend, Refentše jumps twenty stories to his death on a Hillbrow street. His plummet is rendered in a rapid stream of consciousness which interweaves the "liveliness of the place" and "menacing" aspects of the city with the presence of migrants:[21]

> *Makwerekwere* stretching their legs and spreading like pumpkin plants filling every corner of our city and turning each patch into a Hillbrow come to take our jobs in the new democratic rainbowism of African Renaissance that threatened the future of local Bafana Bafana fans momentarily forgetting xenophobia […] investing in the Moroccan team the Nigerian Super Eagles and singing at least they are African.[22]

The organic metaphors are not coincidental; migrant occupation of Johannesburg is naturalized and growing, connecting disparate parts of the city to Hillbrow, and recentering the city toward this marginal community. The potential for spatial and social change is, however, contained by the violent finality of Refentše's suicide, which is echoed by Refilwe's death from AIDS in the book's second half. Pursuing a degree in the UK, and despite her xenophobia, she meets and falls in love with a Nigerian man. However, both she and her new lover have unknowingly suffered from HIV/AIDS for years, and each returns home to die. The book ends by addressing her in the afterlife: "You too have had your fair taste of the sweet and bitter juices of life, that ooze through the bones of our Tiragalong and Alexandra, Hillbrow and Oxford […] Welcome to Our Heaven."[23] These words conjure a relational thread between the local and the global that is anchored by intimate associations, albeit cosmological. In this way, Mpe creates a form of spatial affectivity redolent of the "composite reality of Africans as bridging intimacy and distance, parochialism and cosmopolitanism."[24]

The Restless Supermarket is similarly preoccupied with the rapidly changing Hillbrow of the 1990s. The protagonist, proofreader Aubrey Tearle, is caught against his will in an altered cityscape that, once shaped by white European diasporas (Tearle's local drinking place is "Café Europa") is now home to African immigrants. Tearle's xenophobia is indiscriminate – "Bloody Germans. From Germany out *und so weiter*. Hungarians, Italians, Scots. Immigrants. Foul-weather friends"[25] – although his racism is unwavering: "It was not my imagination: there were more and more people of colour in Hillbrow. And it was obvious to me that they were living in our midst."[26] Sometimes European immigrants and local black South Africans combine in an unholy alliance: "Other black women appeared in the Café. Always women, in the beginning, on the arms of sallow-skinned men wearing gold jewellery and open-neck shirts. Continentals and Slavs, men with overstuffed wallets and easy habits."[27] The threat that these others signify for Tearle is a threat to Johannesburg's (white, Western European) urbanism, mirrored by his obsessive documentation and policing of the English language. But the borders of language are permeable and cannot be fenced, as the borders of the city are also in flux.

The tidy semiotic coordinates which Tearle attempts to impose on Hillbrow's hectic spaces find textual representation in his narrative of the fantasy city "Alibia," inspired by a mural on one of Café Europa's walls. Alibia is a "walled city" and its "narrow streets," "gondolas" and "baroque steeples" are an amalgam of European influences.[28] That is, it embodies a defended and exclusive ideal very unlike the Hillbrow in which Tearle lives. The failure of this imaginary city to inflect the spaces of the real Johannesburg is shown to be a failure, as James Graham puts it, of Tearle's sympathetic imagination. The book concludes without providing any answers as to how a different cityscape may be forged, and "frustrates any attempt to imagine the structural formation of material conditions necessary for a heterogeneous community to cohabit on more equal terms within the post-apartheid city."[29] Indeed, the racialization of Johannesburg spaces continues undisrupted, as one character points out to Tearle after the Café Europa closes down: "It's not the end of civilization, you know. There are new places for whites opening up in Rosebank."[30]

Tearle's futile efforts to order Hillbrow against the incursion of "foreigners," figured as Eastern Europeans and black South Africans, distinguishes another Vladislavic character, the middle-aged, white statistician Budlender of *The Exploded View*. The book is a collection of four interlinked narratives, each of which is focused on the daily experiences of four of Johannesburg's male inhabitants. Budlender is the protagonist of its first story, "Villa Toscana." The characters never meet but their lives intersect coincidentally through the city's houses, restaurants, billboards, and roads. The interweaving of discrete but connected stories and places cue the reader to the existence of alternate spaces between rigid physical and social expressions of difference. Budlender's narrative begins as he is sitting at traffic light in his car, assessing the vendors and beggars on the road outside:

> A man holding a hand-lettered sign asking for money or food came closer between the two lanes of cars, moving from window to window and tap-dancing for each driver in turn [...] Was he a Nigerian? It was time to learn the signs [...] a particular curl to the hair or shade to the skin, the angle of a cheekbone or jawline, the ridge of a lip, the slant of an eye, the size of an ear – it seemed to him that there were Nigerians everywhere. He had started to see Mozambicans too, and Somalis. It was the opposite of the old stereotype: they all looked different to him. Foreigners on every side. Could the aliens have outstripped the indigenes? Was it possible? There were no reliable statistics.[31]

Sandra Saayman has noted the dehumanizing language of Budlender's observations,[32] and his occupation as a census statistician shares uneasy echoes with apartheid's racial taxonomy, but there is something more being suggested here. Budlender's windscreen has, we learn later, been cracked by "a stone" ricocheting from the wheel of a mini-bus taxi, and he views the beggar through its fractured glass in order to break him into pieces or interpretable signs, reinforced by the two sentences, "Was he a Nigerian? It was time to learn the signs." However, the signs are evasive, and their meanings cannot be relied upon: "Could the aliens have outstripped the indigenes? There were no reliable statistics." Budlender's attempts to categorize the man outside his window (who may or may not be a migrant) is correlated by his need, like Tearle, to impose knowability upon Johannesburg. But his efforts are frustrated. The fracture in the windowpane is an "exploded view." It disassembles the whole (the individual, the city) into its components, but these refuse certainty, because they can be manipulated to construct a variety of images that are defined as much by the viewer as by the viewed. Budlender's perspective is as fractured and exploded as the glass in his windscreen.

The Hostile City

In Mpe's and Vladislavic's writing, migrants are aligned with a spatially ambiguous Johannesburg which cannot be pinned to static ways of knowing. Their stylistic inventiveness enables a mode of reading that reveals both the city's mutability and its fixedness. The formal experiments of the early 2000s gives way to a less accommodating realism as the unresolved tensions undercutting Johannesburg's claim to being a "world-class city" exploded in the late 2000s in a series of attacks targeting migrant communities.[33] Deep and persisting economic divisions in South Africa, which are still raced, meant that the already fragile existence of African migrants were rendered even more precarious. As Shose Kessi argued, it is within these persisting structural inequalities and the failures of economic reform that the xenophobic attacks must be understood.[34] Nyathi's *The Gold-Diggers* was written as a direct response to these events,[35] while Tshuma alludes to them elliptically in her poetic prologue to *Shadows* as "Bitter day back in 08."[36] Both authors were born in Bulawayo, and both are now of the Zimbabwean diaspora; Nyathi lives in Johannesburg and Tshuma in the US. Along with writers such as Nuruddin Farah and Yewande Omotoso, they are part of a group of African creatives who live or have lived in South Africa, and whose representations of its cities inscribe migrant perspectives.[37] Fiona Moolla observes, "the potential transnationalism of South African literature from the other direction has escaped attention,"[38] and in what follows the chapter thinks through the implications of reading Johannesburg from "the other direction." This includes paying attention to how the city is traversed by migrant "elsewheres"[39] in which it is only one node in a matrix of other cities and spaces.

The Gold-Diggers is anchored in the real events of 2008 and 2015, during which anti-immigrant sentiment resulted in multiple deaths, looting, and widespread violence. The book's unstinting realism does not shy away from the cruelty and instability of migrant life in Johannesburg. It opens at Bulawayo's Max Garage, "the gateway out of Bulawayo to places like Esigodini, Gwanda, Beitbridge and Johannesburg,"[40] where a group of strangers is about to undertake a dangerous and illegal journey across the border to South Africa. By beginning in Bulawayo, Nyathi effectively redirects the locus of foreign migrant narratives. Even a text as sympathetic to external migrants as *Welcome to Our Hillbrow* omits to account for their origins, so that they attain visibility only once they are in the city. By surfacing the elsewheres of migrant life, the book destabilizes Johannesburg's geographic hegemony. The city's recasting as a periphery is even more pronounced in Tshuma's *Shadows*, a collection of stories beginning with the eponymous novella "Shadows," whose protagonist Mpho also starts his journey from Max Garage. But if *The Gold-Diggers* moves most of its action to Johannesburg, "Shadows" makes the Bulawayo township where Mpho lives the driving force of his narrative, and his time in Johannesburg very brief.

Before turning to the content of the books, it is worth exploring how their titles offer glimpses into the Janus-faced city, what Sarah Nuttall has described as the contradiction between Johannesburg's "surface and underneath."[41] On the one hand, the reference to "gold" suggests surface affluence, tales of which lure migrants to the city. On the other, this conspicuous wealth would not be possible without the hidden labor of those who work underground, the "gold-diggers," of whom Nyathi's grandfather was one such migrant.[42] *Shadows* speaks to the spectrality of those who inhabit the fringes, a material and psychic "underneath" from which the migrant rarely escapes. In both texts, migrants disappear in liminal spaces – the border, the inner city – shadows from which they never emerge. In *The Exploded View*, statistician Budlender's failure to successfully label the possibly migrant beggar is imagined as a failure to impose orderliness on the city; for Nyathi and Tshuma, Johannesburg is simply unnavigable for most migrants, who are ultimately rendered statistical by their violent, premature deaths: "He was just another statistic."[43]

The character arcs in *The Gold-Diggers* are overwhelmed by a somewhat schematic representation of suffering: Malume is eaten by a crocodile trying to cross into South Africa, Thulisiwe is kidnapped at the border by people smugglers, the child Gugulethu is sold into sexual slavery, Lindani is tricked into becoming a drug-mule by her Nigerian boyfriend, Chamunorwa is lynched by a xenophobic mob, Chenai is sexually assaulted by her white employer, and Dumisani, who becomes a successful businessman, barely survives a murder attempt by his South African wife. In this way, the novel rehearses a long-standing debate about the utility of spectacle in African fiction.[44] The tension between authentically capturing the vicissitudes of migrant life without flattening its intricacies is a balance Nyathi struggles to achieve. As the remaining migrants finally arrive in the city, their driver Melusi thinks to himself, "Every encounter [with Johannesburg] was different. No one man could experience Johannesburg in the same way."[45] And yet, what the novel demonstrates is spatial and experiential homogeneity. In attempting to articulate the very real dangers that migrants face, *The Gold-Diggers* reduces non-Zimbabwean characters to caricatures, from Lindani's hustling boyfriend, Kayin, to Dumisani's unscrupulous and sexually rapacious wife, Nomonde.

In "Shadows," the realist aesthetic is threaded with Mpho's poetic observations, "maddening whorls,"[46] in a strategy that thickens the places Tshuma describes, whether the Bulawayo township where he resides with his ailing mother, a prostitute, or his short stay in Johannesburg. Walking through his township, Mpho sees its poverty – "In the gutter, the shit flows" – but also its complexity – "in the midst of all that shit, clumps of wild sugar cane flourish."[47] After his mother dies, he follows his ex-girlfriend Nomsa to Johannesburg, staying with an acquaintance who lives in the inner city. Mpho's first impressions of Johannesburg index the tension between its "surface and underneath." From a distance it is "awash in the light of the morning; a sleepy sun forming a haloed arch over the metropolitan structures protruding from the green landscape – like a postcard,"[48] but this image of an ideal city is punctured by its ruination. The derelict inner-city buildings "squat in the filth of the streets, with broken windows and dingy walls [...] babies wail [....] Sometimes you hear the moans of people making love. The screams of people in pain."[49]

Scenes of decay maintain the trope of the atomizing city evident in Nyathi's writing but the narrative pivots in a chapter called "Joburg streets," where Mpho's first-person perspective is replaced by a second person "You" that brings to mind the collective "You" of *Welcome to Our Hillbrow*. Expanding the narrative perspective enables Tshuma to depict Mpho's experience of the city as shared, and to locate him within an encompassing migrant identity. The chapter describes how the streets are linguistically marked by migrants –"Everywhere you go, you hear loud, rapid Shona and lilting Nigerian-English"[50] – and proceeds to lay claim to the totality of the city: "This is Joburg. The Shona and the Nigerian-English, they are the mortar that holds up this crumbling block."[51] This contention is crucial because it overtly constructs Johannesburg as a migrant city in ways that even Mpe's text does not. Here, the questions arise of which Johannesburgs attain visibility in the domain of world literature, and whether representations such as Tshuma's and Nyathi's impact the ways in which the city is read outside South Africa. While their works do have a local audience, it remains the case that in the global literary market, Johannesburg fictions are South African fictions. Migrant authors rarely appear on British or American university curricula dealing with South African literatures, for example. The realities of whose work is received as belonging to the already under-represented field of "South African" literatures thus shows the insecurity of Tshuma's linguistic claim to the city, a tenuousness that is reflected in her story's final pages.

Although "Joburg Streets" illuminates the mobile walker, the "You," of *Welcome to Our Hillbrow*, it closes with an image of stasis. Caught between the need to survive in the city and fear of persecution, migrant life is reduced to a singular outcome, "The result: immobility."[52] The theme of immobility is revisited at the story's end, in an example of the "double-displacement" of non-belonging.[53] After failing to persuade Nomsa to return with him, Mpho goes back to Bulawayo where he is promptly arrested and jailed for "insulting and undermining the authority of the President of the Republic of Zimbabwe."[54] The book concludes in court, where his guilty verdict seems assured. Mpho's entrapment signals his dislocation from both Bulawayo and Johannesburg, and Tshuma's refusal of narrative closure leaves the reader similarly suspended. His final thoughts drift to his mother: "Mama and I, perhaps we'll find peace in the shadows."[55] Against the heightened visibility declared for migrants on Johannesburg's streets, these final words intimate that, whether in life or death, the invisibility of the shadows may be the safest space for those whom society oppresses.

The Speculative City

The surge in South African speculative fiction over the last decade can be interpreted as responding to the limits of the imagined communities of the early 2000s, while also searching for ways of writing space that extend the parameters of realism, and it is to two examples of the genre that I now turn. Beukes's *Zoo City* and Ntshanga's *Triangulum* should be read within speculative fiction's emergence across the continent, which Joshua Burnett identifies as a continuation of the magical-realist tradition of writers such as Amos Tutuola and Ben Okri.[56] Burnett argues that, "Africans themselves are the descendants of victims of an alien invasion (i.e., colonialism, particularly of the European variety but also other forms), and it is that alien invasion which created the political geography of modern-day Africa."[57] Beukes and Ntshanga track migrant occupation of Johannesburg in quite different ways but they each appropriate the alien motif that Burnett diagnoses: in *Zoo City*, via prejudice against the zoos, or the animalled, which is analogous to the xenophobic treatment of "alien" African migrants,[58] and in *Triangulum* as an extra-terrestrial encounter highlighting historical practices that made black South Africans alien in their own country.[59]

Zoo City is stylistically hybrid, combining science fiction with elements of the noir detective story in a specifically South African lexicon, which the author herself describes as "muti-noir."[60] Its protagonist, Zinzi December, is a former journalist jailed after her involvement in the death of her brother and who has fallen from a comfortable middle-class life into the miasma of Hillbrow, where she lives with her partner Benoit Bocanga, a Congolese refugee. Zinzi and Benoit are "zoos," which means they can be identified as criminals by the presence of animal familiars, in Zinzi's case, a sloth. Zinzi's *shavi*, or magical ability, is to locate lost objects. After one of her clients is murdered, she is drawn into the nefarious world of music producer Odi Huron. Beukes's descriptions of the city show two Johannesburgs, absolutely segregated from one another. If Zinzi's walks through Hillbrow disclose marginalization, they also reveal social networks that operate via public spaces such as the street. AbdouMaliq Simone has called these affiliations "people as infrastructure,"[61] and they map the inner city not through its crumbling built environment but the ways in which inhabitants forge relational systems. Migrants are an integral part of these spatial socialities; on her way to a client in the suburbs, Zinzi buys a "nutritious breakfast, aka a *skyf*" from a Zimbabwean street vendor, and airtime from a local Cameroonian shop owner.[62]

However, migrants' and zoos' occupation of the city is restricted to Hillbrow, and movement through its other spaces is met with hostility: "I walk on up Empire and through Parktown past the old Johannesburg College of Education, attracting a few aggressive hoots from passing cars. I give them the finger. Not my fault if they're so cloistered in suburbia that they don't get to see zoos."[63] The segregation of city space is marked here by the division between walkers and drivers. The drivers are hermetically and antagonistically sealed from the outside world, preventing the kinds of social interaction of the street. The threat to suburbia, to the houses of the drivers, is the walking figure of the "zoo," who is a reminder of the precarity of the status quo and its reliance on exclusion. Societal neglect of the poor is reflected in the flight of capital to the suburbs. In a later scene, Zinzi takes cover from gang warfare in Hillbrow's Palisades Mall, now mostly empty. Her attention is caught by an abandoned travel agency:

> I'm held up by the signage in Go-Go-Go Travel, or more specifically the list of specials. The place names are a list of well-worn exotica: Zanzibar. Paris. Bali. Amazing deals!
>
> These are places that do not feature: Harare. Yamoussoukro. Kinshasa. These are places that require alternative travel arrangements.[64]

As Hillbrow has become home to Zimbabweans, Ivorians, and Congolese, the aspirational discourses of neoliberal South Africa have swiftly relocated elsewhere. Go-Go-Go "took the imperative of its name too seriously, because it's upped and gone."[65] The contrast between international sites of leisure and the "places that do not feature," strongly evokes Zygmunt Bauman's theorization of the hyper-mobile tourist versus the migrant "vagabond," whose movement is enforced and peripheralized.[66] The novel does not envision that these social and spatial segregations will change in Johannesburg; the zoos will remain in "zoo city," and the suburbanites in their gated communities. Rather than refiguring the relationship between its intra-city spaces, Beukes orients Johannesburg in terms of the continent, and the book ends by looking outwards and northwards.

In the final chapter, Zinzi is sitting in a car at Beit Bridge, on the border between South Africa and Zimbabwe. She is heading toward Congo, on a journey that is the inverse of that undertaken by Benoit, to find his wife and children after he is injured trying to rescue her. The book sketches her itinerary:

> Day one: Johannesburg to Harare
> Day two: Harare to Lusaka
> Day three: Lusaka to Mbeya
> Day four: Mbeya to Dar es Saalam
> Day five: Dar es to Nairobi
> Day six: Nairobi to Jinja
> Day seven: Cross into southern Uganda
> Day eight: Mbasa to Kigali.
> The place names sound like new worlds. I have only ever travelled to Europe.[67]

With these words, Beukes repurposes and corrects the vocabulary of Go-Go-Go Travel, forging a connective web between Johannesburg and Kigali that replaces the consumerist geographies of "the tourist" with that of the "vagrant." This is optimistically framed by "new worlds," offering an alternate vision to the scenes of impoverishment and desperation typically associated with the continent. Traveling on a forged Zimbabwean passport as Tatenda Murapata, a young migrant worker returning home for a holiday, Zinzi is transformed from having once been a "tourist" who had only ever "travelled to Europe" to being a migrant. Her symbolic renaming fully deconstructs the boundaries between South Africa and its neighbors, and between locals and "aliens."

Zoo City concludes by looking outwards toward the rest of the continent; *Triangulum* extends this vision to otherworldly spaces. The book's treatment of the migrant labor system connects the homelands to Johannesburg, to the world and finally, exceeds borders of the planet. It centers on the nonlinear coming-of-age story of an unnamed woman, segueing between the years of her adolescence at the turn of the millennium and a series of recorded therapy sessions some thirty years later. From the age of nine, the narrator is haunted by what she calls "The Machine," which appears as an inverted triangle.[68] Much later, in old age, she will learn of the planet's imminent destruction through these extra-terrestrial encounters. Her recollections are framed by the diary of Dr. Naomi Buthelezi, herself a science-fiction writer, who is tasked with decoding the manuscripts in the year 2040; among her discoveries is that the documents predict a global apocalypse in 2050.

As a bildungsroman and speculative imagining of South Africa's near future, *Triangulum* draws on local history to critique global capital and environmental harm. Ntshanga directly addresses the correlation between the structures of apartheid and the themes of science fiction: "South Africa's dystopian future could easily be imagined through its dystopian past. In the sense that we've already been through it—the kind of tiered and oppressive technological society that's a trope in a lot of science fiction narratives about the future."[69] The South African dystopia was spatially enacted in homelands and townships, through which the migrant laborer moved, working in Johannesburg's gold mines and living in the townships, but a citizen of the homeland. The book's first half is set in the former Ciskei, where the narrator lives with her father and then her aunt.[70] Both her parents are employed by the homeland government when her mother develops what is thought to be a psychiatric illness and vanishes. Her father is unable to find work after 1994 and has "dropped an economic class and retreated from the public, avoiding the glares that awaited [him],"[71] thus demonstrating the complex system of cooption by which apartheid operated.

The second part of the book is set in Johannesburg in 2025, "The Metropolis," where the narrator is employed as a programmer for a company whose aims remain mysterious: "The prevailing assumption [...] was that our purpose was data mining: to monitor the rise and decline of the worker population in the metropolis and beyond."[72] The company's methods are expressly linked to the population control strategies of apartheid; "History in the metropolis was a circle."[73] In this future Johannesburg, townships remain spaces of abandonment, discarded by the state and handed over to the private sector: "The townships were meant to serve as micro-cities, we were told: self-contained, privately owned zones."[74] These tactics most obviously echo the "separate but equal" lie of apartheid, although the origins of the Zones are international, having first developed in Asia.[75] In this way, the book establishes ties between the township and the global urban poor, whose lives are controlled by transnational corporates and who are in fact destined for slave labor.[76] The narrator's work turns out to be more sinister than data collection, as she is inducted into clandestine experiments on the minds of marginal persons, justified as eliminating the "self-destructive behaviours of the townships."[77] She joins an eco-terrorist group known as "The Returners," led by her lover D, who is killed along with several others attempting to sabotage

Protopa Paper, a petrochemical plant implicated in the development of the Zones.[78] Ten years later, the narrator learns that her missing mother Nobomi was the first to be contacted by the Machine. She travels to the Cradle of Humankind, where she receives a message from the aliens that Earth will be destroyed by an interstellar object unless humanity ceases its environmental destruction.[79]

Triangulum does not explicitly deal with external migrants but its representation of Johannesburg reveals how the historical treatment of black South Africans as itinerant, disposable labor continues in their relegation to under-resourced townships. The economically disenfranchised majority remain on the edges of the national project, and their protests over service delivery and government corruption are met with violent force.[80] Large numbers of the country's black population inhabit the status of "outsiders" typically ascribed to foreign migrants because they continue to be excluded from socioeconomic citizenship. In 2012, then Democratic Alliance leader Helen Zille tweeted that black school pupils from the Eastern Cape studying in the Western Cape were "education refugees."[81] Zille's conflation of black South Africans with refugees is one example of their persistent designation as "alien," even within national borders. Moreover, *Triangulum* illustrates how the unequal power relations governing the township transcend national borders via its depiction of "Zones" that have been rendered homogenous by global capital. Such correspondences ask us to think about how city spaces everywhere are organized against the interests of the poor, whether in Johannesburg, Harare, or London.

Conclusion

This chapter has sketched the outlines of migrant Johannesburg, paying close attention to how the thematic and formal choices of the city's writers speak to its evolution over the last two decades. In so doing, it considers both internal and external migration, as well as their intersection. The emergence of Johannesburg as a "world" city in the early 2000s was mirrored in the experimental fictions of Mpe and Vladislavic, who cultivated ambiguity between divided spaces. The failure to forge a hospitable Johannesburg, manifested by the xenophobic attacks of the 2000s and 2010s, saw the mutable city replaced by a reinscription of difference in texts by diasporic writers such as Nyathi and Tshuma. Although showing an internally atomized city, their works decenter Johannesburg as only one site in a network of migrant elsewheres, enmeshing it with the geography of the continent. These authors offer us the opportunity to read the city "from the other direction" and to reframe the parameters of what constitutes "South African" in the corpus of "world literature," an intervention to which this chapter responds. The chapter concludes by reading the speculative city of Beukes and Ntshanga, who imagine otherworldly spaces that establish lines of association between Johannesburg, the rest of Africa, the world, and beyond. Finally, the scope and variety of the literatures discussed here can only affirm the deep complexity of the city they represent.

Notes

1 Achille Mbembe and Sarah Nuttall, "Introduction," in Sarah Nuttall and Achille Mbembe, eds., *Johannesburg: The Elusive Metropolis* (Johannesburg: Wits University Press, 2009), 1–33.
2 Philip Harrison and Tanya Zack, "The Power of Mining: The Fall of Gold and Rise of Johannesburg," *Journal of Contemporary African Studies* 31, no.4 (October 2012): 551–570, 554–555.
3 Keith Beavon, *Johannesburg: The Making and Shaping of the City* (Pretoria: University of South Africa Press, 2004), 9–33.
4 Dudu Ndlovu and Loren Landau, "The Zimbabwe-South Africa migration corridor," in Tania Bastia and Ronald Skeldon, eds., *The Routledge Handbook of Migration and Development* (London and New York: Routledge, 2020), 473–478.
5 Phaswane Mpe, *Welcome to Our Hillbrow* (Johannesburg: Picador Africa, 2014), Kindle.
6 Ivan Vladislavic, *The Restless Supermarket* (Johannesburg: Umuzi, 2012), Kindle.
7 Ivan Vladislavic, *The Exploded View* (Johannesburg: Umuzi, 2017), Kindle.
8 Sue Nyathi, *The Gold-Diggers* (Johannesburg: Pan Macmillan South Africa, 2018), Kindle.
9 Novuyo Rose Tshuma, *Shadows* (Johannesburg: Kwela, 2013), Kindle.
10 Lauren Beukes, *Zoo City* (Johannesburg: Jacana Press, 2010).
11 Masande Ntshanga, *Triangulum* (Johannesburg: Umuzi, 2019). Kindle.
12 African migrants make up to 26.6 percent of the inner-city's population, while 25.4 percent of inner-city residents are internal migrants from other South African provinces. See Skosana, "Mayor's claim – undocumented migrants make up 80% of Joburg inner city – 'absurd,'" africacheck.org (September 7, 2017), https://bit.ly/3GD6ro8.
13 Ronit Frenkel and Craig Mackenzie, "Conceptualizing 'Post-Transitional' South African Literature in English," *English Studies in Africa* 53, no.1 (2010): 1–10.
14 Mpe, *Welcome*, 76.
15 Lindsay Bremner, "Re-Inventing the Johannesburg Inner City," *Cities* 17, no. 3 (2000): 185–193.
16 Mpe, *Welcome*, 116.

17 Carrol Clarkson, "Locating identity in Phaswane Mpe's *Welcome to Our Hillbrow*," *Third World Quarterly* 26, no. 3 (2005): 451–459.
18 Mpe, *Welcome*, 90.
19 Gugu Hlongwane, "'Reader, be assured this narrative is no fiction': The City and its Discontents in Phaswane Mpe's *Welcome to Our Hillbrow*," *Ariel – A Review of International English Literature* 37 (October 2006): 69–82.
20 Mpe, *Welcome*, 312.
21 Ibid., 325.
22 Ibid., 343. Bafana Bafana is the name of the South African national football team.
23 Ibid., 1338.
24 Frances Nyamnjoh, "Fiction and the Reality of Mobility in Africa," *Citizenship Studies* 17, nos. 6–7 (2013): 653–680, 669.
25 Vladislavic, *Restless Supermarket*, 81.
26 Ibid., 199.
27 Ibid., 201.
28 Ibid., 28.
29 James Graham, "Ivan Vladislavic and the Possible City," *Journal of Postcolonial Studies* 44, no. 4 (December 2008): 333–344; 336.
30 Vladislavic, *Restless Supermarket*, 458.
31 Vladislavic, *Exploded View*, 4.
32 Sandra Saayman "Imagining the Other – the Representation of the African Migrant in Contemporary South African Literature," *International Journal of Language & Linguistics* 3, no. 6 (2016).
33 Lauren Kruger, *Imagining the Edgy City: Writing, Performing, and Building Johannesburg* (Oxford: Oxford University Press, 2013), 198.
34 Shose Kessi, "Xenophobia and the Politics of Citizenship and Belonging in South Africa," *The Johannesburg Salon* 10 (2015): 10–13; 11.
35 Nyathi, *Gold-Diggers*, 59.
36 Tshuma, *Shadows*, 35.
37 Omotoso's first novel, *Bom Boy* (2011), tells the story of Leke, a Nigerian boy living in Cape Town, while Moolla notes that Farah is working on a novel about Somali migrants living in Johannesburg, yet to be published at time of writing: Moolla, "Introduction: Re-Inscribing Nuruddin Farah in African Literature," *Tydskrif vir Letterkunde* 57, no. 1 (2020): 1–6; 3.
38 Ibid., 4.
39 Abdoumaliq Simone, "On the Worlding of African Cities," *African Studies Review* 4, no. 2 (September 2001): 15–41; 18–19.
40 Nyathi, *Gold-Diggers*, 228.
41 Sarah Nuttall, *Entanglement: Literary and Cultural Reflections on Post-Apartheid* (Johannesburg: Wits University Press, 2009), 83–84.
42 Nyathi, *Gold-Diggers*, 147.
43 Ibid., 552.
44 See, for example, Helon Habila's review of another Zimbabwean author, NoViolet Bulawayo's *We Need New Names* (2013) at *The Guardian* (June 20,

2013), www.theguardian.com/books/2013/jun/20/need-new-names-bulawayo-review, in which he described some of the novel's scenes as "poverty porn."

45 Nyathi, *Gold-Diggers*, 872.
46 Tshuma, *Shadows*, 899.
47 Ibid., 57.
48 Ibid., 1110.
49 Ibid., 1133.
50 Ibid., 1154.
51 Ibid., 1178.
52 Ibid., 1186.
53 Johan Jacobs, "The Trauma of Home and (Non)Belonging in Zimbabwe and its Diaspora: 'Conversion disorder' in *Shadows* by Novuyo Rosa Tshuma," *Literator* 37, no. 1 (2016).
54 Tshuma, *Shadows*, 1390.
55 Ibid., 1651.
56 Joshua Yu Burnett, "'Isn't Realist Fiction Enough?': On African Speculative Fiction," *Mosaic: An Interdisciplinary Critical Journal* 52, no. 3 (2019).
57 Ibid.
58 Shane Graham, "The Entropy of Built Things: Postapartheid Anxiety and the Production of Space in Henrietta Rose-Innes' *Nineveh* and Lauren Beukes' *Zoo City*," *Safundi* 16, no. 1(2015): 64–77;74.
59 It should be noted that the genre has been critiqued for its dominance by white writers, of whom Beukes is the best known. This imbalance gestures towards wider questions about which South African writers are read internationally, and the consequences of historically raced access to educational and financial resources.
60 Cheryl Stobie, "Dystopian Dreams from South Africa: Lauren Beukes's *Moxyland* and *Zoo City*," *African Identities* 10, no. 4 (2012): 367–380.
61 AbdouMaliq Simone, "People as Infrastructure: Intersecting Fragments in Johannesburg," *Public Culture* 16, no. 3 (2004): 407–429; 407.
62 Beukes, *Zoo City*, 13–17.
63 Ibid., 18.
64 Ibid., 68.
65 Ibid., 59.
66 Zygmunt Bauman, *Globalization: The Human Consequences* (New York: Columbia University Press, 1998), 77–102.
67 Beukes, *Zoo City*, 348.
68 Ntshanga, *Triangulum*, 97.
69 Masande Ntshanga, "South Africa's dystopian future could easily be imagined through its dystopian past," interview by Siphiwe Gloria Ndlovu, *The Johannesburg Review of Books* (June 3, 2019), https://bit.ly/3IhpfL4.
70 As Dr. Buthelezi's notes explain, "the Ciskei homeland was a nominal independent state, symptomatic of the apartheid regime, that existed from 1981 to 1994" (Ntshanga, *Triangulum*, 20).
71 Ibid., 30.

72 Ibid., 214.
73 Ibid., 226.
74 Ibid., 215.
75 Ibid., 215; 319.
76 Of course, the blueprint for apartheid was transnational, having been influenced by both European colonialism and the Jim Crow laws of the southern states of America. See for example, David Theo Goldberg, *The Threat of Race: Reflections on Racial Neoliberalism* (Hoboken: John Wiley & Sons, 2008).
77 Ntshanga, *Triangulum*, 248.
78 Ibid., 315.
79 Ibid., 341.
80 Peter Alexander, "Rebellion of the Poor: South Africa's Service Delivery Protests—A Preliminary Analysis," *Review of African Political Economy* 37, no. 123 (2010): 25–40.
81 Osiame Molefe, "Tough lessons for Zille from refugee tweet debacle," *Daily Maverick* (April 4, 2012), www.dailymaverick.co.za/article/2012-04-04-tough-lessons-for-zille-from-refugee-tweet-debacle/.

CHAPTER 13

Russia

Borders and Centers

Anne Lounsbery

Prologue: Kyiv/Kiev, Provinces/Capitals

A fraught question: where are Russia's borders, and where is its center? At the time of this writing, its borders are unstable: the Russian Federation is waging war in an attempt to conquer – or in Russia's representation, take back – territory in the sovereign nation of Ukraine. As for its center, for perhaps half a millennium Russia has imagined itself as, among other things, the inheritor of Kyivan (or Kievan) Rus', a medieval Slavic state located partly in what is now Ukraine.[1] By styling itself as Kyiv's heir or by "absorbing" the Kyivan heritage, the state now governed from Moscow has at times proven itself capable of effecting Kyiv's symbolic erasure, as today's Ukrainians are well aware. One might say that in symbolic terms, Russia has moved the "center" of East Slavic culture out of today's Ukraine and relocated it to a position 500 miles to the east. (Here we see a parallel with Britain, in which the "Celtic fringe" was not only incorporated into "English" literature but also reimagined as central to that "English" tradition.)[2]

Soon after the Kyivan Prince Volodymyr (in Russian, Vladimir) converted to Orthodoxy in 988, the polity known as Kyivan Rus' began to envision itself as successor to the Eastern Empire of Rome and therefore as a "new Jerusalem." Several centuries later, after Kyiv's decline and Constantinople's capture by the Ottomans in 1453, early modern Moscow in turn imagined itself as (another) new Jerusalem: Muscovite theologians developed the idea that Moscow was the "Third Rome," that is, the rightful successor to the Roman and Byzantine empires, and thus the symbolic heart and geopolitical guardian of genuine Christendom. For the tsars who were consolidating power in Russian lands by around 1500, the image of Moscow as the Third Rome sometimes proved useful, and as a result this idea "achieved long-term resonance in the Russian cultural imagination."[3] Russia's elision or absorption of Kyivan heritage is underscored today by the giant monument to the Kyivan ruler Prince Volodymyr that has stood directly across from the Moscow Kremlin since 2016.

The arguments by which Muscovite thinkers laid claim to spiritual and political "centrality" were perhaps convoluted, as such arguments always are, but in the long term the effort to locate legitimacy in Moscow proved quite successful. By the early nineteenth century, the city had indeed come to be seen as central to Russian territory and to Russianness (despite the fact that from 1704 to 1918, Moscow was not even the seat of Russia's government). In the words of one memoirist, Moscow was "the sun around which other towns appear like planets."[4] It was coded as traditional, Orthodox, "eastern," symbolically feminine, a haven of old boyar and merchant cultures, slow-paced, and distant – if not closed off – from the outside world. Even as the boundaries of central or "European" Russia were redrawn in response to the changing extent of the empire, the idea that Russia had a *middle* and that Moscow embodied it was rarely challenged.

And yet Moscow's middle-ness took on its meaning partly in response to the *peripheralness* of Russia's other capital, St. Petersburg, founded *ex nihilo* in 1704 by the coercively westernizing emperor Peter the Great. For more than two centuries – that is, until Lenin moved the seat of Soviet power back to Moscow in 1918 – both cities were described as capitals (*stolitsy.*) Compared to Moscow, Petersburg in the Imperial period was decidedly outward-looking. In effect, it was a state center situated on a geographic periphery: as Nikolai Gogol put it in 1836, "whoever has been to the Russian capital has been to the edge of the earth."[5] Its long, straight avenues and architectural consistency were designed to display the autocracy's might and grandeur by projecting order, symmetry, and permanence. Petersburg was everything Moscow was not – new, coastal, bureaucratic, "Western," symbolically masculine, ethnically hybrid, and thus vaguely foreign. It was, in Alexander Pushkin's words, the empire's "window to Europe."

Strangely, despite its location on a geographic periphery, Petersburg was fully capable of functioning as a symbolic center. In fact, in literary works set outside the capitals, Moscow and Petersburg often play nearly identical roles. In Anton Chekhov's *Three Sisters*, when the Prozorovas stand on their provincial porch and repeat "to Moscow! to Moscow!" they are doing exactly what Gogol's provincials do in *The Inspector General* when they direct their gaze longingly toward Petersburg: they are dreaming of the capital's signifying power. For Chekhov's provincials as for Gogol's, the capital – either capital – can function as a quasi-magical and patently unreal ideal, toward which the characters look in the hope that their insignificant lives will take on meaning when subjected to the center's ordering Logos. The provinces are where nothing can happen, and the capitals are where *real life* is lived. Thus in Chekhov's 1899 story "On Official Business," a Moscow bureaucrat who has been assigned to serve in some far-off town believes that the very remoteness of this place deprives it of any potential meaning. Everything here, he thinks, is "alien," "trivial," and "uninteresting"; "everything here is accidental." Real life, he says to himself, is in the capitals: "our homeland, the real Russia, is Moscow and Petersburg, but here is just the provinces, the colonies."[6]

"Just the provinces, the colonies": it would be hard to miss parallels between the way Russia imagined its provinces' relationship to the metropoles and the way other traditions imagined their colonies' relationship to the imperial center. The Russian empire's geographically contiguous space could blur distinctions between what Europeans confidently designated "provinces" and "colonies," with the result that certain Russian regions could at different times be classified variously as colonies, provinces, or borderlands. (Indeed, while the act of colonizing was taken as a reassuring sign of Russians' Europeanness, "it was not clear in every instance whether they had colonized their own country or someone else's."[7]) In literary representation, Russian provincials – much like characters in, say, British colonial and postcolonial texts who find themselves "stuck" on a periphery they are told is meaningless – often feel themselves to be left out of everything that really matters in the world. Hence the "overwhelming sense of the banality of one's life" that such characters experience (and to experience one's own life as meaningless is, as a scholar of British India reminds us, "a damning marker of economic and ideological subordination"[8]).

"Provincial" places in Russian literature, including cities, often reveal a striking dilution of significance: witness the fact that the designation *provintsiia* can be applied to virtually anywhere that is located outside Moscow and Petersburg but *not* in the exotic non-Russian borderlands (the Caucasus, Siberia, etc.). Places that in other countries' symbolic geographies would perhaps function as regions or regional centers with their own distinct identities (say, for instance, the gritty specificity of Portsmouth as seen in Jane Austen's *Mansfield Park*) can be reduced to homogeneity and placelessness by way of this flattening formulation. And yet many of Russian literature's foundational texts are set "in the provinces," and indeed they rely on the provinces–capitals binary to develop their most important insights; this is true, for instance, of both Gogol's *Dead Souls* (1842) and Fyodor Dostoevsky's *Demons* (1871–72). Insisting on the monotony and banality of provincial places – and hinting that such monotony and banality might well tip over into something worse – allows Russians to think about the consequences of centrality and peripherality more generally, and thus (eventually) about modernity and non-modernity – all crucial issues at times when educated elites are worrying about their relationship to European ways of measuring both time and space.

Here we must emphasize the absurdity of the belief that some lives are meaningful while others are not, depending on where they are lived: this is an ideological construct. The provinces–capitals binary that makes the capitals the sole locus of meaning-making is as imaginary as the colonies–metropole binary we see in systems such as Pascale Casanova's influential *World Republic of Letters*. And indeed, many Russian texts set in the provinces are not really *about* the provinces. Rather, they are about the image of the provinces as it finds expression in Russia's mainstream literary culture – which has often wielded virtually all representational power and whose point of view has almost always been situated in the capitals.

At first glance Russia's provinces–capitals opposition might appear simply to recapitulate world literature's center–periphery opposition. And yet, as I have argued elsewhere, in the end the Russian example undermines such binaries:[9] the ambiguities of Russia's situation – peripheral but not small, European but also Asian, behind but also possibly ahead, Christian but perhaps not exactly Christendom in the sense of "the West," etc. – did not allow it to be definitively located on either center or periphery.[10] This helps to explain why Western ideas of world literature cannot accommodate Russia, which is neither fully "modern" nor straightforwardly "backward." It does not fit anywhere along the timeline of what Arjun Appadurai calls "Eurochronology," the supposedly universal standard that underwrites the normative temporality of world literature (with binaries such as ahead/behind and cosmopolitan/provincial).[11] Such a picture of the literary "world" must leave out Russia altogether, and in fact – rather astonishingly – whole theories of world literature have been articulated with barely a passing mention of writing in Russian.[12] I will return briefly to this problem at the end of the present chapter, but for now, let it serve as another example of how totalizing systems can distort our view of cultural realities.

Moscow: Fortress at the Center of the World

If we look at any transportation map of Russia, we see Moscow situated at the center of a web- or wheel-like system. The ancient capital forms a hub from which spokes (roads) extend outward; a series of concentric rings are formed by roads connecting the spokes. In semiotic terms, this center functions as a condensing force to concentrate significance: as you move away from the middle, meaning is diluted, coherence fades, entropy prevails. Indeed, while Moscow's centrality is geographic, it is also mystical and religious (Eastern Orthodox), as noted above. Its symbolic role is that of preserver and defender. The conservativism reflected in this image is also reflected in the caution and vigilance with which early Russian leaders tended to view the "outside" world.

It is useful to compare the intensely centralized nature of Russia's symbolic and infrastructural geography with how North America was being imagined at around the same time: Thomas Jefferson's 1785 "land ordinance" represents the continent as a space with *no* center. Instead of rings, Jefferson lays down "a mechanical grid over the surface of America," inviting us to see the land as a series of interlocking and interchangeable one-mile squares. In addition to serving as a plan for colonization, the American map is an expression of what has been called "Cartesian social space" – space that is "identical point to point and potentially unlimited in extent." In theory, the grid renders all parts identical, with any section capable of standing for the whole. In this ideal vision – once again, an ideal that is totally imaginary and ideologically loaded – America's democratic social space is imagined as "a universal and everywhere similar medium in which rights and opportunities [are] identical."[13]

One cannot get much further from America's relentlessly equalizing grid than Russia's series of concentric circles radiating out from a single focal point. Moscow's topography mirrors its centrality in the national imaginary, although its beginnings were not grandiose. The city began as a collection of houses and churches along narrow twisting lanes, with neighborhoods diffuse and rambling rather than dense (hence the saying "Moscow is a big village": it did not look like a European capital), all encircled by monasteries linked by a series of ring roads – and always with the Kremlin at its core. Even the huge transformations effected in the twentieth and twenty-first centuries, from Stalin's destruction of churches to today's large-scale demolition of old housing stock, have not obscured Moscow's circular layout or this layout's implicit ideological message: in the words of the Futurist poet Vladimir Mayakovsky, "the earth begins, as is well known, at the Kremlin."[14]

Moscow's symbolic centrality is key to literary texts from the eighteenth century up to our own time. Nikolai Karamzin and Alexander Pushkin, Andrei Platonov and Tatiana Tolstoya – all have incorporated Moscow's middle-ness into their poetics. Pushkin's *Eugene Onegin* (1823–31) and

Tolstoy's *War and Peace* (1865–69) are explicit about the crucial relationship between Moscow and Russianness itself (and about the problematic relationship between Petersburg and Russianness). In Andrei Platonov's story "Doubting Makar" (1929), the peasant protagonist sets off for Moscow "in order to stand *at the very center*," "the middle of the central city and the center of the entire [Soviet] state." Having determined that this point is near the Bolshoi Theatre, Makar goes there and holds perfectly still, "[experiencing] a feeling of respect for himself and for his state."[15] At the end of Venedikt Erofeev's samizdat masterpiece *Moscow-Petushki* (1969–70), the drunken protagonist, himself a Muscovite, wanders around the capital searching for but never reaching the Kremlin, which he says he has never seen: the center is not for marginal types like him. As Erofeev's text implies, sometimes in the Soviet period Moscow's hypercentralization of power could transform "everything outside the Kremlin walls" into a kind of periphery.[16]

Tatiana Tolstoya's late-Soviet story "The Fakir" (1986) is structured entirely around the idea of Moscow – central Moscow, that is – as a concentrating force, the only place in a vast, shabby, meagerly provisioned empire where nothing is in short supply. The main character, Galya, does not live in this magical center: she lives with her family in a grim, bare apartment on the capital's furthest outskirts. In Tolstoya's representation, an exurb might as well be a steppe wilderness. Here everything that matters, from everyday necessities to opera tickets, can be obtained only with great effort, and often not at all, by making humiliating phone calls, standing in line, traveling for hours on crowded buses. And what is procured by way of such efforts is usually just the stuff of bare survival.

Galya experiences life on the periphery as a curse:

> Someone unnamed, indifferent, like fate, had decided: this one, this one, and this one will live in a palace. Life will be good for them. And these, and these, and these ones, too, including Galya and Yura, will live there. No, not there, wa-a-ay over there, that's right, yes. By the ravine, beyond the deserted lots.[17]

Here "in the tortuous mud, in the viscous Precambrian of the outskirts," lies the ragged borderline between civilization and chaos (XX). The term "boundary road" (*okruzhnaia doroga*, literally "circle road") recurs frequently, evoking a fragile barrier meant to stave off encroaching entropy. Beyond there is only "an abyss of darkness," "where the frosty wind howled, the cold of uninhabited plains penetrated your clothes, and the world [...] seemed as horrible as a graveyard."[18]

> And beyond the boundary road, beyond the last weak strip of life, on the other side of the snow-filled ravine, the invisible sky slipped down, resting its heavy edge on a beet field—right there, on the other side of the ravine.[19]

Past the boundary road there is nature, perhaps, but it is a version of nature that is unromantic, rude, and ominous:

> It was impossible, unthinkable, unbearable to realize that the thick darkness extended farther, over the fields that blended into a white roar, over badly constructed fences, over trees pressed into the cold earth where a doomed dull light quivers as if held in an indifferent fist [....] Farther once again, the dark white cold, a crust of forest where the darkness is even thicker, where perhaps a pathetic wolf is forced to live: it comes out on a hill in its rough wool coat smelling of juniper and blood, wildness, disaster, gazes grimly and with disgust at the blind windy vistas, clumps of snow hardening between its cracked claws.[20]

Clearly the outskirts where Galya is condemned to live are marked by a scarcity that is as much spiritual as material.

Thus Galya treasures her connection with their mysterious friend Filin who occupies a "curlicued palace"[21] in Moscow's very middle. (The word *filin* denotes a species of Eurasian eagle owl; it is one of many things about the character that are left unexplained.) His apartment is elaborately provisioned and decorated, and Galya's visits there are her only glimpses of a world of abundance – an abundance of material goods, pleasure, culture, even history and narrative, all of which are scarce on the periphery. At Filin's apartment they eat grapefruit with shrimp (exotic delicacies in Soviet times), sip tea from china cups, and admire their host's "useless but valuable" knickknacks ("a beaded purse, perhaps an Easter egg,"[22]). The building's heavily ornamented exterior represents forms of pleasure and creativity that can only be indulged once basic needs are met:

> Filin's tower nestled in the middle of the capital, a pink mountain, ornamented here and there in the most varied way—with all sorts of architectural doodads, thingamajigs, and whatnots: there were towers on the socles, crenels on the towers, and ribbons and wreaths between the crenellations, and out of the laurel garlands peeked a book, the source of knowledge, or a compass stuck out its pedagogic leg.[23]

As all this embellishment suggests, Filin's world represents not only material abundance but a connection to history and to the narratives – true or not true – that infuse bare life with meaning. Every rarity he offers up to his guests comes with a story, a fanciful provenance that conjures mysterious possibilities. The ring he wears is not a cheap one from a store, but something "from an excavation, Venetian if he's not lying, or a setting of a coin from, God help me, Antioch, or something";[24] the *pirozhki* he serves (for which he uses the French word "tartelettes") are made according to the recipe handed down directly from Pushkin's favorite baker; this is not, Filin says, just a Wedgwood teacup (though that in itself would be a rarity in a Soviet apartment) – no, it is a Wedgwood cup from a Nazi plane that was shot out of the sky by a partisan during the war![25]

Such are the enlivening networks of history and narrative that Galya craves, having found herself stuck on a periphery where material manifestations of culture are few and far between. Filin himself is Orientalized and perhaps effete ("Anatolian eyes," "Mongol slippers"[26]), but his exoticism speaks of magical abilities: he is "the all-powerful gentleman who with a wave of the hand, the flicker of an eyebrow can transform the world to the point of unrecognizability."[27] Ushering chosen guests "into the warmth and light [...] where the hothouse roses refuse to acknowledge the frost, wind, darkness that have besieged [his] impregnable tower, powerless to penetrate,"[28] Filin is an agent of anti-chaos. He pushes back against the anarchy of the surrounding hinterlands, which Russians in the center typically saw as a threat to civilization.

Tolstoya's story reflects elites' inchoate fear of Russia's immense and supposedly empty geographic space. The philosopher Nikolai Berdiaev, writing in 1918, contended that "Russian cultural energy does not want to spread itself out over the boundless expanses of Russia"; rather, "it tries to conserve itself in the centers. There's some sort of fright before the dark and engulfing depths of Russia."[29] (Of course, those outside the center were likely to perceive the imbalance quite differently: the provinces have long seen in the capitals both "a symbol of indispensable political power" and "a spider sucking them dry."[30]) Elites in the capitals not infrequently perceived the rest of the country as an unfillable emptiness, an expanse capable of diffusing meaning to the point of total dissolution. As Maxim Gorky lamented, the "boundless, flat country" preserves no traces of humans' creativity or labor.[31] Where culture is spread so thin, artifacts and ideas risk losing their connections with each other. No energizing encounters or webs of meaning seem possible, and thus no models for transformation or development; whatever has ended up out here is now inert, going nowhere. According to this vision, it takes a Filin in a "curlicued palace" in the center of the center – a powerful centripetal force – to preserve the artifacts and stories that sustain civilization. As we have seen, such a center has most often been located – or rather, imagined – in Moscow.

Petersburg: Civilization at the End of the Earth

Petersburg, too, though emphatically not a geographic center, was conceived as a triumph of civilization over chaos – in this case, the wasteland of the northern swamps where Peter I ordered that his new capital be built from nothing. For a century or so after its founding in 1704, the capital was celebrated in literature precisely as a civilizational victory, its monumentality and Western-ness admired as symbols of Russia's new status as a European empire. The great human suffering occasioned by the city's construction was initially not emphasized: it was the necessary price for Russia's entry into the ranks of European powers.

In the nineteenth century, however, the image of Petersburg became complicated, even paradoxical, uniting in itself a series of polarities – "nature and culture, chaos and order, individual and state, enlightenment and despotism, future and crisis."[32] Behind the city's imposing architectural ensembles and public spaces, writers began to perceive crueler aspects of state power (autocracy, bureaucracy, militarism). Works by Pushkin, Gogol, and Dostoevsky explored how Petersburg's grandeur was inextricable from the powerlessness and oppression experienced by ordinary people. And at the same time, writers began to imagine that behind a façade of order and rationality, Petersburg was a fundamentally irrational and even surreal place, where, as Gogol writes in "Nevsky Prospect," "everything is a cheat, everything is a dream, everything is other than it seems!" and "the devil himself lights the street lamps."[33] The city came to be associated not simply with art but with artifice and artificiality, especially that of an imperial state deploying rituals and rigid hierarchy to obscure brutality. In *War and Peace* and *Anna Karenina* (1877), for instance, Tolstoy sets the pernicious unnaturalness of Petersburg against the naturalness of Moscow, aligning the latter with the countryside, traditional ways, and "authentic" Russianness.

In Dostoevsky's writings (especially *White Nights* [1848] and *Notes from Underground* [1864]), Petersburg's paradoxical combination of the surreal and the aggressively Western is linked to the idea of a problematic modernity being imposed on the "real" Russia by the state. The new capital's conspicuous modern-ness had always represented a disruption of traditional Russian temporality, if not a radical break from it. As if to underscore the rupture, Peter even reformed the calendar Russians had used for centuries (shifting the beginning of the year from September 1 to January 1, among other changes), thereby "enshrining [...] a regime of plural temporalities that has affected the course of Russia's development and [left] it isolated among major European societies."[34] He and his successors, most notably Catherine II, compelled elites to embrace ideas of progress and progressive history that were linked to the West and Westernization (and in 1918 the Bolsheviks would adopt the Gregorian calendar, thereby bringing the Soviet Union into line with European countries). But rupture in the name of progress came to be associated with political precarity and violence, both of which intensified in the half-century following the 1860s Great Reforms. After serfdom was abolished in 1861, industrialization, urbanization, and labor mobility changed Petersburg perhaps more than any other Russian city. The autocracy – still very much identified with Peter's capital – found it impossible to implement economic reform while maintaining stability and preserving its grip on power.

In 1881 Petersburg witnessed the assassination of Tsar Alexander II, and in the last decades of tsarist rule political terrorism claimed many lives. A sense of impending doom was dramatized in texts such as Andrei Bely's eschatological modernist novel *Petersburg* (1913), in which a terrorist bomb and the 1905 revolution figure prominently. Bely's distortion of time and space reflects the era's volatility, an instability that was to extend even to the city's name: from 1914 to 1924 Petersburg was called Petrograd, and from 1924 to 1991, Leningrad. The bloody period surrounding the 1917 Revolution was memorialized by a number of great poets (including Alexander Blok, Osip Mandelshtam, and Anna Akhmatova) who bore witness to their city's historic catastrophes. Their works often invoked themes of apocalypse and broken time: as the "secular Western city of the Antichrist" that had displaced holy Moscow and fractured its mythical temporality, Petersburg/Petrograd/Leningrad was a good setting for exploring the ends of various worlds.[35]

After the Bolsheviks transferred the seat of government back to Moscow, the city they left behind continued to function as a cultural capital (and thanks to its secondary status, it was not subjected to the same radical infrastructure interventions as Moscow). Between 1941 and 1944 the Nazi blockade martyred Leningrad, killing between 600,000 and a million civilians – yet another apocalypse. After the war the siege was ideologized and aestheticized both in an official state cult and in private and underground writings, with poets, prose writers, and diarists describing how Leningraders' suffering and heroism transpired against a backdrop of beauty and monumentality, rich in cultural associations.[36] In the later Soviet period, Leningrad's "second city" status helped make it a haven for underground and semi-underground cultural movements. No longer tightly linked to state power, postwar Leningrad and post-Soviet

Petersburg were often seen as the repository or custodian of an almost-sacred high culture (architecture, poetry, music), and whatever happened in the city happened within this living archive.

Evgeny Zamiatin's story "The Cave" (1920) takes place during one of the twentieth century's cataclysms: winter in Civil War-era Petrograd, most likely 1919–20, during which the city froze and starved while surrounded by the White army, which was trying to retake it from the Reds. These facts of time and place go unexplained, however, in the story's opening lines, which simply deposit us in what seems to be a prehistoric Ice Age world:

> Glaciers, mammoths, wastes. Black, nocturnal cliffs, somehow resembling houses; in the cliffs—caves. And no one knows what trumpets at night on the stony path among the cliffs, who blows up white snow-dust, sniffing out the path. Perhaps it is a gray-trunked mammoth, perhaps the wind. Or is the wind itself the icy roar of the most mammoth of mammoths? One thing is clear: it is winter. And you must clench your teeth as tightly as you can to keep them from chattering; and you must split wood with a stone ax; and every night you must carry your fire from cave to cave, deeper and deeper. And you must wrap yourself in shaggy animal hides, more and more of them.
>
> A gray-trunked mammoth roamed at night among the cliffs where Petersburg had stood ages ago.[37]

A string of nouns, no human speech, few man-made artifacts, little movement: this is all the opening lines give us, perhaps because so little is left to the characters, who are trying to stay alive with an absolute minimum of resources at a moment when civilization itself is in retreat.

Huddled in a freezing apartment, a man named Martin Martinych must decide what to save and what to burn, and whether or not to steal his neighbor's wood, in order to give his dying wife one last hour of warmth. What used to be furniture, letters, and sheet music (Scriabin, among the most spiritual and "civilized" of Russian composers) is now just fuel for the stove, the "greedy cave god"[38] to which they sacrifice one thing after another. Having gradually boarded up the apartment, room by room, they now occupy a bedroom crammed with a motley assortment of objects. Desk, books, Scriabin opus 74, a flatiron, five potatoes "scrubbed lovingly to gleaming whiteness":[39] the objects' worth has been radically altered by the collapse of the civilization on which their meaning once depended, and obviously potatoes are now more valuable than cultural artifacts.

The ghosts of high culture haunt the story, just as they haunt Petersburg when times are too bleak to allow for producing the surplus value on which high culture depends.[40] Even as "civilized" ways of ordering space and time break down, for example, echoes of the Orthodox liturgical calendar survive in the cave: "On the feast of the Intercession of the Holy Virgin, Martin Martinych and Masha shut up the study; on the Day of the Kazan Virgin they made their way out of the dining room and huddled in the bedroom."[41] And it is on his wife's saint's day, October 29, that Martin decides to steal wood in order to warm the apartment for her one last time. The man who used to play Scriabin is now "reverting to Adam," his face "crumpled and clay-like"; he is a "cave dweller" who will steal from his neighbor's woodpile.[42] At the end Martin gives his wife, who wants to die, the single vial of poison they have saved for this eventuality; then he walks outdoors to freeze to death himself. As he steps outside – where "the world [is] one vast, silent cave" – the final lines leave the reader alone in the dark, estranged city: "A light icy draught blows white dust underfoot, and unheard by anyone – over the white dust, the boulders, the caves, over the crouching humans – goes the huge, measured tread of some unknown monster mammoth."[43]

Before the Revolution Zamiatin was allied with a subset of avant-gardists who generally insisted on art's autonomy and non-utility – an insistence that is hard to maintain when one is freezing and starving. Nonetheless the story reveals traces of avant-garde literary concerns. While the chaos of objects piled around the apartment signals the breakdown of cultural categories in the wake of catastrophe ("In the Petersburg bedroom-cave things were much as they had been in Noah's ark not long ago – the clean and the unclean thrown together by the flood"[44]), it also allows Zamiatin to muster a "succession of heterogeneous images"[45] of the sort favored by Futurists. For some writers both before and after the Revolution, such juxtapositions served modern art's imperative to break apart familiar "logical, causal-temporal, spatio-temporal and even syntactic" relationships.[46] Certainly Petrograd in the winter of 1919–20 – which in Zamiatin's text is at once a cave in the Ice Age, the ark of Noah, the age of Adam, and the graveyard of twentieth-century cultural treasures – is an appropriate place to stage such ruptures.

Petersburg/Petrograd/Leningrad is also a place for contemplating how culture survives or does not survive when it is besieged in any way, including ideologically. What forms of memory can best preserve legacies under attack? What does it mean for a former political capital to become a reliquary, charged with safeguarding vestiges? In this sense Zamiatin's text prefigures Leningraders' accounts of the German blockade twenty years later; indeed, later artistic treatments of the two sieges – 1919–20 and

1941–44 – at times almost merge them into one catastrophe, with accounts of the second siege "[using] the first as a template."[47] But to skip from 1920 to 1941 is to erase the city's experience of the 1930s, when the Soviet regime was purging the intelligentsia and Leningrad's population was moving to the industrial outskirts.[48] And it was in the 1930s that Leningrad's second-city status was more or less codified, rendering it symbolically "provincial" in much the same way Moscow had been provincial in the nineteenth century – slightly off the beaten path of history, more traditional, a preserver of the past.

Conclusion

Here we return to the question of provinciality. In systems like Casanova's, Paris is at once the undisputed "center" of the literary world and the "Greenwich meridian" of culture.[49] In this as in other models that draw on Immanuel Wallerstein's "world systems theory," spatial peripheries are dependent and sterile. But the Russian example goes a long way toward dismantling such systems. For one thing, it shows that centers are slippery: thanks to the autocrat's absolute power to "transfer his seat to a specially created or minimally populated 'center,'" even capital cities can go from being provincial to unprovincial and back again, losing or gaining their "centralness" in the world.[50]

The Russian case teaches us that there is more than one way of imagining the "world" of world literature. If in the West, world literature tends to be conceived as centripetal, with centers that represent themselves as the source of all creative energy, Russian and Soviet versions of this world are likely to be centrifugal, attentive to the peripheries, boundaries, and contact zones that are perceived as more lively and artistically productive than the comparatively rigid centers. Thinkers such as Alexander Veselovsky, Mikhail Bakhtin, Yuri Tynianov, and Yuri Lotman are examples of this willingness to refocus attention on peripheries of various sorts, so that "the boundary rather than the center" becomes the site of "literary and cultural transformation."[51]

Nineteenth-century Russian writers foretold this development when they learned to make conscious use of their supposed provinciality, thereby providing a basis upon which later thinkers could develop a more nuanced understanding of center–periphery relations than did those who occupy undisputed centers. As a result Russia's "provincial" literature can suggest ways of reimagining not only ideas of4 peripherality and Eurochronology, but also the world in world literature.

Notes

1 Serhii Plokhy, *Lost Kingdom: The Quest for Empire and the Making of the Russian Nation from 1470 to the Present* (New York: Basic Books, 2017). Kyiv is the transliteration from Ukrainian; Kiev from Russian. Since Rus' was located in territory now divided among Ukraine, Belarus, and Russia, all of these present-day states can claim it as their ancestor.

2 Katie Trumpener, *Bardic Nationalism: The Romantic Novel and the British Empire* (Princeton, NJ: Princeton University Press, 1997). As Trumpener points out, through the eighteenth century Britain (like Russia) was primarily an "internal" empire. British literary dynamics resulting from internal political inequalities resonate strongly with those in Russia – an empire without a fully developed sense of nation.

3 Andrew Kahn et al., eds., *A History of Russian Literature* (Oxford: Oxford University Press, 2018), 44–45, 102. See also Daniel B. Rowland, "Moscow—The Third Rome or the New Israel?", *Russian Review* 55, no. 4 (October 1996): 591–614.

4 F.N. Glinka, 1786–1880, was the cousin of the composer and the author of a widely read memoir of the Napoleonic Wars. Cited in Leonid Gorizontov, "The 'Great Circle' of Interior Russia: Representations of the Imperial Center in the Nineteenth and Early Twentieth Centuries," in Jane Burbank, Mark von Hagen, and Anatolyi Remnev, eds., *Russian Empire: Space, People, Power, 1700-1930* (Bloomington, IN: Indiana University Press, 2007), 69.

5 Nikolai Gogol, "Petersburg Notes from 1836," in Laurence P. Senelick, ed., *Russian Dramatic Theory from Pushkin to the Symbolists, An Anthology* (New York: University of Texas Press, 2021), 16, https://doi.org/10.7560/770256-005.

6 Anton Chekhov, *Selected Stories,* Cathy Popkin, ed. (New York: W.W. Norton & Company, 2014), 395.

7 Willard Sunderland, *Taming the Wild Field: Colonization and Empire on the Russia Steppe* (Ithaca, NY: Cornell University Press, 2004), 171.

8 Saikat Majumdar, *Prose of the World: Modernism and the Banality of Empire* (New York: Columbia University Press, 2013), 32.

9 See Anne Lounsbery, *Life is Elsewhere: Symbolic Geography in the Russian Provinces, 1800–1917* (Ithaca, NY: Cornell University Press, 2019), especially 249–255.

10 Casanova's scenario in *The World Republic of Letters* has been described as "underdog nations battling for a place in a literary sun blocked by the shadow of tyrant languages and literatures": not a model that works well for Russia. Christopher Prendergast, ed., "The World Republic of Letters," in *Debating World Literature* (New York: Verso, 2004), 17.

11 Arjun Appadurai, *Modernity at Large: Cultural Dimensions of Globalization* (Minneapolis, MN: University of Minnesota Press, 2000), 30, 1.

12 See for example the *Routledge Companion to World Literature*, the index of which reveals virtually no mention of either Russia or the Soviet Union. Theo D'haen, David Damrosch, and Djelal Kadir, eds., *The Routledge Companion to World Literature* (New York: Routledge, 2012).

13 Philip Fisher, *Still the New World: American Literature in a Culture of Creative Destruction* (Cambridge, MA: Harvard University Press, 2000), 43–44.
14 V.V. Maiakovskii, "Prochti i katai v Parizh i v Kitai," *Polnoe sobranie sochinenii Maiakovskogo v 13 tomakh* (Moscow: Goslitizdat, 1955), 10: 257.
15 Cited and translated in Yuri Slezkine, *The House of Government: A Saga of the Russian Revolution* (Princeton, NJ and Oxford: Princeton University Press, 2017), 317 (emphasis added).
16 Emily D. Johnson, *How St. Petersburg Learned to Study Itself: The Russian Idea of Kraevedenie* (University Park, PA: Penn State University Press, 2006), 178.
17 Tatyana Tolstaya, "Fakir," in *White Walls. Collected Stories*, trans. Antonina W. Bouis and Jamey Gambrell (New York: New York Review of Books Classics, 2007), 165.
18 Ibid., 152.
19 Ibid., 161.
20 Ibid., 161–162.
21 Ibid., 161.
22 Ibid., 151.
23 Ibid., 160–161.
24 Ibid., 151.
25 Ibid., 159.
26 Ibid., 152.
27 Ibid., 160.
28 Ibid., 155.
29 Nikolai Berdiaev, *Sud'ba Rossii* (1918), http://krotov.info/library/02_b/berdyaev/1918_15_07.html.
30 C.E. Simonovich, "Rovesniki voiny tsentra i provintsii—istoriia i psikhologiia," in S.N. Poltoraka, ed., *Tsentr-provintsiia. Istorichesko-psikhologoicheskie problemy. Materialy vserossiiskoi nauchnoi konferentsii, 6–7 dekabria 2001 g* (Petersburg: Nestor, 2001), 157.
31 Maxim Gorky, "On the Russian Peasantry," *Journal of Peasant Studies* 4, no. 1 (October 1976): 12–13 (first published Berlin, 1922).
32 Polina Barskova, "The Spectacle of the Besieged City: Repurposing Cultural Memory in Leningrad, 1941–1944," *Slavic Review* 69, no. 2 (Summer 2010): 334. Such are the defining paradoxes of what Russian cultural critics have dubbed "the Petersburg text," i.e., the image of Petersburg generated by a long line of markedly intertextual works of literature about the city (and about one another).
33 *The Complete Tales of Nikolai Gogol*, vol. I, trans. Constance Garnett; Leonard J. Kent, ed. (Chicago and London: University of Chicago Press, 1985), 238.
34 Andreas Schönle, "Calendar Reform under Peter the Great: Absolutist Prerogatives, Plural Temporalities, and Christian Exceptionalism," *Slavic Review* 80, no. 1 (Spring 2021): 70.
35 David M. Bethea, *The Shape of Apocalypse in Modern Russian Fiction* (Princeton, NJ: Princeton University Press, 2014), 19.
36 See Barskova, "Spectacle."

37 Yevgeny Zamiatin, "The Cave," in *The Dragon. Fifteen Stories*, ed. and trans. Mirra Ginsburg (Chicago: University of Chicago Press/ New York: Random House, 1966), 135. I have adjusted some of the translations.
38 Ibid., 136.
39 Ibid.
40 Timothy Langen, "Zamiatin's 'The Cave,'" *Philosophy and Literature* 29, no. 1 (April 2005): 214.
41 Zamiatin, "Cave," 135–136.
42 Ibid., 137, 139.
43 Ibid., 145.
44 Ibid., 136.
45 Ibid.
46 Jan van der Eng, "The Imagery of the Avant-Garde: Zamyatin's 'The Cave,'" in Fernand Drijkoningen and Klaus Beekman, eds., *Avant Garde No. 0: Presentation Revue interdisciplinaire et international* (Leiden: Brill, 1987), 105.
47 Barskova, "Spectacle," 336.
48 Ibid.
49 Pascale Casanova, *The World Republic of Letters*, trans. M.B. DeBevoise (Cambridge, MA: Harvard University Press, 2004), 87–88.
50 Mikhail Epstein, *Bog detalei: Narodnaia dusha i chastnaia zhizn' v Rossii na iskhode imperii* (New York: Slovo, 1997), 32. Not unrelated here is the argument first put forth by nineteenth-century historians that Russia "colonized itself": a highly problematic statement in that it elides the non-Russian peoples who occupied spaces that the Russian state conquered, but nonetheless evocative of the autocracy's relationship to "its own" people.
51 Kate Holland, "Narrative Tradition on the Border: Alexander Veselovsky and Narrative Hybridity in the Age of World Literature," *Poetics Today* 38, no. 3 (September 2017): 429.

CHAPTER 14

"Cityful Passing Away"

Resituating Dublin

Christopher Morash

In the "Lestrygonians" episode of James Joyce's *Ulysses*, the character of Leopold Bloom walks along College Green in the center of Dublin, past the façade of Trinity College, when a cloud passes in front of the sun. "His smile faded as he walked, a heavy cloud hiding the sun slowly, shadowing Trinity's surly front. Trams passed one another, ingoing, outgoing, clanging. Useless words." As he walks, the movement of the trams and the movement of the clouds mutates into a reflection on change, which in turn opens up the question of time, and which very quickly pushes up against the limits of language ("useless words"):

> Cityful passing away, other cityful coming, passing away too: other coming on, passing on. Houses, lines of houses, streets, miles of pavements, piledup bricks, stones. Changing hands. This owner; that. Landlord never dies they say. Other steps into his shoes when he gets his notice to quit. They buy the place up with gold and still they have all the gold. Swindle in it somewhere. Piled up cities, worn away age after age.[1]

"Cityful passing away, other cityful coming, passing away too": there are perhaps few lines in any literature dealing with any city that encapsulate so precisely that paradox of the city *per se*: that seemingly contradictory combination of continuous loss and vibrant life, of nostalgia for what is gone in the midst of the continual celebration of the new. In these lines from *Ulysses*, this paradox does not so much take the form of knowledge, as of a sudden epiphanic awareness, an eruption of metaphor that brings us to one of the definitional qualities of the city. And yet, in spite of the complexity, and abstraction of the questions that take shape in Bloom's mind here in relation to temporality, change, and repetition, the entire passage is grounded in the physical fabric of Dublin: the trams, the brick of the buildings, the pavements on the streets.

For the reader of *Ulysses*, this will be no surprise. The entire novel, for all of its complex allusiveness and games with language, is firmly grounded in what Stephen Dedalus elsewhere in the novel calls the "ineluctable modality of the visible"[2] (to which we might also add the modality of the auditory): here, the "surly front" of the College, the visible movement of light, and the moving tramcars, supplemented by the sound of the "clanging" trams. As a novel of a city, *Ulysses* sits atop, but never transcends, the immediate data of sensory perception. At the same time, while each perceptual sensation is a singularity (this cloud at this moment, that particular tram at that moment), both cloud and passing tram also signal multiplicity; there are always more clouds (especially in Ireland), and one tram is distinguishable from another only by virtue of the time at which it arrives or departs. The aptness of passing trams in sparking Bloom's reflection on repetition and difference may well remind us of the well-known passage in Saussure's *General Course in Linguistics*, where Saussure explains the play of "differences and identities" in language by "drawing some comparisons with facts taken from outside speech." His chief example is that of "two 8:25 p.m. Geneve-to-Paris trains that leave at twenty-four hour intervals. We feel that it is the same train each day, yet everything – the locomotives, coaches, personnel – is probably different."[3] Less well known is the passage that follows, in which Saussure develops his argument by suggesting that the city itself provides us with yet another exemplary case of the play of difference and repetition in signifying structures, where it is relative position that confers significance. "If a street is demolished," Saussure argues, "then rebuilt, we may say that it is the same street even though in a material sense, perhaps nothing of the old one remains. Why can a street be completely rebuilt and still be the same? Because it does not constitute a purely material entity."[4]

The point here is not to suggest some hitherto unremarked affinity between Joyce and Saussure; it is to open up the possibility of imagining a city as we would imagine signification in Saussurean linguistics; both as a material entity (the 8:25 train is still made of steel) and an entity that is not entirely material, but rather is a series of repetitions and differences with no positive term. The comparison with Saussure allows us to understand the play of repetition and difference in the passage from "Lestrygonians" in the context of a distinction that Saussure makes elsewhere, and which is central to his thought: it extends not only along the synchronic axis, extending outwards through "lines of houses [...], miles of pavements," but also diachronically, along a temporal axis: "Changing hands. This owner; that. Landlord never dies they say. Other steps into his shoes when he gets his notice to quit." The city multiplies outward not only spatially, from this street to the next, but also temporally over time. As Saussure observed, the 8:25 train each morning achieves its identity not because of when it arrives (it can be late, and still be the 8:25 train, as any commuter will tell you) but because of its place in a structure, so that a train (or a street) is both itself and all of the other individual railway carriages or combinations of specific buildings that occupy that space, not only at a given moment, but also those which have occupied the space in the past and will occupy it in the future. We could pursue this thought further in Joyce, by following his diversion to the related reflection that the city as a site of repetition and difference is also the site of an accumulation of capital ("swindle in it somewhere"). However, of more direct relevance to the argument here is Joyce's final, vertiginous move: Dublin is not simply *a* city; it is, in fact, "piled up cities," multiple repetitions of itself "piled up" over time, so that the city is never singular; it is always, to some extent, both itself and other than itself.

Were it the case that these lines from *Ulysses* were the only instance in the literature of Dublin where we find this perception of the city as an agglomeration of "piled up cities," we might simply chalk it up as another instance of Joycean idiosyncratic genius, and leave it there. However, the sense of the city as multiple that Joyce conjures up is one that recurs in the work of other writers in relation to Dublin, across a range of contexts and historical moments. For instance, one of the best-known poems about the city is "Dublin," by the Northern Ireland-born writer Louis MacNeice. At one point in the poem, he admits: "This never was my town, / I was not born or bred / Nor schooled here and she will not / Have me alive or dead / But yet she holds my mind." Arriving in Dublin in 1939, just as the Second World War was beginning, MacNeice writes Dublin as a city that is never singular, but is instead a multiplicity of "piled up" cities. The poem ends with one of the most lasting literary images of Dublin:

> Port of the Dane,
> Garrison of the Saxon,
> Augustan capital,
> Of a Gaelic nation,
> Appropriating all
> The alien brought,
> You give me time for thought
> And by a juggler's trick
> You poise the toppling hour –
> O greyness run to flower,
> Grey stone, grey water,
> And brick upon grey brick.[5]

This is, on one level, Joyce's "cityful passing away, other cityful coming"; it is Dublin as a site of sedimentary memory, with layers of history sitting upon one another, in which the city's past exists in the present as a kind of spectral effect; the city as edifice. In terms of poetic structure, MacNeice uses his line breaks to create the effect of the "piled up" city on the page, visually stacking the layers of Dublin's history in three- or four-word lines like so many stacked slices of time. MacNeice's poem also makes explicit something that is abundantly obvious elsewhere in Joyce, but perhaps only implicit in the "Lestrygonians" passage: each of these past moments not only connects to the others in a vertical line; they also all connect outwards to other cities, other places. So, for instance, when we read the line "Port of the Dane," it reminds us that the first known literary reference to Dublin (admittedly, an oblique reference) comes from the Icelandic poet Óttar *svarti*, writing in Old Norse in 1026, who includes Ireland (where Dublin was the main Viking settlement) in a poem of praise to the Danish king, Cnut the Great: "Skal svá kveðja / konung Dana, / Íra ok Engla / ok Eybúa, / at hans fari / með himinkröptum, / löndum öllum / lof viðara" ["I will greet the king of the Danes, the Irish, the English, and the Islanders; so his praise may travel through all the lands under heaven"].[6] From its earliest origins as a Viking settlement, then, Dublin was part of a network that encompassed the known world at the time (at least from a Viking perspective). It would be wildly anachronous to call it a "transnational network" (well before the historical advent of the nation-state), much less a "global network"; the phrase "imperial network" might be closer, but that too would require a bit of nuance in terms of structure of the Norse expansion. The point is that at the deepest sedimentary level, Dublin is a city connected to a wider world before the terms "global" or "transnational" had any meaning.

This sits uneasily with what was for so many years the dominant colonial and postcolonial narrative of Irish literary history, in which a Gaelic (or, in some formulations, a "Celtic") culture constitutes an indigenous soil. While there were traces of a small, earlier Gaelic settlement on the site of Dublin, Dublin as a city (even on the comparatively modest scale of an early medieval city) owes its original existence to Viking settlement, and hence to networks of trade and settlement that extended to what is now Iceland, and throughout the Viking world across continental Europe. All of this is implicit in the rich suggestiveness of that four-word line – "Port of the Dane." Something similar is at work in the succeeding lines. The word "Saxon" in the phrase "Garrison of the Saxon" most immediately suggests the discourse of Irish nationalism, where "Saxon" functioned as pejorative synonym for English (or even British), as in the phrase "to take the Saxon shilling" (which meant to join the British Army). However, the Saxons were also a Germanic tribe from central Europe, and juxtaposing "Saxon" with "Dane" keeps alive that earlier meaning, with its evocation of migrating tribes. Likewise, just as "Augustan" is the term for an architectural style of the eighteenth century, it also references Caesar Augustus, and Rome. In short, these few lines not only layer history through time, they also extend the tendrils of the city outwards, to Iceland, to the Caucasus, and to Rome. What is more, as with Joyce, this temporal and spatial connectedness is embedded in the immediate sensory experience of the physical fabric of the city, where both the past and its outward reach are piled up, "grey brick upon grey brick."

Here, once again, the play of repetition and difference – how can the same city be a port of the Danes, garrison of the Saxon, and Augustan capital? – opens up the experience of time as change. MacNeice moves into the question of time adroitly, through what seem to be almost throw-away phrases: "by a juggler's trick / You poise the toppling hour." In a moment of direct apostrophe (the city addressed as "you"), we are told that Dublin provides "time for thought." As is so often the case in MacNeice's writing, the phrase "time for thought" seems conversational, almost banal; but it is freighted, carrying here its mirror image: "thought for time." This implied inversion is supported by the lines that follow, where the key word is "poise": "You poise the toppling hour." Two different senses of "poise" are held in balance here – appropriately enough: "to poise" means both "to weigh" and also "to keep in equilibrium."[7] In terms of the word's history, the link between the two ideas can be imagined through the idea of weighing with a set of balances. The poem thus bears the implication that Dublin's "grey bricks" both "weigh" time (in the sense of assessing it, or even by acting as ballast to the flow of time) and leave it momentarily "poised" (paused) – waiting, expectant, but ready at any moment to continue its irresistible onward toppling movement: "poise the toppling hour." Again, as with Bloom and the trams in College Green, the experience of the city is both of constant change and yet of moments that "poise" that "toppling hour," if briefly, where time itself becomes tangible, part of the phenomenological fabric of the city.

We might well ask at this point what it is about Dublin that makes these imaginative extensions through time and space possible. The answer that Dublin has a long history will not suffice: there are many cities as old, or much older, particularly once we move outside Europe. Instead, what these texts suggest is that the scale of Dublin's past is manageable enough to be grasped in a single thought; and, more importantly, that the past can be physically present in a particularly immediate way. This latter feature is due to the city's waves of development and under-development. The old medieval streets of the city, built up from the original Viking settlement, had the original "garrison of the Saxon" appended to them in the form of Dublin Castle, which was built on land created by filling in what had been a basin in which Viking longboats had moored. When the city began to expand outside its city walls in the so-called "long eighteenth century" (from about 1660 to 1820), the "Augustan capital" that MacNeice evokes was built, and as historian David Dickson puts it, "defensive concerns had little bearing on Dublin's growth."[8] New streets, squares, and public buildings were laid out to the east and north of old medieval center. However, Ireland never experienced the boom in population that we find in other European cities (notably London) in the nineteenth century, so not only did the medieval streetscape remain, so too did its successor, the Georgian city, often repurposed as tenements and offices, but shaping the city nonetheless. This meant that by the time Joyce and MacNeice were writing in the 1920s and 1930s, traces of the "Saxon garrison" remained, as did the edifices of the "Augustan capital / Of a Gaelic nation," decades after the Gaelic nation itself had come into being. Again, this kind of physical layering of the city is far from unique to Dublin (one might think here of Barcelona, or of Beijing); however, in Dublin, each of these layers not only sits on the surface; they also each radiate outwards, whether it be to the Atlantic world of the Vikings, or to the imperial world of the British Empire, or beyond.

What Dublin makes available to its writers, then, is a complex, spatially expansive past-as-present that can be mobilized in moments of crisis. This might seem like a version of Pascale Casanova's influential argument in *The World Republic of Letters*, which would hold that "in the space of a few decades the Irish literary world traversed all the stages (and all the states) of rupture with the literature of the center, providing a model of the aesthetic, formal, linguistic, and political possibilities contained within outlying spaces."[9] In fact, the argument here is closer to Joe Cleary's more recent critique of Casanova in *Modernism, Empire and World Literature*, in which he takes issue with a model in which "two centuries of 'peripheral' revolutions [...] have not, in her account at least, proved sufficient to change in any really substantive way the basic institutional structures of the world literary system or the dominance of the core regions of the system." Instead, Cleary argues, the modernist period constitutes one in which the Western European literary system "was in fact decisively restructured."[10]

It is not so much that Dublin literary culture challenged the center of a literary system from the periphery; instead, it could be argued that by absorbing elsewhere to itself, Dublin deconstructs the oppositional structure that made it possible to think in terms of center and periphery in the first place. It is this, then, that we see in MacNeice at the onset of the Second World War, or in Joyce in the crisis of subject/object relations that underpins the modernist novel.

What is more, that sense of crisis in which the past-as-present could be put to use did not end in Dublin with the period to which we typically assign literary modernism. In the mid-1970s, when the conflict in Northern Ireland was at its most actively violent, we find Seamus Heaney making influential use of it in a poem from his 1975 collection *North*. *North* includes a series of poems, including "Bog Queen" and "The Grauballe Man," that resituate current political violence through the use of images of the mummified bodies of sacrificial victims from long before the Viking period that have been discovered in bogs throughout the world that extended from Iceland across northern Europe evoked by Óttar *svarti* more than a thousand years earlier. These figures allow Heaney to resituate "the exact / and tribal, intimate revenge"[11] of the Irish complex internecine and anti-imperial conflict of the 1970s, so that it both retains its particularity and immediacy, and in the same gesture is framed by a perspective that is distanced, both temporally and spatially.

Heaney's poetry is not usually connected with Dublin (although he lived in the city for much of his life). Instead, it is known for being grounded in his "home place" (as he referred to it), in rural County Derry, and it was his complex sense of connection to a rural community with a sense of belonging that contributed to the resonance of his work for so many Irish readers. It is significant, then, that one of the pivotal poems in *North* (placed immediately after the title poem), is "Viking Dublin: Trial Pieces." This was very much a public poem, appearing not only in the pages of *North*, but also in *The Irish Press* newspaper in 1975:

> Like a long sword
> sheathed in its moisting
> burial clays,
> the keel stuck fast
>
> in the slip of the bank
> its clinker-built hull
> spined and plosive
> as *Dublin*.[12]

The keel of the Viking longboat, the sword, and the carved pieces of bone were, in fact, all objects that were excavated at the site of the site of the original Viking settlement in Dublin during excavations in the 1970s. However, Heaney focuses on one such object: the trial piece, the section of bone upon which an apprentice carver would learn his craft. These pieces of carved bone are, for Heaney, "trial pieces" in at least two senses: they are objects produced through hardships endured ("trial"); and they are the products of ceremonial proceedings – trials – whose outcomes were bodies and weapons buried in the mud. As we might expect from Heaney, as a writer so attuned to the physical qualities of language itself, it is the sound of words that connects these objects to the present. The word "plosive" is precisely resonant here: it is both a term from phonetics for the sudden puff of air produced by consonants "d" and "b" in the word "Dublin," as well as carrying a suggestion of the word "explosive" in a city in which three no-warning bombs had exploded the previous year, 1974, killing twenty-six people. At the time when "Viking Dublin: Trial Pieces" was published in a city where the possibility of sudden violence was a lived reality, the poem provided a metaphor for understanding what he calls elsewhere in *North* those "who would connive / in civilised outrage / yet understand the exact / and tribal, intimate revenge."[13] However, placing "Viking Dublin" in the context of MacNeice's "Dublin," or of *Ulysses*, read from the perspective of Dublin in 2021, a curious contradiction comes into focus: that which he uses as an image of the indigenous, the "tribal" and "intimate" is, in fact, its opposite: a site of settlement for a culture that came from outside Ireland. Here, perhaps, the lines from MacNeice's "Dublin" come back into focus: "Appropriating all / The alien brought." In other words, as well as functioning as a commentary on the nature of Irish internecine conflict in the 1970s, Heaney's "Viking Dublin" reminds us that in Dublin – and here the city differs from much of the rest of the country – when you dig down to the deepest strata, you find not the native; instead you find (to use MacNeice's word) "the alien," uneasily appropriated.

The implications of this paradox have long worried at Irish culture, particularly during the period of the Irish Literary Revival a little over a century ago, where the sense that Dublin was in some way alien to itself extends not only backward in time, but also forward. Writing in 1937 (almost contemporaneously with MacNeice), W.B. Yeats saw in Dublin's main thoroughfare, O'Connell Street, an emblem of all that was the antithesis (for him, the hated antithesis) of the ancestral, the indigenous. "When I stand upon O'Connell Bridge in the half-light," he wrote, "and notice that discordant architecture, all those electric signs, where modern heterogeneity has taken physical form, a vague hatred comes up out of my own dark."[14] Whether it be in the plays of his contemporaries such as J.M. Synge or Lady Gregory, or in the poetry of successors such as Patrick Kavanagh, perhaps the most firmly established narrative of Irish literary history in the twentieth century is structured around an opposition between the rural and the urban, with the weight of authority – Joyce notwithstanding – firmly on the side of the rural. Of course, the fuller picture is more complex than this, and, as Declan Kiberd once remarked, "it might make more sense to see the assault on urban values in revivalist and nationalist literature less as an attack on the city as such than on the idea of a colonial or imperial capital, less as an assault on the city as a non-Irish phenomenon than an attempt to imagine an Irish alternative."[15] Nonetheless, the narrative persists.

When others looked up O'Connell Street (or Sackville Street, as it was known until 1921), they saw it with a different kind of vague hatred. Originally laid out as Drogheda Street in 1728, it was named for Henry Moore, Earl of Drogheda, whose name is literally inscribed in the map of the city, with the surrounding streets still known as Henry Street, Moore Street, and Earl Street; there was once even an Of Lane (to complete the topographical signature, Henry Moore, Earl *of* Drogheda), which has since become Henry Place.[16] The main thoroughfare was renamed in 1756 for Lionel Cranfield Sackville, the 1st Duke of Dorset, who served twice as Lord Lieutenant of Ireland. By 1862, however, as Yvonne Whelan notes in her account of Dublin street names, the *Irishman* newspaper was calling for "a thorough reform of the nomenclature of Dublin street names [...] most of them foreign and anti-national."[17]

The call to rename the streets was mixed with a wider debate about naming in nineteenth-century Ireland, which the playwright Brian Friel has memorably explored in a rural context in his play *Translations* (1980), set during the British Ordinance Survey mapping of Ireland in the late 1830s. As one character asks another in Friel's play, "Do you know where the priest lives," to which the reply is: "at Lios na Muc." He is immediately rebuked, for the name has changed. "No, he doesn't. Lois na Muc, the Fort of the Pigs, has become Swinefort. And to get to Swinefort you pass through Greencastle and Fair Head and Strandhill."[18] In rural Ireland, there had been a dense weave of Irish-language place-names, often down to the level of individual fields, stones, or ditches, over which English-language names were superimposed in the nineteenth century, leading Douglas Hyde, founder of the Gaelic League (and later Ireland's first President), to proclaim in 1892 that "on the whole our place-names have been treated with about the same respect as if they were the names of a savage tribe which never before had been reduced to writing." Consequently, one of the initiatives of the cultural revival involved the reclamation and restoration of the original Irish place-names, and this inevitably extended to Dublin, where, as Whelan comments, campaigns to rename streets "served as an act of political propaganda of enormous symbolic value [....] By 1900 the text of Dublin's street names had come to reflect the increasingly contested nature of space in the city."[19] The decision of Dublin Corporation to rename Sackville Street after Daniel O'Connell – the leading Catholic nationalist political leader of the nineteenth century, born into the Irish-speaking Ó Conaill family from rural County Kerry – was a declaration of a shift of power (even if the actual name change was not made until after Irish Independence in 1921).

However, conflating the situation in which a lane or a field in rural Ireland whose name has been acquired through tradition and local association over generations, with one in which a greenfield site was laid out and the new place named – as happened with Drogheda/Sackville Street – is to confuse two very different (indeed, one might say opposite) states of affairs. As with MacNeice or Heaney digging down into the Dublin's deepest archaeological strata and finding a Viking trial piece, if you dig down into the soil of O'Connell Street, you find not the traces of a precolonial indigenous culture with its traditional patterns of naming, but its antithesis. And, from a certain kind of cultural nationalist perspective, which valued the indigenous and the original, this was problematic. However, as the readings of Joyce and MacNeice with which we opened suggest, there is another way of reading the situation. Likewise, in Oliver St. John Gogarty's memoir, *As I Was Going Down Sackville Street*, first published in 1937 (the same year in which Yeats raged against the street's "modern heterogeneity"), Gogarty recalls:

> I gazed up Sackville Street. The grandest thing we have in Dublin, the great Doric column that upheld the Admiral, was darkened by flying mists, intermittent as battle smoke; [...] That pillar marks the end of a civilization, the culmination of the great period of eighteenth-century Dublin, just as the pillar at Brindisi marks the end of the Roman road.[20]

The "great Doric column" here is the monument to Admiral Horatio Nelson, which stood in the center of Dublin's main thoroughfare from 1809 until it was blown up in 1966, and was in some respects the monumental embodiment of the street's colonial past. However, Gogarty draws out the classical associations of an architectural style – Doric – which (through a small sleight of hand) allows him to connect the British Empire with the Roman Empire, so that Dublin (and, more particularly Sackville/ O'Connell Street) becomes equated with Brindisi, where the Via Appia that ran from Rome literally ran out of road before it met the sea, its hero stranded by the ebbing tide. However, unlike in rural Ireland, where the receding tide of empire could be imagined to have left behind the original, indigenous culture it originally swamped, in Dublin there is no original, authentic ground to reveal. Its layers are its authentic being; there is no bedrock.

It is at this point that the Dublin trams in *Ulysses* return (as trams always do). In a 1907 guidebook to the city, the author notes of the monument to Nelson that "the pillar forms a sort of landmark, and is the starting-place of several lines of trams."[21] It is here that Joyce sets the "Aeolus" episode of *Ulysses*, which takes place in the offices of the *Freeman's Journal* newspaper, just around the corner on Abbey Street. The *Freeman's Journal* was, of course, where Leopold Bloom worked, selling advertisements, and Stephen Daedalus also drops into its offices in this episode, which takes its name from the "keeper of the winds" in the *Odessey* – suggesting both that journalism is so much hot air, but also that it is the wind that makes the city move. The whole chapter is written like a series of short newspapers stories, and the entire section gives the impression of the constant circulation of words and stories, all against the ineluctable auditory background of the tramlines. So, we have a section with the headline "In the Heart of the Hibernian Metropolis":

> Before Nelson's pillar trams slowed, shunted, changed trolley, started for Blackrock, Kingstown and Dalkey, Clonskea, Rathgar and Terenure, Palmerstown, part and upper Rathmines, Sandymount Green, Rathmines, Ringsend and Sandymount Tower, Harold's Cross. The hoarse Dublin United Tramway Company's timekeeper bawled them off.[22]

It is not simply that Dublin is internally connected to its own constituent elements, as the timekeeper calls out the names of Dublin neighborhoods and suburbs. The O'Connell Street tram stop is also opposite the General Post Office. Of course, there is another history in that building, as one of the principal sites of the 1916 Rebellion, connecting the street in complex ways to a history of anti-imperial resistance; it is also the case in *Ulysses* that the Post Office is the site of a global connectivity. Under the headline "The Wearer of the Crown," Joyce both absorbs the irony of writing about the General Post Office in 1922 (six years after the 1916 Rising) in a novel set in 1904, and moves past the irony, to use the Post Office as a way of writing Dublin as a city that is both itself, and part of multiple networks, connected globally:

> Under the porch of the general post office shoeblacks called and polished. Parked in North Prince's street His Majesty's vermillion mailcars, bearing on their sides the royal initials, E.R., received loudly flung sacks of letters, postcards, lettercards, parcels, insured and paid, for local, provincial, British and overseas delivery.[23]

As well as the ghostly proleptic presence of the Rising, the Post Office is the point at which the city connects not just to the Empire, but to the world beyond.

That connectivity would be unremarkable (what city does not have a post office?) were it not for the reader's equally proleptic awareness that lying ahead of *Ulysses* is *Finnegans Wake*, where the city as part of a grid connecting it outwards in multiple and complex ways is incorporated into the structure of language itself. Consider, for instance, the *Wake*'s opening:

> riverrun, past Eve and Adam's, from swerve of shore to bend of bay, brings us by a commodius vicus of recirculation back to Howth Castle and Environs. Sir Tristram, violer d'amores, fr'over the short sea, had passencore rearrived from North Armorica on this side the scraggy isthmus of Europe Minor to wielderfight his penisolate war: nor had topsawyer's rocks by the stream Oconee exaggerated themselse to Laurens County's gorgios while they went doublin[24]

As with the other Dublin texts we have considered, so too is the opening of *Finnegans Wake* grounded in the physical fabric of the city, in this case the River Liffey, which from the opening word "riverrun" takes us through topography, architecture (Eve and Adam's is a church on the river bank), and their intersections (Howth Castle is located on a peninsular spur that protrudes out into Dublin Bay). Then we have "Sir Tristam," who is both Tristan from the story of Tristan and Isolde, for whom is named the Dublin suburb of Chapelizoid (Isolde's chapel), where much of the *Wake* takes place, but also Sir Amory Tristam, the first Earl of Howth (linking to Howth Castle), who was a soldier in the Peninsular Wars in Spain ("the penisolate war"; Howth is also a peninsula), and whose first name – "Amory" – becomes a pun on "America," which leads to the pun "doublin," and hence to the town of Dublin in Laurens County, Georgia, on the banks of the Oconee, founded by a Dubliner, Peter Sawyer. And so it goes, for more than 600 pages.[25] The point is this: what *Finnegans Wake* does at the level of language is already implicit in *Ulysses* and also in MacNeice's "Dublin": it writes Dublin as a multiply connected space, composed of structures of repetition and difference with no absolute terms.

And it is at this point that the possibilities created by Dublin's literary imagining become a resource in the present, in that the absence of an absolute term invalidates any mythic point of authentic origin, any original inhabitant. This in turn collapses the distinction between the native and the alien that constituted the binary opposition through which Irish culture was read in a colonial context, most powerfully during the period of the Irish Literary Revival. To walk through Dublin today is to live this kind of rhizomatic urban experience. To put it simply, Ireland has moved within two decades from being a society defined by a colonial binary and outward emigration, to being a space of inward migration, principally from elsewhere in Europe, but also from Africa, Asia, and South America. Much of this has been focused in Dublin, and more than 20 percent of the city's population was foreign-born in 2018; that same year, for instance, the city ranked eighth among ninety-three cities in Europe taking part in the Council of Europe's Intercultural Cities Index (and fourth among cities with populations over 200,000).[26] As this change has occurred, it has become necessary to rethink narratives of Irish culture that posit an authentic ground of Irishness, located in some primal moment before colonization. In some respects, it has been remarkable with what little apparent cultural dissonance that transition has been made, and it may be the case – at least with regard to Dublin – that part of the reason lies in the recognition on the part of its writers that the city has never had an authentic, indigenous origin. Instead, the city has always been composed of the sedimented appropriations of "all the alien brought"; and while traces of each layer linger in the city's physical fabric, they also radiate outwards from each layer like the language of the *Wake*, extending their tendrils beyond the city, connecting Dublin to its elsewhere in what might be thought as a reversal of colonization, a post-postcolonial condition.

One way this might constitute a resource for the city in the twenty-first century can be found in a text by a spoken-word poet, Stephen James Smith, who opens his 2018 poem "Dublin You Are" with his own reworking of MacNeice's "Dublin":

> Dublin you are grey brick upon grey brick,
> full of tarmac and hipster pricks?
> Just face it, all other places Pale in comparison,
> you are more than some former Saxon garrison.

He then exhorts his city, "Dublin don't be scared / to change," building a vision of the city extending outwards, not only to its new outer suburbs, but also to the new "grey bricks" as it were, adding their own worlds to those of the Danes and the Saxons:

Dublin you are full of Polish,
and Brazilians speaking Portugese,
and now the Chinese
have turned Parnell Street into Chinatown.
Dublin don't let them down.[27]

Notes

1 James Joyce, *Ulysses* (Richmond, London: Alma, 2012), 120.
2 Ibid., 30.
3 Ferdinand de Saussure, *Course in General Linguistics*, Charles Bally, Albert Sechehaye and Albert Reidlinger, eds., trans. Wade Baskin (New York: Philosophical Library, 1959), 108.
4 Ibid.
5 Louis MacNeice, *Collected Poems* (London: Faber and Faber, 1966), 178–180.
6 Benjamin Hudson, "Knúte and Viking Dublin," *Scandinavian Studies* (1994): 319–335.
7 Oxford English Dictionary, *s.v.* "poise"; www.oed.com.
8 David Dickson, *The First Irish Cities: An Eighteenth-Century Transformation* (New Haven: Yale University Press, 2021), 28.
9 Pascale Casanova, *The World Republic of Letters*, trans. M.B. Debevoise (Cambridge, MA.; Harvard University Press, 2004), 304.
10 Joe Cleary, *Modernism, Empire, World Literature* (Cambridge, MA: Cambridge University Press, 2021), 11.
11 Seamus Heaney, *North* (London: Faber, 1975), 38.
12 Ibid., 22.
13 Ibid., 38.
14 W.B. Yeats, "An Introduction for My Work," in William H. O'Donnell, ed., *The Collected Works: Vol. V: The Later Essays* (New York: Simon and Schuster, 2007), 215.
15 Declan Kiberd, "The City in Irish Culture," *City* 6, no. 2 (2002): 219–228; 221.
16 Neal Doherty, *The Complete Guide to the Streets of Dublin City* (Dublin: Orphen House, 2016), 63–64.
17 Cited in Yvonne Whelan, *Reinventing Modern Dublin: Streetscape, Iconography and the Politics of Identity* (Dublin: University College Dublin Press, 2003).
18 Brian Friel, *Collected Plays: Volume II*, Peter Fallon, ed. (Oldcastle, Co. Meath: The Gallery Press, 2016), 458.
19 Cited in Whelan, Reinventing, 100–101, 102.
20 Oliver St. John Gogarty, *As I Was Going Down Sackville Street* ([1937] London: Sphere, 1968), 263.
21 Samuel A. Ossory Fitzpatrick, *Dublin: A Historical and Topographical Account of the City* (London: Methuen, 1907), 298–299.
22 Joyce, *Ulysses*, 88.
23 Ibid., 88.

24 James Joyce, *Finnegans Wake* (London: Penguin, 1992), 3.
25 Roland McHugh, *Annotations to Finnegans Wake*, 4th ed. (Baltimore, MD: Johns Hopkins University Press, 2016), 3.
26 "Intercultural Cities Index: Dublin," Council of Europe (2018), https://rm.coe.int/dublin-ireland-results-of-the-intercultural-cities-index-2nd-report-ju/16808c5366.
27 Stephen James Smith, *Fear Not* (Dublin: Arlen House, 2018), 12–15. See: https://youtu.be/UNQcwcb1saU.

CHAPTER 15

From Altepetl to Megacity

Narrating Mexico City as World Literature

María Moreno Carranco and José Ramón Ruisánchez Serra

As Ignacio Sánchez Prado has categorically stated, there is no such thing as a singular world literature. What he means is that every literary system entails a world literature, not in the sense of exerting an influence, but in the way it reads the productions of the sum of literary systems that reach it: "The worldliness of world literature is neither a self-evident, ideal nor an utopian pursuit. It is, rather, a concretely existing category related to specific cultural locations and material practices[:] the limits of one's world literature are the limits of one's material access to the world."[1]

To us, this idea is put to better use when we allow the set of material conditions and practices, and the cultural location shaping the worldliness of Mexican literature to become one and the same thing. Mexico City, historically, has had its own unique literary culture, made up of a network of writers, publishing houses, bookstores, and libraries, that has created a literary world defined by the imagined boundaries of the city. Even more importantly, the city itself ciphers the wager of literature. Mexican literature has always attempted to express the promise and complexities of life in Mexico City. Often the challenges posed by the sheer size of the city and by its several centuries of existence have defeated the literary attempt. In contrast, a number of texts not originated in belles-lettres but in different fields of knowledge, have successfully captured crucial traits of the ever-changing texture of Tenochtitlan, Mexico, DF, CDMX. Moreover, Mexico City has been the place to embody the country's attempts for global recognition. Our understanding of the global is delineated as much by local material conditions as by how we narrate them.

In the following pages, we explore different strategies that have been used to write Mexico City in literary texts. As these literary strategies can be tied to the peculiarities of the city itself, it is valuable to recapitulate them together.

The City from the Distance

We shall first focus on *distance*, either physical or personal, as that which allows the author to write the city as a whole from an outside vantage point.

The *Tira de la peregrinación* or *Boturini Codex*, dating from circa 1535, documents the migration of the Aztec from the northwest of modern Mexico and their very slow approach to the site prophesied by their god Huitzilopochtli. This codex, with its myriad footsteps arriving and departing from endless toponyms signaled with dates, institutes a crucial operation regarding the future capital. The city is first and foremost a promise. Tenochtitlan possesses textual formulation even before it is founded. Just as importantly, its remote location prevents any rapid or direct approach. Even when the Aztec at last arrive in the Basin, they spend decades trying to find a place to settle on the already heavily populated shore of Lake Texcoco – in fact, a system formed of five interconnected bodies of water fed by forty-eight rivers – before finally finding the islet in the sweetwater portion of the lake that was to become their city in 1325.

The physical traits of the islet where the city was founded created a unique environment. Sweet water made *chinampas* – floating gardens used for agriculture and construction – possible. Conversely, the Aztec capital was at the mercy of floods. The establishment of Mexico-Tenochtitlan in this particular location is the most relevant factor shaping the city through its more than 700 years of history, it explains for instance the devastation wreaked by later earthquakes.[2]

Two centuries after its foundation, the city was one of the largest in the world. By 1521 it had an estimated 300,000 inhabitants.[3] In the chronicles of the conquest, Tenochtitlan is once again presented as a promise. Richness and fame await there, but simultaneously the capital is repeatedly described as an inexpugnable deathtrap. The fraught approach of Cortés and his men creates the main narrative impetus of a sizable part of these *crónicas*, fueling the desire of his readers to finally see the forbidden city.

Distance, thus, creates the vision of the city as a whole and launches both Díaz del Castillo and Cortés into their marveled (and marvelous) descriptions. These tracts remain intensely engaging because they capture the moment when the city is on the cusp of its worlding. The talisman word Mexico-Tenochtitlan finally reveals itself as an image, and this image must be signified. Díaz del Castillo says it seemed to him that he was visiting the dreamworlds of Amadís de Gaula. Cortés, when describing Tlatelolco market, states it is twice as large as Salamanca's main square. These comparisons connect this gleaming city to the world of poor Spaniards who had migrated to the colonies in search of a better life, and perhaps explain in part why, despite its complicated geographical location, Cortés decided to rebuild the city in the same place, understanding the political and symbolic weight of Tenochtitlan.[4] Barbara Mundy analyzes the codexes Mendoza (ca. 1542) and Aubin (ca. 1576–1608) as the first documents addressing the city and illustrating the continuities between Tenochtitlan and Mexico City. Even if in his letters, Cortés described Tenochtitlan as "destroyed and razed to the ground" – which would equate the existence of the city with the prevalence of its built environment – it is likely that Cortés understood the city as both a physical entity and an assemblage of citizens and practices. The latter make it possible to understand the city as "a single entity, the island space called Tenochtitlan in the fifteenth century, and Mexico City by the seventeenth."[5]

As early as the sixteenth century, we see a crucial difference in terms of the conception of the city. The pre-Hispanic city-states in the Valley of Mexico were named *altepetl(s)* in Nahuatl, literally meaning "mountain-water." An important aspect of the conception of altepetl is lost in the translation into Spanish as city or town. In Mesoamerica, as stated by James Lockhart,[6] the altepetl did not distinguish between urban centers and the countryside. Federico Navarrete Linares explains that the concept of altepetl encompassed what we call a political entity and its people, natural as well as supernatural elements, such as the patron god.[7] Bernardino de Sahagún, to whom we shall return later, explained the term succinctly in his *Historia general de las cosas de la Nueva España* or *Florentine Codex* (1540–85):

> And they said that the hills are not real, only above they are earthy, stony; inside they are like vessels, like houses that are filled with water. And if at some point they wanted to destroy the hills their world would be flooded.
>
> And so they named where men live, altepetl.[8]

The Altepetl's conceptualization of natural elements as constitutive of the city suggested a harmonious relationship with the lake and the sweet-water source in Chapultepec hill. Perhaps more importantly, it implied the lasting capacity of the city to grow its own food locally. The expansion of early capitalism entails the destruction of preexisting modes of production and exchange.[9] The very landscape preserved by these modes is similarly eroded. Its consequences for Mexico City have been ecologically devastating.

The Layered City

This sustained destruction explored by Chea creates a sort of historiography that is already deeply literary. According to Kojin Karatani, nation is the collection of possibilities renounced, ruined, or otherwise destroyed by the State in order to better serve the expansion of Capital. Yet, these remainders do not entirely disappear. Nation as narration, as Homi Bhabha put it already a few decades ago, produces the condition of affectivity that allows citizens to love the capitalist State.[10] Certain historiographies, then, are in fact histories of nation rather than of State, and thus better lend themselves to literary treatment and reception.

It is precisely in these histories of nation that the forming of the city and its literature into a dense palimpsest of history, materiality, and practices can be better traced. The past is always conditioning, modeling, and shaping the present. Mexico City's layers, including its natural environment, built elements, and social practices, are at times partly erased, as with the destruction of Tenochtitlan, the constant floods that led to the abandonment of the city center for five years in the seventeenth century, or the massive damage of several earthquakes intensified by the unstable subsoil of the desiccated lake bed. Yet, the reappearance of the past – qua nature or previous urban configurations –creates a constant demand on memory that appears prominently in literary texts. The first to fully understand this demand were the Franciscan friars. The aforementioned Sahagún trained the first generation of Nahua intellectuals in the Colegio de Santa Cruz in Tlatelolco. Able to write Spanish, Latin, and Nahuatl with Roman characters, these young scholars became invaluable in compiling his encyclopedic *Florentine Codex*, one of the more important sources to this day for everything pertaining to the (lost) world of Tenochtitlan, including its conquest.

This story is attempted again by Father Francisco Xavier Clavijero's *Historia Antigua de México* (*History of Mexico*, 1780). It is worth reconstructing the circumstances that lead to Clavigero's publication. For nearly 300 years, the colonial city was the capital of New Spain. Mexico became the main cultural and economic center in the Americas and one of the most important cultural centers of the West. Exceptionally big and well-supplied libraries were formed. It is not surprising that shortly after the first edition of *Don Quijote* (1605), more volumes were circulating in New Spain than in the peninsula. Baroque art flourished in sculpture and architecture.[11] By the eighteenth century, when half of the population was European, a quarter mestiza, and a quarter Indian, the colonial administration of the city started several modernization projects. The *traza* [grid] was improved with the opening of new avenues and bridges, sidewalks built, plazas and markets reordered, facades painted, and street lighting installed. Additionally, the potable water and sewage networks were improved through the building of new canals, and garbage dumps were created in an attempt to clean and sanitize the capital.[12]

This was part of the Bourbon dynasty's effort to regain control over transatlantic trade, modernize state finances to benefit royal coffers, and establish tighter political and administrative control within the empire. In order to decrease the church's power, the Jesuits were expelled. They had been in charge of educating the elites of New Spain. Jesuit exiles in Bologna echoed the temporal chasm of the ancient city with the geographical distance instituted by the new political order. This led to important works, such as the *Rusticatio Mexicana* (*Mexican Country Scenes*, 1781), a landscape poem written in Latin by Rafael Landívar: "I have been telling of the flower gardens which grow in the middle of the lake, of Vulcan's wrath, of waters streaming from the hills, of clothes steeped in various dyes."[13] As this short passage shows, the poem, written in Latin, followed classic models perhaps too closely.

The momentous *Historia Antigua* by Clavijero is a gallant attempt to make sense of available materials with scholarly rigor. His project, however, was marred by the use of scripture as ultimate authority. The most memorable passages in *Historia* occur when Clavijero forgets his religious identity and allows his prose to become almost novelistic when narrating the adventurous life of young Nezahualcóyotl in exile.

The Forastero's Gaze

Clavijero's *Historia* was carefully studied by Alexander von Humboldt when he arrived in the capital of New Spain, a city that remained relatively small – a population of 200,000 at the dawn of the nineteenth century – which allowed him to measure it thoroughly. His multi-volume *Essai politique sur le royaume de la Nouvelle-Espagne* (*Political Essay on the Kingdom of New Spain*, 1808) radically and durably changed Mexicans' perception not only of their capital, but also of their territory. Humboldt had a gift for comparison. For instance, he states that Mexico is five times the size of Spain; he reminds his readers that Popocatepetl is more than 600 meters taller than Mount Blanc; and was the first to call Mexico the City of Palaces. Through him, Mexico City became not only the capital of a country but part of a continent, the mountains surrounding it a continuation of the Andes.

The *forastero* (outsider) embodied the distance which made the totalization of the city possible. The *forastero* was not only an author but also the implied reader of an entire genre, that of the early travel guide. One such guide is Marcos Arróniz's *Manual del viajero en México* (*Mexico's Travel Guide*, 1858), which attempted to portray the city, its attractions and amenities, for an imagined visitor who is ultimately the reader of world literature.

One of the more fascinating *forasteros*, writing for other readers of the world, was indeed a *forastera*: Frances Calderón de la Barca, in her witty *Life in Mexico* (1842). In the following passage, Calderón de la Barca narrates how she and her husband traveled to Mexico City for the first time. As they do so, the chronicles of the conquistadors come to mind, with the help of the hazy weather: "as we strained our eyes to look into the valley, it all appeared to me rather like a vision of the Past than the actual breathing Present. The curtain of Time seemed to roll back, and to reveal to us the great panorama that burst upon the eyes of Cortés when he first looked down upon the table-land."[14] Yet, as they approach the city, Calderón de la Barca notes that present-day Mexico is no longer what Cortés saw: "The scenery on this side of Mexico is arid and flat, and where the waters of the Lagunas, covered with their gay canoes, once surrounded the city, forming canals through its streets, we now see melancholy marshy lands, little enlivened by the great flights of wild duck and waterfowls."[15] Notice how the past simultaneously offers a tantalizing presence but then recedes behind its impossibility. This oscillation is an important worlding device of Mexico City literature.

In the verse of Guillermo Prieto (1818–97), the most powerful poet of the Mexican nineteenth century, the *forastero* finds a new avatar: the "I" of the poems (or a character in the poems that stands in for this "I") is an outsider that witnesses the lives of the popular classes and transcribes their expressions with gusto. But he remains foreign, a verse ethnographer that perceives the charm of these scenes, precisely because he is not part of the class he celebrates. This can be studied in "Trifulca," a short narrative poem. When Cayetano seems about to kill his wife Bartola, Pablo, "the most beloved grocer / of the neighborhood," admonishes Cayetano against hitting women and punches him to the ground for good measure. But immediately Bartola,

> Like lightning, like a lion
> opened the blade
> of her concealed knife,
> her eyes ablaze,

and so she addressed don Pablo,
"What does a grocer have to do with this
marriage breaker, party pooper?
"Don't you know he is my husband,
we were wedded by the church
and he just governs what he owns
and there he is master?"[16]

In the end, Pablo has to make himself scarce and the happy couple leaves the scene arm in arm. Pablo stands for the "I" of the poet, who can tell the story and capture the voices, but at the cost of remaining barred from the communities upon which he spies. He is closer to the elites than to the *pueblo* that triumphantly remains true to its opaque self. This is the reason why Prieto's *Musa callejera* (*Streetsmart Muse*, 1883) signaled the perception that Mexico was not a homogeneous city. Its popular classes spoke and behaved differently, and this difference warranted literary attention. Thus, in Prieto, instead of the city as a whole, we find that different spaces within it are privileged.

Prieto was not only a poet. His *Memorias de mis tiempos* (*Memoirs*, published posthumously in 1903) is a wonderful, lively, and messy memoir where Prieto recalls the years 1828–40. The coinciding of his youth with the invention of independent Mexico makes the book a key document for understanding both the intellectual processes of his generation and the structures of feeling, shared by the first romantics in Mexico.

One would be hard pressed to choose between *Memorias* and *Los bandidos de Río Frío* (*The Bandits from Río Frío*, 1891) by Prieto's friend Manuel Payno, as the ultimate book on nineteenth-century Mexico. Both are grand narratives that include a multitude of characters and a wealth of information regarding everyday existence in Mexico. The main difference is that, while Prieto wrote a memoir of his formative years, Payno decided to pen a feuilleton-novel to reminisce about the dying century. Yet *The Bandits* is not quite a historical novel in the sense that, even though most of its central subplots are historical, they were not in reality contemporary with each other. But this point precisely defines the world of the novel: the city is made of racialized layers that in turn belong to non-synchronous stages: the mostly Indian periphery communicates via the aquatic thoroughfare that the mestiza Cecilia uses to bring fruits into the modernized Criollo downtown. Payno insists that the lagoons and canals were in the same state in which Cortés first saw them, but coexist with modern shops, markets, and churches. He describes fields with medicinal herbs at the east of the city, the city's garbage dump by the northern gate of Vallejo, and an inhospitable salty marsh, while the palaces in central streets resemble those of a medieval city. These descriptions reveal the coexistence of urban elements in colonial and even precolonial times, and the presence of the countryside that, as noted before, was excluded from the city.

The Growing City

Changes in the last quarter of the nineteenth century made writers of the Porfiriato feel that the colonial city, and not only Tenochtitlan, was already irreparably modified. The certainty that the old city was lost forever became widespread, creating a desire for literary restoration. Both Luis González Obregón and Artemio de Valle Arizpe understood this and were able to exploit the fascination exerted by the colonial past in palatable texts not unlike the influential *Tradiciones peruanas* (*Peruvian Traditions*, 1872) of Ricardo Palma. The colonial city was an ideal landscape to profit from the increased sophistication of *Modernismo*. The sumptuous lexicon of poets at the turn of the century, together with the exotic commodities that often appear in their verse, were conducive to recreating a city where baroque architecture was in dialogue with the commodities brought from the Nao de China from Asia, and from Europe via the Andalusian merchants.

Texts on charming or terrifying corners of the city, brand new or laden with tradition, were abundant even before the Porfiriato. Given the lack of sufficient news, and the slow development of professional journalism, newspapers consumed shorter texts where the descriptive and narrative elements carried similar weight in the text. Yet the genre culminates only with the appearance of the Modernista *crónica*, an eminently literary form of journalism that Manuel Gutiérrez Nájera was the first to masterfully practice. The *crónica* allowed distinguished contemporary Spanish American authors, including Rubén Darío and José Martí, to make a living. Yet, it must also be understood as the laboratory for their poetry. The cross-pollination of the two genres is evident in the joyful "La duquesa Job" ("Duchess Job", 1884), the most beloved of Gutiérrez Nájera's poems, predicated on his *flâneries* in the fashionable streets of the city. This set a precedent for what would become a significant tendency in Mexican poetry of the twentieth century, which we explore later in this chapter. For now, it suffices to say that the tension between offering an encompassing view of the city and concentrating on a certain neighborhood became more visible at the onset of the twentieth century, when the city was about to lose its clearly defined physical borders.

Mexico City, with a population of over half a million, began to sprawl across its peripheral landscape to undergo a major transformation during the Porfiriato. Porfirio Díaz, who served seven terms as president of Mexico from 1876 to 1911, was a clear example of a Latin American "progressive dictatorship," combining limited political freedom and silencing of the press with extensive modernization projects, such as the expansion of the railroad system and the development of industries, especially textiles and mining. More importantly, during his rule, Mexico became one of the main oil producers in the world. Díaz promoted foreign investment, particularly from the United States but also from Great Britain and France, which caused resentment among nationalists. This discontent, combined with the fact that his rule benefited mainly the middle and upper classes, led to popular discontent and ultimately to the Mexican Revolution.

Díaz had a great influence in the city's development. He made a substantial effort to turn Mexico City into an "ideal city," setting urban trends that continue to shape the city's fabric today. In this period urban expansion went beyond the lake, by then almost totally desiccated. Many of the planned areas or *colonias* were developed in the 1900s. The process increased after the Mexican Revolution, and the subsequent industrialization of the city led to the disappearance of the last remains of the altepetl or indigenous city and its agricultural and lacustrine characteristics.[17]

As Mauricio Tenorio-Trillo noted, the Porfirian elite blended French and local architecture, preexisting urban planning, and symbols from pre-Hispanic times with a Housmannized urban landscape.[18] The urban reshaping also meant a civilizing process since it aimed to change people's behaviors by making them more European and therefore "better." The aspiring global metropolis is also the space for intimate everyday events and encounters that at times bridge its new sociospatial stratification. This spatial separation continues today, with a wealthy and powerful West and a poor and disadvantaged East.

Federico Gamboa's novel *Santa* (1903) was the first bestseller of twentieth-century Mexico. It tells the story of an exurban girl, born in Chimalistac, a small town in the outskirts of the city later swallowed by urban expansion. Santa, the protagonist, is raped in the wild lava fields of the Pedregal, which Gamboa describes thus:

> A volcanic landscape dotted with bushes, colossal monoliths, and sloping stones so smooth that not even goats could pause when crossing them, the Pedregal possesses serpentine, crystal-clear streams that flow from unknown springs, disappearing occasionally, only to reappear some distance away,

> then plummet silently and permanently into cavernous openings that the weeds disguise with seemingly criminal intent.[19]

It is worth noting how Gamboa, while incorporating this place (the future site of the national university) into the written city, inscribes moral dangers to the very features of the non-urban landscape. These pitfalls force Santa to work as a prostitute in the city. There, she first gains fame, only to later face decline and disease. This attempt to rewrite Emile Zola's *Nana* (1880) was, in our view, widely successful, not because of the moral tale but rather because it offered a tantalizing panorama of Mexico City as a Latin American Babylon, where pleasures could be bought and sold, and eroticism pierced the rigid structure of social classes – even if temporarily. The brothel where Santa begins her journey as a prostitute marks the middle space between the new and exclusive areas of the city and the ones excluded from all progress: it connects two disparate worlds.[20]

The Boundless City

When Carlos Fuentes published his inaugural novel, *La región más transparente* (*Where the Air is Clear*, 1957), Mexico City was on its way to become a modern metropolis. This encompassing fiction captures the lives of the ambitious *capitalinos* competing for money and sex in the prosperous city created by the economic policies which concentrated industry, finance, and higher education in the Valley of Mexico. But for young Fuentes, it was no longer possible to make a single character the axis of the novel. Instead, *Where the Air is Clear* breaks with this convention in favor of a novel where the city itself is the protagonist, represented by a plethora of characters. Fuentes adapted this approach to the choreography of urban life from John Dos Passsos's fiction.

In the years following *Where the Air is Clear*, the population of the city exploded, caused to a great extent by a developmentalist model that equated modernization with industrialization, with the hope of economic growth, accompanied by increased urbanization. By the end of the twentieth century, the population of the city had reached about eight million inhabitants. The population of its central districts has since remained stable, but the metropolitan region has grown forty-fold: from 8.5 km^2 to about 3,400 km^2, containing a population of over 20 million. Today it is a city where there are few vestiges of the lake, and the rivers and canals that were navigated up to the beginning of the twentieth century are only present in the names of avenues such as Rio de La

Piedad, Canal de la Viga, or Río Churubusco, which have been built over remaining waterways and the aqueous remnants of the lake. The apparent absence of the lake marks the texture of the fragility of the city, as in the caves of air prone to collapse; the unstable soil; the layers of colonial and Aztec debris. The city experiences floods every year, earthquakes have devastating effects, the buildings in the historic center are sinking. Thus, we see how the city is constituted of historical layers, including its natural and built environments, and its social practices. Many elements of the present city are embedded and conditioned by elements of its past. Catholic churches were often built on the locations of prehepatic temples, reusing the same stones. The buildings and city space have mutated over time without disappearing, and other practices have similarly adapted; for example, churches are heavily adorned with flowers, which is a continuation of the way temples in Tenochtitlan were decorated, with elaborate arrangements of roses and other flowers picked from the floating gardens.

The way these historical processes become *embodied* is brilliantly plotted by Carlos Fuentes in the two books he published in 1962. In *La muerte de Artemio Cruz* (*Death of Artemio Cruz*), Fuentes' narration of the contemporary city of *Where the Air is Clear* is replaced with a more generous representation of the past. The plethora of characters is also replaced by a single protagonist that embodies Mexican history. The arc of Artemio Cruz's rags-to-riches story matches that of modern Mexico: from the Porfiriato to the success story of industrialized Mexico and its underside of former revolutionaries turned corrupt politicians and entrepreneurs. Here, instead of neighborhoods or houses, it is the citizen who is abolished by time and a change in circumstances.

Artemio Cruz should be read in tandem with Fuentes's second (and short) novel of 1962, *Aura*. In this ghost story, a historian is seduced by a mysterious young woman who turns out to be a reincarnation of the ancient lady who hires him to investigate a nineteenth-century archive. So while in *Artemio Cruz* the protagonist remembers from his deathbed, in *Aura* memory has the power to come back from beyond the grave and impose its (sexual) power on the present.

Fuentes's early narratives owe a great deal to Octavio Paz's essays and his poetry about Mexico City. Paz celebrates the colonial splendor and the neighborhood of Mixcoac where he grew up in "Pasado en claro" ("A Draft of Shadows," 1975) or "Nocturno de San Ildefonso"("San Ildefonso Nocturne") and "Vuelta" ("Return") (both included in *Vuelta* in 1976), which we partially quote here:

I am
in Mixcoac
The letters rot
in the mailboxes
The bougainvillea
flattened by the sun
against the wall's white lime
a stain
a purple
passionate calligraphy
I am walking back
back to what I left
or left me.[21]

In these poems the "I" finds a cipher for the narrator's subjectivity and memory in the city.

The strong connection between place and subject can be read, in turn, as the basis of a new narrative form, especially as novelists renounce the attempt of urban totality to concentrate on the fragments of the city that define the characters of their narrative. This concentration reaches its climax in *El apando* (*The Hole*, 1969), the brief masterpiece published by José Revueltas just after the student movement was quashed in a bloodbath in October 1968. The claustrophobic fiction takes place inside a punishment cell in the Lecumberri jail[22] shared by three men, addicted to and deprived of drugs. This hyper-confined space successfully allegorizes the life of the "have-nots" in the city.

Even Fuentes himself in later books such as the fine "narrative quartet" *Agua quemada* (*Burnt Water*, 1980) opted for a partial account of the city. Other writers chose a neighborhood, an age-group, or protagonists with a shared sexual orientation, and used these as a vantage point from which to construct a different understanding of city life. Once this was established as a common practice, parts of the city outside the central districts were explored by post-1985 fiction writers such as Juan Villoro and Emiliano Pérez Cruz, and poets such as Fabio Morábito and more recently Inti García Santamaría.

But before moving this far into the present we must go back into the literary genre of the chronicle to explore instances when text privileges a moment when the whole city beats in unison, rather than a single location. This synchronization becomes all the more miraculous in the gargantuan city of the second half of the twentieth century. The more salient chronicles narrate the crucial events of the 1968 student movement and the 1985 earthquake from the standpoint of urban totality.

In Poniatowska's *La noche de Tlatelolco* (*Massacre in Mexico*, 2007) we find the following passage where political participation is *felt*:

> As soon as we left Chapultepec Park, just a few blocks farther on, hundreds of people began to join our ranks. All along Paseo de la Reforma, the sidewalks, the median strips, the monuments, and even the trees were full of people, and every hundred yards our ranks were doubled. And the only sound from those tens of thousands of people, were their footfalls.[23]

The multitude crosses the very route of privilege, the park where the viceroy would hunt, and the boulevard created by the Empress, and as it does so, it becomes only its togetherness, what its members share.

Poniatowska's chronicles, as well as those influenced by Carlos Monsiváis – the recently translated *Vértigo horizontal* (*Horizontal Vertigo*, 2019) by Juan Villoro comes to mind – powerfully reveal the immediate present, but also use it as a standpoint from which to explore the events that caused this revelation. In other words, in these texts the moment when a diverse citizenry coalesces into a people can (and should) be read as the moment when the present offers a tight connection to the past.[24]

Even when the city has grown beyond what is possible to experience, some of the more ambitious books on Mexico City still successfully strive to provide an image of its totality. These books, it must be noted, have been penned by foreign authors. Jonathan Kandell's *La Capital* (1988) remains not only immensely informative but also thoroughly enjoyable, especially the sections devoted to the indigenous and viceroyal city. Its rigorous chronology contrasts with Serge Gruzinski's labor of love in *La ciudad de México: una historia* (*A History of Mexico City*, 1996) where chaos and a multitude of perspectives including archaeology, art, theater, literature, painting, film, and television convey a (mostly) faithful mimetic representation of the Mexico City palimpsest. More recently, David Lida has cleverly divided his books on Mexico City into different monographic chapters that deal with topics such as money, sex, and violence.[25] So instead of a chronology or a cartography, they update the nineteenth-century *Guías del viajero* (*Travel Guides*) and seem equally attractive for Mexican and English-speaking audiences.

Conclusion

Mexico City has been portrayed as an urban tsunami referencing the endless waves of autoconstruction houses that go up and down the hills in the city's periphery. These extensive areas are largely absent from the city's literature and cultural production. The rest of the city encompasses more or less planned neighborhoods, several of which originated as towns or quadrants of Tenochtitlan in precolonial times while others were the result of the city's expansion. In the twenty-first century, the Santa Fe urban megaproject, located in the western periphery, epitomizes the global city.[26] Corporate buildings, luxurious shopping centers, hotels, restaurants, and high-end gated communities sit adjacent to traditional towns and poor settlements. The privileged enclave follows international trends of urban development that, particularly in the Global South, heighten the inequalities of neoliberal capitalism. This local version of a global city has yet to inspire its own literature. It is, however, the material expression of the city's desired worldliness.

Mexico City, similar to other major cities in the Global South, is and has been a milieu in constant (trans)formation, drawing on diverse connections, and subject to national and world forces. It is thus the site for instantiating the country's claims to global significance. Mexico City's literature, qua world literature, conditions our understanding of the global. An examination of literature by both Mexican writers and *forasteros* shows the specific ways in which the local and the global constitute each other here and, in turn, condition the ways in which the city has been produced, imagined, and consumed there. Not all the city's geographies are part of its literary construct; while some places are represented in detail, others are not (yet) part of its literary making. This can be explained by how Mexico City itself has absorbed or rejected different mores in literature in its journey from the altepetl to megacity.

This chapter is an attempt to better understand the dialogue between the materiality of Mexico City and the complex mirrors literature has held up to it. Cities inspire stories, imaginaries, and situations bound to specific territories. As cities are complex processes that cannot be simply described, tropes that unveil different aspects of their texture are required. In consequence these tropes almost never appear in isolation.

Thus, the attempts to look at Mexico City from comprehensive perspectives give rise to specific details: think of Moctezuma allowing Hernán Cortés to touch him, to prove he was human. In the same way, the catastrophic occurrence of an earthquake harks back to the foundation of the city on the lake seven centuries ago, as a necessary explanation of the city's tectonics. In other words, what we analyze separately for heuristic reasons is usually found together, mimicking the perpetually changing Mexico City palimpsest.

Urban texts are artifacts which co-form the city using both situated and global connections ranging from the symbolic to the material. Literature acts on and contributes to different forms of spatialization; it has the capacity to plot, preserve, and alter the urban experience, simultaneously *here* in the actual Mexico City and *there* in the ways Mexico City is imagined. We therefore return to our initial statement that there is no such thing as a singular world literature. Mexico City's literary system configures its own particular world literature. The specific material conditions – libraries, bookstores, archives, of course, but also aspects of everyday life in Mexico City, such as its food and architecture, its streets and public spaces, its spatial stratification – found in the urban and historical context of Mexico City produce a nonconforming, quite singular model of world literature.

Notes

Special thanks to C. Greig Crysler for his detailed comments to an earlier version of this chapter.

1 Ignacio M. Sánchez Prado, *Strategic Occidentalism* (Evanston, IL: Northwestern University Press, 2018), 15.

2 María Moreno Carranco and Rocío Guadarrama, "La ciudad en un lago," in Rocío Guadarrama and María Moreno Carranco, eds., *Mundos habitados: espacios de arquitectura, diseño y música en la Ciudad de México* (Mexico City: Universidad Autónoma Metropolitana, 2020), 49.

3 Paris and Seville had around 200,000 inhabitants at this time, while larger cities such as Beijing and Cairo had about 670,000 and 400,000 inhabitants, respectively.

4 María José and Rodilla León, *Aquestas son de México las señas* (Mexico City: Universidad Autónoma Metropolitana, 2014), 51–52.

5 Barbara Mundy, *The Death of the Aztec Tenochtitlan. The Life of Mexico City* (Austin, TX: University of Texas Press, 2015), 8–10.

6 James Lockhart, *The Nahuas after the Conquest* (Stanford, CA: Stanford University Press, 1992), 19.

7 Federico Navarrete Linares, *Los orígenes de los pueblos indígenas del Valle de México: los altépetl y sus historias* (Mexico City: Universidad Nacional Autónoma de México, 2011), 27–28.

8 Cited in ibid., 25.

9 Pheng Chea, *What Is a World? On Postcolonial Literature as World Literature* (Durham, NC: Duke University Press, 2016), 60–99. Chea also discusses the modification of space and time as consequences of capitalist expansion.

10 Homi Bhaba, ed. *Nation and Narration* (London and New York: Routledge, 1990). Kojin Karatani, *The Structure of World History* (Durham, NC: Duke University Press, 2014), 209–227.

11 Louis Panabiére, *Ciudad Águila, Villa Serpiente* (Mexico City: Fondo de Cultura Económica, 1996), 59.

12 Leonardo López Luján, *El ídolo sin pies ni cabeza* (Mexico City: El Colegio Nacional, 2020), 13–14.

13 Rafael Landívar, "Grandeza Mexicana" in Andrew Laird, ed., *The Epic of America: An Introduction to Rafael Landívar and the Rusticatio Mexicana* (London: Bloomsbury, 2020), 256.
14 Frances Calderón de la Barca, *Life in Mexico* (Berkeley, CA: University of California Press, 1982), 60.
15 Ibid., 61. Alfonso Reyes's essay "Visión de Anáhuac" (1915) revisits the same panorama.
16 Guillermo Prieto, *Atentamente* … (Mexico City: Promexa, 1979), 32. The translation is ours. For further exploration of this topic, see José Ramón Ruisánchez, "We, the Romantics" in José Ramón Ruisánchez, Anna M. Nogar, and Ignacio Sánchez Prado, *A History of Mexican Poetry* (Cambridge: Cambridge University Press, in press).
17 Serge Gruzinski, *La Ciudad de México: una historia* (Mexico City: Fondo de Cultura Económica, 2004), 487.
18 Mauricio Tenorio-Trillo, *I Speak of the City: Mexico City at the Turn of the Twentieth Century* (Chicago: University of Chicago Press, 2012), 13.
19 Federico Gamboa, *Santa: A Novel of Mexico City*, John Charles Chasteen, ed. (Chapel Hill, NC: University of North Carolina Press, 2010), 32.
20 Guadalupe Pérez-Anzaldo, "La representación del espacio urbano en relación con el personaje femenino en *Santa* de Federico Gamboa," *CiberLetras: revista de crítica literaria y de cultura* 16 (2007).
21 Octavio Paz and Eliot Weinberger, "Return," *The Hudson Review* 25, no. 1 (1972): 9, https://doi.org/10.2307/3849774.
22 The Lecumberri prison is one of Porfirio Diaz's modernization projects, which along with the mental hospital La Castañeda were meant to house the "undesirables" who could not be present in the "ideal city."
23 Elena Poniatowska, *Massacre in Mexico* (Columbia, MO: University of Missouri Press, 2007), 54.
24 For more on this, see Ruisánchez Serra and José Ramón, *Historias que regresan* (Mexico City: Fondo de Cultura Económica, 2012).
25 See David Lida, *Las llaves de la ciudad* (Mexico City: Sexto piso, 2008) and *First Stop in the New World: Mexico City the Capital of the 21st Century* (New York: Riverhead Books, 2008).
26 For an extensive discussion of the Santa Fe area, see María Moreno-Carranco, "Global Mexico under Construction," in Clara Irazabal, ed., *Transborder Latin Americanisms* (New York: Routledge, 2014), 187–214; and María Moreno Carranco, *Geografías en construcción: el megaproyecto de Santa Fe en la Ciudad de México* (Mexico City: Universidad Autónoma Metropolitana, 2015).

CHAPTER 16

(In)Visible Beijing Within and Without World Literature

Weijie Song

Beijing's Inner City, or the Forbidden City, stimulated Franz Kafka (1883–1924), a German-language writer, to compose "An Imperial Message" (1919, posthumous publication 1930; English, 1933),[1] imagining an Oriental, absurdist, and epistemological impasse where the message about the emperor's death can never be delivered from the heart of the "Great Within" to the outer circles of the royal order and imperial control.

Beijing's Outer City and the vast land beyond inspired Italo Calvino (1923–85), an Italian author and journalist, to write *Invisible Cities* (1972; English, 1974),[2] envisioning the conversation between Marco Polo, the Italian explorer, and Kublai Khan, the aging Mongolian ruler, about the imaginary mapping and (im)possibility of understanding the "tracery of a pattern" of the wondrous capital and the immeasurable empire.

Horizontally, Beijing's spectacular walls and gates fascinated Oswald Sirén (1879–1966), a Finnish-born Swedish art historian, to write in Paris in 1924 about his study of the city's topography:

> [T]he origin of this book is the beauty of the city gates of Peking; their importance as characteristic elements in some of the finest views of the Chinese capital; their wonderful setting amid old buildings, fresh trees, and decaying moats; their decorative architectural character. Some of these gates may still be called landmarks of Peking, historically as well as topographically they reflect, together with the adjoining walls, much of the early history of this great city, and they form, together with the streets and landscapes in which they are set, the most relevant spots of characteristic and beautiful scenery.[3]

Vertically, French writer and ethnographer Victor Segalen's (1878–1919) posthumous *René Leys* (1922; English, 1974, 1988)[4] imagines a secret city underneath the Forbidden City to express his spatial exoticism, describing the (in)tangible capital and the impediments of trans-cultural (dis)enchantment and border-crossing (mis)representation.

Since the 1900s, on and off the map of "the world republic of letters,"[5] literary Beijing, from the exotic configurations to the multivalent self-portraits in Chinese-language writing, has unfolded, historically and geopolitically, as an ancient capital of traditional China, a Republican city of new thought and everlasting memories, a fallen city under Japanese military control, a socialist capital of Maoist ideology and Cultural Revolution, and a rejuvenated city and cosmopolitan megacity in the post-Cold War era and the new millennium. The methods of imagining Beijing have developed along the multilayered trajectories of writers and their city-texts in terms of variegated genres, ideas and trends, moments and movements, places and spaces, emotional entanglements, materiality, and urban chronotopes. This chapter aims to situate Beijing writing in the enlarged and entangled contexts of Chinese-language literature and world literature in terms of evidenced influences, implicit connections, and paralleled representations.

Unlike treaty cities such as Shanghai, Tianjin, Hankou (Hankow), and Guangzhou (Canton), which are mainly the hubs of new knowledge and modern lifestyles, the significance of Beijing in the late Qing Dynasty lay in the symbiosis of the old and the new, the negotiation between the officials and the commoners, the coexistence of the ruling Manchu bannermen and the Han Chinese people, and the integration of traditional politics and modern civilization. Without losing its inherent political resources, this cultural space had a special symbolic significance during a series of confrontations and communications, such as the advantage and disadvantage, or substance and function, of Chinese and Western learning; the conflicts between the old and the new society; the hierarchical changes in upper and lower classes; the reshaping relationship between government and the common people; and the complications in Chinese and foreign contacts.

In August 1900, Beijing was violently conquered and looted by the Eight-Nation Alliance of Austria-Hungary, France, Germany, Italy, Japan, Russia, the United Kingdom, and the United States. The humiliating and traumatic incident and its aftermath triggered a widespread sense of shame, humiliation, and catastrophe, and left an open wound in the minds of Beijing's inhabitants and the larger Chinese populace. It also led to the collapse of the Manchu Empire and thereafter the haunting ghost of imperial consciousness, the rise of broad and narrow nationalisms, and the dissemination of superstitions in popular folklore in the imperial capital at the turn of the century.[6] On May 4, 1919, the Chinese New Cultural Movement (with the controversial name of Chinese Enlightenment or

Renaissance) took place in Beijing, posing the question: Why did the radical new cultural movement take place in Beijing, then an ancient capital, rather than in Shanghai, a modern metropolis and the city of Chinese modernity? On June 20, 1928, Beijing was renamed Beiping after the nationalist government (Kuomintang or KMT) moved its capital to Nanjing. The former capital was slowly losing its original distinction as a political center, whereas its cultural aura had gradually spread outward in various spaces and directions.

Among the tumultuous social-political milieu of the 1920s, in terms of urban colors, sounds, animals, humans, and moments of epiphany and disillusionment, contrasting images of Beijing can be seen between Tsurumi Yūsuke's (1885–1973) Japanese travelogue "Beijing Charms" (1922) – which was translated into Chinese ("*Beijing de meili*") by Lu Xun (1881–1936), the founding father of modern Chinese literature, in 1925 – and Lu Xun's own Beijing stories and essays published in the same year. Tsurumi, a politician, orator, author, playwright, and internationalist, provides a cosmopolitan and comparative portrayal of Beijing derived from his abundant travels in East Asia, Europe, and America. "Beijing Charms" captures the sharp distinctions between the gray hues of Beijing's everyday life and the splendid imperial grandeur. The sound of bells tied to donkeys indicate a pastoral lifestyle, and the cheerful journey from the suburb to the city reverberates with innocent children's giggles – and the not-so-distant rumbles of cannons from large-scale warlord combat. Tsurumi also foregrounds the majestic manners of city animals, in particular camels, to emphasize the lack of Japanese urban scenes and as an example of Platonic elitism. He reveals his identity as a Japanese traveler, situates himself as the object of curious gazes from innocent girls behind bamboo curtains, and describes the discoveries of his observations as a foreigner. At the end of "Beijing Charms," he discloses an exoticist and pseudo-loyalist obsession with Beijing,[7] a viewpoint shared by George Ernest Morrison (1862–1920) and other foreign fans of Beijing in the early twentieth century. For instances, William Somerset Maugham's (1874–1965) collection of essays *On a Chinese Screen* (1922) and Sir Reginald F. Johnston's (1874–1938) *Twilight in the Forbidden City* (1934) also betray a continued obsession with a mysterious, Orientalist, and eternal Beijing as an ancient capital, and project their own anxieties, doubts, and hopes from the declining Great Britain onto the screens and images of ancient Beijing.[8]

Lu Xun translates and criticizes Tsurumi's "colonial gaze" and pseudo-loyalist enchantment. His own Beijing writing depicts a bleak and desolate city with market noises and acoustic distress in "Brothers" (*Xiongdi*, 1925).

In "Regret for the Past" (*Shangshi*, 1925), he parallels the desperate human condition with a brutal world of animals and pets, where the chicks grow into hens and start to appear as meals on the table, and the pet dog is eventually abandoned and homeless. Lu Xun also reflects the apathetic collective gaze from and toward the crowds in silent China in "A Public Spectacle" (*Shizhong*, 1925). The recurrent images of "dark room" and "solitary lamp" serve as the entry point into Lu Xun's further understanding of "inner illumination" (*neiyao*), a term he coined in "Toward a Refutation of Malevolent Voices" in 1908.[9] If "inner illumination" could appear as part of material existence, then in the mid-1920s, it was incarnated as a solitary lamp in a dark room of a home. Lu Xun's Beijing narrative brings to light the narrator's epiphany from the gloomy chamber in the "forsaken corner of the hostel" and the allegorical form of resilient "inner radiance" – an illumination from the heart, be it dead fire or pale flame, which, in Lu Xun's tenacious struggle against the darkness of modern China, waits to be rekindled and reawakened, in Beijing and beyond.

Lu Xun's impressionist sketches present a gloomy and melancholic picture of modern Beijing's psychological reality, profoundly echoing the city image and story conceived by Zhang Henshui (pen name of Zhang Xinyuan, 1895–1967), arguably the most prolific and popular writer between the 1920s and the 1930s. Zhang turned many of his experiences in modern Beijing into fiction, serialized in literature supplements of newspapers and later published in book form. These bestsellers, including *Unofficial History of Beijing* (*Chunming waishi*, 1924–29), *Grand Old Family* (*Jinfen shijia*, 1926–32), and *Fate in Tears and Laughter* (*Tixiao yinyuan*, 1929–30), feature new protagonists in a mix of flâneur, dandy, modern journalist, classical poet, and modern-day "infatuated monk"-like hermit. Zhang Henshui's storytelling captures fleeting moments in Beijing's quotidian and transient everyday life – the enduring imagery of the city, its modern urbanism, and its feelings, emotions, and "stream of consciousness." From the end of the Manchu Qing Empire to the early Republican period, the indigenous literary topography of ancient and modern Beijing was evidenced and manifested in conventional chapter-linked[10] vernacular narrative genres including martial arts fantasy, court-case story, scholar-beauty romance, and novels of social manners and human emotions, among many others.

Fate in Tears and Laughter, Zhang's most popular work in Republican China, contains both traditional and modern viewpoints and showcases romantic love and desire, urban landscapes and spectacles, chivalrous intervention and assassination, and the profound darkness in a chaotic Beijing during the warlord period. A quadrilateral romance unfolds between the male protagonist (a young student and sojourner from the south) and three women: a drum singer from a humble family in the poor district of Heaven's Bridge in southern Beijing, an innocent and gullible girl who becomes the mistress of a brutal warlord; a modern girl from a wealthy distinguished family who endeavors to accommodate both traditional and modern manners; and a woman knight-errant who also comes from Heaven's Bridge. A skilled martial artist, she is a fervent reader of traditional martial arts novels. Reading enables her to hone her emotions by indulging in the chivalrous mentality that has begun to vanish from the modern city.

High on her reading list is the Qing Dynasty writer Yanbei Xianren's (pen name of Wen Kang) martial arts fiction, *A Tale of Lovers and Heroes* (*Ernü yingxiong zhuan*, 1878).[11] The author was a Manchu bannerman and erudite literatus. His consistent use of the colloquial Beijing dialect marked the beginning of a rise in popularity of the "Beijing-flavor" writing style. He idiosyncratically blends heroic minds and deeds, affectionate love and passion (the cult of *qing*), and orthodox Confucian virtues (loyalty, filial piety, chastity, and righteousness) in this tapestry of urban imaginations. The narrative mode comes to terms with legal, political, and urban (in)justice through a love-triangle story: a talented Confucian scholar wins the hearts of a virtuous fair lady and a female knight-errant. This romantic harmony also signifies the social and moral order in Beijing, the capital of the Manchu Empire.

Similarly, Zhang Henshui incorporates martial arts fantasy into his modern Beijing story. For him, this genre best conveys everyday practices and escapist daydreams in the urban milieu: having nowhere to ask for redress of injustices and no way to assuage their indignation, city readers turned to ambiguous and fabricated heroism for comfort and redemption. Zhang situates a transitional Beijing in the larger contexts of social and cultural transformation, elite and lower-class divisions, the fantastic and the everyday, amorous transgression and moral values, and the (un)taming of chivalrous women in the popular martial arts genre and widely circulated literary texts.

If Zhang Henshui's storytelling leans toward traditional narrative conventions and reflects on the everlasting human interests and emotions in the modern urban milieu, then Lao She (pen name of Shu Qingchun, 1899–1966) can be understood as a more "modern" writer who puts into practice a variety of new genres such as allegorical satire, science fiction, counter-martial arts story, modernist epic, new drama, and pseudo-biographical accounts from the 1930 to the 1960s. As a Manchu bannerman, Beijing native, and one of the most important writers in twentieth-century China, Lao She was an avid reader and creative admirer of Charles Dickens (1812–70) and Joseph Conrad (1857–1924). He presents images of a city tortured by the tension between the charming legacy of old Beijing and the intruding advent of modernization. His Beijing narratives are colored by a Dickensian comprehensive cognitive mapping of his beloved hometown,[12] and a Conradian imagination of darkness and horrors from the urban interiority.

In the year 1934, on the eve of the Second Sino-Japanese War, Lao She wrapped up an anti-martial arts story, "The Soul-Slaying Spear" (*Duanhun qiang*, 1935; English, 1985), with a famous and apocalyptic paragraph:

> The time had come for Asia to wake up from its dream. The sound of rifle firs overpowered the roaring of tigers in the jungles of the Malay Peninsula and India. Half awake, the peoples of Asia rubbed their sleepy eyes and offered prayers to their ancestors and gods; but before long, they lost all of their land, their freedom, and their rights. Men with different-colored faces stood outside their doors, the barrels of their guns still warm. Of what use were their long spears, powerful bows and poisonous arrows, and thick shields covered in gorgeous snakeskin? Their ancestors and the divinities worshipped by their ancestors were totally impotent. China, with its dragon banners, was no longer the great mystery it had been in the past. New China had railroads running through its graveyards, destroying all auspicious geomantic influences. The fringed maroon banner of the escort, the steel sword in a green sharkskin sheath, the horse hung with a string of bells, the accumulated wisdom and argot of the escort trade as well as the code of justice and pride of reputation – for Dragon Sha, all of these things, including his mastery of the martial arts and his career as a swordman – had vanished like a dream. This was the age of the iron horse, of automatic rifles, of treaty ports and of terrorism. There were even rumors about that people were out to chop off the emperor's head! [13]

Lao She delivers a sophisticated yet disappointing message to indicate the reluctant transformations in Beijing, China, and Asia. The story focuses on Dragon Sha, a self-denying yet stubborn martial arts master, who witnesses the great transformation yet refuses to be assimilated into the ongoing changes of the world. At the end of the story, Dragon Sha chooses to dishonorably ignore the challenge from his peer, remain an outsider and stranger to this new time, and abandon the duty of passing the martial arts to the young generation:

> Leaning on his spear in the middle of the courtyard, he gazed up at the stars and thought back on the good old days, when he enjoyed a fine reputation in the country inns and all through the wilderness. Sighing, he rubbed his

> hands over the cool, smooth handle of his spear and smiled. "No, I won't teach this to anyone. I won't teach this to anyone."[14]

The knight-errant-turned-hermit confronts social-cultural adversity and upholds his persistent resistance to the unending urban and national chaos. By radically challenging the literary conventions of martial arts narratives, Lao She performs a "soul-slaying" and melancholic mourning for bygone chivalrous temperaments and bids farewell to the disappearing old Beijing culture threatened by the advent of industrial civilization and modernization at large.

Another salient and controversial example is Lao She's novel *Cat Country* (*Maocheng ji*, 1933; English 1970, 2013),[15] which mixes multiple genres, such as dystopian fiction, political allegory, and science fiction. In so doing, the author displays his speculative, apocalyptic, and cynical view of the city and the nation. As Ian Johnson states, "Lao She himself had an ambivalent feeling about *Cat Country*, seeing it as a detour away from his roots as a humorist who came out of Beijing's storytelling tradition."[16] More importantly, Lao She also addresses the dilemma and predicament of individualism, labor, family, and the city evidenced in his major novel *Rickshaw Boy* (*Luotuo Xiangzi*, 1937; different English translations in 1945, 1949, 1981, and 2010),[17] which portrays the fate of rickshaw puller Xiangzi, an orphan of Beijing and a pauper protagonist, and maps the trajectories of a symbolically homeless individual who encounters a desperate process of dream-making and dream-waking irony. Lao She's literary topography of Xiangzi presents a naturalist, modernist, and realist saga of a pauper orphan's frustration and failure in the hostile urban milieu.

Through the oeuvres of Zhang Henshui and Lao She, Beijing narratives develop along two major routes: traditional chapter-linked narratives on the one hand, and modern-form novels, novellas, and short stories on the other. Another emerging and important new genre is "drama" (*xiju*), which serves as an umbrella term to comprehend both spoken drama (*huaju*), a Western-style theater introduced to China at the turn of the twentieth century, and modern rendition of traditional Chinese opera (*xiqu*), such as Peking opera, Kun opera, and other local operas. It also encompasses theatrical adaptation of fiction and other literary genres. In this vein, Cao Yu (1910–96), a distinguished dramatist, is hailed as China's Shakespeare, and contributes to modern Beijing literature one of his most celebrated plays *Peking Man* (*Beijing ren*, 1940; English, 1986).[18] Cao was deeply influenced by Eugene O'Neill (1888–1953) and Henrik Ibsen (1828–1906).[19] In *Peking Man*, he comes to term with the destruction of the traditional gentry family and the rise of the new capitalist class in the semicolonial, semi-feudalist

Beijing. The cannibalistic, patriarchal traditional family has been the main site onto which various literary imagined realities of Chinese modernization have been projected.

During the Second Sino-Japanese War and the Chinese civil war, Lao She finished his pivotal trilogy, *Bewilderment* (*Huanghuo*), *Ignominy* (*Tousheng*), and *Famine* (*Jihuang*), which were published together as his wartime epic entitled *Four Generations under One Roof* (*Sishi tongtang*, 1944–50). The *magnum opus* charts the spatial trajectories of wartime emotions, such as nostalgia, mourning, shame, anger, and hatred, and thus creates an affective mapping of military violence, family degeneration, urban misery, and national suffering in a warped and wounded city under Japanese occupation. In Lao She's Second World War atlas of emotions, one can decipher the entanglements of family and city, self and society, individual and nation-state, and urban history and traumatic memory. Alongside the Little Sheepfold Lane, a typical Beijing courtyard house linked to an alleyway, and other real and fictional places and spaces ranging from a small clandestine room in a family house to the gigantic Tiananmen Square in the heart of the city, readers are presented with the vicissitude of urban emotions and cultural memories shaped by war and violence. The novel navigates the emotional tension between private obsession and public passion, personal desire and collective guilt, and quasi-loyalist affection and nationalist sentiment. Therefore, it invokes a performative psychogeography of pain and catharsis, trauma and redemption, nostalgia and longing, loss and epiphany, and melancholy and hope.

On January 31, 1949, Beijing entered the socialist period under a communist regime. From the Maoist period (1949–66) to the Cultural Revolution (1966–76), Beijing writings were sporadic and marginalized, and the literary connection with the Soviet Union can be found in Wang Meng's (1934–) *Long Live Youth* (*Qingchun wansui*, 1956) and Yang Mo's (1914–95) *Song of Youth* (*Qingchun zhige*, 1958). An exceptional example is Lao She's three-act play *Teahouse* (*Chaguan*, 1957; English, 1980, 2010),[20] which embodies the decline of the Manchu Empire, the failure of the warlord regime, and the downfall of the nationalist government, recapitulating and condensing fifty years of history and politics into a pessimistic miniature of old Beijing. The teahouse functions as a physical and psychological place and space, and a warped space–time continuum that presents the interactions between material deformations and emotional vicissitudes (nostalgic sympathy, a sense of loss, as well as melancholia and self-mourning before death arrives). His *Beneath the Red Banner* (*Zhenghongqi xia*, 1980; English, 1982),[21] an epic, encyclopedic yet incomplete autobiographical, testimonial, and ethnographic work, as well as a tribute to Cao Xueqin's (ca. 1715–63) great novel of manners *The Story of the Stone* (ca. 1760), was written in the early 1960s and published years after he committed suicide in 1966, on the eve of the Cultural Revolution.

Mao passed away in 1976 and China stepped into the Reform Era after 1978. Literary Beijing rejuvenated itself in the 1980s, proliferated in the 1990s, and has flourished in the twenty-first century. Liu Xinwu (1942–), a leading voice of contemporary Beijing literature, has become one of its most representative figures. Liu confesses that he is indebted to Thomas Hardy (1840–1928), Romain Rolland (1866–1944), Hans Christian Andersen (1805–75), Anton Chekhov (1860–1904), and Ernest Hemingway (1899–1961). His *The Bell and Drum Towers* (*Zhonggulou*, 1985; English, 1993, 2021) exhibits a transformative time–space continuum:

> Keep in mind that at the northernmost of central Beijing stand the ancient Bell and Drum Towers. The Drum Tower in front, red walls and gray tiles. The Bell Tower behind, gray walls and green tiles. The Drum Tower is squat, the Bell Tower slender [....] The Bell and Drum Towers have been silent for fifty-eight years. It's 5:00 p.m. on December 12, 1982, and they continue to stand mightily there, as if they might strike at any moment. [...] In the rush of time passing, how many people have felt or will feel this sacred sense of history, this solemn sense of fate? [...] The two towers stand tall, eternally awaiting the next moment, the next day, the next month, the next year, the next generation.[22]

Liu's Mao Dun literary award-winning novel sets this one single day in 1982, focuses on a compound (*siheyuan*) occupied by multiple households with different pasts and backgrounds, and reveals Beijing urbanites' pain, trauma, sorrows, joys, dream, and hope in their individual and collective memories in turbulent modern times. This saga colorfully depicts how many Beijing inhabitants suffered and survived the catastrophic Cultural Revolution and eventually obtained their urban identity and historical consciousness, as multigenerational citizens position themselves in a long span of stormy histories, and around the Bell and Drum Towers, the obsolete time-telling center that lost its original function in 1924, the year the last emperor of the Qing Dynasty was forced to leave the Forbidden City.

Wang Shuo (1958–), a contemporary successor of Lao She, a fan of Raymond Carver (1938–88) and a secret admirer of Jorge Luis Borges (1899–1986), tells his Beijing stories in a cynical and bold manner pervaded with dark humor. His major work includes *The Troubleshooters* (*Wanzhu*, 1987), *Playing for Thrills* (*Wande jiushi xintiao*, 1989; English, 1998), *No Regrets about Youth* (*Qingchun wuhui*, 1991), and *Wild Beasts* (*Dongwu xiongmeng*, 1991).[23] Wang's poignant Beijing narratives focus on rebellious youth culture and resistance against authority as well as perplexing configurations of individuality, collectivity, sexual imagination, and political fantasy. His urban adventures unfold in different locations, ranging from the military compound to the mean streets, from leisure parks to political monuments. Wang's Beijing style is characterized by a flaunting use and abuse of Maoist propagandist terms, ideological cliché, and revolutionary emotions.

Lao She's works written from the 1930s to the 1960s constitute an encyclopedia of literary Beijing and create a tradition of modern Beijing taste, with Beijing-flavor narratives colored by the local dialects, customs, and details of everyday urban life. Representative Beijing writers in the Reform Era after 1978, such as Deng Youmei (1931–), Wang Zengqi (1920–97), Chen Jiangong (1949–), Su Shuyang (1938–2019), Han Shaohua (1933–2010), Liu Suola (1955–), Xu Xing (1956–), Shi Tiesheng (1951–2010), Liu Heng (1954–), and Ye Guangcen (1948–), continued the legacy of Lao She's Beijing writing, adopting Beijing dialect to showcase the regional characteristics and charms of the old city and document its changes, evidenced in different types of place and space from shabby alleyways to grand avenues, from the ethnic Manchu bannerman's lifestyle to the old Beijing culture at large.

At the end of the twentieth century, Zhang Beihai (1936–2022), a unique diasporic writer living in New York's Chinese community, attempted to rejuvenate the chivalrous imagination once evidenced in Zhang Henshui's literary mapping of the Heaven Bridge district and the city as a whole, and in Lao She's soul-slaying sentiment about the bygone Beijing culture and spirit. His novel *The Last Swallow of Autumn* (*Xia yin*, 2000; a literal translation of the original Chinese title is *Reclusive Knight-Errant*)[24] invokes and revives the soul of old Beijing and the city's charm by rewriting, if not revolutionizing, the martial arts genre, reorienting the chivalrous interventions and romantic deeds in various urban places and spaces on the eve of the Second Sino-Japanese War in the 1930s. Like Zhang Henshui and Lao She, Zhang Beihai navigates a chivalrous Beijing through a distinctive literary mapping of imbricated human emotions and their geographical locales, imaginary or real; in so doing, he showcases his understanding of urban transformation, personal/historical violence, and social (in)justice amid political, martial, and cultural crisis. Through illuminating storytelling strategies and idiosyncratic obsession with everyday practices, Zhang Beihai's literary text, together with its theatrical reworking and cinematic adaptation (for instance, Jiang Wen's creative and controversial film *Hidden Man* in 2018, based on Zhang's novel), creates and charts a nuanced and quotidian Republican Beijing colored by martial arts trajectories, the protagonists' predicament, and the larger process of coming to terms with the ongoing challenges and changes in the macro- and micro-urban environments.

Since the beginning of the twenty-first century, and especially after the 2008 Olympic Games, contemporary Beijing writing has paid more attention to the city's consumer society, market economy, political control, unequal development, large-scale immigration, and uneven globalization. Yingjin Zhang has argued that "previously prevailing imaginaries of Beijing as a traditional walled city and a sacrosanct site of China's imperial power and socialist enterprises have been transmuted by the forces of globalization and transfigured into new imaginaries of Beijing as a global city wrought with ambivalences and contradictions."[25] Liu Zhenyun (1958–) contributes neorealist representations tackling rapid urbanization and its discontents. Feng Tang (1971–), who has lived abroad for many years, relies on the genre of bildungsroman to construct and confirm an imaginary return to his hometown, Beijing. Shi Yifeng (1979–) has been deeply involved in the urban environment, juxtaposing the city's transformation and simultaneous attachment to ongoing change. Wen Zhen (1982–)'s 2014 Beijing love stories, including "We Date at Night in the Art Gallery" (*Women yeli zai meishuguan tan lianai*) and "A Love Affair on Anxiang Road" (*Anxiang lu qingshi*), focus on the othering of female characters such as marginal figures, migrants in the lower society, and young women from outer provinces: names of places, sites, and landmarks, serve as a literary index to understand the transitional capital. Qiu Huadong's (1969–), a spokesman of Beijing's rapid urbanization, adores John Updike (1932–2009), John Cheever (1912–82), Margaret Atwood (1939–), and Alice Munro (1931–). His up-to-date urban records and romances of new citizens, and his ongoing passion for the city's past and present, culminate in a work partially inspired by Peter Ackroyd's *London, The Biography* (2001). Qiu's nonfictional *Beijing, The Biography* (*Beijing zhuan*, 2020) spans three thousand years of Beijing's history, moving from the Liuli River to the final destination of China Zun (CITIC Tower), the tallest and flagship skyscraper and an icon of the capital located in the heart of Beijing's new 30-hectare central business district.

Environmental humanities, eco-criticism, and nature writing include environmental philosophy, ecosophy, and environmental ethics in the 1970s; environmental history in the 1980s; and environmental literature, cultural studies, anthropology, geography, and political ecology since the 1980s. The three waves of environmental humanities shift the focus and scope of investigations from the "natural" and "non-human world" to urban life and environmental justice, and to transnational and multiethnic ecological crisis and sustainable futures. Urban ecological injustice is a major theme in the second wave of environmental humanities, and also the topic of a unique collection of essays, *Garden No. 711: The Ultimate Last Memo of Beijing* (*711 hao yuan: Beijing zuihou de zuihou jinian*, 2011), by Yan Lianke (1958–), winner of Franz Kafka and Newman prizes, who coined the term "mythorealism" to describe the Kafkaesque and Márquezan mix of reality and absurdity in contemporary China. For him, mythorealism

> abandons the seemingly logical relations of real life, and explores a "nonexistent" truth, an invisible truth, and a truth concealed by truth. Mythorealism keeps a distance from any prevailing realism. The mythorealist connection with reality does not lie in straightforward cause-and-effect links, but rather relies on human souls, minds [...] and the authors' extraordinary fabrications based on reality [....] Imaginations, metaphors, myths, legends, dreams, fantasy, demonization, and transplantation born from everyday life and social reality can all serve as mythorealist methods and channels.[26]

Yan's *Garden No. 711*, a tribute to Henry David Thoreau's (1817–62) *Walden; or, Life in the Woods* (1854), depicts the creation and destruction of an ecotopia in the suburban era of Beijing and the impossibility of poetic dwelling in the post-Maoist capital marred by crazy and greedy developers and their damaging impacts.[27]

Chan Koonchung (1952–), an interpreter of George Orwell's (1903–50) dystopia and Michel Foucault's (1926–84) heterotopia, distributes outside mainland China his banned yet brave works *The Fat Years* (*Shengshi*, 2009; English, 2011) and *Zero Point Beijing* (*Beijing ling gongli*, 2018).[28] Both works expose the political censorship, dystopian reality, governmental control, and cultural amnesia in the postmodern totalitarian state, and the author's unfailing search for the historical truth.

Praised as the most accomplished of the post-1970 writers, Xu Zechen (1978–), a passionate reader and subtle follower of Italo Calvino, Gabriel García Márquez (1927–2014), William Faulkner (1897–1962), and Orhan Pamuk (1952–), published *Running Through Beijing* (*Paobu chuanguo zhongguangcun*, 2006; English, 2014), *Jerusalem* (*Yelu saleng*, 2014), and *The Deep Imperial City* (*Wangcheng ruhai*, 2017), illustrating the underground world of underprivileged strangers, wanderers, migrants, and their inevitable misfortunes and strategies of urban struggle and survival.[29] Xu's *Northward* (*Beishang*, 2018), a contemporary literary reference to the classic

Marco Polo story, covers a hundred years of adventure along the Beijing-Hangzhou Grand Canal, ending in Beijing, and highlighting the protagonists' pilgrimage to the city and voyage of self-discovery in Beijing, China, and the wider world.

Literary imaginings of Beijing can be found in works of diverse genres (conventional chapter-linked vernacular novel, avant-garde prose and play, mainstream propaganda, news reportage, crime story, martial arts narrative, science fiction, diasporic writing, utopian and dystopian imagination, etc.) against the larger backdrop of modern literary trends, societies, schools, and movements (naturalism, realism, modernism, expressionism, socialist, postmodernism, neorealism, diasporic writing, and popular culture).[30] Literary urban narratives in Chinese-language representation are intricately intertwined, in both visible and invisible ways, with the traces and (dis)connections in world literature, and tease out the encoding and decoding of Beijing as a real, imagined, mythical, metaphorical, and semiotic city surviving barbarianism, exoticism, Orientalism, (mis)understanding, (over)interpretation, and (un)translatability.

Notes

1 See Franz Kafka, "An Imperial Message," Ian Johnson's translation at www.kafka-online.info/an-imperial-message.html.

2 Italo Calvino, *Invisible Cities*, trans. William Weaver (New York: Harcourt, 1974).

3 Osvald Sirén, *The Walls and Gates of Peking* (London: John Lane the Bodley Head Limited, 1924), vii. See also David Strand's exemplary research, *Rickshaw Beijing: City People and Politics in the 1920s* (Oakland, CA: University of California Press, 1989).

4 Victor Segalen, *René Leys: A Novel*, trans. J.A. Underwood (New York: Overlook Press, 1988).

5 See Pascale Casanova, *The World Republic of Letters*, trans. M.B. DeBevoise (Cambridge, MA: Harvard University Press, 2004).

6 For the two lootings of Beijing at the end of the Manchu Qing dynasty, see James Hevia's post-colonial decoding, "Looting Beijing: 1860, 1900," in Lydia Liu, ed., *Tokens of Exchange* (Durham, NC: Duke University Press, 2000), 192–213.

7 Tsurumi Yūsuke, "Beijing Charms," in *Thoughts, Landscapes, Figures (Sixiang, shanshui, renwu)*, trans. Lu Xun from Japanese into Chinese (Shanghai: Beixin shuju, 1929), 245–265.

8 See Chunmei Du, "Travel Along the Mobius Strip: Somerset Maugham and Gu Hongming East of Suez," *The International History Review* 36, no. 1 (2014): 1–18.

9 The term has also been translated as "inner brilliance" (Cheung Chiu-yee), "inner brightness/light" (Jon von Kowallis), "hidden glow" and "powers and secrets" (Pu Wang), and "inner life" or "an enlightened inner life" (Ban Wang). For English translations of Lu Xun's works, see *Selected Works of Lu Xun*, trans. Gladys Yang and Yang Xianyi (Beijing: Foreign Languages Press, 1980).

10 Chapter-linked (*Zhanghui*) style is a traditional Chinese literary genre and pattern for long novels from the Ming Dynasty onwards, with each chapter headed by a summary couplet.

11 See David Der-wei Wang, *Fin-de-siècle Splendor: Repressed Modernities of Late Qing Fiction, 1849–1911* (Stanford, CA: Stanford University Press, 1997), chapter 4, and Elena Suet-Ying Chiu, *Bannermen Tales (Zidishu): Manchu Storytelling and Cultural Hybridity in the Qing Dynasty* (Cambridge, MA: Harvard University Asia Center, 2018).

12 For the Dickensian vision and manifestation of Beijing, see Lao She's oxymoronic description, "Filthy, beautiful, decrepit, lively, chaotic, peaceful, and charming, that was the magnificent early summer city of Beiping," in *Rickshaw Boy*, trans. Howard Goldblatt (New York: Harper Perennial Modern Chinese Classics, 2010), 290.

13 Lao She, "The Soul-Slaying Spear," in *Crescent Moon and Other Stories*, trans. Sidney Shapiro (Beijing: Chinese Literature Press, 1985), 149–150.

14 Ibid., 164.

15 Lao She, *Cat Country: A Satirical Novel of China in the 1930s*, trans. William Lyell (Columbus, OH: Ohio State University Press, 1970; rpt. Penguin Modern Classics, 2013). For a recent study, see Lena Rydholm, "Cosmopolitan and Vernacular Dynamics in Modern Chinese Fiction and Lao She's satirical novel *Cat Country*," in Christina Kullberg and David Watson, eds., *Vernaculars in an Age of World Literatures* (New York: Bloomsbury Academic, 2022), 153–180. Lao She once confessed that he was influenced by Jonathan Swift's *Gulliver's Travels* and Aldous Huxley's *Brave New World*. The literal translation of this novel title should be *Records of Cat City*. The word "records" (*ji*) indicates Lao She's ambition of writing a history for an allegorical dystopia of the city and its soul, and the nation-state/China, reminding readers of the great historian Sima Qian, the father of Chinese historiography, and his classic *Records of the Grand Historian*. For a recent historical, journalistic, and architectural effort of writing records for Beijing, see Wang Jun, *Beijing Record: A Physical and Political History of Planning Modern Beijing* (Singapore: World Scientific Publishing Company, 2011).

16 Ian Johnson, "China: When the Cats Rule," *The New York Review of Books* (August 26, 2013), www.nybooks.com/daily/2013/08/26/china-when-cats-rule/.

17 See Lau Shaw, *Rickshaw Boy*, trans. Evan King (New York: Reynal & Hitchcock, Inc., 1945); Lao She, *Rickshaw: The Novel of Lo-t'o Hsiang Tzu*, trans. Jean M. James (Honolulu, HI: The University Press of Hawaii, 1979); Lao She, *Camel Xiangzi*, trans. Shi Xiaoqing (published in association with Beijing: Foreign Languages Press and Bloomington, IN: Indiana University Press, 1981); and Lao She, *Rickshaw Boy*, trans. Howard Goldblatt.

18 Cao Yu, *Peking Man*, trans. Leslie Nai-kwai Lo et al. (New York: Columbia University Press, 1986).

19 See Joseph Siu-ming Lau's pioneering study, *Ts'ao Yu, The Reluctant Disciple of Chekhov and O'Neil: A Study in Literary Influence* (Hong Kong: Hong Kong University Press, 1970); Edward Gunn, "Cao Yu's Peking Man and Literary Evocations of the Family in Republican China," *Republican China* 16, no. 1 (1990): 73–88.

20 Lao She, *Teahouse: A Play in Three Acts*, trans. John Howard-Gibbon (Beijing: Foreign Languages Press, 1980; rpt. New York: Columbia University Press, 2004), and "Teahouse," trans. Ying Ruocheng, rev. Claire Conceison, in Xiaomei Chen, ed., *The Columbia Anthology of Modern Chinese Drama* (New York: Columbia University Press, 2010), 547–597.

21 Lao She, *Beneath the Red Banner*, trans. Don J. Cohn (Beijing: Panda, 1982).

22 Liu Xinwu, *The Wedding Party*, trans. Jeremy Tiang (Seattle, WA: Amazon Crossing, 2021), 7, 341, 343, 378. An earlier excerpt translation appears as "The Bell and the Drum Tower," in Jianing Chen, ed., *Themes in Contemporary Chinese Literature* (Beijing: New World Press, 1993), 93–204.

23 Wang Shuo, *Playing for Thrills*, trans. Howard Goldblatt (New York: William Morrow, 1998). For a recent study, see Yiran Zheng, *Writing Beijing: Urban Spaces and Cultural Imaginations in Contemporary Chinese Literature and Films* (Lanham, MD: Rowman & Littlefield, 2016).

24 See Michael Berry, "A Tale of Two Cities: Romance, Revenge, and Nostalgia in Two Fin-de-siècle Novels by Ye Zhaoyan and Zhang Beihai," in Carlos Rojas and Eileen Chow, eds., *Rethinking Chinese Popular Culture* (London: Routledge, 2008), 127–143.

25 Yingjin Zhang, "Remapping Beijing: Polylocality, Globalization, Cinema," in Andreas Huyssen, ed., *Other Cities, Other Worlds* (Durham, NC: Duke University Press, 2008), 221. See also Zhang's *The City in Modern Chinese Literature and Film: Configurations of Space, Time, and Gender* (Stanford, CA: Stanford University Press, 1996); Yomi Braester, *Paint the City Red: Chinese Cinema and the Urban Contract* (Durham, NC: Duke University Press, 2010); Robin Visser, *Cities Surround the Countryside* (Durham, NC: Duke University Press, 2010), and Weijie Song, *Mapping Modern Beijing: Space, Emotion, Literary Topography* (New York: Oxford University Press, 2018).

26 Yan Lianke, *Faxian xiaoshuo* (Tianjin: Nankai daxue chubanshe, 2011), 181–82. See Weijie Song's English translation and critical discussion, "Yan Lianke's Mythorealist Representation of the Country and the City," *Modern Fiction Studies* 62, no. 4 (2016): 644–658.

27 Authors of ecocritical reports and non-fiction writing about the environmental challenges and crisis include Sha Qing and Ye Guangcen. For recent studies of ecocriticism and environmental humanities, see Rob Nixon, *Slow Violence and the Environmentalism of the Poor* (Cambridge, MA: Harvard University Press, 2011); Karen L. Thornber, *Ecoambiguity: Environmental Crises and East Asian Literatures* (Ann Arbor, MI: University of Michigan Press, 2012); Ursula K. Heise, Jon Christensen, and Michelle Niemann, eds., *The Routledge*

Companion to the Environmental Humanities (London: Routledge, 2017); Chia-ju Chang, ed., *Chinese Environmental Humanities: Practices of the Margins* (London: Palgrave, 2019); Sheldon H. Lu and Haomin Gong, eds., *Ecology and Chinese-Language Cinema: Reimagining a Field* (London: Routledge, 2019).

28 See Chan Koonchung, *The Fat Years*, trans. Michael Duke (New York: Doubleday, 2011). For a science fiction imagining of contemporary Beijing, see Hao Jingfan, "Folding Beijing" ("Beijing zhedie," 2012), trans. Ken Liu, *Uncanny Magazine* no. 2 (2015), rpt. in Ken Liu, *Invisible Planets: An Anthology of Contemporary Chinese SF in Translation* (New York: Tor Books, 2016), 219–261.

29 See Xu Zechen, *Running through Beijing*, trans. Eric Abrahamsen (San Francisco, CA: Two Lines Press, 2014).

30 Scholar Chen Pingyuan proposes five critical approaches to literary Beijing through: local documents, travel guidance, memory culture, literary imagination, and critical methods; Chen Pingyuan, *Beijing Memories* (*Beijing jiyi yu jiyi Beijing*) (Beijing: Sanlian shudian, 2008).

CHAPTER 17

Worlding Lagos in the Long Twentieth Century

Madhu Krishnan

In a 1960 essay published in the periodical *West Africa*, the Nigerian novelist and chronicler of city life Cyprian Ekwensi describes Lagos at the mid-century:

> The noise in the shimmering sun. The bustle. The mixed stenches in the slum drains that open to the sky. These things become—after a few weeks of living in Lagos—as acceptable as bouquets to the bride. It is all part of an atmosphere that, at first encounter, hits the eyes with the consciousness of a trained left. The heat in no way brings comfort to the harassed senses of sight and smell. Sweat drips off the face and water condenses on beer bottles in the hotels where the thirsty gather and lounge away the hours. All this in an atmosphere of *Bonsue* (a new "kill-me dance"), *Ropopo* (another name for the same thing) and all the surrealist attempts to squeeze the last ounces of enjoyment from the cooler hours of the evening when the bicycle bells have slackened their jangling and the loco-man's siren is only a faint threat for tomorrow's ten-past-six.[1]

Constituted under the phantasmagoric effects of a "shimmering" sun, full of hustle and bustle, rife with stenches and filth which are transformed into the alluring spectacle of a bride's bouquet, the city is less a place in which life happens and more the spatial medium through which existence is mediated. Recalling Henri Lefebvre's conception of the trialectics of space as constituted by the interplay of spatial practices, representations of space, and representational space, Lagos functions as a space lived, perceived, and conceived all at once. The city is both a space of expropriation and a site where spatial strategies, "the calculus of force-relations" through which power attempts to administer social production,[2] meet their match in the tactical energy of its inhabitants:

> The roads are crowded to effusion with petty traders and it is quite impossible for Town Planning Committees to restrict any areas to the residential. The Town Planning Committees came in far too late with their modernisation and therefore have been able to capture only the virgin areas like

> Apapa and Itire and parts of Okoyi where the new Housing Estates—at first derided by evicted slum-dwellers—are now sold out before the faintest tracing has appeared on the architect's board. Ikoyi has long been the white man's resurrection but now the robe and the turban, the slipper and the head-tie have invaded it and the long lines of washing waving colourfully are sure signs of what has transpired since the beginnings of national consciousness.[3]

Through its environments, both built and natural, its inhabitants develop new routines, learning the rhythms and temporalities of a space both unforgiving and indiscriminate in its embrace of its people. Space becomes the medium through which "the weak [...] turn to their own ends forces alien to them."[4] Town Planning Committees, with their zeal for imposing some kind of order on the city sprawl, find themselves thwarted, belated in their efforts and relegated to margins which eventually become new centers. The city is a carnivalesque site where improvisation and agility intertwine with the strictures of its spatial parameters.

Confounding attempts at cartographical categorization, neither region nor town, once political capital and still economic center, as much a part of the Nigeria as it is exceptional, Lagos embodies the conception of the world as "an ethos, a habitus and an inhabiting," less an enclosure than a utopian projection whose own sense of being and meaning "does not occur as a reference to something external to the world."[5] Lagos, in this manner, has long functioned in global literary imagination as a "significant geography."[6] Dunton, for instance, notes that "by the early years of the twenty-first century, [Lagos had] become established as one of the world's preeminent fictionalized cities, as with London and Paris more than a hundred years before" through what has elsewhere been termed "its power over the imagination and its capacity to engender a broad range of affected responses."[7] A megacity among megacities, whose actual geographical size and contours remain unknowable, Lagos stands as a synecdoche for modernity itself, being all things to all people, impossible to pin down, always on the move, always changing, alluring and terrifying in equal measure. The irresistible pull of the city is captured in the epigraph to the 1964 African Writers Series edition of Cyprian Ekwensi's *People of the City*: "the city attracts all types and how the unwary must suffer from ignorance."[8] Open to all, yet governed by unwritten codes and practices only readable to those attuned to its particular rhythms, Lagos is as much an idea or symbol as it is an actual place. Often associated with images of poverty and social degradation, on the one hand, or the opulence of a hyperactive late capitalism, on the other, Lagos is also a city of dualities, a place where incongruent modes of social production appear in simultaneity, entangling spatial scales even as the divisions between them accelerate.

The "Problem" of Lagos: A Brief History

In a 1955 letter to the Colonial Office recounting a meeting with Sir Musendiku Buraimoh Adeniji Adele II (then the Oba of Lagos), J.W. Robinson articulates the so-called "problem" of Lagos at the mid-century:

> Lagos, which used to think and legislate for Nigeria, has now no influence either in the Regions or in the Federal Council of Ministers. In fact no Lagos member of the House of Representatives can, under the Constitution, be a member of the Council. In the Regions, as a result of regionalising the Public Services, Lagosians are to have less and less chance of finding employment. [...] Ottawa though capital of Canada is just a town in one of the Canadian states, and there is no reason why Lagos should not be the same.[9]

Lagos, as Robinson's comments make clear, has always been an exceptional site in the Nigerian – and, indeed, world – imaginary. While there has been evidence of human settlement in the area now known as Lagos (or Èkó to its indigenous populations) long before the first colonial invasion, the city as it appears today began to take its contours with the arrival of the Portuguese in the fifteenth century. In the centuries that followed, Lagos became an important trading port, first in commodities and later in the trafficking of enslaved people. The city's development accelerated rapidly with the arrival of the British during the second wave of colonialism-imperialism in the eighteenth century. In 1914, with the amalgamation of the Northern and Southern Protectorates, the Colony of Lagos was named capital of the Colony and Protectorate of Nigeria, having previously acted as a protectorate in its own right over much of southwestern Nigeria. Over the subsequent years, the status of Lagos shifted on several occasions. In 1950, for instance, a town council was established as the primary administrative unit of the city, led by an elected mayor. With the 1951 Constitution, Lagos was merged for a time with the Western Region (then one of the Nigeria's three major regions: Northern, Eastern, and Western). Following complaints of neglect and protest, in the main from Lagos's large non-Yoruba populations, Lagos was reverted to local government status in 1959, and, by 1963, had attained official city status for the first time. Since 1967, Lagos has functioned as a recognized and official sub-state of the Nigerian federal structure.

None of these shifts were without controversy and, indeed, Lagos has always been a contested site in the Nigerian geopolitical landscape. A 1955 letter from the Colonial Office justifies the continued absence of representation for the capital in the National Assembly, noting that "if Lagos, or Lagos and the Colony districts were to be separately represented it would upset the North/South balance [through which the National Assembly operated]."[10] Another letter, dated late 1956, warns that "if the United Kingdom were to press for [extending the boundaries of Lagos territory], we should run the risk of opening wide the door to other boundary changes [...] and thence [...] to 'fragmentation'."[11] The very conceptual demographics of the city remained a point of tension, with various parties noting the delicate balance that maintained Lagos's ability to act as a home to populations from all ethnic groupings and across the nation. In possession of what had been characterized in the middle of the twentieth century as "the best harbour on the West coast of Africa,"[12] Lagos, from the start, has been defined through its entanglements with multiple spatial scales, critical to the region, the empire and, indeed, the world. A key site for understanding the dynamics of extraversion,[13] territorialization and deterritorialization,[14] Lagos has for centuries been irreversibly implicated in the constitution of the modern world system. Yet, Lagos's extraverted orientation belies the complexity of its spatial entanglements and particularly the simultaneity of scalar entanglements at the level of nation, region, and continent, including its role as host to a range of important pan-African and internationalist movements and a built environment constituted as a specifically Nigerian space through the construction of monumental sites.

Literary Lagos in the Mid-Century

Akin Adesokan notes the ways in which extant discourse around Lagos has bifurcated around two seemingly opposed paradigms: that of an urban apocalypse, degradation and squalor, and that of resilience, creativity, and innovation.[15] This sense of the city as both and neither, everything and nothing, repeatedly emerges in its literary representations. Early in the pages of Teju Cole's *Every Day is for the Thief* (2007), the narrator muses over the contradictory impulses of the city while on a bus journey from the mainland to islands: "The bus crosses from Yaba over the Third Mainland Bridge into Lagos Island. In the shadow of skyscrapers, half-nude men in dugouts cast nets into the lagoons. The work of arms and shoulders. I think of Auden's line: *Poetry makes nothing happen.*"[16] Lagos is a place of all things. It's a site of poetry, but a poetry that effects nothing. It is a place both bewildering and familiar, pastoral and ultra-modern, as much the space of fisherman and manual labor as it is of engineering marvels and hyperactive development. Defined by the rhythms of its inhabitants but also unable to fully contain them, the Lagos of the literary imagination over the last hundred years speaks to a range of anxieties, contradictions, and moments of creativity and spontaneity which themselves attest to the larger anxieties and tensions of the world literary field and its constitution more broadly.

In early examples of Onitsha Market pamphlets, the city is portrayed as a place of corruption through Westernization. A pamphlet titled *Life Turns Man Up and Down: Money and Girls Turn Man Up and Down* features early in its pages a black and white block print captioned "A picture of a Lagos Boy greeting his bar Lady friend." The couple in the photo are notable for their Western clothing, the man smoking a cigarette and his companion in high heels and a minidress. Described further as "A Highlife man and his Lover," the text warns us:

> This man is a womanizer and a smoker. He can finish ten packets of C.G. a day and can not pass a night without any lady. He does not care for anybody. He doesn't know his home town again. He does not care for his parents. What he knows is to take his C. G. and to chase girls all about. Just look at his waist.
>
> He hasn't known that C.G. is dangerous to human beings and girls are poisonous to boys. He will one day suffer them.[17]

Onitsha Market literature arose in a context of increasing literacy rates and urban migration in West Africa in the wake of the Second World War. Influenced by an influx of returning servicemen flocking to the city and the moralistic aesthetics of Indian and Victorian chapbooks, market literature, as Newell has shown, "depict[s] the non-elite man's experience of Nigeria at a time of immense social and economic change."[18] In the example noted above, it is significant that the corrupted "Lagos boy," unaware of the suffering to come, is characterized by his estrangement from the allegedly grounding influence of his home town and family, what is purported, in contrast to the city, to be authentically Nigerian and African. Instead, he focuses his cares on his material desires, the decadent – but fleeting and ultimately fatal – pleasures of the body. The pamphlet both sets up a spatial duality between the "traditional" and "pure" space of the village home and the corrupting and corrosive materialism of the city, and emphasizes the ways in which space functions not as an inert container but rather as a driver of subjectivity. This notion, that the city shapes its inhabitants, who then shape the city, also emerges across a range of early novels.[19] In

Ekwensi's *People of the City*, the narrative makes repeated references to the constitution of a "city man – fast with women, slick with his fairy-tales, dexterous with eyes and fingers," accompanied by a

> girl who belonged strictly to the city. Born in the city. A Primary education, perhaps the first for years at secondary school; yet she knew all about Western sophistication – make-up, cinema, jazz [...] content to walk her shoes thin in the air-conditioned atmosphere of department stores, to hang about all day in the foyer of hotels with not a penny in her handbag, rather than live in the country and marry Papa's choice.[20]

In Chinua Achebe's *No Longer At Ease* (1960) and *Man of the People* (1966),[21] the city remains a space of alienation, made visible through the forced assimilation into a particular brand of Euro-modernity of its elite classes. As in *Life Turns Man Up and Down: Money and Girls Turn Man Up and Down*, identification with the city is rendered through the idiom of consumption, symbolized through commodities and cultural objects tied to the global scale, and utterly opposed to the values of tradition and family of the countryside.

Internal migration was a major preoccupation for colonial administrators and town planners alike in the middle of the twentieth century, seen both as a possible means for the creation of a productive labor force and as a potential moral danger. In the 1950s, Lagos was home to some 8,000 migrants per year from the rest of Nigeria. Described as "com[ing] because it provides them with work or trade, work or trade which is not localized but for the benefit of the whole Federation of Nigeria,"[22] by the 1960s anxieties resounded around "the universal problem of finding employment for people drifting from rural to urban areas."[23] A 1963 Christian Aid report complains of young male migrants to the city that "nothing will induce them to go back to live in the villages. The briefest taste of the most uninspiring form of urban life is enough to whet their appetites for more and at once anything seems better than the tight discipline of the family and the dreary monotony of village life in the bush."[24] Likewise, a 1965 report commissioned by the United Nations sums up the "disease of urbanism":

> If West African countries do not raise their urbanisation rates, the rural settlements will collapse under the pile-up of unproductive numbers. If they do raise them, the growth of the towns will take on the dimensions of a disaster. Such, crudely formulated, is yet another of West Africa's menacing dilemmas. The growth of towns is out of gear with the growth of the economy. Urban development is unhinged from rural development. A permanent urban unemployment problem is being created, without alleviation of the rural predicament.[25]

By 1971, Lagos was experiencing a growth rate of 14 percent per annum, expanding, by 1972, to a Metropolitan Area "includ[ing] the city of Lagos and the neighbouring districts located within a radius of 17 to 20 miles from the city."[26] With its growth in population and geographical footprint, Lagos became an increasingly important site for the concentration of fixed capital. As "the focus of railway, road and air transportation to different parts of the country," Lagos at that time held a central importance "in assembling raw materials and for the distribution of finished products either internally or as exports."[27] Far from an expression of its natural environment, this unprecedented concentration of spatial resources accelerated largely due to "deliberate government activities [...] aimed at the promotion of industries and the participation of government in industrial establishments within metropolitan Lagos,"[28] that is, spatial strategies and representations of space.

Despite the trials and tribulations of city life, in its mid-century literary depictions the city remains a site of reinvention and communion beyond the taxonomies imposed under coloniality. In *People of the City*, The All Languages Club, a nightspot where protagonist Amusa Sango and his band play, is articulated through the desire of its proprietor, a former member of the Civil Service, "to take a practical step towards world unity [....] To create a place where men and women of all languages and social classes could meet and get to know one another more intimately. It was [the proprietor's] earnest desire that the spirit of fellowship created here would take root and expand."[29] Through a shared participation in music, "the spirit of fellowship," and conviviality, an alternative space develops here which, though not entirely sheltered from the privations of city life (it is telling that this description of the club is juxtaposed, lines later, with another series of evictions from Molomo Street at the hands of greedy landlord Lajide), nonetheless demonstrates the desire for a spatial practice rendered through a different logic. Despite the modesty of its scale, moreover, it is imagined as a space which might reverberate outwards, transforming the larger social organization through its own model and projecting a world formed on communion and solidarity.

Neil Smith observes that "the construction of geographical scale is a primary means through which spatial differentiation 'takes place'".[30] In the case of Lagos in the twentieth-century literary imaginary, a range of interlocking scales appear which, taken as a whole, do not necessarily imply a congruence or totality. In Buchi Emecheta's *The Joys of Motherhood* (1979), protagonist Nnu Ego's focalization initially suggests a drastic opposition between the city and her home in rural Igboland. Much of the novel's early depiction of Nnu Ego's marriage foregrounds the ways in which the city has fundamentally altered the family unit, displacing traditional gender roles, flexible models of labor, and social (re)production with colonialist norms based on the nuclear family and wage labor.[31] Yet, as the narrative progresses, a more complex picture emerges. Notable here is the importance of the village association for the ordering of Nnu Ego's social life. In the novel's opening pages, it is through her identifiable status as a member of the Ogboli village that Nnu Ego's suicide is stopped. Later, it is from the women of the village association that she learns the art of marketing, and is able to provide, for a time, for her family. During domestic disputes and familial unrest, the village association operates as a sounding board and judicial organ. In a similar vein, in Achebe's *No Longer at Ease*, it is the Umuofia village association that demands financial support and filial piety from Obi Okonkwo, which he uses to justify his slide into corruption. As much as these examples might lend credence to the simplified view of African political economies as essentially "patrimonial" in nature,[32] a more nuanced picture emerges at the level of spatial analysis that points to the complex interconnections across seemingly incompatible scalar ecologies in the service of social production.

The specter of the global through Lagos's entanglement in a commodities-driven capitalist world system is emphasized in mid-century portrayals of the city. As a burgeoning market woman, Nnu Ego establishes herself through the trade of cigarettes sold to sailors passing through Lagos's port during the Second World War. Elsewhere, in *People of the City*, even the most tranquil images are undercut by the ever-present fact of combined and uneven development represented in the movement of "ships and cargo vessels" at the lagoon and roads rife with "lorries from the hinterland, loaded with produce to be stacked in the adjoining warehouses," cutting through the "still, oppressive air" of the city.[33] The movement of commodities, people, and ideas, moreover, creates a sense in which the city is simultaneously defined through the social processes of "lesser" scales (the family, the household, the village, the tribe) while becoming embedded in "larger" scales of the world system.

Writing Contemporary Lagos Under Neoliberalism

In his exploration of the Lagos novel, Dunton proposes "a historical progression" from the middle of the twentieth century to the present day which "not[es] both how images of entropy become more prominent [...] and how [...] fresh energies are foregrounded in an attempt to address the experiential realities of life in a city such as Lagos."[34] A key factor in the narratological shifts which Dunton identifies is, of course, the evolution of the city itself. From the oil boom years of the 1970s to the present day, Lagos, like Nigeria, can best be defined by the impact of neoliberalization and, specifically, structural adjustment on social production and the spatiality of the city. As has been well documented, following the bursting of the oil bubble in the early 1980s Nigeria fell subject to a series of dictatorial governments, whose austerity policies effectively eroded anything resembling public services and public goods – the commons – in favor of privatization intended to enrich the few at the expense of the many. Culminating in the excessive corruption of the Abacha regime, among whose many crimes include the murder of Kenule Saro-Wiwa, the period leading into the new millennium can be seen as one of increased fragmentation, accelerated divisions, and an entrenchment of combined and uneven development which continues into the present day. It is perhaps no surprise, then, that contemporary renderings of the city display far less of the optimistic sense of utopian promise that older representations might have held, even tacitly. One particular literary manifestation of the neoliberalization of the city, echoed more broadly in the constitution of world literature, is the increased significance of genre fiction and particularly the depiction of the city in crime thrillers.

In these texts, the city functions as a fundamentally ungraspable space, both sinister in its inner workings and somehow irresistible. In novels such as Leye Adenle's *Easy Motion Tourist* and Toni Kan's *The Carnivorous City* (both published in 2016), the city "is a beast with bared fangs and a voracious appetite for human flash," a place where "life is not just brutish – it is short." And yet,

> like crazed moths disdaining the rage of the flame, we keep gravitating towards Lagos, compelled by some centrifugal force that defies reason and willpower. We come, take our chances, hoping that we will be luckier than the next man, willing ourselves to believe that while our fortune lies here, the myriad evils that traverse the streets of Lagos will never meet us with bared fangs.[35]

Where, in earlier works, the city's attractions appear at the scale of its material possibilities, registered through coloniality and modernity, in these more recent texts the city is itself likened to a creature of black magic, hypnotic and irresistible in a different kind of logic more specular, attuned to the despoliation of late capitalism. Contemporary Lagos emerges through a neoliberal ontology, one in which (de)privation defines everything and nothing remains to be seen that is not a commodity. The promise and magic of the boom years, with the utopian projection of some kind of pan-African horizon through which to imagine the future, is utterly absent; instead, redemption is only possible by succumbing to material wealth and the enterprise of the self. Lagos, then, is little more than "a city of dissemblers," where "everyone was hiding some deception that would, like a pebble flung against a mirror, shatter the image of their fake lives."[36] "Fake lives," like the "fake" wealth of the post-structural adjustment era and its neoliberal economy produces a version of the contemporary defined by liquid modernity (the replacement of the solid, statist social structures of the past with a finance-driven and elitist sense of fluidity) and the encroachment of non-places (spaces which "cannot be defined as relational, or historical, or concerned with identity") upon what were once thick social spaces.[37]

Genre fiction, however, is not alone in registering the neoliberalization of everyday life in Lagos. In an early passage in *Looking for Transwonderland* (2012), a creative non-fiction travelogue, author Noo Saro-Wiwa recounts her own potted history of the city:

> Once upon a time, Lagos was a placid cluster of islands and creeks separated from the Atlantic by lagoons, where local men caught fish, the cry of white ibis could be heard and snakes shimmied among the bushes. By the fifteenth century, the area had become a busy slave port. Under British colonial rule it became Nigeria's economic and political capital. The grasses, wild birds and trees were quickly devoured by urbanization, its wild metastasis cluttering the cityscape so densely it seems to have made a crater that has sent the rest of the country tumbling into it. Nobody knows how many people live in Lagos; it could be 10 million, it could be 17 million – no one is counting the teams of street urchins and shanty dwellers, or the illegal buildings erected under the distracted eyes of previous governments.[38]

Critical in this depiction are a series of moves which constitute the neoliberalization of social production and the constriction of its imaginative and material possibilities. We see, for instance, the transformation of space into time through the production of a single, teleological narrative of the city, beginning in a "placid" time defined by pastoral and atemporal mystifications, transforming, somehow, through urbanization on an undisciplined pathway through modernity, the riches of which are forever frustrated by the teeming masses and their ungovernability. Despite passing referencing to Lagos's time as "a busy slave port" and its subjugation "under British colonial rule," moreover, there is a strong sense of detachment here from the larger structures of the world economy and world system. Rather than foreground the ways in which coloniality has produced a particular spatiality through which the city and its many scales of existence emerge, instead appears an almost inevitable sense of disorder. The city is a cancer subject to a "wild metastasis"; opening up and swallowing all around it like a "crater," a space that "devours" and destroys. Across *Looking for Transwonderland*'s early sections, Lagos is repeatedly depicted in such terms, foregrounding the chaos and disorder which drive its daily rhythms, and lamenting the lost possibilities signaled by its decaying infrastructure and corrupted public spheres. The sole site for something resembling relief appears when narrator Noo visits Victoria Island. On Victoria Island, "residential mansions lay strategically inconspicuous behind guarded security gates, and the okadas wove at deferential speeds between the tinted-windowed 4 x 4s. Here, Nigeria dusts itself down and shakes hands with world commerce: Chinese, Thai, and Italian restaurants, foreign banks, art galleries, and sports bars lined the streets' embassies, boat clubs."[39] Set off from the squalor of the city, shielded from its ungovernable pulsations, the wealthy neighborhood stands as one of the few spaces of redemption in the city. Tellingly, however, this is a redemption that speaks in the language of commerce and commodities: restaurants, galleries, banks, and sports bars of foreign provenance which, taken together, call to mind a vision of Afropolitanism predicated on "a certain glow of access, affluence and mobility [...] that signals particular class and cultural inflections" and rooted in "its attendant consumer cultures, urban cultures, as well as a deep-seated investedness in connectivity to the so-called global metropolis."[40]

And yet there is another way in which the city comes into being in contemporary literary texts, neither rooted in an allegiance to a cosmopolitan brand of commodity fetishism nor defeatist in its capitulation to the inevitable failure of corruption. This alternative vision of the city is one not quite of utopian promise, but acknowledges the improvisatory tactics of its inhabitants and their ability to, somehow, form sites of world-making and belonging even as they experience the realities of material degradation. A prime example of this strand of Lagos-writing appears in Chibundu Onuzo's *Welcome to Lagos* (2017).The primary action of the novel takes place as the lives of five newcomers to the city become rather unexpectedly entangled with that of a newly-disgraced national politician. While much of the plot focuses on themes of corruption and censorship, the novel's conclusion is notable. Having lost their temporary home, the novel's five central characters find themselves back on the streets. Among them, former soldier Yemi takes it upon himself to explore the city every day, encountering in it an opportunity for a kind of education once denied to him as a child:

> He would enter a bus, not minding the destination the conductor was calling, riding all over the city. He had been to beaches, sinking into loose sand, gathering shells into his pockets; drawing near the worshippers in white garments that fluttered like wings; stepping at last into the ocean and gasping as the cold water surged round his feet. He had walked in a protected forest, plunging into the emerald silence of seventy-eight hectares of undisturbed habitat, his guide pointing out the reserve's animals: monkeys, snakes and the half-submerged head of an alligator, lying in wait for its prey. He had visited a small village of artists, cane weavers, painters, sculptors, moving through their exhibitions for free.[41]

Immersing himself in the city, Yemi is transformed, becoming, as his friend and colleague Chike thinks, "a historian, an anthropologist, a sociologist" whose engagement with the city's rhythms offers him salvation.[42] Through his daily encounters with the city's histories, Yemi eventually discovers a place he refers to only as "the water city." At first glance, this place looks "like any slum" to Yemi;[43] on closer scrutiny, however, it becomes transformed into a symbol of resilience:

> He soon saw his first house. It stood high on its stilts, its wooden ankles bathing in salt water. He had seen villages built on the sea in the Delta but nothing of this magnitude. Everywhere he looked, the grey houses and their rusted roofs spread like a sheet. Lightweight canoes moved between the buildings, their owners paddling lightly to steer. They were selling things, drifting from door to door, passing up plates of food and fresh fish, sliced and wrapped in cellophane.[44]

This place, we learn, is Makoko, one of Lagos's largest informal settlements. As a place appearing on no map, but "here nonetheless, their residence defying cartographers,"[45] Makoko functions as a representational space, a symbolic site that "need obey no rules of consistency or cohesiveness,"[46] but instead contains within it the imaginative possibilities for a different kind of social order and unity. In a novel explicitly concerned with the differential spaces of the city, it is significant that *Welcome to Lagos* ends here, now the home of its five central characters. If, in *Looking for Transwonderland*, moments of respite can only be found through participation in a particular kind of global consumer culture whose apparent celebration of fluidity belies its limited access, here redemption comes through a tactical escape from the strictures of maps and cartography itself. Spatial practices based on invention and improvisation become the means through which some sort of relief can be achieved, even as these practices remain under threat from the larger structures of administration which seek to impose their own representations of space and spatial strategies upon the city.

Across the last seventy years, the ways in which Lagos has come into being in the literary imagination point toward a series of tensions, dualities, and irresolvable contradictions which have evolved over time along with – if not always at pace with – the city's own development. As the proliferation of its literary representations indicate, Lagos, like world literature itself, remains a space too capacious to imagine, always rendered through its various myths and ultimately ungraspable. At once terrifying and fascinating, simultaneously a place of infinite inventiveness and a place of destruction and despoliation, the city's ungovernability is made manifest in the cacophony of spatial practices and tactics to which it gives rise. Continually growing, its boundaries pressed outward by new settlements and new spaces of life, the city, much like the very concept of the world, is amorphous, at times appearing utopian in its projection of an imagined but impossible future. At the same time, Lagos is very much a real place, subject to attempt after attempt at governability through town planning schemes, slum clearance schemes and, today, reclamation and luxury compound schemes. Its literary manifestations are diverse and sometimes divergent, but they exemplify the ways in which the material and the imaginative operate through a dialectic mode of ordering, even as they demonstrate the impossibility of a total or final representation.

Notes

1 Cyprian Ekwensi, "Lagos: City in a Hurry," *West African Review* 31, no. 394 (September, 1960): 14–18; 14.
2 Michel de Certeau, *The Practice of Everyday Life* (Berkeley, CA: University of California Press, 1984), xix.
3 Ekwensi, "City in a Hurry," 14.
4 de Certeau, *Practice*, xix.
5 Jean-Luc Nancy, *The Creation of the World, or Globalization*, trans. François Raffoul and David Pettigrew (Albany, NY: State University of New York Press, 2007), 42–43.
6 Karima Laachir, Sara Marzagora, and Francesca Orsini, "Significant Geographies: In lieu of World Literature," *Journal of World Literature* 3 (2018): 290–210.
7 Chris Dunton, "Entropy and Energy: Lagos as City of Words," *Research in African Literatures* 39, no. 2 (2008): 68–78, 68; Femi Eromosele, "Lagos in Contemporary Nigerian Music Video: Brymo's '1 Pound (The Documentary),'" *Social Dynamics* 47, no. 1 (2021): 7–22, 7.
8 Cyprian Ekwensi, *People of the City* (London: Heinemann, 1963), frontmatter.
9 United Kingdom National Archives (NA), file FCO 141/13392, "Letter from J. W. Robinson to Colonial Office, 29 September 1955."

10 NA, file FCO 141/13392, "Letter from A.F.F.P. Newns to R. F. A. Grey, 30th September, 1955."
11 NA, file FCO 141/13392, "Letter from Tom Williamson to James Robinson, 10 December 1956."
12 Josephine Olu Abiodun, "Urban Growth and Problems in Metropolitan Lagos," *Urban Studies* 11, no. 3 (October 1974): 341–347, 345.
13 Jean-François Bayart, "Africa in The World: A History of Extraversion," *African Affairs* 99, no. 395 (2000): 217–267.
14 Frederick Cooper, "What is the Concept of Globalization Good For? An African Historian's Perspective," *African Affairs* 100, no. 399 (2001): 189–213.
15 Akin Adesokan, "Anticipating Nollywood: Lagos circa 1996," *Social Dynamics* 37, no. 1 (2011): 96–110, 97.
16 Teju Cole, *Every Day is for the Thief* (Abuja: Cassava Republic Press, 2007), 38.
17 Okenwa Olisah, *Life Turns Man Up and Down: Money and Girls Turn Man Up and Down* (Onitsha: Njoku and Sons Bookshop, 1964?), 6.
18 Stephanie Newell, *West African Literatures: Ways of Reading* (Oxford: Oxford University Press, 2006), 110.
19 Ekwensi, *People*, 5.
20 Ibid., 23.
21 Chinua Achebe, *No Longer at Ease* (London: Heinemann, 1960); Achebe, *A Man of the People* (London: Heinemann, 1966).
22 NA, file FCO 141/13392, "The Position of Lagos (first draft)."
23 NA, file DO 177/29, "Letter from E. I. Oliver to Eric A Midgley, 26 September 1960."
24 School of Oriental and Asian Studies (SOAS), Christian Aid, file CA/A/6/4, Nigeria 1961–68, "The Church in Urban Nigeria: Report on a visit of Canon R.S.O. Stevens to Nigeria during May and June, 1963," 4.
25 SOAS, file PP MS 9/65, "Draft of 'Problems of Modernisation in West Africa,'" 167.
26 Olu Abiodun, "Urban Growth," 341.
27 Ibid., 345.
28 Ibid.
29 Ekwensi, *People*, 30.
30 Neil Smith, "Homeless/Global: Scaling Places," in Jon Bird, Barry Curtis, Tim Putnam, George Robertson, and Lisa Tickner, eds., *Mapping the Futures: Local Cultures, Global Change* (London: Routledge, 1993), 87–119, 97.
31 Buchi Emecheta, *The Joys of Motherhood* (London: George Braziller, 1979).
32 This argument has been influentially put forward in Patrick Chabal and Jean-Pascale Daloz, *Africa Works: Disorder as Political Instrument* (Oxford: James Currey, 1999).
33 Ekwensi, *People*, 100.
34 Dunton, "Entropy and Energy," 70.
35 Toni Kan, *The Carnivorous City* (Abuja: Cassava Republic Press, 2016), 34–35.
36 Ibid., 213.

37 See Marx Augé, *Non-Places: An Introduction to Supermodernity* (London: Verso, 2009), 77; Zygmunt Bauman, *Liquid Modernity* (Cambridge: Polity Press, 2000).
38 Noo Saro-Wiwa, *Looking for Transwonderland: Travels in Nigeria* (London: Granta, 2012), 13.
39 Ibid., 37.
40 Grace Musila, "Part-Time Africans, Europolitans and 'Africa lite,'" *Journal of African Cultural Studies* 28, no.1 (2016): 109–113, 111, 110.
41 Chibundu Onuzo, *Welcome to Lagos* (London: Faber & Faber, 2017), 295–296.
42 Ibid., 351.
43 Ibid., 296.
44 Ibid., 297.
45 Ibid., 350.
46 Henri Lefebvre, *The Production of Space*, trans. Donald Nicholson-Smith ([1974] Malden, MA: Blackwell, 1991), 41.

CHAPTER 18

Haunted Vitality
Sydney, Colonial Modernity, and World Literature

Brigid Rooney

Christina Stead's *Seven Poor Men of Sydney* (1934) begins with an arresting image of South Head at the entrance to Sydney Harbour: "The hideous low scarred yellow horny and barren headland lies curled like a scorpion in a blinding sea and sky."[1] This unpunctuated battery of adjectives conjures a foreboding environment in which landforms appear animated and hostile, repelling the visitor. Stead drafted this, her first novel, in London and Paris after her 1928 departure from Sydney. Her narrative gaze crosses time and space, traveling like returning memory toward the Heads from the open ocean beyond. The direction of this approach recalls the passage of the British invaders who, in 1788, sailed through the Heads into Sydney's many-lobed Harbour, its drowned river valley. Guided by the Gadigal (Cadigal) people of the Eora Nation, the invaders set down at some distance from the Heads, at the place known to its people as "Warrane," a sheltered cove with an abundant supply of wood and fresh water (the soon-polluted, now subterranean Tank Stream).[2] Today, high above this cove towers the central business district of the contemporary global city. Looking out from Circular Quay, where road, railway, and ferries meet, the cove's estuarine waters form a bowl, at the rim of which stand Sydney's two great architectural icons. On the western side the Harbour Bridge, opened in 1932, joins southern to northern shores. A monumental feat of interwar engineering, the Bridge was an aesthetic wonder that facilitated Sydney's suburban expansion. At Bennelong Point on the eastern side stands the Opera House, opened in 1973, its iconic white sails mirroring yacht-filled waters, signaling Sydney's global postmodernity. Circular Quay, Bridge, and Opera House form a theatrical dress-circle, an amphitheater that frequently serves as visual synecdoche for city and nation at large.

Seven Poor Men of Sydney at once registers and undermines the city's claims to modernity: it "was and remains a military and maritime settlement."[3] Sydney's inauspicious penal beginnings evolved rapidly as officers became landholders, convicts became emancipists, and free settlers arrived. The invaders spread, year by year, into the hinterland, over the Great Dividing Range, establishing colonies around the coastline and inland, encountering Aboriginal people no matter where they went. The menace of Stead's South Head, and her depiction of the city's still raw condition, suggests the spectrality of Sydney, a ghosting that lingers still, almost two and a half centuries on from British invasion. Sydney's buried waterways and ubiquitous sandstone speak of the deep millennial time of an ancient land, bearing the traces of its First Nations peoples whose immemorial tenure makes theirs the world's oldest continuing culture. Aboriginal people today still seek justice, recovery of their languages and culture, and recognition of their unceded sovereignty. In pockets of remnant bushland, under everyday urban and suburban places, carvings in sandstone and other markings attest to the not-quite-complete erasure of Aboriginal country. These layers make a palimpsest of Sydney, manifesting themselves in and shaping the contours of its literature.

Sydney's colonial past is integral to the nation's history, and Sydney's literature likewise contributes to the formation of the national literature. As a collective project, Australian literature took shape in the 1920s and 1930s, and consolidated institutionally from the mid-century onwards, developing density and diversity with accelerated globalization. Sydney's literature, however, like that of other cities, is not entirely contained by the category of nation. Cities are simultaneously subnational, operating below nation at regional level, and supranational, transcending nation via city-to-city global circuits. Sydney is a node in a global web formed by the transnational histories and logics of capitalism and settler-colonial modernity. These conditions are inscribed in Sydney's literature. Some works have circulated well beyond their local context of writing and production, garnering international readers. Others less traveled may anticipate local-global relations through a kind of double vision in which the particularized "here" is ghosted by spaces or times more distant. So, for example, Sydney in Stead's novel is ghosted by Paris, the place of its writing. Meanwhile Stead's narrative regards Sydney's (read Australia's) status as provincial: it suffers from cultural belatedness relative to the Greenwich Meridian time that, for Pascale Casanova, is set by the world literary capitals of Paris, London, or New York.[4] Yet Stead is a prime example of how Sydney's writers traffic in modernist and realist modes, repurposing world literary forms and genres. Double vision is also generated in Sydney's texts through citations, or what Wai Chee Dimock identifies as the looping or threading of texts into distant spaces and deep time.[5] To trace double vision in Sydney's texts is thus to recognize their defamiliarizing qualities, their opening toward an otherness that dispels illusions of autonomy.[6]

The "deep time" invoked in world literature is dwarfed by ancestral Aboriginal time, a temporality that challenges and haunts settler literature. In *Sydney* (2010), Delia Falconer describes the city as both vital and haunted: "This is not a simple haunting [....] It is not just its human past that seems to well up. There is a sense that everything has an extra layer of reflection, of slip beneath the surface."[7] Responding to Falconer's ghosted, refracted city, this chapter takes several slices through time, focusing on texts that conjure Sydney's spectral layers and map its broader dynamics. I consider 1930s texts that exhibit Falconer's haunted vitality, exploring modes of temporality other than those of regulated urban modernity. Their representations of the watery depths of the Harbour, its "slip beneath the surface," summon the colonial past even as they submerge its full import. Next, bridging mid-century and contemporary moments, I review layered temporalities in historical fictions that imagine Sydney's colonial frontier, works concerned with both the making and unsettling of nation. Last, I touch briefly on contemporary texts of a spatially expanded, culturally diverse Greater Sydney that reworld the city while threading its scenes through world literature.

Haunted Harbour: Interwar Sydney

Interwar texts set in Sydney produce what Meg Brayshaw calls an "aqueous poetics" through which the estuarine Harbour becomes "'vitally entangled' with human society and the built environment."[8] In Stead's *Seven Poor Men of Sydney*, Kenneth Slessor's "Five Bells" (1939), and Eleanor Dark's *Waterway* (1938), modern city and watery abyss form a chronotope, a space–time figure that relays modernist themes of subjective interiority and crisis. The city-harbor chronotope, figuring the watery abyss, relays anxiety about belatedness as not-quite-yet modernity, even as texts engage modernist forms and concepts. Their sense of Sydney as derivative of its Euro-Western parent culture vies with the vibrant energy of its social and natural environment. Such tensions are implicated in recurring scenes of drowning in the Harbour that memorialize specific historic events. In May 1927, a young man named Joe Lynch, linked to Sydney's bohemian circles, drowned after falling overboard from a ferry somewhere between Circular Quay and Mosman. In November that year, forty lives were lost in Sydney Harbour's worst maritime accident when the *Greycliffe*, a wooden ferry on its after-school run between Circular Quay and Watsons Bay, was split in two by the larger, metal-hulled, outward-bound *Tahiti*. Fictive renditions of these fatal events invoke yet also displace the colonial past, allegorizing the settler-colonial condition.[9]

In Stead's *Seven Poor Men of Sydney*, maritime traffic joins Sydney to the world: "little boys run out to name the liners waiting there for the port doctor, liners from Singapore, Shanghai, Nagasaki, Wellington, Hawaii, San Francisco, Naples, Brindisi, Dunkirk and London."[10] Thus oriented to the world, Sydney is modern, but also hampered, as suggested earlier, by its isolation and provinciality. The novel's young adults are figuratively (in one case literally) paralyzed, stuck in a parochial society, under the sway of their parents. The horror of their near-incestuous entrapment is explicitly linked to a painting in the city's art gallery, *The Sons of Clovis* by Évariste Luminais (1880), in which two young men, hamstrung by their father as punishment for rebellion, are set adrift on a barge in the Seine.[11] Despite their stranded condition, Stead's seven poor men (and one rebellious woman) engage in political debate that courses through gatherings, workplaces, and socialist organizations, and marvel at scientific wonders: in one brilliant setpiece, the humblest among them, Joseph Baguenault, attends a proto-Einsteinian lecture on light at the university.[12] The narrative climaxes with the suicide of Joseph's cousin Michael, a sensitive, brooding young man who – trapped in cycles of involution, futility, and despair – plunges in delirium from the notorious bluff at South Head. Michael's suicide fulfills the menace in the novel's first image, and in recurring images of South Head Signal Station's flagstaff. Michael deems the flagstaff "a monstrous pale tree, bitterly infinite, standing footless in the earth and headless in the heavens, a splinter sterile and sapless, a kind of scarecrow, a rack for cast vestments, a mast castaway: underneath the sea ran."[13] From the colony's beginnings, the Signal Station was used for semaphore communication with approaching ships. In Stead's novel, it looms in triumph over doomed youth, locked within the colonial outpost. Yet the final chapters, a series of nested narratives told in Michael's memory, generate perspectives at prehistoric, geological, and continental scales. Against the flagstaff's giddy verticality, the text delivers its horizontal vision of a vast interconnected mesh, its threads "woven of the bodies of flying men and women with the gestures interlocked in thousands of attitudes of passion,"[14] before coming to rest on Joseph who emerges as the implied keeper of the tale.

If there is a work of settler literature that presides over Sydney Harbour, it is Kenneth Slessor's "Five Bells."[15] An elegy occasioned by the 1927 drowning of Slessor's friend Joe Lynch, the poem may also stem from the wreck of the *Greycliffe*.[16] Musical compositions, artworks, and literary texts have constellated around this iconic poem. The Opera House's northern foyer, for example, features the "Salute to Five Bells" mural by Australian artist John Olsen, and has inspired composers such as Peter Sculthorpe.[17] Gail Jones's novel *Five Bells* (2011), to which I will return, meditates on Slessor's poem.[18] Slessor was a poet and journalist affiliated with Sydney's "Vision" group, a vitalist, anti-modernist, bohemian circle.[19] Notwithstanding his association with "Vision," Slessor forged a poetics in dialogue with the modernisms of T.S. Eliot and Ezra Pound. Published on the eve of war, "Five Bells" meditates on time, being, and mortality, yielding unforgettable images of the Harbour at night and fusing natural and built environment in gestures of dissolution, inversion and backward movement:

> Deep and dissolving verticals of light
> Ferry the falls of moonshine down. Five bells
> Coldly rung out in a machine's voice. Night and water
> Pour into one rip of darkness, the Harbour floats
> In air, the Cross hangs upside-down in water.[20]

Figuring backward-running time, Harbour waters reflect the skies in a double inversion, using the antipodean trope of the "upside-down world." For a Sydney reader, the word "ferry" pivots from verb to noun, as the vertical "falls of moonshine down" cross the horizontal passage of the commuter ferry. The poem works across temporalities, setting the "little fidget wheels" of modern machine time against subjective Time, "the flood that does not flow." In deathly refrain, the phrase "*Five bells*" – "time's bumpkin calculus" – demarcates breaks, like cinematic jump cuts, between one passage of thought-memory and the next.[21] Philip Mead pinpoints Slessor's emulation of cinematic modes of time – "its language of recollection is framed as a series of projected, inter-dissolving scenes" – and notes its kinship with Walter Benjamin's sense of the past as that which "can be seized only as an image which flashes up at the instant when it can be recognized and is never seen again."[22] The poet-speaker summons the dead man who continually dissolves on the brink of appearing, becoming a "something" that "hits and cries against the ports of space, / Beating their sides to make its fury heard."[23] These revenant images, like time and water flowing over the dead man, implicate the poet-speaker who is at once the watcher from a distance and bodily bound by the deathly element: "I felt the wet push its black thumb-balls in, / [...] I felt your eardrums crack [...] / I was blind and could not feel your hand."[24] Reading the poem as masculine elegy, Kate Lilley identifies the poet-speaker's concern with his own future posthumousness, and the poem's Orphic scene of looking backward as one that recuperates and legitimates the survivor-poet.[25] For Leigh Dale, Lilley's reading opens recognition of the poem's settler consciousness, through which the violence of colonialism is eclipsed by the elegiac script of white masculine loss.[26]

The *Greycliffe* shipwreck inspired a potent short story by Stead, "The Day of Wrath" (1934)[27] as well as Eleanor Dark's novel *Waterway* (1938), published during the Sesquicentenary (150th anniversary) of First Fleet invasion.[28] The title, "waterway," designates the Harbour as an everyday thoroughfare vital to the city even as it signals the narrative's aqueous poetics and its function as theatrical amphitheater for action and event. *Waterway* folds time into space, deploying the twenty-four hour scheme of modernist fictions of the city such as James Joyce's *Ulysses* and Virginia Woolf's *Mrs Dalloway*.[29] Yet Dark also sought to make her fiction accessible for readers. In *Waterway*, as Melinda Cooper observes, this involved blending "modernist introspection and middlebrow romantic plotline."[30] Relaying their thoughts, circumstances, and exchanges, the narrative follows multiple characters across a single day as they leave and return home to Watsons Bay. Its concerns span local and national matters of social justice and progress as well as international fears of looming world war. *Waterway* offers a cross-sectional portrait of Sydney's settler society and class cleavages, dramatizing the gap between the vulgarly rich and desperately poor. The novel's climactic event is the wreck of the ferry, a catastrophe through which the tangled impasses within its conflicted settler community are resolved. The wreck allows symbolic redress of classed and gendered injustices. Yet, as we will see in the next section, the redemption of *Waterway*'s settler community beyond this calamity also subsumes or displaces recognition of the colonial violence registered in the narrative's framing scenes.

Rolling Year Zero: Fictions of Sydney's Colonial Frontier

Even as interwar urbanization gathered pace, Sydney's frontier past became a focus of national narration. During the 1938 Sesquicentenary, narratives of Sydney's foundations sought to affirm its modernity and futurity. In Sesquicentenary posters, the Bridge appears as a colossus of progress, astride the Harbour and the past.[31] Modernity was palpable not only in design, music, cinema, and architecture but also, paradoxically, in a surge of cultural nationalism typified by the Jindyworobaks, a group of writers, artists, and intellectuals who adopted motifs from Aboriginal culture to indigenize the settler nation. Settler appropriation of Aboriginal culture was twinned with the discourse of extinction, the presumption that Aboriginal people themselves were destined to die out. Meanwhile, Aboriginal people in cities like Sydney were subjected to "structural genocide" through racialized regimes of surveillance, "protection," segregation, child removal, and assimilation.[32] Yet, forced to the fringes, Aboriginal people did not remain silent. On January 26, 1938, as the city celebrated its anniversary with street parades and a First Fleet reenactment, a group of Aboriginal activists met in a landmark protest that would sound down the decades, declaring a "Day of Mourning" and petitioning the Commonwealth Government for their civil and human rights.

The appropriation of Aboriginal culture to indigenize the modern settler nation was yoked to the genocidal erasure of Aboriginal people who, dispossessed and displaced, became internal refugees. Patrick Wolfe describes settler colonialism – in Australia, North America, and Israel – as deploying a "logic of elimination" enabling settler acquisition and exploitation of territory. Because the settler means to stay, argues Wolfe, invasion is best understood as "a structure not an event," one that persists into the present.[33] Yet colonization is also eventful, unfolding in time as well as space.[34] In *The Colony*, a multidisciplinary history of early colonial Sydney, Grace Karskens cites anthropologist Deborah Bird Rose's metaphor for "the process by which Aboriginal country, long known, occupied and managed, was rendered 'empty', 'timeless' and 'wild' by colonisation," a process imagined "as a rolling Year Zero that is carried across the land cutting an ontological swathe between 'timeless' land and 'historicised' land."[35] Karskens observes how the wheel of colonization rolled through the Sydney region between 1788 and the 1830s, bringing violence into "new" country, "its heavy freight of dispossession, abduction and loss of food sources setting off new cycles of bloody attacks, which in turn triggered 'rituals of terror' from the Europeans."[36] Continent-wide frontier violence rolled on for at least 150 years, with the last recorded massacre occurring as late as 1928 in Coniston, in the Northern Territory.

That settler-colonial desire for indigeneity is the counterpart of a logic of elimination cannot be excluded from consideration of Eleanor Dark's fiction – both *Waterway* and her subsequent *Timeless Land* trilogy – even as we recognize Dark's groundbreaking attention to the acquisitive greed and violence of colonial invasion. *The Timeless Land* (1941), the first novel in the trilogy, maps Sydney's colonization to its perimeters. Coinciding with a new appetite for historical sagas, *The Timeless Land* was successful in the USA: Dark's Australian settler-frontier story resonated across continents.[37] Dark's research on Sydney's colonial archive for *The Timeless Land* overlapped with her completion of *Waterway*. Though the latter concerns contemporary Sydney, Dark drew epigraphs for each of its five sections from the archive. The first is from an eyewitness account as the fleet sailed into the Harbour: "the natives everywhere greeted the little fleet with shouts of defiance and prohibition, the words 'Warra warra' – Go away, go away – resounding wherever they appeared."[38] The narrative proper opens with the panorama of the contemporary city and Harbour at dawn from the perspective of Oliver Denning, the novel's ethical touchstone. In a moment of double vision, the reader is invited to inhabit Oliver's perspective, as he imagines himself inhabiting the place of an Aboriginal warrior, a century and a half earlier:

> Now, with the aid of dim light, narrowed eyes, and a little imagination, you could annihilate the city, the growth whose parent cells had fastened upon the land that day. You could become a different kind of man, tall and deep-chested, black-skinned and bearded, standing upon some rocky peak with the dawn wind on your naked body, your shield and spear and throwing-stick in your hands.[39]

This temporal doubling yields the past in palimpsest: the Harbour's inner headlands of "Blue's Point and Potts Point, Longnose Point and Slaughter-house Point" come into view with their Aboriginal names and implied cultural histories: "Warringarea and Yarranabbe, Yeroulbine and Tarrah."[40] Dark launched her next novel, *The Timeless Land*, by moving from this momentary doubling to the full inhabitation of Aboriginal perspectives, via figures such as Bennilong (based on the historical figure Wularaway Bennelong, c.1764–1813), and imagining both sides of the frontier. At one point, Governor Arthur Phillip, who resembles Dark's fictive Oliver Denning, is afforded a vision of the modern city to come: "[D]azzled by the sun and by something which had been near enough to an hallucination," Phillip "had seen a city on these shores. He had seen wharves crowded with shipping. He had seen wide streets and lofty buildings, and the homes of a free and happy people."[41] Phillip's vision of Sydney enacts a future anterior that also doubles and reverses Denning's vision in *Waterway*, in which the Aboriginal past, submerged beneath the everyday settler world, ghosts the present city.

Dark's unapologetic use of "invasion" in both novels rather than the euphemistic "settlement" may surprise readers today. Even so, *Waterway*'s Oliver turns from the "blasting revelation" of "lovely places violated," away from grief "for a brave and ancient race fading slowly to extinction"[42] to seek joy in the city's present community, signified in the domestic scene of red roofs cascading to the Harbour shore. This turn is conditioned, ironically, by imminent world war, indeed by the threat of invasion, but the return of a spectral past is superseded by the narrative's sense of irreversible modernity. Oliver's response is at once an admission and a turning away, a moving on, discursively continuous with a progressive, modern settler logic of elimination. At the novel's end, Oliver gazes again upon the now darkening Harbour, recalling "the conflict which had begun from a century and a half ago" that had "painted it with colours of flame and blood," while affirming that "the land will win, [...] must always win."[43] This formulation tends to naturalize settler belonging, incorporating the past, blocking (im)possible recognition, and resting hope in settler community and futurity. Although it recognizes past injustice, the narrative remains silent about Aboriginal people in the present of Dark's own time.

In 1968, anthropologist W.E.H. Stanner called out "the Great Australian Silence," the nation's decades-long cult of disremembering the colonial frontier.[44] Although both *Waterway* and *The Timeless Land* effect a partial break with this collective amnesia, Stanner's criticism holds, given Dark's representation of Aboriginal culture as timeless and unchanging, and its people as regrettably fading away. Her fictions do not recognize the contemporaneity, the coevality, of Aboriginal culture. Since the 1980s, Indigenous and non-Indigenous researchers and writers have broken the silence to highlight the injustice and brutality of the frontier and Australia's genocidal history. These revisionist histories informed the Australian High Court's 1992 Mabo judgment that swept away *terra nullius* as legal justification for colonization. The popular impact of revisionist history was demonstrated in a nationwide "Walk for Reconciliation" on May 28, 2000, "the biggest expression of public support for any cause."[45] In Sydney, hundreds of thousands walked across the Harbour Bridge. Among them was novelist Kate Grenville, whose historical fiction, *The Secret River* (2005), inspired by the Walk, took contemporary readers to Sydney's Hawkesbury-Nepean River frontier during its peak period of violence. Like Dark, Grenville drew on the colonial archive, and *The Secret River* found a wide readership. The novel attracted controversy, however, not only from historians who disputed Grenville's claims about the superior imaginative power of fiction, but also from those who saw in her novel a failure to reckon with historical and cultural difference. Sensitive to unethical forms of appropriation, Grenville (unlike Dark) avoided inhabiting the perspective of her Aboriginal characters, but this problematic absence was mitigated by the performance of Aboriginal actors when her novel was adapted for the stage.[46]

The Secret River in turn inspired Julie Janson, a Burruberongal woman of the Darug Nation, to write *Benevolence* (2020).[47] Recalling the fiction of both Dark and Grenville, Janson's reconstruction of Sydney's frontier not only attends to its colonial archive but also reaches beyond official written records.[48] Putting Aboriginal people at the center of Sydney's history, Janson draws on her own family's story and on the knowledge and guidance of Darug, Gundungurra, and Wonnaruah Elders.[49] *Benevolence* dramatizes the "rolling wheel" of colonization through the story of Muraging, based on Janson's ancestor, Mary Ann Thomas.[50] The narrative opens in 1816 when Muraging is given by her father to the missionary Shelleys, husband and wife custodians of the Parramatta Native Institution, in exchange for a brass kingplate and the understanding that his daughter will learn the language and ways of the *waibala* (white colonizers). Muraging swiftly acquires a new identity as "Mary," as well as command of English and skill in playing the violin. Janson's portrait of the Shelleys exposes the irony of Christian "benevolence": their desire to convert Aboriginal charges to *waibala* ways is undercut by brutal frontier realities.

Following Muraging, Janson's narrative maps an expansive territory, from relatively settled Sydney town to the far reaches of the Hawkesbury-Nepean River, Muraging's (and Janson's) ancestral country. Muraging senses the violation of the land itself: "The hot air smells of burning gum leaves as men clear the bush of the beloved trees. Crack, crack, crack as tree spirits fall [….] It rips apart the spirit pathways to the sky. An endless cracking of death to the Darug."[51] Muraging emerges not as a victim, however, but as a spirited survivor. Amid the trauma and chaos, the narrative holds fast to the central thread of Muraging's will to survive and reconnect with kin and country. By the end, reaching Palm Beach at the mouth of "the great sacred Deerubbin [Hawkesbury-Nepean River], the shining silver track that binds and links her people from the Blue Mountains to Freemans Reach, from South Creek to Marra Marra Creek, and then to Barrenjoey," Muraging envisions the "interconnected lines of marriage, kinship and a cluster of mixed-up clans"[52] and is here, at last, reunited with her surviving kin.

In narrating bare life on the colonial edge, Janson's historical novel resonates with other Aboriginal and Torres Strait Islander people's writings. Its patterns of itinerancy, precarity, and survival recall, for example, the memoir of Ruby Langford Ginibi. Published in the Bicentenary year, *Don't Take Your Love to Town* (1988) tells of life on the margins of mid-to-late twentieth-century urban Australia, attesting to the interconnected world of Aboriginal kin and enduring links to country despite dispossession and disadvantage.[53] Not unlike Muraging, Ruby is constantly on the move between her ancestral Bundjalung country in northern New South Wales, her housing commission home in the outer Sydney suburb of Green Valley, and the inner city suburb of Redfern, then a vital hub for Aboriginal activism. On January 26, 1988, Redfern was the gathering place for the largest-ever protest by Aboriginal people, one that recalled Sydney's 1938 activists by declaring the Bicentenary "A Year of Mourning." Caring for her extended family, kin, and mob, Ruby is another spirited survivor. These works contribute to and contest Sydney and its literature. They are not just "Australian literature" but participate in transnational indigenous literatures, testifying to the perspectives, histories, and experiences of First Nations people, asserting still-unmet demands for justice and recognition of sovereignty.

Greater Suburban Sydney: A Tale of Two Cities

Beyond its city-harbor precinct, then, Sydney is a larger, more diverse entity. Bounded by mountains, rivers, and national parklands, its 12,000 km^2 house a multiethnic population of more than 5.3 million people. Greater Sydney has historically tended toward sprawl rather than density, manifesting the suburban ideal of detached dwelling on a quarter-acre block. The "great Australian dream" of home ownership has been integral to the nation's modern cultural identity and its political (class) "settlement," a dream now increasingly out of reach, with skyrocketing property values, rampant speculation, and social housing shortfalls.[54] Suburbia is often aligned with insular complacency and amnesia about the past, and not without reason. In *The Colony*, Karskens observes how: "Violence and bloodshed underpinned the spread of settlers over stolen ground; modern suburbs are built over battlefields."[55] Writers have sometimes drawn on suburbia to challenge settler amnesia, or hint at what lies buried beneath everyday suburban place. Patrick White famously used suburban sprawl as his metaphor for national parochialism: "In all directions stretched the Great Australian Emptiness," he wrote in 1958.[56] White's suburban Castle Hill, at the outer metropolitan edge of Sydney where he then lived, is encoded in his "Sarsaparilla" writings, including *The Tree of Man* (1955), *Riders in the Chariot* (1961), and *The Solid Mandala* (1966). White's fictional Sarsaparilla is populated with the grotesque, the corrupt and the malevolent, the closeted and the prudish, yet also with eccentrics, mystics, and outsiders, the migrant, the refugee and the Aboriginal outcast. White's cosmopolitanism is integral to the way his fictions extend the imagined reach of suburbia while interrogating the parochial fabric of mid-century Australia.[57]

No longer at Sydney's outer edge, Castle Hill now stands at the tip of a swathe of newer suburban estates reaching to the foot of the Blue Mountains. Sydney's suburbs may seem uniform but in reality form a mosaic of subregions shaped by environmental, cultural, and socioeconomic factors. The most contentious divide, between Sydney's East and West, was amplified in the city's 2021 battle against the COVID-19 pandemic. Mridula Amin's report, "Why Sydney's COVID-19 response could be a tale of two cities," touches on the long-standing stigmatization of Greater Western Sydney, highlighting the area's young demographic, its multilinguistic, multicultural character, its economic precarity, and its indispensability to the whole city's everyday functioning.[58] Resisting stigmatization, Western Sydney writers have been producing a vibrant literature. Some connect outer suburban terrain with world literature, as in Luke Carman's *An Elegant Young Man* (2013), while others relay intimate, playful, or searing narratives expressive of culturally diverse communities. Among the latter are Michael Mohammed Ahmad's bildungsroman trilogy, *The Tribe* (2014), *The Lebs* (2018), and *The Other Half of You* (2021), Peter Polites's *Down the Hume* (2017) and *The Pillars* (2019), and Yumna Kassab's *The House of Youssef* (2019). These writers are redefining and recentering Sydney's literature, expanding its horizons and reading local place through diasporic, global experience.

With Gail Jones's *Five Bells* – in which her character Pei Xing journeys by train from her home in Sydney's southwestern suburb of Bankstown to Circular Quay – we come full circle. As Jones's characters move through the city, their memories bring the past into the present and scenes from other cities into Sydney. Revisiting Sydney's haunted harborside, the novel at once compresses space and expands it outward, threading the urban center into far-flung multicultural suburbs and places elsewhere. Four characters converge on the Quay. Ellie, recently arrived from Western Australia to write a thesis, is renting in inner-suburban Glebe. She heads to the Quay to meet her former lover James (Gennaro) DeMello, also from Western Australia, a young man bearing an unspeakable burden of grief and guilt. Formerly from China, Pei Xing is a survivor of the Cultural Revolution. By train, then ferry across to the Harbour's north shore, she makes her weekly visit to the bedside of Dong Hua, her erstwhile persecutor from the camps. Last is Catherine Healey from Dublin, who has come to Sydney hoping to extricate herself from a "mire of grief"[59] after the death of her beloved brother. Following the characters' ruminations as they traverse the city in a single day, the novel recalls both Eleanor Dark's *Waterway* and such modernist novels as Woolf's *Mrs Dalloway* (1924). Pei Xing reads *Doctor Zhivago* (1957) aloud to Dong Hua, while Ellie reads *Petersburg*

(1913) by Andrei Bely, thinking to compare the latter to Joyce's *Ulysses*, to find "intelligible links between cities rendered in words."[60] Likewise, each character renders the Opera House in words: as a many-chambered fan, a bowl of blown roses, a gleaming stack of washed dishes.

The narrative's concerns with backward-flowing time and memory are enacted in its design, while its prose is infused with the language of "Five Bells." Jones turns Slessor's poem, however, to quite other ends. While the fate of James echoes that of Joe Lynch, the narrative averts the poem's existential darkness and white-masculinist settler melancholy, instead enfolding James in elemental, maternal imagery. The poignancy of James's death is balanced by the life-affirming orientation of the three women, Catherine, Ellie, and Pei Xing. Jones's vision of Sydney registers the ethical claims of the past in the present. While steadfast in its witnessing of trauma, however, *Five Bells* refuses the temptation to succumb to an immobilizing, self-indulgent fixation on guilt, bitterness, or grief.

Five Bells weaves together the seemingly divergent threads of this discussion. Jones's novel is cosmopolitan in the very material sense of having traveled into the wider world, appearing in translated editions in French, German, and Spanish. But this mobility is already anticipated by the narrative, with its neomodernist patterning of simultaneities, time–space compressions, and interior consciousness. *Five Bells*'s city-wide, continental, even planetary span, threads Shanghai and Dublin, Chinese and Irish diasporas into contemporary Sydney, and historic trauma into its incandescent Harbour. As Robert Dixon observes, *Five Bells* "creates a thread of comparison between the lost white settler child, the stolen Aboriginal children, and the stolen children of China's Cultural Revolution."[61] But the narrative also demonstrates how local-global perspectives on historic trauma can be generated without collapsing difference into sameness. Dimensions of settler colonialism and historic trauma are threads that connect Sydney's texts across time, producing the city's meanings. In *Five Bells*, meanwhile, legacies of trauma meet small acts of forgiveness, compassion, and grace. That Pei Xing forgives her torturer, offering instead care and companionship, is mirrored in the narrative's seemingly glancing mention of the 2008 apology delivered by then Prime Minister Kevin Rudd to Australia's First Nations people. As each character passes through the Quay – that historic ground zero of invasion – a busker, never seen, always heard, plays the didgeridoo. Each is arrested by the haunting sound, both an everyday city sound and signal of a surviving ancestral culture and its people. The sound invites visitors, migrants, and settlers alike to open their ears and their hearts to all that it carries, and the claims that it makes.

Notes

I thank Meg Brayshaw and Monique Rooney for their insightful comments on drafts of this chapter.

1 Christina Stead, *Seven Poor Men of Sydney* ([1934] South Carlton, Victoria: The Miegunyah Press, 2015).
2 First Nations people living in the Greater Sydney area included not only the Gadigal, but the Guringai, the Darug, the Dharawal, and the Gundungurra, within which are numerous clan groups, each connected with its ancestral country.
3 Stead, *Seven Poor Men*, 1.
4 Pascale Casanova, *World Republic of Letters*, trans. M.B. DeBevoise (Cambridge, MA: Harvard University Press, 2004), 87–91.
5 Wai Chee Dimock, *Through Other Continents: American Literature Across Deep Time* (Princeton, NJ and Oxford: Princeton University Press, 2006), 3–6.
6 For discussion of "double vision" see Robert Dixon and Brigid Rooney, eds., "Introduction: Australian Literature, Globalisation and the Literary Province," in *Scenes of Reading: Is Australian Literature a World Literature?* (North Melbourne: Australian Scholarly Publishing, 2013), ix–xxv.
7 Delia Falconer, *Sydney* (Sydney: New South Press, 2010), 21.
8 Meg Brayshaw, *Sydney and its Waterway in Australian Literary Modernism* (Cham: Springer International Publishing/Palgrave Macmillan, 2021), 6–8.
9 See also Brigid Rooney, "Time's Abyss: Australian Literary Modernism and the Scene of Ferry Wreck," in *Scenes of Reading*, 101–114.
10 Stead, *Seven Poor Men*, 2.
11 *Sons of Clovis II* was purchased in 1886 by the Art Gallery of NSW; see image online at www.artgallery.nsw.gov.au/collection/works/712/.
12 Sam Matthews, "'Lights All Askew in the Heavens': Einsteinian Relativity, Literary Modernism and the Lecture on Light in Christina Stead's *Seven Poor Men of Sydney*," *Australian Literary Studies* 31, no. 6 (December 2016), https://bit.ly/3WVyowX.
13 Stead, *Seven Poor Men*, 43.
14 Ibid., 332.
15 Kenneth Slessor, "Five Bells," in *Selected Poems* (London, Sydney: Angus & Robertson, 1975), 121–124.
16 See Rooney, "Time's Abyss," 103.
17 See also the singular painting by John Olsen, *Five Bells*, 1963, Art Gallery of New South Wales, Sydney, www.artgallery.nsw.gov.au/collection/works/133.1999/; Peter Sculthorpe, "*Harbour Dreaming: For Solo Piano*" (alternative title "Between Five Bells") (London: Faber Music Ltd, 2000).
18 Gail Jones, *Five Bells* (North Sydney: Vintage/Random House, 2011).
19 See Peter Kirkpatrick, *The Sea Coast of Bohemia: Literary Life in Sydney's Roaring Twenties* ([1992] Perth: Australian Scholarly Publishing, 2007), 83.
20 Slessor, "Five Bells," 121.

21 On "cinematism" in "Five Bells" see Philip Mead, *Networked Language: Culture & History in Australian Poetry* (North Melbourne: Australian Scholarly Publishing, 2008), 73–86.
22 Ibid., 73.
23 Slessor, "Five Bells", 121.
24 Ibid, 124.
25 Kate Lilley, "'Living Backward': Slessor and Masculine Energy," in Anthony J. Hassall, ed., *Kenneth Slessor: Critical Readings* (St. Lucia, Queensland: University of Queensland Press, 1997), 246–264.
26 Leigh Dale, "No More Boomerang? 'Nigger's Leap' and 'Five Bells,'" *Journal of Australian Studies* 37, no. 1 (March 2013): 48–61 [49–50, 57].
27 "The Day of Wrath" appears within Stead's *The Salzburg Tales* (London: Peter Davies, 1934); see also Rooney, "Time's Abyss," 104–106.
28 Eleanor Dark, *Waterway* ([1938] Sydney: F.H. Johnston Publishing, 1949).
29 For debate about *Waterway*'s Joycean references see Paul Giles, *Backgazing: Reverse Time in Modernist Culture* (Oxford: Oxford University Press, 2019), 201–209; and Brayshaw, *Sydney and its Waterway*, 14 (note 3).
30 Melinda J. Cooper, *Middlebrow Modernism: Eleanor Dark's Interwar Fiction* (Sydney: Sydney University Press, 2022), Kindle edition, Location 4827.
31 See Rooney, "Time's Abyss," 107, on Charles Meere's poster, "1788–1938, 150 years of progress" (1937). See image online at National Library of Australia website: https://nla.gov.au/nla.obj-135780425/view.
32 For "structural genocide," see Patrick Wolfe, "Settler Colonialism and the Elimination of the Native," *Journal of Genocide Research* 8, no. 4 (2006): 387–409 [403].
33 Ibid., 388.
34 See Philip Steer on the relevance of "event" in his *Settler Colonialism in Victorian Literature: Economics and Political Identity in the Networks of Empire* (Cambridge: Cambridge University Press, 2020), 27.
35 Rose is cited in Grace Karskens, *The Colony* (Sydney: Allen & Unwin, 2009), 455–56.
36 Ibid., 456.
37 Dark read and enjoyed Margaret Mitchell's *Gone with the Wind* (1936). For this point and detail about the American reception of Dark's fiction, see David Carter and Roger Osborne, *Australian Books and Authors in the American Marketplace 1840s–1940s* (Sydney: Sydney University Press, 2018), 262–270.
38 Dark, *Waterway*, 10.
39 Ibid., 11.
40 Ibid., 11–12.
41 Eleanor Dark, *The Timeless Land* ([1941] London: Collins, 1954), 67–68.
42 Dark, *Waterway*, 12.
43 Ibid., 384.
44 W.E.H. Stanner, *After the Dreaming* ([1969] Sydney: Australian Broadcasting Commission, 1974), 24–25.

45 For details, see "Walk for Reconciliation," National Museum of Australia website, www.nma.gov.au/defining-moments/resources/walk-for-reconciliation.

46 See, for example, Clarissa Sebag-Montefiore's review of the play: "The Secret River review – A Masterful Portrayal of Australia's Past," *The Guardian* (February 10, 2016), www.theguardian.com/stage/2016/feb/10/the-secret-river-review-a-masterful-portrayal-of-australias-dark-past.

47 Julie Janson, *Benevolence* (Broome, Western Australia: Magabala Books, 2020). Janson discusses Grenville's *The Secret River* in "The NIB Presents: Australian Indigenous Voices in Literature," Waverley Council (2020), www.youtube.com/watch?v=WrhQDmO9TEU.

48 Janson contributed to a Western Sydney University team researching Sydney's Aboriginal history: see "Acknowledgements," *Benevolence*, 339–340.

49 Ibid., 340.

50 Ibid., 339.

51 Ibid., 48.

52 Ibid., 334.

53 Ruby Langford [subsequently known as Ruby Langford Ginibi], *Don't Take Your Love to Town* (Ringwood, Victoria: Penguin, 1988).

54 For explanation of "Australian settlement" see Brendan Gleeson, *Australian Heartlands: Making Space for Hope in the Suburbs* (Sydney: Allen & Unwin, 2006), especially 12–20.

55 Karskens, *The Colony*, 449.

56 Patrick White, "The Prodigal Son," *Australian Letters* 1, no. 3 (April 1958): 37.

57 For more about Patrick White, and the literature of Greater Western and suburban Sydney, see Brigid Rooney, *Suburban Space, the Novel and Australian Modernity* (London: Anthem Press, 2018).

58 Mridula Amin, "Why Sydney's COVID-19 response could be a tale of two cities," ABC (July 10, 2021), www.abc.net.au/news/2021-07-10/nsw-covid-19-response-is-a-tale-of-two-cities/100281710; Diane Powell, *Out West: Perceptions of Sydney's Western Suburbs* (St. Leonards, New South Wales: Allen & Unwin, 1993).

59 Jones, *Five Bells*, 17.

60 Ibid., 214.

61 Robert Dixon, "Invitation to the Voyage: Reading Gail Jones's Five Bells," *Journal of the Association for the Study of Australian Literature (JASAL)* 12, no. 3 (2012): 15.

Select Bibliography

Chicago Schools: The Skyscraper in Translation

Abu-Lughod, Janet L. *New York, Chicago, Los Angeles: America's Global Cities*. Minneapolis, MN: University of Minnesota Press, 1999.

Cronon, William. *Nature's Metropolis: Chicago and the Great West*. New York: W. W. Norton & Co., 1991.

Drake, St. Clair and Horace R. Cayton. *Black Metropolis: A Study of Negro Life in a Northern City* [1945]. Chicago: University of Chicago Press, 2015.

Elsheshtawy, Yasser. *Dubai: Behind and Urban Spectacle*. New York: Routledge, 2010.

Goodman, Nelson. *Ways of Worldmaking*. Indianapolis, IN: Hackett Publishing Co., 1978.

Huyssen, Andreas. *Miniature Metropolis: Literature in the Age of Photography and Film*. Cambridge, MA: Harvard University Press, 2015.

Munif, Abdelrahman. *Cities of Salt* [1984]. Translated by Peter Theroux. New York: Vintage International, 1989.

Norris, Frank. *The Pit: A Story of Chicago* [1902]. New York: Penguin Books, 1994.

Wright, Richard. *Native Son* [1940]. New York: HarperCollins, 1993.

Writing the Manichean City from Colonial to Global Metropolis

Adiga, Aravind. *The White Tiger: A Novel*. New York: Free Press, 2008.

Chi-ha, Kim. "Five Bandits." Translated by Brother Anthony of Taizé, *Manoa* 27, no. 2 (2015): 94–104.

Fanon, Frantz. *The Wretched of the Earth*. Translated by Richard Philcox. New York: Grove, 2004.

King, Anthony. *Urbanism, Colonialism and the World Economy: Cultural and Spatial Foundations of the World Urban System*. London: Routledge, 1990.

Rizal, José. *Noli Me Tangere (Touch Me Not)*. Translated by Harold Augenbraum. New York: Penguin, 2006.

Warwick Research Collective, *Combined and Uneven Development: Towards a New Theory of World-Literature*. Liverpool: Liverpool University Press, 2015.

Watson, Jini Kim. *The New Asian City: Three-Dimensional Fictions of Space and Urban Form*. Minneapolis, MN: University of Minnesota Press, 2011.

The Urban Itinerary and the City Map: The Experience of Metropolitan Space

Calvino, Italo. *Invisible Cities*. Translated by William Weaver. New York: Harcourt, 1974.
de Certeau, Michel. *The Practice of Everyday Life*. Translated by Steven Rendall. Berkeley, CA: University of California Press, 1984.
Elkin, Lauren. *Flâneuse: Women Walk the City in Paris, New York, Tokyo, Venice, and London*. New York: Farrar, Strauss, and Giroux, 2016.
Jameson, Fredric. *Postmodernism, or, the Cultural Logic of Late Capitalism*. Durham, NC: Duke University Press, 1991.
Linde, Charlotte and William Labov, "Spatial Networks as a Site for the Study of Language and Thought," *Language* 51, no. 4 (December 1975): 924–939.
Quayson, Ato. *Oxford Street, Accra: City Life and the Itineraries of Transnationalism*. Durham, NC: Duke University Press, 2014.
Ryan, Marie-Laure, Kenneth Foote, and Maoz Azaryahu, *Narrating Space/Spatializing Narrative: Where Narrative Theory and Geography Meet*. Columbus, OH: Ohio State University Press, 2016.

The Neighborhood and the Sweatshop: Immigrant and Diasporic Rites of Passage in the Literature of New York

Bender, Thomas. *The Unfinished City: New York and the Metropolitan Idea*. New York: The New Press, 2002.
Homberger, Eric. *The Historical Atlas of New York City: A Visual Celebration of 400 Years of New York City's History*, 3rd ed. New York: St. Martin's Griffin, 2016.
Koolhaas, Rem. *Delirious New York: A Retroactive Manifesto for Manhattan*. New York: The Monacelli Press, 1997.
Lindner, Christoph. *Imagining New York City: Literature, Urbanism, and the Visual Arts, 1890–1940*. Oxford: Oxford University Pres, 2015.
Miller, Stephen. *Walking New York: Reflections of American Writers from Walt Whitman to Teju Cole*. New York: Empire State Editions, 2015.
Wilson, Ross, ed. *New York: A Literary History*. Cambridge: Cambridge University Press, 2020.

"The Whole World in Little": London as the Capital of World Literature

Casanova, Pascale. "Literature as a World." *New Left Review* 31 (Jan/Feb 2005): 71–90.
Emecheta, Buchi. *Second Class Citizen*. London: Penguin Classics, 2021.

Evaristo, Bernadine. *Girl, Woman, Other*. London: Hamish Hamilton, 2019.
Selvon, Sam. *The Lonely Londoners*. London: Penguin, 2006.
Warwick Research Collective, *Combined and Uneven Development: Towards a New Theory of World-Literature*. Liverpool: Liverpool University Press, 2015.
Williams, Raymond. *The Country and the City* [1973]. London: Hogarth Press, 1985.

Unworlding Paris: *Flânerie* and Epistemic Encounters from Baudelaire to Gauz

Achille, Etienne, Charles Forsdick, and Lydie Moudileno, eds. *Postcolonial Realms of Memory: Sites and Symbols in Modern France*. Liverpool: Liverpool University Press, 2020.
Casanova, Pascale. *The World Republic of Letters*. Translated by M.B. DeBevoise. Cambridge, MA; London: Harvard University Press, 2004.
Jules-Rosette, Bennetta. *Black Paris: The African Writers' landscape*. Urbana, IN: University of Illinois Press, 2000.
Kane, Cheikh Hamidou. *L'Aventure ambiguë* [1961]. Paris: Juillard, 2003.
Niang, Mame-Fatou. *Identités françaises: Banlieues, féminités et universalisme*. Leiden: Brill Rodopi, 2020.

Sketching the City with Words: Istanbul Through Time in Turkish Literary Texts

Altuğ, Fatih. "Istanbul in Modern Ottoman Literature: 1870–1923." *History of Istanbul from Antiquity to XXIst Century*, vol. 7, *Literature, Arts and Education*. https://istanbultarihi.ist/611-istanbul-in-modern-ottoman-literature-1870-1923.
Avcı, Mustafa. "Istanbul of the Orientalists." *History of Istanbul from Antiquity to XXIst Century*, vol. 7, *Literature, Arts and Education*. https://istanbultarihi.ist/624-istanbul-of-the-orientalists.
Aynur, Hatice. "Portraying The City with Words: Istanbul in Ottoman Literary Texts." *History of Istanbul from Antiquity to XXIst Century*, vol. 7, *Literature, Arts and Education*. https://istanbultarihi.ist/609-potraying-the-city-with-words-istanbul-in-ottoman-literary-texts.
Elger, Ralf. "Istanbul in Early Modern Muslim Arabic Literature," *History of Istanbul from Antiquity to XXIst Century*, vol. 7, *Literature, Arts and Education*. https://istanbultarihi.ist/626-istanbul-in-early-modern-muslim-arabic-literature.
Pamuk, Orhan. *İstanbul: Memories and the City*. Translated by Maureen Freely. New York: Random House, 2005.
Uysal, Zeynep. "Re-writing the City: Five Istanbuls From the Republican Era." *History of Istanbul from Antiquity to XXIst Century*, vol. 7, *Literature, Arts and Education*. https://istanbultarihi.ist/612-re-writing-the-city-five-istanbuls-from-the-republican-era.

Romance and Liminal Space in the Twentieth-Century Cairo Novel

Allen, Roger. *The Arabic Novel: An Historical and Critical Introduction*. Syracuse, NY: Syracuse University Press, 1995.

Hawas, May. *Politicising World Literature: Egypt, between Pedagogy and the Public*. New York: Routledge, 2019.

Kilpatrick, Hilary. "The Egyptian Novel from Zaynab to 1980," in M. M. Badawi, ed., *Modern Arabic Literature*, 223–69. Cambridge: Cambridge University Press, 2012.

Mehrez, Samia. *The Literary Atlas of Cairo*. Cairo: The American University in Cairo Press, 2016.

The Literary Life of Cairo. Cairo: The American University in Cairo Press, 2016.

Rakha, Youssef. "In Extremis: Literature and Revolution in Contemporary Cairo (An Oriental Essay in Seven Parts)," *The Kenyon Review* 34, no. 3 (2012).

Bombay/Mumbai and its Multilingual Literary Pathways to the World

Kolatkar, Arun. *Kala Ghoda Poems*. Mumbai: Pras Prakashan, 2004.

Nerlekar, Anjali. *Bombay Modern: Arun Kolatkar and Bilingual Literary Culture*. Evanston, IL: Northwestern University Press, 2016.

Pinto, Jerry and Naresh Fernandes. *Bombay, Meri Jaan: Writings on Mumbai*. New Delhi: Penguin Books, 2003.

Prakash, Gyan. *Mumbai Fables*. Princeton, NJ: Princeton University Press, 2010.

Rushdie, Salman. *The Moor's Last Sigh*. New York: Pantheon, 1995.

At Home in the World: Singapore's Literary Translocality

Bakri, Annaliza, ed. *Sikit-Sikit Lama-Lama Jadi Bukit*. Singapore: Math Paper Press, 2017.

Koh Tai, Ann, Tan Chee Lay, Hadijah Rahmat, and Arun Mahizhnan. *Literature*. Singapore: Institute of Policy Studies, 2018.

Patke, Rajeev S. and Philip Holden. *The Routledge Concise History of Southeast Asian Writing in English*. London: Routledge, 2010.

Poon, Angelia, Philip Holden, and Shirley Lim, eds. *Writing Singapore: An Historical Anthology of Singapore Literature*. Singapore: NUS Press, 2009.

Quah, Sy Ren and Hee Wai Siam, eds. *Memorandum: A Sinophone Singaporean Short Story Reader*. Translated by Dan Feng Tan. Singapore: Ethos Books, 2020.

Wee, C.J.W-L. *The Asian Modern: Culture, Capitalist Development, Singapore*. Hong Kong: Hong Kong University Press, 2007.

Imagining the Migrant in Twenty-First-Century Johannesburg

Beukes, Lauren. *Zoo City*. Johannesburg: Jacana Press, 2010.
Kruger, Lauren. *Imagining the Edgy City: Writing, Performing, and Building Johannesburg*. Oxford: Oxford University Press 2013.
Mpe, Phaswane. *Welcome to Our Hillbrow*. Johannesburg: Picador Africa, [2001] 2014. Kindle.
Ntshanga, Masande. *Triangulum*. Johannesburg: Umuzi, 2019. Kindle.
Nuttall, Sarah and Achille Mbembe. *Johannesburg: The Elusive Metropolis*. Johannesburg: Wits University Press, 2009.
Nyathi, Sue. *The Gold-Diggers*. Johannesburg: Pan Macmillan, 2018. Kindle.
Tshuma, Novuyo Rose. *Shadows*. Johannesburg: Kwela, 2013.
Vladislavic, Ivan. *The Restless Supermarket*. Johannesburg: Umuzi, [2001] 2012. Kindle.
The Exploded View. Johannesburg: Umuzi, [2004] 2017. Kindle.

Russia: Borders and Centers

Djagalov, Rossen. *From Internationalism to Postcolonialism: Literature and Cinema between the Second and the Third Worlds*. Montreal: McGill-Queen University Press, 2020.
Eliot, T.S. "What Is a Classic?" in Frank Kermode, ed., *Selected Prose of T. S. Eliot*, 115–131. New York: Farrar, Straus, and Giroux, 1975.
Gogol, Nikolai. *Plays and Petersburg Tales*. Translated by Christopher English. Introduction by Richard Peace. Oxford: Oxford University Press, 2009.
Lounsbery, Anne. *Life is Elsewhere: Symbolic Geography in the Russian Provinces, 1800–1917*. Ithaca, NY: Cornell University Press, 2019.
Tihanov, Galin. *The Birth and Death of Literary Theory: Regimes of Relevance in Russia and Beyond*. Stanford, CA: Stanford University Press, 2019.
Tolstoy, Leo. *War and Peace*. Translated by Richard Pevear and Larissa Volokhonsky. London: Vintage Classics, 2008.

"Cityful Passing Away": Resituating Dublin

Casanova, Pascale. *The World Republic of Letters*. Translated by M.B. DeBevoise. Cambridge, MA: Harvard University Press, 2004.
Dickson, David. *Dublin: The Making of A Capital City*. London: Profile, 2014.
Joyce, James. *Ulysses*. Catherine Flynn, ed. Cambridge: Cambridge University Press, 2022.
Kincaid, Andrew. *Postcolonial Dublin: Imperial Legacies and the Built Environment* (Minneapolis, MN: University of Minnesota Press, 2006).
Sakr, Rita. *Monumental Space in the Post-Imperial Novel: An Interdisciplinary Study* (London: Bloomsbury, 2012).
Whelan, Yvonne. *Reinventing Dublin: Streetscape, Iconography, and the Politics of Identity* (Dublin: University College Dublin Press, 2003).

From Altepetl to Megacity: Narrating Mexico City as World Literature

Calderón de la Barca, Frances. *Life in Mexico*. Berkeley, CA: University of California Press, 1982.
Díaz del Castillo, Bernal. *True History of the Conquest of New Spain*. Translated by Alfred Percival Maudslay. New York: Cambridge University Press, 2015.
Fuentes, Carlos. *Where the Air is Clear*. Translated by Sam Hileman. Funks Grove, IL: Dalkey Archive, 2014.
Gruzinski, Serge. *A History of Mexico City*. Translated by Stephen Sawyer. Berkeley, CA: University of California Press, 2014.
Mundy, Barbara. *The Death of the Aztec Tenochtitlan. The Life of Mexico City*. Austin, TX: University of Texas Press, 2015.

(In)Visible Beijing Within and Without World Literature

Braester, Yomi. *Paint the City Red: Chinese Cinema and the Urban Contract*. Durham, NC: Duke University Press, 2010.
Lee, Leo Ou-fan Lee. *Shanghai Modern: The Flowering of a New Urban Culture in China, 1930–1945*. Cambridge, MA: Harvard University Press, 1999.
Shih, Shu-mei Shih. *The Lure of the Modern: Writing Modernism in Semicolonial China, 1917–1937*. Berkeley and Los Angeles, CA: University of California Press, 2001.
Song, Weijie. *Mapping Modern Beijing: Space, Emotion, Literary Topography*. New York: Oxford University Press, 2018.
Visser, Robin. *Cities Surround the Countryside: Urban Aesthetics in Postsocialist China*. Durham, NC: Duke University Press, 2010.
Zhang, Yingjin. *The City in Modern Chinese Literature and Film: Configurations of Space, Time, and Gender*. Stanford, CA: Stanford University Press, 1996.

Worlding Lagos in the Long Twentieth Century

Barrett, A. Igoni. *Blackass*. London: Granta, 2015.
Cole, Teju. *Every Day is for the Thief*. Abuja: Cassava Republic, 2007.
Ekwensi, Cyprian. *People of the City*. London: Heinemann, 1963.
Lefebvre, Henri. *The Production of Space*. Translated by Donald Nicholson-Smith. Malden, MA: Blackwell, 1991. First published 1974.
Massey, Doreen. *For Space*. London: Sage, 2005.

Haunted Vitality: Sydney, Colonial Modernity, and World Literature

Dark, Eleanor. *The Timeless Land*. Sydney: A&R Australian Classics, 2013. First published 1941.

Ginibi, Ruby Langford. *Don't Take Your Love to Town. St Lucia*: University of Queensland Press, 2007. First published 1988.
Janson, Julie. *Benevolence*. Broome, Western Australia: Magabala Books, 2020.
Jones, Gail. *Five Bells*. North Sydney: Vintage/Random House, 2011.
Karskens, Grace. *The Colony*. Sydney: Allen & Unwin, 2009.
Stead, Christina. *Seven Poor Men of Sydney*. South Carlton, Victoria: The Miegunyah Press, 2015. First published 1934.
White, Patrick. *Riders in the Chariot*. London: Vintage, 1996. First published 1961.

Index

Cambridge Companions To ...

AUTHORS

Edward Albee edited by Stephen J. Bottoms
Margaret Atwood edited by Coral Ann Howells (second edition)
W. H. Auden edited by Stan Smith
Jane Austen edited by Edward Copeland and Juliet McMaster (second edition)
Balzac edited by Owen Heathcote and Andrew Watts
Beckett edited by John Pilling
Bede edited by Scott DeGregorio
Aphra Behn edited by Derek Hughes and Janet Todd
Saul Bellow edited by Victoria Aarons
Walter Benjamin edited by David S. Ferris
William Blake edited by Morris Eaves
James Baldwin edited by Michele Elam
Boccaccio edited by Guyda Armstrong, Rhiannon Daniels, and Stephen J. Milner
Jorge Luis Borges edited by Edwin Williamson
Brecht edited by Peter Thomson and Glendyr Sacks (second edition)
The Brontës edited by Heather Glen
Bunyan edited by Anne Dunan-Page
Frances Burney edited by Peter Sabor
Byron edited by Drummond Bone
Albert Camus edited by Edward J. Hughes
Willa Cather edited by Marilee Lindemann
Catullus edited by Ian Du Quesnay and Tony Woodman
Cervantes edited by Anthony J. Cascardi
Chaucer edited by Piero Boitani and Jill Mann (second edition)
Chekhov edited by Vera Gottlieb and Paul Allain
Kate Chopin edited by Janet Beer
Caryl Churchill edited by Elaine Aston and Elin Diamond
Cicero edited by Catherine Steel
J. M. Coetzee edited by Jarad Zimbler
Coleridge edited by Lucy Newlyn
Coleridge edited by Tim Fulford (new edition)
Wilkie Collins edited by Jenny Bourne Taylor
Joseph Conrad edited by J. H. Stape
H. D. edited by Nephie J. Christodoulides and Polina Mackay
Dante edited by Rachel Jacoff (second edition)
Daniel Defoe edited by John Richetti
Don DeLillo edited by John N. Duvall
Charles Dickens edited by John O. Jordan
Emily Dickinson edited by Wendy Martin
John Donne edited by Achsah Guibbory
Dostoevskii edited by W. J. Leatherbarrow
Theodore Dreiser edited by Leonard Cassuto and Claire Virginia Eby
John Dryden edited by Steven N. Zwicker
W. E. B. Du Bois edited by Shamoon Zamir
George Eliot edited by George Levine and Nancy Henry (second edition)
T. S. Eliot edited by A. David Moody
Ralph Ellison edited by Ross Posnock
Ralph Waldo Emerson edited by Joel Porte and Saundra Morris
William Faulkner edited by Philip M. Weinstein
Henry Fielding edited by Claude Rawson
F. Scott Fitzgerald edited by Ruth Prigozy
F. Scott Fitzgerald edited by Michael Nowlin (second edition)
Flaubert edited by Timothy Unwin
E. M. Forster edited by David Bradshaw
Benjamin Franklin edited by Carla Mulford
Brian Friel edited by Anthony Roche
Robert Frost edited by Robert Faggen
Gabriel García Márquez edited by Philip Swanson
Elizabeth Gaskell edited by Jill L. Matus
Edward Gibbon edited by Karen O'Brien and Brian Young
Goethe edited by Lesley Sharpe
Günter Grass edited by Stuart Taberner
Thomas Hardy edited by Dale Kramer
David Hare edited by Richard Boon
Nathaniel Hawthorne edited by Richard Millington
Seamus Heaney edited by Bernard O'Donoghue
Ernest Hemingway edited by Scott Donaldson
Hildegard of Bingen edited by Jennifer Bain

Homer edited by Robert Fowler
Horace edited by Stephen Harrison
Ted Hughes edited by Terry Gifford
Ibsen edited by James McFarlane
Henry James edited by Jonathan Freedman
Samuel Johnson edited by Greg Clingham
Ben Jonson edited by Richard Harp and Stanley Stewart
James Joyce edited by Derek Attridge (second edition)
Kafka edited by Julian Preece
Kazuo Ishiguro edited by Andrew Bennett
Keats edited by Susan J. Wolfson
Rudyard Kipling edited by Howard J. Booth
Lacan edited by Jean-Michel Rabaté
D. H. Lawrence edited by Anne Fernihough
Primo Levi edited by Robert Gordon
Lucretius edited by Stuart Gillespie and Philip Hardie
Machiavelli edited by John M. Najemy
David Mamet edited by Christopher Bigsby
Thomas Mann edited by Ritchie Robertson
Christopher Marlowe edited by Patrick Cheney
Andrew Marvell edited by Derek Hirst and Steven N. Zwicker
Ian McEwan edited by Dominic Head
Herman Melville edited by Robert S. Levine
Arthur Miller edited by Christopher Bigsby (second edition)
Milton edited by Dennis Danielson (second edition)
Molière edited by David Bradby and Andrew Calder
Toni Morrison edited by Justine Tally
Alice Munro edited by David Staines
Nabokov edited by Julian W. Connolly
Eugene O'Neill edited by Michael Manheim
George Orwell edited by John Rodden
Ovid edited by Philip Hardie
Petrarch edited by Albert Russell Ascoli and Unn Falkeid
Harold Pinter edited by Peter Raby (second edition)
Sylvia Plath edited by Jo Gill
Plutarch edited by Frances B. Titchener and Alexei Zadorojnyi
Edgar Allan Poe edited by Kevin J. Hayes
Alexander Pope edited by Pat Rogers
Ezra Pound edited by Ira B. Nadel
Proust edited by Richard Bales
Pushkin edited by Andrew Kahn
Thomas Pynchon edited by Inger H. Dalsgaard, Luc Herman and Brian McHale
Rabelais edited by John O'Brien
Rilke edited by Karen Leeder and Robert Vilain
Philip Roth edited by Timothy Parrish
Salman Rushdie edited by Abdulrazak Gurnah
John Ruskin edited by Francis O'Gorman
Sappho edited by P. J. Finglass and Adrian Kelly
Seneca edited by Shadi Bartsch and Alessandro Schiesaro
Shakespeare edited by Margareta de Grazia and Stanley Wells (second edition)
George Bernard Shaw edited by Christopher Innes
Shelley edited by Timothy Morton
Mary Shelley edited by Esther Schor
Sam Shepard edited by Matthew C. Roudané
Spenser edited by Andrew Hadfield
Laurence Sterne edited by Thomas Keymer
Wallace Stevens edited by John N. Serio
Tom Stoppard edited by Katherine E. Kelly
Harriet Beecher Stowe edited by Cindy Weinstein
August Strindberg edited by Michael Robinson
Jonathan Swift edited by Christopher Fox
J. M. Synge edited by P. J. Mathews
Tacitus edited by A. J. Woodman
Henry David Thoreau edited by Joel Myerson
Thucydides edited by Polly Low
Tolstoy edited by Donna Tussing Orwin
Anthony Trollope edited by Carolyn Dever and Lisa Niles
Mark Twain edited by Forrest G. Robinson
John Updike edited by Stacey Olster
Mario Vargas Llosa edited by Efrain Kristal and John King
Virgil edited by Fiachra Mac Góráin and Charles Martindale (second edition)
Voltaire edited by Nicholas Cronk
David Foster Wallace edited by Ralph Clare
Edith Wharton edited by Millicent Bell

Walt Whitman edited by Ezra Greenspan
Oscar Wilde edited by Peter Raby
Tennessee Williams edited by Matthew C. Roudané
William Carlos Williams edited by Christopher MacGowan
August Wilson edited by Christopher Bigsby
Mary Wollstonecraft edited by Claudia L. Johnson
Virginia Woolf edited by Susan Sellers (second edition)
Wordsworth edited by Stephen Gill
Richard Wright edited by Glenda R. Carpio
W. B. Yeats edited by Marjorie Howes and John Kelly
Xenophon edited by Michael A. Flower
Zola edited by Brian Nelson

TOPICS

The Actress edited by Maggie B. Gale and John Stokes
The African American Novel edited by Maryemma Graham
The African American Slave Narrative edited by Audrey A. Fisch
African American Theatre by Harvey Young
Allegory edited by Rita Copeland and Peter Struck
American Crime Fiction edited by Catherine Ross Nickerson
American Gothic edited by Jeffrey Andrew Weinstock
American Horror edited by Stephen Shapiro and Mark Storey
American Literature and the Body by Travis M. Foster
American Literature and the Environment edited by Sarah Ensor and Susan Scott Parrish
American Literature of the 1930s edited by William Solomon
American Modernism edited by Walter Kalaidjian
American Poetry since 1945 edited by Jennifer Ashton
American Realism and Naturalism edited by Donald Pizer
American Short Story edited by Michael J. Collins and Gavin Jones
American Travel Writing edited by Alfred Bendixen and Judith Hamera
American Women Playwrights edited by Brenda Murphy
Ancient Rhetoric edited by Erik Gunderson
Arthurian Legend edited by Elizabeth Archibald and Ad Putter
Australian Literature edited by Elizabeth Webby
The Australian Novel edited by Nicholas Birns and Louis Klee
The Beats edited by Stephen Belletto
Boxing edited by Gerald Early
British Black and Asian Literature (1945–2010) edited by Deirdre Osborne
British Fiction: 1980–2018 edited by Peter Boxall
British Fiction since 1945 edited by David James
British Literature of the 1930s edited by James Smith
British Literature of the French Revolution edited by Pamela Clemit
British Romantic Poetry edited by James Chandler and Maureen N. McLane
British Romanticism edited by Stuart Curran (second edition)
British Romanticism and Religion edited by Jeffrey Barbeau
British Theatre, 1730–1830, edited by Jane Moody and Daniel O'Quinn
Canadian Literature edited by Eva-Marie Kröller (second edition)
The Canterbury Tales edited by Frank Grady
The City in World Literature edited by Ato Quayson and Jini Kim Watson
Children's Literature edited by M. O. Grenby and Andrea Immel
The Classic Russian Novel edited by Malcolm V. Jones and Robin Feuer Miller
Comics edited by Maaheen Ahmed
Contemporary Irish Poetry edited by Matthew Campbell
Creative Writing edited by David Morley and Philip Neilsen
Crime Fiction edited by Martin Priestman
Dante's 'Commedia' edited by Zygmunt G. Barański and Simon Gilson

Dracula edited by Roger Luckhurst

Early American Literature edited by Bryce Traister

Early Modern Women's Writing edited by Laura Lunger Knoppers

The Eighteenth-Century Novel edited by John Richetti

Eighteenth-Century Poetry edited by John Sitter

Eighteenth-Century Thought edited by Frans De Bruyn

Emma edited by Peter Sabor

English Dictionaries edited by Sarah Ogilvie

English Literature, 1500–1600 edited by Arthur F. Kinney

English Literature, 1650–1740 edited by Steven N. Zwicker

English Literature, 1740–1830 edited by Thomas Keymer and Jon Mee

English Literature, 1830–1914 edited by Joanne Shattock

English Melodrama edited by Carolyn Williams

English Novelists edited by Adrian Poole

English Poetry, Donne to Marvell edited by Thomas N. Corns

English Poets edited by Claude Rawson

English Renaissance Drama edited by A. R. Braunmuller and Michael Hattaway, (second edition)

English Renaissance Tragedy edited by Emma Smith and Garrett A. Sullivan Jr.

English Restoration Theatre edited by Deborah C. Payne Fisk

Environmental Humanities edited by Jeffrey Cohen and Stephanie Foote

The Epic edited by Catherine Bates

Erotic Literature edited by Bradford Mudge

The Essay edited by Kara Wittman and Evan Kindley

European Modernism edited by Pericles Lewis

European Novelists edited by Michael Bell

Fairy Tales edited by Maria Tatar

Fantasy Literature edited by Edward James and Farah Mendlesohn

Feminist Literary Theory edited by Ellen Rooney

Fiction in the Romantic Period edited by Richard Maxwell and Katie Trumpener

The Fin de Siècle edited by Gail Marshall

Frankenstein edited by Andrew Smith

The French Enlightenment edited by Daniel Brewer

French Literature edited by John D. Lyons

The French Novel: from 1800 to the Present edited by Timothy Unwin

Gay and Lesbian Writing edited by Hugh Stevens

German Romanticism edited by Nicholas Saul

Global Literature and Slavery edited by Laura T. Murphy

Gothic Fiction edited by Jerrold E. Hogle

The Graphic Novel edited by Stephen Tabachnick

The Greek and Roman Novel edited by Tim Whitmarsh

Greek and Roman Theatre edited by Marianne McDonald and J. Michael Walton

Greek Comedy edited by Martin Revermann

Greek Lyric edited by Felix Budelmann

Greek Mythology edited by Roger D. Woodard

Greek Tragedy edited by P. E. Easterling

The Harlem Renaissance edited by George Hutchinson

The History of the Book edited by Leslie Howsam

Human Rights and Literature edited by Crystal Parikh

The Irish Novel edited by John Wilson Foster

Irish Poets edited by Gerald Dawe

The Italian Novel edited by Peter Bondanella and Andrea Ciccarelli

The Italian Renaissance edited by Michael Wyatt

Jewish American Literature edited by Hana Wirth-Nesher and Michael P. Kramer

The Latin American Novel edited by Efraín Kristal

Latin American Poetry edited by Stephen Hart

Latina/o American Literature edited by John Morán González

Latin Love Elegy edited by Thea S. Thorsen

Literature and the Anthropocene edited by John Parham

Literature and Climate edited by Adeline Johns-Putra and Kelly Sultzbach

Literature and Disability edited by Clare Barker and Stuart Murray

Literature and Food edited by J. Michelle Coghlan

Literature and the Posthuman edited by Bruce Clarke and Manuela Rossini

Literature and Religion edited by Susan M. Felch

Literature and Science edited by Steven Meyer

The Literature of the American Civil War and Reconstruction edited by Kathleen Diffley and Coleman Hutchison

The Literature of the American Renaissance edited by Christopher N. Phillips

The Literature of Berlin edited by Andrew J. Webber

The Literature of the Crusades edited by Anthony Bale

The Literature of the First World War edited by Vincent Sherry

The Literature of London edited by Lawrence Manley

The Literature of Los Angeles edited by Kevin R. McNamara

The Literature of New York edited by Cyrus Patell and Bryan Waterman

The Literature of Paris edited by Anna-Louise Milne

The Literature of World War II edited by Marina MacKay

Literature on Screen edited by Deborah Cartmell and Imelda Whelehan

Lyrical Ballads edited by Sally Bushell

Medieval British Manuscripts edited by Orietta Da Rold and Elaine Treharne

Medieval English Culture edited by Andrew Galloway

Medieval English Law and Literature edited by Candace Barrington and Sebastian Sobecki

Medieval English Literature edited by Larry Scanlon

Medieval English Mysticism edited by Samuel Fanous and Vincent Gillespie

Medieval English Theatre edited by Richard Beadle and Alan J. Fletcher (second edition)

Medieval French Literature edited by Simon Gaunt and Sarah Kay

Medieval Romance edited by Roberta L. Krueger

Medieval Romance edited by Roberta L. Krueger (new edition)

Medieval Women's Writing edited by Carolyn Dinshaw and David Wallace

Modern American Culture edited by Christopher Bigsby

Modern British Women Playwrights edited by Elaine Aston and Janelle Reinelt

Modern French Culture edited by Nicholas Hewitt

Modern German Culture edited by Eva Kolinsky and Wilfried van der Will

The Modern German Novel edited by Graham Bartram

The Modern Gothic edited by Jerrold E. Hogle

Modern Irish Culture edited by Joe Cleary and Claire Connolly

Modern Italian Culture edited by Zygmunt G. Baranski and Rebecca J. West

Modern Latin American Culture edited by John King

Modern Russian Culture edited by Nicholas Rzhevsky

Modern Spanish Culture edited by David T. Gies

Modernism edited by Michael Levenson (second edition)

The Modernist Novel edited by Morag Shiach

Modernist Poetry edited by Alex Davis and Lee M. Jenkins

Modernist Women Writers edited by Maren Tova Linett

Narrative edited by David Herman

Narrative Theory edited by Matthew Garrett

Native American Literature edited by Joy Porter and Kenneth M. Roemer

Nineteen Eighty-Four edited by Nathan Waddell

Nineteenth-Century American Poetry edited by Kerry Larson

Nineteenth-Century American Women's Writing edited by Dale M. Bauer and Philip Gould

Nineteenth-Century Thought edited by Gregory Claeys

The Novel edited by Eric Bulson

Old English Literature edited by Malcolm Godden and Michael Lapidge (second edition)

Performance Studies edited by Tracy C. Davis

Piers Plowman by Andrew Cole and Andrew Galloway

The Poetry of the First World War edited by Santanu Das

Popular Fiction edited by David Glover and Scott McCracken

Postcolonial Literary Studies edited by Neil Lazarus

Postcolonial Poetry edited by Jahan Ramazani

Postcolonial Travel Writing edited by Robert Clarke

Postmodern American Fiction edited by Paula Geyh

Postmodernism edited by Steven Connor

Prose edited by Daniel Tyler

The Pre-Raphaelites edited by Elizabeth Prettejohn

Pride and Prejudice edited by Janet Todd
Queer Studies edited by Siobhan B. Somerville
Renaissance Humanism edited by Jill Kraye
Robinson Crusoe edited by John Richetti
Roman Comedy edited by Martin T. Dinter
The Roman Historians edited by Andrew Feldherr
Roman Satire edited by Kirk Freudenburg
Science Fiction edited by Edward James and Farah Mendlesohn
Scottish Literature edited by Gerald Carruthers and Liam McIlvanney
Sensation Fiction edited by Andrew Mangham
Shakespeare and Contemporary Dramatists edited by Ton Hoenselaars
Shakespeare and Popular Culture edited by Robert Shaughnessy
Shakespeare and Race edited by Ayanna Thompson
Shakespeare and Religion edited by Hannibal Hamlin
Shakespeare and War edited by David Loewenstein and Paul Stevens
Shakespeare on Film edited by Russell Jackson (second edition)
Shakespeare on Screen edited by Russell Jackson
Shakespeare on Stage edited by Stanley Wells and Sarah Stanton
Shakespearean Comedy edited by Alexander Leggatt
Shakespearean Tragedy edited by Claire McEachern (second edition)
Shakespeare's First Folio edited by Emma Smith
Shakespeare's History Plays edited by Michael Hattaway
Shakespeare's Language edited by Lynne Magnusson with David Schalkwyk
Shakespeare's Last Plays edited by Catherine M. S. Alexander
Shakespeare's Poetry edited by Patrick Cheney
Sherlock Holmes edited by Janice M. Allan and Christopher Pittard
The Sonnet edited by A. D. Cousins and Peter Howarth
The Spanish Novel: from 1600 to the Present edited by Harriet Turner and Adelaida López de Martínez
Textual Scholarship edited by Neil Fraistat and Julia Flanders
Theatre and Science edited by Kristen E. Shepherd-Barr
Theatre History by David Wiles and Christine Dymkowski
Transnational American Literature edited by Yogita Goyal
Travel Writing edited by Peter Hulme and Tim Youngs
Twentieth-Century American Poetry and Politics edited by Daniel Morris
Twentieth-Century British and Irish Women's Poetry edited by Jane Dowson
The Twentieth-Century English Novel edited by Robert L. Caserio
Twentieth-Century English Poetry edited by Neil Corcoran
Twentieth-Century Irish Drama edited by Shaun Richards
Twentieth-Century Literature and Politics edited by Christos Hadjiyiannis and Rachel Potter
Twentieth-Century Russian Literature edited by Marina Balina and Evgeny Dobrenko
Utopian Literature edited by Gregory Claeys
Victorian and Edwardian Theatre edited by Kerry Powell
The Victorian Novel edited by Deirdre David (second edition)
Victorian Poetry edited by Joseph Bristow
Victorian Women's Poetry edited by Linda K. Hughes
Victorian Women's Writing edited by Linda H. Peterson
War Writing edited by Kate McLoughlin
Women's Writing in Britain, 1660–1789 edited by Catherine Ingrassia
Women's Writing in the Romantic Period edited by Devoney Looser
World Literature edited by Ben Etherington and Jarad Zimbler
World Crime Fiction edited by Jesper Gulddal, Stewart King and Alistair Rolls
Writing of the English Revolution edited by N. H. Keeble
The Writings of Julius Caesar edited by Christopher Krebs and Luca Grillo
Edward Albee edited by Stephen J. Bottoms
Margaret Atwood edited by Coral Ann Howells (second edition)

For EU product safety concerns, contact us at Calle de José Abascal, 56–1°,
28003 Madrid, Spain or eugpsr@cambridge.org.

www.ingramcontent.com/pod-product-compliance
Ingram Content Group UK Ltd.
Pitfield, Milton Keynes, MK11 3LW, UK
UKHW042143130625
459647UK00011B/1163